SPACE:1999 ™

MAYBE THERE

THE LOST STORIES
FROM SPACE: 1999

Anderson Entertainment Limited
The Corner House, 2 High Street, Aylesford, Kent, ME20 7BG

Maybe There – The Lost Stories From Space: 1999
by David Hirsch and Robert E. Wood.

Hardcover edition published
by Anderson Entertainment in 2022.
Paperback edition published
by Anderson Entertainment in 2022.

www.gerryanderson.co.uk

ISBN: 978-1-914522-62-8

Editorial director: Jamie Anderson
Cover design: Marcus Stamps

Typeset by Michał Olędzki

SPACE: 1999™

MAYBE THERE

THE LOST STORIES FROM SPACE: 1999

By David Hirsch & Robert E. Wood

Foreword by

Christopher Penfold

'Terra Nova' (detail)
Original *Space: 1999* pre-production artwork by Keith Wilson.

CONTENTS

ACKNOWLEDGEMENTS

The authors would like to extend our deepest thanks to the following people:

Jamie Anderson
Tim Collins
Martin Willey
Steve Warnek
Warren Friedrich
Renèe Feit
Jorge Carmo
Victor Marino, Jr.
Simon Rhodes
Kit Bevan
Chris Bentley
and most importantly,
Christopher Penfold, whose generous assistance and input has been invaluable and an inspiration to both of us.

FOREWORD

Can there possibly be anything new to say about the remarkable phenomenon that is *Space: 1999*? This was the question that first occurred to me when Robert E. Wood and David Hirsch invited me to write this foreword for *Maybe There*. But, looking at these gems from the seemingly bottomless treasure chest of archives that Robert and David have brought up from the deep, convinced me that there is always something new to say about an endeavour which attempted to examine the behaviour of our human species in the present through the speculative lens of science fiction and our unleashed imagining about how we might perform in our future as pioneers in space.

Memory can play funny tricks and my own memory is long and increasingly fragile. When I first read Gerry and Sylvia's pitching script for '*Zero G*', I told Robert and David that I couldn't recall ever having read it. But now, having read the novelisations and original storylines collected here, I realise I must have done so. The basic concept of casting 300 humans out into space by blasting the Moon out of Earth's orbit and leaving them adrift without any "*Enterprise*" means of controlling their direction of travel and utterly at the mercy of whatever the deep unknown had to throw at them is present with remarkable clarity in '*Zero G*'. And that is the visionary concept with which we had to work when George Bellak and I began the process of turning that concept into a produceable and (almost) credible reality.

The threat of nuclear apocalypse was very real to us in 1973 at the height of the Cold War. Yet here we are again, facing the shattering of what we ought to describe as Gorbachev's Peace by Putin's murderous invasion of Ukraine and his venomous threat to deploy nuclear weapons in the interests of his own ego. That war has already had the catastrophic effect of distracting us from the climate crisis and providing what must surely be the final bonanza for the prime polluters of our planet – the fossil fuel industry.

With those twin damoclean swords hanging over our heads we have, as a species, begun to react in wildly different ways. On the one hand we have a young generation who, seeing their own futures under threat, are mobilising by impressively non-violent means to persuade their un-listening rulers to take action on their behalf. And, on the other hand, we have tech billionaires attempting to use their obscene wealth either to provide "safe havens" on Earth or to make their escape into space.

Space exploration is, of course, expensive and there is always the powerful argument that the money would be better spent on improving the conditions for human life on Earth. Others see space exploration as a challenge – a new frontier which stretches human ingenuity to its limits and beyond. When Elon Musk talks about his ambition to lead a manned expedition to Mars, he suggests that the vehicle in which he will travel will be constructed at a base on the Moon and, in acknowledgement of the influence of *Space: 1999* on his childhood imagination, he proposes to call that facility '*Moonbase Alpha*'. I regard that as a huge compliment to the original vision of Gerry and Sylvia Anderson, the development of which is powerfully documented in the scripts, both used and rejected, which Robert and David have collected here.

One very powerful memory I have about the process of that development is the nightmare of trying to work from Pinewood with scriptwriters in America long before the days of the internet and email when we were dependent on crackling toll calls across the Atlantic time zones. There is nothing like working together as editor and writer face-to-face and in the same room and I eventually found the problems of trying to hear Art Wallace, let alone talk to him, insuperable. We abandoned the working relationship with many regrets and the quality of his writing on display here in his original draft of '*Siren Planet*' only sharpens those regrets. But the fallback process whereby Johnny Byrne took over the writing of what became '*Matter of Life and Death*' produced the first of his many outstanding contributions to the series.

I have written elsewhere about the very great contribution that George Bellak made to the evolution of the series. The first requirement of any writer of fiction is the creation of a credible world and that world is very much on display here in David Hirsch's adaptation of '*The Void Ahead*'. What we might call the moral universe of *Space: 1999* was largely George Bellak's creation and I found it so interesting to read Robert's adaptation of Irving Gaynor Neiman's script '*A Breath of Death*'. I really don't think my memory is failing on this because I am certain I have never read it before. It must have been commissioned by George – and then abandoned by George because, I suspect, its moral universe would have been anathema to him.

I have now had the great pleasure of re-reading David Weir's script for '*The Black Sun*'. It is one of my favourite episodes and my first recollection of it was that I had written much of the production version. Not so, it seems, and David Hirsch's adaptation shows just how much of the original remained in the final version. I very much enjoyed working with David Weir who was, possibly, the most talented contributor to the series. He had a restless and vivid imagination and we spent many pleasurable hours at his Hampstead home just shooting the breeze – about the series, yes, but also about what Douglas Adams describes as 'Life, the Universe and Everything'. So it's very possible, as David Hirsch suggests in his observation about my original storyline for '*Guardian of Piri*', that David Weir had something to do with the development of that story as well.

I would be quite a rich man if I had a dollar for every time someone had said to me that *'Dragon's Domain'* was their favourite episode. On a recent visit to my cardiologist I confessed to having been involved in the making of *Space: 1999*. He was impressed and confessed to having re-watched the whole of series one during the COVID-19 lockdown. And when he was enthusing about *'Dragon's Domain'* he showed me the hairs standing up on his arm! So I hope that you all will have as much pleasure as I have had in re-acquainting myself with my original storyline.

The politics of dumping nuclear waste on the Moon as portrayed by George Bellak in '*The Void Ahead*' are distressingly familiar and are all too comparable with today's politics of climate crisis denial and failure to act. So many of the themes we attempted to deal with in the first series of *Space: 1999* are just as relevant now as they were in 1974. I am grateful to David and Robert for disinterring these relics and I am full of admiration for the way in which they have "novelised" them for readers who may be unfamiliar with screenplay formats.

So a heartfelt '*Yes*' is the answer to my original question. It has been a real joy to discover that there is indeed still something new to say about this remarkable series which you – readers and fans – have all kept alive for so long by your dedication and enthusiasm. I hope and confidently expect that you will find yet more to enthuse over in this remarkable re-emergence of both made and unmade scripts.

We created the fictional Moonbase Alpha nearly fifty years ago and now we are looking forward to that base becoming a reality in the not too distant future. As I write this I am holding my breath for a successful launch of Artemis – and that would be a wonderful step in the right direction. Fingers crossed!

Christopher Penfold
6 September 2022

INTRODUCTION

CREATING A NEW UNIVERSE

by David Hirsch & Robert E. Wood

At the end of *Space: 1999's* first episode, the camera pans up from Moonbase Alpha into the void of space, where a familiar title is superimposed: 'series created by Gerry and Sylvia Anderson.' As they had done many times before, a concept, sometimes a brief outline of format and characters, was initially pitched to Lew Grade at ATV in London (and/or Abe Mandell of ITC New York). Once this project was approved, it needed to be fleshed out into a series 'Guideline' or 'Bible'. Ofttimes, this was the result of inputs from many, many voices. The financiers want something they can easily sell to TV broadcasters, the filmmakers want a show that stands out with memorable stories and visuals, and the actors need a character that challenges their skills. The genesis of any sci-fi genre show requires more than just simply setting up a format and recurring cast, an entire world must be created. Futuristic technology has to be imagined that will believably support a self-sufficient Moonbase and its spacecraft.

In 1969, the Andersons had begun filming on their first live-action series, *UFO*. This lavish production saw the secret SHADO organisation protect the Earth from a hostile Alien invasion. When the program reached the United States in the fall of 1972, it became an immediate hit, airing Saturday nights at 7:00pm on the CBS-TV Network's 'Owned and Operated' stations. The success was due in part thanks to preceding

America's number one comedy, *All in the Family* (the US adaptation of *Till Death Do Us Part*).

After filming was completed on the initial 26 episodes of *UFO*, Gerry Anderson had moved on to the Robert Vaughn adventure series, *The Protectors*. It was during this time that he was asked to develop a second series of *UFO*, but with the caveat that no episode could be set on Earth. Abe Mandell felt that the terrestrial-bound stories were the weakest and demanded some kind of guarantee. Despite the character driven '*A Question of Priorities*' being his favourite episode, Anderson agreed to re-envision SHADO's tiny Moonbase as a large Lunar city, whose inhabitants would now be cast adrift, at the mercy of a hostile universe.

Film and TV production is, after all, a cooperative effort. The Andersons had a special talent for surrounding themselves with a team who excelled in their art. By the time *UFO 2* went into pre-production, Derek Meddings, who had supervised the visual effects, had moved on to the James Bond film, *The Man with the Golden Gun*. Production Designer Bob Bell was also tied up on *The Protectors*, so the producers turned to two other key employees that had been with them since *Fireball XL5*. Brian Johnson and Keith Wilson were now tasked with creating the look of the new 'Moon City'. Christopher Penfold was also brought on as original Script Editor Tony Barwick was also committed to *The Protectors*.

ITC suspended development on *UFO 2* when the ratings dropped later in the American run, believing interest had waned. Gerry Anderson was not willing to let all their hard work go to waste and pitched an entirely new series that could make use of the time and money already invested. Initially, the thought was to tailor the series to take advantage of the new American FCC 'Primetime Access Rule'. This gave early evening time slots (7:00pm to 8:00pm) back to local TV stations. *The Protectors* was already filling the demand for fresh 30-minute programs. Gerry and Sylvia Anderson set about writing the pilot script for the series now titled *Space: 1999*, in that format.

Not long after, the new series was again reimagined with a potential, and highly profitable, network sale in mind. ITC New York demanded an American writer be brought on board to make the show more desirable to CBS, NBC, or ABC. New York based writer George Bellak was brought in to flesh out the main characters and pen a captivating first episode that would keep viewers coming back week after week. Christopher Penfold remained on as Story Consultant and together they would seek out other writers who could join them and provide new stories, or flesh out plot lines initially conceived by the Andersons. As much of this development occurred before shooting began, Bellak's pilot script would go through multiple revisions to accommodate feedback from various sources. Eventually, Bellak had to part company and left the production before shooting began. Penfold resumed running the Writer's Room, performing uncredited work on the first episode's final shooting script.

Scripts submitted by other writers would also have to receive alterations, due to budget limitations or casting changes. There were also others that had to be abandoned. Changes like these are not something out of the ordinary in the world of TV production. Once a series is off and running it must be constantly fed with new material. When one department, whether it be art, visual effects, or especially the shooting stage, finishes one episode, the next must be ready to go. A production stoppage is money wasted. The script department is, therefore, under enormous pressure to always have something ready to shoot. Feeding this beast often means rewriting material up until the last moment, handing it in, and moving on to attack the next script in line. Naturally, every script writer will admit that anything can happen after that which may alter what they intended. A scene cut out in the editing process might spoil the narrative, or an actor fails to deliver a performance that sells the gravitas of the situation.

For this volume, we have adapted several scripts from the early days of *Space: 1999* that had to be altered to the ever evolving casting, set design, and visual effects requirements. One script, Irving Gaynor Neiman's '*A Breath of Death*', never made it beyond the initial writing phase.

All these stories are presented here as originally written, with the proposed names and every word of dialogue intact.

Sometimes, the scriptwriters would use multiple names and spellings for the same character, prop or location. A handy guide to these changes can be found at the back of this book. We have endeavoured to translate the action lines of the scripts into a novelised narrative format as gently as possible in order to preserve their original tone. These stories provide glimpses into the lost and alternate early visions of *Space: 1999*, had the series taken a slightly different path and gone, 'Maybe there'.

ZERO G

First Episode, 1973
by Gerry & Sylvia Anderson
Adapted by David Hirsch

ACT ONE

Somewhere in deep space, a man-made reconnaissance probe, marked C. 42, approached its destination, a fiery orange planet, ringed by coloured light.

Far across the universe, the arrival was being monitored by the men and women of W.A.N.D.E.R., the World Association of Nations Defending Earth Rights. The operation was housed within the vast complex of Moon City, humanity's first outpost in space. The year was 1999.

Space Commander Steve Maddox sat in his spacious, futuristic office. It was of modular construction, similar in design to much of the base. He was a man in his prime, an ex-astronaut who had led the first manned expedition to Mars, highly trained, tough, dedicated, space oriented. A man of the future – in the future.

Activating his intercom, Maddox called out, 'Moon City to Earth Control… Space Commander Maddox reporting on Deep Space Probe C. 42… All systems are go. We are ready to receive first transmission 14.35 Earth time.'

'Right, Steve,' Earth Control responded, 'Will await your next report… Good Luck!'

Maddox rotated his chair and depressed a button. The office wall behind him divided, and his room became an integral part of the control centre beyond. Banks of computers and highly sophisticated control consoles marked this as the nerve centre of Moon City. The Controller and his team busily made last minute checks before the reception of transmitted information from Probe C. 42. Maddox hadn't failed to notice the atmosphere was tense.

'C. 42 transmission in 60 seconds,' the Controller announced. A female operator followed with, 'T minus 55.'

The probe was very close to the planet, whose surface detail became more evident to the onboard cameras.

'T minus 40,' the female operator said as Doctor Marc Miller entered the control centre and crossed the room to join Maddox at his desk. His vast knowledge of space science afforded him a key position in Moon City. Both men had developed a strong bond during their tours of duty, despite vastly different responsibilities within the W.A.N.D.E.R. organisation.

The countdown continued, 'T minus 30.'

'Everything checks out, Steve,' Miller informed his friend. 'It looks good.'

Maddox smiled, 'Thanks, Marc.'

'T minus 25,' the female operator said.

Maddox called out, 'Roll recorders.'

Immediately, the response came back, 'Recorders rolling.'

'Lock on to Master Computer.'

'Master Computer – green.'

'T minus ten,' the woman began counting the seconds as the tension rose higher, '5… 4… 3… 2… 1… transmission!'

The atmosphere was electric as a weird cacophony of sound emitted by the C. 42 transmission filled the control room.

Then, abruptly, it ceased.

'Transmission 5.23 seconds in duration,' the female operator confirmed.

Maddox smiled to Doctor Miller. 'Good, that means we've got all the information we expected.' He nodded to the Controller, 'Commence Data Processing.'

'Yes, sir!' came the crisp acknowledgment. Maddox swivelled back in his chair to face the Doctor as the wall slid shut once more, affording the men some privacy.

'Six hours before we get the Computer Analysis,' sighed Maddox. 'It's gonna be a long wait.'

Doctor Miller shrugged, 'That probe's taken two years to make that journey – I guess another six hours is not gonna make much difference.'

Maddox rose, crossed to the panoramic window, and thoughtfully stared out at a green pulsating light, much larger than a star, hanging motionless above the Moon's horizon.

'Well, Marc, *They've* been watching us ever since we set up Moon City.' He turned to stare at his friend, 'How are They gonna react now that we are watching them?'

In space, an Alien ship hovered silently.

Several hours later, a mass of paperwork and computer data littered Maddox's office. He stared intently into Miller's eyes, 'It would appear there's very little doubt.'

'I agree,' the Doctor concurred.

'There's a mass of information, but I'll only relay the relevant facts to Earth.'

Miller nodded, 'The closer shots of the planet due to be transmitted tomorrow should confirm our theories beyond doubt.'

Maddox hit the intercom. 'Yes, Commander?' acknowledged a female voice.

'Earth Report 26240 – transmit Priority One.' Maddox began to dictate, 'Probe C. 42 reconnaissance – Planet Uranus. Instrumentation reports gas mixture similar to Earth's atmosphere… presence of water… surface temperature 20 degrees centigrade… first pictures show…'

He paused briefly, picking up a photo among the mass on the table and continued, 'What appears to be transportation systems… buildings and vegetation. Second transmission from closer range should confirm the above. Signed, Space Commander Maddox, 27th February 1999.'

As he gazed out the window, Doctor Miller pointed, 'Our ever watchful friend sitting up there just out of range – maybe now we've made our move, they'll make theirs.'

'Yeah,' Maddox agreed thoughtfully. He hit the intercom again. 'Control, I'm going on standby until…' Checking his watch he continued, '20:00 hours. Keep intensive surveillance of that Alien ship. <u>Any</u> sign of activity report immediately.'

He looked back at Miller and commented, 'It's been quite a day!'

As the Alien ship continued to hold its position, silently pulsating away, Maddox entered his quarters. He approached the communications console and reported, 'Control, Commander Maddox – I'm in my quarters.'

'Location recorded,' acknowledged the voice of Control.

Maddox reached for a decanter and began to make himself a drink. As he raised the glass, a green light on the wall caught his attention. It appeared as if it was made to shimmer by the moving liquid in the decanter.

Drawn to the window, he approached and stared out in the direction of the Alien vessel. Suddenly, he became aware his face was covered in beads of perspiration.

The Commander rushed to the air conditioning control, then frowned as it clearly read **COOL**. He mopped his brow and began to have difficulty breathing, as if the air in the room was leaking out into space.

He turned back to the communications console, punched the intercom button, and called out, 'Control – this is Commander Maddox…'

No reply! All systems appeared dead.

He keyed another button, 'Marc? This is Steve, are you there?'

His further pleads brought no response.

Aware that something was very wrong, Maddox moved across the room to the door. Instead of automatically opening upon his presence, he was shocked to hear the electronic bolts lock instead. He tried the manual override button but that too failed to respond.

Drenched in sweat, his body slumped against the doors as his lungs struggled to gasp for air in a thinning atmosphere. Panic took over as he used all his remaining energy to bang against the bulkhead. Exhausted, his body slid to the floor.

A voice suddenly came from everywhere – and nowhere, 'Relax, Commander…,' it said. 'Keep calm.'

Before Maddox, a strange network of geometrical, brilliantly coloured, three-dimensional shapes with no beginning or end, began to form. Every angle was the same, all tailing off into a black void. He struggled to his feet and found himself transfixed into a dazed disbelief.

The voice echoed again, 'It's been a long journey – you've been subjected to enormous stresses… but the process of transference is almost complete.'

From within that black void, Maddox could see a ray of green light reach out and touch him. As it made contact with his body, he found it was no longer difficult to breathe. The ray vanished and he began to cautiously move through the coloured geometric shapes.

'There is no escape, Commander.'

Maddox could not accept this possibility and carefully stepped around what he perceived as a large tubular structure. Beyond it, a sight stopped him dead in his tracks. In the distance, through a strange structure, he could see an opening, the exterior of an Alien planet. Exotic foliage covered the landscape beneath a vivid flame-coloured sky.

Maddox spotted what appeared to be an exit and attempted a run for it, only to painfully strike an invisible shield that knocked him to the ground.

'There is no escape, Commander,' the voice repeated once again.

Undeterred, Maddox got back on his feet and began to cautiously test the area covered by the shield. He realised he was hopelessly trapped, reached for his laser beam generator, and crouched down into a firing position. A pencil-like beam struck the shield and caused a bright halation but it remained intact.

'Your Earth weapons are useless here, Commander. You are on the planet you call Uranus.'

That voice! It had surely come directly from behind him!

Maddox spun around to face The Uranus Leader. The creature wore a skin-like material of geometric design that matched his environment. Maddox couldn't help but be impressed by his great presence.

'Uranus?' he asked, still unsure of where he was.

'Yes, Commander. The planet you have under surveillance, but we have been watching you.'

'Then it is your spaceship,' Maddox said, referring to the object parked above Moon City.

'It is, and we don't like what we see, Commander. Since the beginning of your civilisation, Earthmen have been shrouded by their atmosphere. Now that shroud has been pierced. You have colonised your Moon. You have established a launching platform that will enable you to journey into space. We have no intention of allowing that to happen, Commander.'

'But you don't…' Maddox stopped in his tracks as the creature instantly disappeared.

'Oh! But we <u>do</u> understand,' came the voice, once again from behind him. He whipped around and saw The Uranus Leader standing in another part of the complex.

'Our intentions are not war-like,' Maddox explained. 'The building of Moon City was an achievement only made possible by the peaceful co-operation of the major nations on Earth. The concept of Moon City is, and always has been defensive, <u>not</u> offensive.'

'Defensive?' the Alien scoffed. 'Look!'

Maddox turned in the direction The Uranus Leader pointed and saw an image appear in mid-air, not part of any console or screen, of a military installation within Moon City.

'Defensive, Commander?'

'Yes, defensive… We are stepping into the unknown. This is Man's first encounter with another life form in the universe – how do we know that you aren't hostile?'

'You don't,' said the Alien as it suddenly spun around to face Maddox. 'Why don't you kill me, Commander? You're armed… I'm not.'

The Space Commander frowned at the unexpected dare, 'I have no reason to kill you.'

'Wrong!' the Leader said in an aggressive tone. 'You recognise my power is greater than yours. You are unsure how effective your weapons would be, or how I might retaliate.'

Maddox remained silent. He reluctantly had to admit to himself that there was a grain of truth in the accusation.

The Leader challenged again, 'What if the position were to be reversed, Commander?'

'You have a very poor opinion of us, whatever action you may take, you will never stop Man's progress. You're right, Earth's shroud has been pierced. We are already in Space.'

'But you will go no further… Believe me, Commander… we mean what we say.'

The Leader paused for a moment, his tone softened, 'My first encounter with an Earthman… I'm impressed… I would like to believe your version of Man's interest in Space. But unfortunately, your Earth's history does not bear this out. You say that your base is defensive – you are the Commander. What is your brief?'

Suddenly, Maddox was enveloped in a bright circle of light – he was about to respond when the Alien stopped him, 'You don't need to answer, Commander.'

'Space Commander Maddox,' came another voice from all around. It had a familiar strict militaristic tone he had heard once before. 'You are hereby appointed Head of Operations, Moon City. You are to investigate and probe deep space in a quest for new mineral and energy sources, so that ultimately Man may exploit and colonise habitable planets. It is the beginning of a new and exciting era – the conquest of Space.'

The Alien Leader raised his hand, 'You have seen all you will ever see of this planet, Commander.'

The band of light disappeared and Maddox dropped to the floor, then blacked out.

When he eventually awoke, Maddox found himself back in his Living Quarters. He hauled his aching body up, and reached for the communications console.

'Control? Commander Maddox.'

'Yes, Sir?' the voice replied.

'Everything OK?' he asked warily.

'Yes, sir,' came a confused reply. 'Same as it was when you checked two minutes ago.'

He was stunned and barely heard the voice call out, 'Commander?'

'Right… thanks…,' he acknowledged.

Maddox cautiously moved toward the window. The Alien ship still hovered beyond the horizon, its position unchanged. A reflex action caused him to shield his eyes when the green light pulsated but it was no brighter than normal.

Maddox approached his door with suspicion, only for it to open upon his approach. Assured that all was normal again, the Commander slumped onto the bed, exhausted. Cupping his chin in his hands, he tried to make sense of all that had happened.

Upon hearing the whole story of the encounter in Maddox's office, Doctor Marc Miller opined, 'Sure, we live in an artificial environment. We generate gravity to simulate Earth conditions. Our air, water and waste materials are recycled. We have no day and night as we know it on Earth. Of course, it is possible these conditions could cause disorientation but, in the three years this base has been operational, psychological side effects have been practically nil.'

'So what's the explanation, Marc?'

Miller shrugged, 'Without conducting extensive medical tests, I'm as bewildered as you are.'

'Maybe I can save you the trouble – the C. 42 is about to transmit its second batch of information – if it doesn't come through, then what I experienced was a reality!'

'Well, all systems are fully operational. I suppose there is a remote chance of a collision with a meteorite, although the "On Board" guidance systems should take care of that. Yes… if that information doesn't come through, I admit that would leave some question marks.'

'T minus 20,' the female technician announced as Maddox and Miller entered the control centre. '5… 4… 3… 2… 1… transmission.'

Instead of the expected data burst sound that previously came from the probe, the room filled with an electronic tone that rose in volume.

The Controller shouted over the din, 'We have Radio interference, sir.'

Maddox's mind raced as he turned to Miller then ran up the stairs to the observation gantry. He instinctively shielded his eyes as he looked out at the Alien spaceship, still pulsating brightly. He turned away and called down, 'Lieutenant! Check if interference is being generated by the Alien ship.'

The Controller turned to an operator and ordered, 'Scan all frequencies Star Map Area Green Zero Four.'

The operator's fingers danced across their control console until the requested data spewed out. 'Computers confirm interference from the direction of the Alien craft.'

Miller looked up at Maddox. Behind the Commander, the Alien pulsation had undeniably become brighter.

ACT TWO

'Earth Control from Moon City,' Maddox reported into his desk radio link, 'Moon Ship Zero Three in orbit… about to commence landing sequence. Will advise when General Heineman has disembarked.'

'Transmission acknowledged. Earth Control out.'

Maddox toggled the base's internal intercom. A female voice responded professionally, 'Yes, sir?'

'Verify with all Section Commanders the meeting scheduled for 18:00 hours Moon Time.'

'Right away, sir.'

He rose from his desk, crossed the control centre to Miller's station, and asked, 'Any further transmissions from the Alien ship?'

Miller shook his head, 'Nothing…'

He reached down to the intercom on the Doctor's desk, 'Space Commander Maddox to Moon Ship Zero Three. Scan all radio frequencies. If there is any transmission other than from Moon City, abort the landing immediately.'

'Moon Ship Zero Three – message acknowledged,' came the reply as he turned and mounted the stairs to the observation gantry.

Flying low above the Lunar surface, Moon Ship Zero Three, a standard Modular Transport Unit, began its final approach. Maddox saw the vessel through the panoramic window as it hovered barely a hundred feet above the surface and slowly manoeuvred for its landing at Moon City.

The M.T.U.'s downward thrusters fired and Maddox's face grimaced in horror. The ship uncharacteristically reared nose up, hung stationary for what seemed a brief moment, before shattering into a fiery mass of small projectiles. The impact violently shook the control centre.

'We're out of control,' said the voice of the pilot.

He was immediately followed by the co-pilot, 'Thrust on Number 2 exceeding maximum.'

'Reduce power!' came a panicked shout. 'Bring the nose down.'

'I can't – there's too much thrust – I just can't…'

The recording ended, no doubt as the M.T.U. exploded.

Maddox, Miller and Lt. Caron stood in silence until the Commander observed thoughtfully, 'Hmm! Thrust on Number 2 exceeding maximum… Lt. Caron, what does the Flight Recorder tell us about the motors?'

'All motors were delivering their normal thrust, sir.'

Miller frowned, 'Are you sure?'

'I've checked and double checked – yes, I'm sure.'

Maddox paced the room as he worked the problem out in his head. 'The downward thrust motors develop full power on landing. How can a motor suddenly deliver more power than its optimum performance?'

'It would only have to be a marginal increase in thrust to upset the ship at such a critical time,' Lt. Caron pointed out.

'And at that altitude the crew would almost certainly panic,' Miller added.

The statement shocked Maddox, 'Panic?'

'I've investigated many crashes, sir,' Lt. Caron concurred. 'Even the most experienced crews can panic when a ship's out of control at that height.'

'OK,' he said, reluctantly accepting the possibility. 'Now tell me under what circumstances does a proven rocket motor deliver more thrust than its known maximum capability?'

Caron stood silent, unable to answer the Commander's question.

The silence in the room was broken by the electronic chirp of the video intercom. They looked up at the twin TV monitors. One displayed a constant scan of the Lunar surface. The other, which normally displayed a stand-by graphic labeled MOON CITY INTERCOM, displayed the face of the Medical Officer, Doctor Gordon.

'Dr. Marc Miller required urgently in Medical Bay,' she called out.

'This is the Medical Report on Lt. Caron.' Dr. Gordon said as she handed a printout to Miller. 'I thought you ought to see it right away.'

'How long was he on the Moon surface?' he asked as he scanned the data.

'It took him about four hours to recover the Flight Recorder from the wreckage.'

'Stress factors amazingly low,' he marvelled.

'The lowest recorded on a post-Moonwalk check,' she pointed out. 'What does it mean, Doctor?'

'I don't know, but there could be a link… Recall Lt. Caron immediately for further checks and…'

Before he could complete his instructions, Maddox's voice blasted over the intercom.

'Moon Alert!… Moon Alert!… All personnel to action stations!' The Commander's face appeared on Communications Columns across Moon City.

'Repeat – all personnel to action stations.'

Miller made his way briskly back to the control centre, dodging personnel as they scrambled to get to their posts. The wall separating the office from the control centre once again slid open as Miller arrived.

'Stand-by for further instructions,' Maddox said, then turned to the Controller, 'Give me Video-scan.'

The giant control centre screen displayed an image of the Alien ship in motion.

'Moving in for the kill?' Miller observed.

Without answering, Maddox turned to the Controller, 'Trajectory?'

The Controller just had to glance at his team. They immediately went into action, fingers dancing across their consoles. The Controller analysed all the gathered data then reported, 'Trajectory termination… approximately 200 miles south of Moon City. Missile Guidance Systems locked onto Alien ship. Awaiting firing instructions.'

'Are you going to attack?' Miller asked Maddox.

'Not unless they do,' he replied. Once again, he asked for an update, 'Trajectory?'

'Landing position still forecast 200 miles south of Moon City.'

Maddox keyed the intercom, 'Space Commander Maddox to Modular Transportation Unit – prepare an M.T.U. for immediate take-off…'

With all Moon City personnel manning their posts, Maddox and Miller moved quickly through empty corridors to the Travel Tube Unit. Selecting the button marked M.T.U. on the control console, a hiss of compressed air signalled the start of the small, six-seater cylindrical compartment. It raced along the sealed tunnel toward the launch pad.

'They think we're hostile, Marc,' the Commander said. 'I think the only chance we stand is to prove to them we're not.'

'But they can hardly be planning an attack with only one ship.'

'You're thinking in terms of Earth technology,' Maddox reminded him. 'We don't know what power that ship's got.'

The Travel Tube car arrived at an array of large buildings containing vertical take-off launch platforms. This was the M.T.U. Section of Moon City where a number of the versatile craft, in a variety of work configurations, sat ready to go at a moments notice on their pads.

As the large boarding tube extended and locked on to one vessel, the Travel Tube Unit, with Maddox and Miller, ran up to the docking hatch. The two men entered the M.T.U. Command Module, with the Commander taking the pilot's seat. The Travel Tube Unit then disengaged from the M.T.U. hatch and, after the boarding tube retracted clear, the downward thrust motors ignited. The Moon Ship rose to about a hundred feet above the Lunar surface then transitioned to horizontal flight.

In the control centre, Lt. Caron watched the progress of the Alien ship from his temporary position at the Commander's console.

'Commander,' he reported into the radio, 'tracking report on the Alien ship. Landing position unaltered. All radio frequencies scanned – all clear.'

'Right,' came the Commander's reply, '20 miles from landing zone.'

'There it is!' Maddox announced. He guided his ship to a landing some distance away from the Alien craft. Moon dust rose around them, partially obscuring the intruder from their view.

'Program our missiles on the target and keep your finger on the button, Marc.'

As Miller punched in instructions to the on-board computer, Maddox noticed the green light began to pulsate once more on the Alien ship.

Urgently, he cried out, 'Stand by to fire.'

No reply came from the other man. He turned and saw Miller's hand slide off the firing button. His body began to slump forward, eyes eerily wide-open. Maddox grabbed his friend's shoulder, but the Doctor did not react.

The Commander reached over and pushed the firing button.

Nothing happened, there was no missile launch, only that now familiar voice, once again all around him. 'Man's first instinct,' it scoffed.

He pulled his hand away and looked back at the Alien ship, only to need to shield his eyes from the now blinding light.

'Although in this case <u>defensive</u>, Commander.'

Maddox found himself before the Alien Leader, back in the Uranus control room. He was still strapped into his M.T.U. pilot's seat, helpless.

'We have decided on our course of action. It is within our power to destroy Earth totally but that is not our way,' the creature began.

'You are about to start your journey into the unknown – we do not believe that you are a threat, Commander. You represent the scientists, explorers – you believe you are defending right against wrong. It is because of your politicians and war-like leaders that we wish to leave Earth incapsulated in its atmosphere.

'You have learned to use energy through machines – we have found that the greatest source of energy is through the human body and mind. In the Universe there is a wealth of power to draw from – power that you do not yet know exists. But nothing is without sacrifice – energy cannot be destroyed – it can only be converted.

'We will never meet again, Commander.'

Maddox watched as the Alien Leader stared intently at a light source in deep concentration. The pulsation increased greater and greater in strength, enveloping his features in the green light.

Maddox, now back in the M.T.U. Command Module, recoiled from the light. He was able, somehow, to perceive that the rapidly pulsating light was simultaneously in synch on both the Uranus Leader's face and the Alien ship.

Miller remained inert in the co-pilot's chair.

The Moon's surface was bathed in the same glow, as if the Sun itself had turned the colour green. Even within Moon City's command centre, the eerie light poured in from the windows.

A piercing electronic sound filled the Commander's ears. Through the green haze, he saw the Alien Leader apparently wracked in awful pain.

Then suddenly, the light, the sound, all vanished. The Alien Leader's face was tranquil. The creature's body slowly became translucent. Eventually, both he and the Alien spacecraft, faded from existence.

The M.T.U. rested alone on the Lunar surface. Within the Command Module, Maddox stirred. He transmitted a call to Moon City, 'Commander Maddox to Control – Maddox to Control.'

Lt. Caron reacted as the voice the broke the silence, 'Control here, Commander.'

'Everything OK at Moon City?'

'As far as I can tell, sir,' he replied as he looked around, unsure what had just occurred.

'Run a complete personnel check – I want a full report when I get back… keep the base on full alert.'

In the M.T.U. Command Module, Miller finally stirred.

'Marc, you OK,' asked Maddox.

Miller nodded with bewilderment, 'What happened – same as before?'

Lt. Caron rallied the troops back at Moon City. 'Survival check… all Section Commanders report to Control Centre immediately…'

He asked the Controller for an instrumentation check, but the man only shook his head in disbelief at the readings. 'Nothing makes any sense – but it's gonna take us a while to analyse exactly what's happened.'

Miller listened to the Commander's tale of his second encounter with the Alien Leader and then responded, 'None of it adds up, Steve.'

'But I've got a feeling it soon will. Let's return to base.'

Maddox fired the downward thrusters and the M.T.U. rose with surprising violence into the Space Sky. The nose had reared up, just as they had earlier observed with the stricken Moon Ship from Earth.

Alarmed, Maddox applied even more power, but he only succeeded in rolling the M.T.U. on its back. Realising a crash was inevitable, Miller lunged for the duplicate controls before him, forcibly changing the Space Commander's settings.

'Have you gone crazy?' Maddox exploded. 'What are you doing?'

Lazily, the M.T.U. rolled over again then dropped hard, nose first, into the Lunar dust. The space vehicle was down but intact. It was the proverbial "Crash you could walk away from."

There was a moment of silent relief in the Command Module. Miller turned to Maddox, 'Don't you see, Steve... the other Moon Ship... didn't the Pilot say the thrusters were exceeding maximum power? And when Lt. Caron went out to the Moon Surface to recover that Flight Recorder, his stress factor was far below normal.'

The answer hit Maddox like an asteroid strike, 'Of course... gravity!'

Returning to Moon City, the Commander found that tonnes of new data had been collected and fed to the computer. The Controller pulled the latest read-out and scanned it.

'Well,' asked Maddox, 'Does it check?'

'I'm afraid it does.'

Maddox read aloud, 'Moon Gravitational pull down by 70 percent... looks like it's still dropping. Moon's axis tilted forty degrees.'

'Have we re-established contact with Earth?'

'We're sending out distress calls every two minutes,' the Controller replied, shaking his head. 'No response.'

'Keep transmitting.'

The Controller acknowledged and returned to his console.

'Are you going to attempt an evacuation?' Miller asked. 'We haven't got a lot of time, Steve.'

Alone in his office, Maddox stared in thought at the kinetic light patterns that danced across his personal computer screen. He reached out, pressed a control, and spoke, 'Computer – Voice Print Identification.'

In a low feminine voice, the computer responded, '*Space Commander Maddox... Code One... Moon City.*'

'Isolate from Main Computer Bank.'

'*Isolated.*'

'Subject – evacuation of Moon City. All relevant information has been transferred into your memory circuit from Central Control – Code 21B2.'

'*Understood – go ahead.*'

'Request forecast effect of complete loss of gravity on the Moon.'

He waited in silence as the computer gathered all data at its disposal. Finally, it gave an unemotional report, '*Centrifugal force unopposed by the gravitational pull will cause the Moon to break Earth's orbit. This process has already commenced.*'

'Request information on the Sun's ability to retain the Moon in the Solar System,' he asked.

There was another pause, then it said, '*Computation shows Moon's velocity and trajectory with 'Zero G' condition will result in complete breakaway from Solar System.*'

Maddox tensed, carefully formulating his next question, 'Request flight plan for ten M.T.U.s flying at 30-minute intervals from Moon to Earth… lift off commencing 17:30 Earth time.'

Judging by the amount of time and frantic computer activity he saw on his monitors, Maddox knew this was the most complicated question to date. Finally, the computer replied, '*Unable to compute – no precedent of similar conditions in memory bank. Request further information.*'

'No further information available,' Maddox responded helplessly. He was sure he knew what was coming next.

'*Unable to compute – requires human decision.*'

He shut the system down. The Commander then sat a bit longer in silence contemplating that the finale decision was his and his alone.

Maddox returned to the control centre and asked the Controller, 'Any contact with Earth?'

'We have a complete communications breakdown, Commander.'

'How long?'

'Approximately 30 seconds, sir.'

The Commander turned and climbed the stairs to the Observation Gantry where Miller reacted to his approach.

'Have you reached a decision?' he asked.

'Yes…'

'Well?'

Silently, Maddox turned towards the Moon horizon where a giant halo of light was forming. The Earth rose from behind the rim on the crater that Moon City had been constructed within.

'The Moon has turned its blind side towards Earth,' said Miller philosophically.

'For the first and last time,' Maddox agreed. 'Take a good look, Marc… We're never gonna see it again.'

The Space Commander turned to a nearby console, unaware all eyes in the control centre below were upon him. He had made his decision.

'Space City,' he began, 'This is your Commander speaking… you all know by now that as a result of Alien action, the Moon has been robbed of its gravity and is leaving the Solar System…

'I have carefully considered the possibility of attempting an evacuation of Moon City and returning you to Earth – not only would this operation be hazardous in the extreme, but it would appear that we would have very little chance of success.

'There is, therefore, in my opinion – only one course open to us – to remain here in Moon City. Whatever our personal feelings may be at this time, we now commence a battle for survival – Survival in Deep Space.'

Outside the viewports, they all watched as the Earth receded from view…

OBSERVATIONS

This 30-minute format script is atypical of the majority of
opening episodes Gerry and Sylvia Anderson have written for
their earlier 'Supermarionation' puppet series. It concentrates
more on setting up the series' format; a) the Moon thrown out
into space, b) the humans as the actual invaders. Due to the
limitations of cramming so much information into such a limited
time, the script is also typically weak on character development.
The Andersons tended to leave much of that to subsequent
episodes. It's interesting to note that the word 'breakaway'
appears in the dialogue here, prior to the pilot episode going
through multiple title variations including '*Zero G*', '*The Last
of the Earth Men*', '*The Void Ahead*', and '*Turning Point*' before
settling on '*Breakaway*'. – David Hirsch and Robert E. Wood.

I honestly can't recollect having read it before, perhaps because
Gerry and Sylvia chose to keep it to themselves. Although the
idea that Aliens should consider confining humans to Earth's
atmosphere because of their history of man's inhumanity to man
clearly found its way somehow into '*War Games*' – Christopher
Penfold.

THE VOID AHEAD

First Draft
by George Bellak
Adapted by David Hirsch

ACT ONE

The N.D.U. 2. Area was an eerie sight on the dark side of the Moon. A Nuclear Disposal Unit, harshly lit by constant floodlights and surrounded by a physical fence. It was sealed off from the surrounding Moonscape, with glaring warning signs, mounted in equidistant spaces screaming:

DANGER

STAY AWAY

RADIATION

BY AUTHORITY OF NUCLEAR DISPOSAL

AUTHORITY BOARD

1999

Despite the inherent danger, an operation was in progress. A spacecraft hovered above and, at the end of its attached line, the crew lowered a massive container into a hole dug into the Lunar soil. All around, ominous structures rose up, mounds of concrete-like material that had covered other holes. This was the newest burial ground for Earth-used atomic fuel waste.

At some distance outside this radiation-dangerous area, two Disposal Unit crewmen stood in standard outside Moon surface gear. The control panel of a complicated sensing unit stood open between them as they attempted to repair it.

At the same time, Professor Bergman was in his private quarters on Moon Base Alpha. He was an intellectual, somewhat austere man with a face that had seen some time. He wrote in his notebook, dictating to himself in a voice that was a combination of science and humanity, of logic and controlled emotion, but now tinged with shock.

"September 9, 1999. It has been only thirty days since I arrived here on Moon Base Alpha... thirty days of events almost impossible for the mind to encompass... incredible events... proving, once again, that immutable law of nature... every advance in our technology brings us closer to some new threshold of danger..."

One of the Disposal Unit crewmen finished checking the electronic device and closed the panel. From the nearby window of the Depository Building, Helena Russell watched the entire operation with deep concentration.

'This unit's operating now,' came the report over the comm system. 'And...'

The voice suddenly cut off and Russell tensed, apprehensive of the rather sudden and unexpected silence. Peering forward through the viewport, she could just make out the puzzled and confused expression on the face of the crewman in his bubble helmet.

'Where is...?' came his voice in a strange, throaty rattle. 'Oh... I...'

The crewman, eyes vacant, face tight, appeared to be moving away, almost floating.

'It's happening,' Helena cried out. 'Look!'

Depot Chief Gundlach, the youthful but heavy-set commander of the N.D.D. called into his communicator, 'Steiner... Get Nordstrom. Get him in here.'

'He just lost touch . . .' she breathed.

The crewman, Nordstrom, eyes glazed over, continued to drift towards the wire fence that surrounded the storage site. He struggled to lift his right hand, but found the simple move difficult.

Steiner ran as fast as he could, bounding in the low Lunar gravity as Gundlach's voice echoed in his helmet, 'Grab him . . . damn it!'

A crewman in the nuclear shuttle's doorway watched helplessly from above as Steiner moved toward Nordstrom, grabbed him, and they began to struggle awkwardly in the low gravity. Their bodies tumbled toward the fence.

Suddenly, Steiner's protective suit was caught by a sharp pointed link on the fence. Pulled, it began to rip. Aware of what was happening, Nordstrom scrambled to prevent his own suit from becoming entangled.

Helena and Gundlach could only watch helpless and horrified from the depot. Nordstrom's voice wailed from the speakers, 'His suit's gone... God... He just... It wasn't my fault...'

'Get in here,' Gundlach ordered and then turned to Helena. 'Doctor . . .'

At that moment her communicator beeped, and Dr. Fujita's voice announced, 'Commander Koenig's E.T.A. is nine minutes.'

'Leaving now.' She paused, then added, 'We've had an… accident here.'

'Like the other two,' Gundlach whispered to himself in agreement.

Without a further word, Helena pointed her commlock unit at the interlock door and buzzed it open. As she moved to the door, Nordstrom silently entered and ripped off his headpiece. His breath was heavy, his face distorted with fear.

Great excitement and hubbub filled Central Control as men and women moved about, tense with apprehension. Vorkonen, the high-ranking member of the Command staff, turned to Probe Section Pilot Sergio Catani. The two men exchanged a dubious look before leading two men and a woman to the Launching Pad.

The group watched and waited as the arriving craft settled down. The walk tube then moved into position and, as the hatch opened, a ladder descended. As John Koenig stepped out at a brisk pace, his eyes caught everything about him.

The group surged forward, and their leader began, 'Commander… I'm…'

'Vorkonen, my adjutant,' Koenig broke in, a trifle impatient, as he walked directly toward Central Control. 'I know… we talked from the Earth Station…'

'Right,' agreed Vorkonen, as the group followed behind Koenig. 'We got the final order for your takeover and arrival only at eighteen hundred hours, yesterday, so the paperwork's not exactly in order.'

Ignoring that, Koenig asked, 'Is Probe Captain Catani here?'

'I'm Catani, Commander,' said a man walking next to Vorkonen.

'I want to see you, immediately.'

'It's mutual.'

One of the women in the group chimed in, 'I'd like to see you, immediately, Commander...'

Koenig looked her over for a moment and then asked, 'Medical Section. Dr. Russell?'

'I hope my Earth Station photo was flattering.'

'Commissioner Symonds described you,' he said as he continued to examine her.

'And an old teacher of yours described you,' she returned the look of inspection.

Koenig was confused for a moment, 'Teacher? Of mine?'

'Professor Bergman.'

'Here?' he asked with a surprised expression.

'Came last week, yes. And described you perfectly.' Pleasantries now aside, her voice switched back to business, 'Can we set up a meeting as quickly as possible? Now, for instance.'

Instead of replying, Koenig turned to Vorkonen, 'One, I'll want Professor Bergman to come as soon as possible. Two, I want to tour the installation. Set that for sixteen hundred hours.

'Catani? I'll see you at the Probe Section at fifteen hundred hours.'

'Commander...' began the Computer Technical Chief, an intensely austere looking man.

'I do want to have a session with you, Mr. Ouma,' acknowledged Koenig. 'I'll want a lot of new inputs for Central Computer. But I'll have to call you about when.'

'Fine.'

'You haven't answered my question, Commander,' said an annoyed Helena.

'It wasn't a question at all,' came a dismissive reply as he walked into a Travel Tube car. Through its viewports, the Moonscape and some buildings of the installation were visible.

'Ten people have contracted this, Commander,' she persisted as the entire group followed on board. 'Ten people in just a little over two months. Eleven, with the man this afternoon.'

'I've read your reports, Doctor,' he stated in a chilly tone.

'Am I boring you? We have no idea where this is coming from, who it will attack next or why…'

'We have a few notions.'

'So do I. I expressed them to the former Commander, but he chose to ignore them. Will you?'

'Only if it's prejudice – without hard evidence.'

As the Travel Tube car engaged, it was evident to the rest of the group that a battle of wills was brewing.

'Yes… Earth Station orders <u>have</u> been followed. All reports on these… "accidents" have been reported on an "eyes only" basis, but no-one can keep a tight lid on this, Commander, not Commissioner Symonds, not you. It's spread out too far.'

Koenig's voice dropped to a quiet tone, 'I want to see the files on the two Advanced Probe men, Doctor… then we'll talk.'

'That's the whole point, isn't it? The setback in the Deep Probe schedule because those two super-trained Probe men are in my section right now turned into semi-catatonics.'

'That's a factor in my being sent up here, yes, I can hardly deny it.'

'And the others? And the possible others?'

Choosing his words carefully, Koenig replied, 'Dr. Russell, I am concerned with the present and the future of this Moon Base, and everyone on it. I worked on the first establishing settlement ten years ago… I set up the first deep space probes from here.'

'I know all about your efforts, but…'

He cut her off, 'I was one of those who <u>knew</u> we could create a stable environment for ourselves on the Moon and jump off from here for every star out there, I <u>knew that</u>.'

'In light of what's been happening,' she asked in a whisper, 'Are you still sure you're right?'

A video screen in the Medical Section was split between two separate patients. Both men on beds were covered in sensors. Their faces stared vacantly with the right sides waxy... shrunken... repellent. Information supplied by the sensors scrolled beneath each image.

'That's how they became within twenty-four hours of the onset.' Helena's voice broke the sombre air. Koenig was fixed on the monitor images, a look of disbelief on his face.

'I knew... I know both of them,' he muttered. 'They trained for eight months for the new mission.'

'In five cases, people just lost control of themselves, and had a fatal accident – as of this afternoon. In three cases, we brought them in, and they had odd brain damage effects... causing death.'

'You said there were some recoveries?'

'One. No special treatment. A recovery as mysterious as the attack.'

'And these two?'

'Suddenly stricken. Surviving for six days in this state. That's twelve out of three hundred personnel... one percent in two months, Commander... One and a quarter. For a controlled environment like this, that's incredible.'

Helena pushed a button on a diagnostic panel and brought up a huge, detailed set of scans. 'Brain X-ray Holographs... The right hemisphere is tremendously swollen... all functions collapse.'

'Have you ever seen that before, in your practice?'

'Never. But it's as though the genetic restrictions have been removed – destroyed, as though by atomic radiation.'

'I'm aware of your ideas, Doctor...' he said dismissively.

Helena snapped off the X-rays and said, 'All the victims either worked at the Nuclear Disposal Depot, or they visited, for some reason.'

'The two Probe men did neither,' he snapped back. 'Not even one visit to the Depot. Their logs would tell us. And what about everyone else who works there or has visited... even you?'

'We know, Commander, that there are different radiation tolerances among human beings.'

'Doctor, Earth Base gets all the metering reports for the Nuclear Waste Depot. It's part of our responsibility up here to operate and maintain that installation.'

'Spare me the lecture, Commander,' she said coldly, 'I've been on Alpha almost a year, I know what our functions are.'

'But you obviously don't know that there are <u>no</u> changes in fission levels. There's no rise in radiation from that pile of waste. And your autopsy reports on the victims indicate no trace of neutron activity whatsoever.'

'I agree that it's not conventional radiation. But it is a cell affecting process, I'm convinced, and its source is in that depot.'

'Your opinion, Doctor... and this interview is to be held confidential, of course.'

Helena stared at him in disbelief, 'I knew Symonds would send <u>his</u> man, I knew it.'

Controlling his anger, Koenig growled, 'What did you say?'

'Everything's political with him. The Depot... The Probe... Alpha Base itself. And it's all turning into a hot potato. You're up here to <u>handle</u> it... because you're clever and your predecessor was a bungler. But before you handle anything, it may kill us all.'

Koenig met with Catani at the elevator gantry to the Probe ship. As the lift rose, Catani explained, 'They were both on a routine training flight in the special T.U. Five. Nothing unusual happened at all because we tracked them all the way, as always. Then when they came down, it was on automatic and when the hatch opened, they were almost stiff. It was terrible.'

'That was three days ago.' Catani nodded in agreement and Koenig continued, 'And they didn't go near the N.D. Installation.'

'So far as I know. Their flight logs have been fed into Central Computer, so you can examine them yourself.'

The lift stopped at the main hatch and the two men entered the impressive interior of the Probe Ship while a technician on board adjusted a piece of equipment.

'The new drive design is terrific,' Catani said proudly, 'We are all set to go. Those two were the best Probemen we have in the section, and now…'

'How long a delay do you figure?' asked Koenig.

'Take four months to feed the backup men the program.' Catani's voice turned angry, 'I told Commander Grodno… I said let's train First crews and the back-up at the same time, but he…'

'Forget him. He's gone. We have to deal with it now.'

'I tell you this. I think the sickness is something connected with the new Probe… with these Meta Frequency Signals we're trying to trace.'

'I'm considering that.'

'What else can it be? It comes so suddenly. When did we compute that these were inner Galaxy signals, one year ago? And Alpha had been on the Moon now, for over ten years. And the Nuclear Depot for over twenty.'

The technician ceased working and moved over to them. 'Commander?' he asked apprehensively. 'I'm Sensor Tech. Four Allison…'

'Oh…' responded Koenig, slightly puzzled at the interruption. 'Looks like you're doing a fine job on this ship.'

'Commander, Sensor Tech. Three Manitis was at N.D. Installation duty and died three weeks ago… The Medical Section said it was an accident – gravity mis-operation.'

THE VOID AHEAD   Act One

Catani tried to intervene, 'Allison, Commander Koenig's not here to…'

'I don't believe it was gravity mis-operation,' the Tech. persisted. 'Because I heard that someone suddenly froze at one of the lift units at the N.D. and he died, and they called that gravity mis-operation.'

'Allison, you're talking about very serious things,' Koenig said calmly, 'And either…'

'I'm all over this base on sensor repair,' he interrupted. 'And I want to know the truth about what's going on.'

'Calm down,' Koenig said in an attempt to reassure Allison. Instead, he became even more agitated.

'I'm not the only one who wants to know, either.'

Catani had had enough with the man, 'I want you off this ship. Report to your Section Commander.'

'Listen to me,' the technician pleaded.

'Allison…' Koenig tried again.

'Manitis was a good friend of mine. We did a tour here, together. And now he's…'

Grabbing the man's hands, Koenig tried to calm him, 'Allison, I sympathise, but your behaviour's irrational…'

'There have been more deaths than those two… I know that…'

Catani moved in to help restrain the hysterical technician, but he continued to struggle against them.

'Allison, listen to me… Allison!' The man froze after the Commander shouted his name. 'There are certain… unexplained situations occurring. But it's not going to do anybody any good to go off the deep end about them. Alpha Base isn't New York or London or Peking. You sign on to come up here and it's still something of an unknown frontier. Understand? Now either I believe you're going to maintain confidence about what I just said or you're going to be confined to your quarters until further notice.'

'I will… Yes,' he said too quickly. 'I will.'

'You won't,' Koenig sighed, almost sadly. He turned to Catani, 'Captain, take him in to Security, yourself. I'll call in the orders.'

Koenig was still tense when he stalked into Central Control and asked Vorkonen, 'You locate Professor Bergman?'

'He's over at the A.G.S.'

'Is he?' A small smile came as his face relaxed, perhaps for the first time. He noticed Vorkonen's puzzled look and explained, 'He conceived the mathematics for the Gravity system here, you know.'

'I didn't.'

'All out of his head... and so here we are...' Koenig returned to a business-like composure and gestured, 'I want to see you in my office.'

As they started to turn, Ouma came over and handed Koenig a folder. 'This is a check list of new inputs to facilitate High Priority Decisions from Computer Services, and I'd like your opinion, Commander.'

Taking the folder, he said, 'I want a read-out of the flight logs on all Probe Training Flights in the last two months.'

'Fine.'

In his office, Koenig placed Ouma's file upon a pile of others and undid his collar.

'How much talk's going around about the situation?' he inquired.

Vorkonen shrugged, 'I think we have it under control, basically.'

'Don't agree. And my gut feeling is it's getting worse. I want a Security Section meeting as soon as possible.'

'I'll arrange it.'

Koenig jabbed the comm. console and impatiently called to Ouma, 'I want those flight logs… <u>now</u>. Not half an hour from now.'

He released the button and turned back to Vorkonen. 'We have everything feeding into that Comp. One A instantly, but extracting something is another story. Now…'

The buzzing of his intercom unit interrupted him. 'Yes?'

'There's an Earth call on the scrambler line, Commander… Commissioner Symonds,' said a technician's voice. Vorkonen raised his eyebrows and took that as his cue to leave.

Koenig moved to the video screen and watched as the bar scrambler obscured the image, at first. After a series of bleeps, the imposing, middle-aged, worried face of Commissioner Symonds appeared.

'Koenig, I hope this isn't a bad time to call, but I wanted to get your first impressions of the situation.'

'Tense. There was another death, this morning at the N.D.'

'Oh, Lord…'

'The Medical Section… Dr. Russell… she absolutely feels…'

'We know what she feels, Commander,' Symonds broke in. 'But she's mis-diagnosing. She has no reliable data to go on… You agree with that, I'm sure.'

'Tentatively,' Koenig cautiously responded. 'But you know, to facilitate investigation, it might be a good idea to stop shipping the waste up here… temporarily…'

Symonds was shocked, 'Are you serious?'

'I'm exploring the possibilities,' Koenig shrugged.

'Koenig, Earth uses prodigious amounts of energy and we produce great atomic waste. What do you suggest we do with it, in the meantime?'

'Alternative methods'

Symonds scoffed, 'Forgetting the cost, which would be astronomical, where do you think we could put it? Koenig, the fact is that no nation wants it within its boundaries on air, sea or land.'

'You're talking politics,' Koenig said a little grimly.

'Politics?' came the angry response. 'Do you think we would have gotten world co-operation for the establishment of Base Alpha without politics?'

'I am aware of certain realities, but…'

'You're a space adventurer, Koenig, but it takes vast sums of money and negotiations to support those adventures. And a find of failure chops us dead. Which is the important point.

'How are the two Probe men doing?'

'No change.'

'We've put out a statement that they've had a minor training accident, nothing serious. It's being bought by the media… and that's important because we have a Lunar Finance meeting coming up on the fifteenth.'

'How are you explaining the fatalities up here?'

Symonds' response was blunt, 'We're ignoring them. That's not really important. The Probe men are. The public is buzzing about the Meta Signals from Space and the mission you're mounting and all the rest and…'

'Commissioner… Just a moment. Please,' Koenig interrupted as the door to his office buzzed and then opened. A white-faced Vorkonen rushed in, important news obviously necessitating the interruption. He handed a computer printout to the Commander, who scanned it and then turned back to Symonds' image.

'Commissioner, we've just had a computer fatality report. Both Probe men suffered cardiac arrest thirty seconds ago…'

Symonds was absolutely in shock. 'What?'

'They're dead.'

'Both of them?'

Koenig's mind raced as he slumped into his chair and asked out loud, 'Both of them. Dead. From what?'

ACT TWO

A Moonship rose from the base and headed outwards toward the dark horizon. Commander Koenig, at the controls, eased the ship into a smooth horizontal flight. Professor Bergman, sitting in the co-pilot's position, watched the Moon slip by below.

'We've been shipping atomic waste up here for almost twenty years now, Professor, and there have been very few radiation accidents.'

'My friend,' sighed Bergman, 'If neutrons were causing that brain damage, and were jumping about in U-392 fuel-rods, the counters would detect them. Undoubtedly.'

'I know that. I get the same nagging feeling, in a way, that Dr. Russell does... the illness hit people mostly connected with the Depot site... So we'll take a look, and make sure.'

Bergman had noticed that the ground below had begun to darken as the spacecraft approached the terminator. 'What...' he began to search for the right phrase, 'A desolate feeling once Alpha disappears.'

Koenig took in his statement. The module was silent for a moment, save for the tell-tale bleeps of the controls. 'You know,' he finally said, changing the subject, 'I couldn't believe it when she said you were here. You've never visited the base. Ever.'

Bergman shrugged and confessed, 'Perhaps a little... frightened... of the reality.'

'Weren't you ever curious to see the hardware you helped dream up... in action?'

'Well, I suppose so... Because I did come up here, didn't I?' he smiled. 'I'm surprised to see so many of my old students grown up, doing important things... Time must go by faster than I calculate.'

Something suddenly attracted Bergman's attention back to the direct vision port. 'What is that down there... is that the N.D.?'

Koenig looked out at the strange, fenced off area, far below. Grave-like mounds, piled high, stood bathed under eerie floodlights. It looked very primitive amongst the barren landscape.

'Hardly,' Koenig scoffed. 'That was the first nuclear waste area up here. It was closed down five years ago. It was a pilot operation basically, and they learned a lot. It's all closed and sealed now.'

'By the time we're finished, Earth will have pocked and polluted this too... all in the name of survival.'

'There's where we're going,' Koenig said pointing, 'Just a hundred miles on...'

Bergman glanced at bright lights blazing on the horizon. 'Aren't you worried about putting down there? After the history?'

'Are you?'

'Somewhat... But I'm very curious.'

'I'm more than that,' replied Koenig, correcting their flight path into a sweeping curve toward the Waste Depot.

Gundlach led Koenig and Bergman, all three suited-up, to a vantage point within the Waste Storage Area. They had a clear view of another load of atomic waste as it was slung into a hole. 'The sensors are all buried in the ground,' Gundlach explained. 'They detect the slightest rise in radiation count. But that's never happened. Never.'

'Let's go inside,' Koenig indicated toward the Depot Station airlock.

A technician monitored the exterior operation from the Depot control room. Partially out of their suits, Gundlach explained as he led them in, 'The waste ships come up twice a week, average.

All the used-up U-392 atomic fuel on Earth is collected at the Keye's Point Energy Centre in Australia and the launch is from there, directly to here.'

The Depot Chief pressed a button on a wall panel and a steaming cup appeared. 'Coffeesub?' he offered.

'No, thanks,' Koenig dismissed the beverage.

'These monitor all the inputs,' Bergman asked, indicating a bank of scopes and meters.

'Microsecond by microsecond, of radiation and consequent heat rise,' answered Gundlach. 'Real time computations. You can see for yourself, there's no variation from base normal.'

'None at all. No,' the Professor agreed after scanning the panels.

'I get a rad check every day, and I read negative all the time, but…' Gundlach shrugged, somewhat worriedly. 'I keep thinking about what's happening… Maybe the worst is having to keep quiet about it.'

Bergman was drawn to two scopes, one labelled "**R**", the other "**H**". Both displayed steady lines. Next to them, another scope had shaggy lines. 'This measuring magnetic fluctuation?' he asked, pointing to the second display.

'That's right. It's a check on the A.G…. the artificial gravity control system.'

'Do you produce your own environment?'

'Yes… Gravity changes and atmosphere production are all independent here.'

'Interesting,' the Professor mused while staring out the panoramic window, watching as the crane dropped yet another load into the ground. As the waste disappeared into the pit, Bergman spotted a perceptible upward movement on the shaggy lines.

'Very…,' he mumbled, motioning for Koenig to take a look at the read-out. He pointed back to the scope and asked, 'Mr.

Gundlach… These levels are a point higher than ordinary… have you noticed that?'

'Not really,' he shrugged. 'So long as we don't go below the red zone, the gravity operation is satisfactory… so we've been told.'

'That's below… but what about above?'

The Professor's question mystified Gundlach.

Doctor Fujita completed his medical checks on Koenig and Bergman, all under the impassive observation of Doctor Russell. 'No… nothing,' he reported. 'The scan indicates your patterns are normal. No problems.'

Koenig attempted a poor joke at Helena's expense, 'You sorry to hear that, Doctor?'

She ignored him and walked over to Bergman. 'I didn't realise you had one of the new alloy hearts implanted.'

'Oh yes… My artificial self. As opposed to my artificial real self… It was done two years ago. Just when an old friend perfected the possibility. Without it…' he shrugged.

'You didn't think I'd go to the Depot, did you?' Koenig asked Helena.

'I hoped you would.'

'There's nothing there, believe me.'

'What's Commissioner Symonds going to say about the Probe Men… died of a bad cold?' she scoffed.

'I'm going to recommend he tell the truth.'

'It's congenitally impossible for him to do that,' Bergman said. 'He's a politician.'

Walking from Medical Centre to the Travel Tube interlock door, Koenig asked Bergman, 'The Meta Signals… You know about them, of course.'

'Very exciting… in principle.'

'Probe Captain Catani feels they may have something to do with what's happening. Do you think there's any basis to that?'

'It's an interesting speculation.'

Koenig buzzed the interlock door with his commkey, and they entered the car. As it started to accelerate, they took their seats.

'All we can do is speculate,' Koenig mused. 'We don't know where those Meta Signals are coming from, what their quality is… is it a communication or a by-product of an energy system…'

'Is it measurable, that's the point… can we measure it, see its effects. At this point, no. So how can we deal with it as a cause?'

In an angry, frustrated voice, Koenig suddenly blurted out, 'She says radiation from the Depot…'

'She says radiation damage,' Bergman corrected him.

'Without radiation? Have you ever come across that?'

'No.'

'I'll tell you this… the two Probe Men who were not at the Depot, they're the key to this. They're the key.'

In Koenig's office, a screen displayed a kind of simulation, a recreated electronic flight recording. They watched a pilot's P.O.V. of the Lunar landscape. From high up, it swooped down and then back up into the stars. Running alongside the video image were notations for heading and altitude.

'This is the last training flight,' Koenig explained to Bergman. 'Flight recorder simulated reproduction.'

'They go quite low at times,' observed the Professor. 'That's surprising.'

'They shouldn't move to low altitudes, but they do… All pilots play around.'

'I seem to recognise some of the landscape…'

'That's over at Mare Librum,' Koenig pointed out. 'But they're nowhere near the N.D. Nowhere near…'

Suddenly, the screen went blank and remained blank for a surprising amount of time.

'What the…' Koenig exclaimed as he checked the device.

'Recorder failure?'

'Never known it to happen… Never. We have double tape systems.'

Koenig rewound the tape and impatiently pressed the "Play" key.

Blank again.

'Nothing there,' observed Bergman.

'Incredible,' Koenig agreed. He hit the intercom button, 'I want Section Head Ouma in here. Right now.'

Koenig was incredulous, 'It's blank, just damn blank.'

The door buzzed and a worried Ouma entered, 'Commander?'

'The Probe Recorders. Computer's done something to them, a whole section is wiped out.'

'What?' Ouma blanched.

'They were fed in, weren't they? And you extracted them.'

'Yes, but nothing was destroyed… we would have had a notation if that happened.'

Without a word, Koenig hit "Play" once again on the recorder and showed Ouma the blank spot.

'I don't understand it.'

'Recheck,' Koenig ordered.

'Immediately. But it goes beyond just this. If we're getting information slippage from the Com A. One…' Ouma stopped and shook his head at the thought. 'No… I cannot accept that…'

'Recheck. Now,'

Bergman quietly added, 'It could have been fed in that way.'

'Blank?' Ouma was astonished at the possibility.

The comm. unit buzzed, and Koenig responded, 'Yes?'

'Control Tech has Level Nine readings on the N.D. 1…' came the filtered voice.

Koenig was amazed. 'N.D. 1?'

'Repeat, Level Nine readings. The Section Tech thinks you should observe.'

'The old Depot,' an aghast Koenig reminded Bergman and Ouma. 'Emergency readings.'

In Central Control, the three men gathered around Sabatini, an extremely worried female tech, who pointed to a bank of scopes and meters.

'They just started to click off…,' she explained. 'We don't have too many sensors on that old Depot, just for emergencies… but look…'

'Is that neutron emission?' asked Bergman, whose eye caught a needle moving past a red line.

'That's the point,' she said and indicated another meter. 'Neutron emission is normal…'

'You mean the pile isn't fissioning?' asked Koenig.

'The heat level is building… and every now and then there's something happening I can't make out.'

'Bring in the N.D. 1 on video…'

Another technician punched a series of buttons and the main screen brought up a surprisingly odd image. The ground around the old waste pits trembled strangely. A blue flash suddenly burst out from one mound, then another erupted.

'That's incredible heat in the bottom layer,' observed Sabatini.

'And still no radiation?' asked Bergman.

'No… Fission is within normal range.'

'It's incomprehensible,' exclaimed Koenig. 'Heat with no atomic action… Professor, that pile of U-392 is completely inactive. Inactive.'

'But it's burning up, somehow,' objected Sabatini. 'Look at it…'

More blue flashes criss-crossed the area as the Lunar soil heaved upward. The image suddenly flared and disappeared.

'Burnout,' reported Sabatini. 'The camera's gone…'

The needles on her panel vibrated furiously then all slammed over to the highest point and remained fixed there.

'The sensing units are burned out, too.'

'Is there any way of pulling in other circuits?' Bergman asked her. 'If we could, at least, see what's happening there…'

Koenig turned to the Comm man and ordered, 'Get a message to Probe Captain Catani. I want him on the launch pad in ten minutes.'

He turned to Bergman and said, 'We'll fly over with a relay camera and tape the information.'

'Koenig, we don't know what's happening there,' the Professor cautioned. 'Stay well up.'

Catani manoeuvred the Moonship high over N.D. 1.

'Suddenly, after all these years… Here we are,' Koenig mused.

He watched the ground below quiver and shake until some kind of explosion rocked an interior section. Blue and yellow flashes lashed out and a series of flood lights collapsed to the ground in another section. The Lunar soil continued to heave in waves around the tortured landscape.

The module hovered high near the centre of the disturbance, its interior illuminated by more and more of the lightning that continued to dance about.

'The heat is fantastic down there,' observed Catani. 'It must be burning up inside.'

'We're coming right over it, now… Better go up so we don't get burnout on the video, too…'

'Right,' agreed Catani. He tried to raise the ship, but there was no response.

'Get up!' Koenig shouted as the module began to pitch and yaw.

'The guidance system's gone wild. We can't…' Suddenly, the module heaved dreadfully. Koenig, not strapped into his chair, was thrown outward as the craft gyrated violently out of control.

'Back-ups failing,' shouted Catani. 'All guidance is out… We…'

Catani's body broke free of his safety straps. He slammed into the module's ceiling, then dropped back down, unconscious and bleeding from a head wound. Koenig grabbed a hand-hold and made an attempt to reach the control panel. Despite the fact that everything pitched and reeled around him, he battled for control and fired a series of thrusters to steady the craft.

Illuminated now only by the flashes of lightning from N.D. 1 below, the Moonship module jerked around the space sky. It shot sideways, stopped, then hovered before it finally limped away and gained speed.

Having miraculously regained control of the spaceship, Koenig sat back in silence, then glanced at the unconscious Catani. The Comm. Tech's desperate plea on the radio went ignored, 'Command ship… video is out… Are you all right? Please report. Please report.'

ACT THREE

The Command Module pitched and yawed almost in limbo, but the image before them was only an illusion. In reality, they were watching a recreation mounted within the 3-D holographic simulator of a Technical Section shed, where all experimental equipment was built and studied. Koenig stood alongside the Tech Section Chief, an intense, somewhat impatient Frenchman named Murneau.

'Yes… that's how she acted,' confirmed Koenig. 'Just like that.'

'You're very lucky to have made it out of there, Commander… You had only two thrusters operating,' the man observed as the simulation ended.

A technician approached with a computer printout. He handed it to the Chief and reported, 'We've got the diagnostic printout on the navigation system… Automatic just blanked out on overload… And the first backup, too…'

'I see that, I see it,' said Murneau a little impatiently, 'But why?'

The technician shrugged, 'Heat didn't do it, that's for sure… All cables were intact… insulation clean.'

The door opened and Catani entered, his face covered with a few contusions and a small bandage.

'How are you feeling, Captain?' Koenig asked.

'Foolish. I kept telling them at Medical Section that I was just knocked out, but they gave me a complete check, up and down the scale. Have they come up with anything here?'

'The Navigation system blanked out.'

Catani was incredulous. 'How the hell could that happen?'

Another technician approached and handed Koenig a slip of paper. 'There's an I.C. for you, sir… from Central Control… The N.D.1 seems to be subsiding… heat levels going down.'

'Up… and down,' he mused as he stared at the puzzling sensor log. 'Just like that.'

Walking into a Travel Tube car with Catani, Koenig told the pilot, 'I want tests on that site. Ready a ship and we'll fly the people in as soon as we can.'

'I'll ferry them, myself.'

Koenig gave him a concerned look. Catani only shrugged, 'If it happens again, I'll resign.'

As the car began to accelerate, Koenig inquired, 'Dr. Russell ask you about what's going on?'

'No… all medical business. But she looks, you know, with those eyes,' Catani said with an almost spooked look, then he shrugged once more. 'Interesting woman. Did you know her husband was Captain Telford Russell?'

That information was news to Koenig. 'The man who led the Venus Probe?'

'Surprise you, eh?'

'He was lost, I remember, five years ago, on a mission. Blasted off – and never came back. I never connected the name.'

'That's right. She comes by her… worry… honestly then…'

Catani went quiet for a moment, then repeated, 'Very interesting woman.'

Koenig's beeper broke the silence. He pressed the button and responded, 'Commander Koenig.'

'Professor Bergman, sir,' the Comm. Section voice announced.

'Accept.'

'John,' came the Professor's voice, 'I must see you as soon as possible.'

'Well, I'm on my way to a Section Head meeting right now and…'

'John, I strongly suggest you come here first.'

'Where are you?'

'In my quarters… Oh… It might be helpful to bring the head of the Technical Section with you…'

'He'll be there.'

Bergman held up a burned-out device before the two men. 'This meter was burned out, on the Central Control monitoring board when the N.D. 1 erupted.'

'It's an almost obsolete gauge,' Murneau scoffed while taking the device from him. 'We installed them years ago when the N.D. 1 was operating and had a Depot Building with Environment and Gravity Production.'

'This was measuring magnetic output,' Bergman pointed out. 'When the installation flared, the needle went right off the dial.'

Murneau was still skeptical, 'Are you saying there was a twentyfold rise in magnetic output at that point?'

'Yes.'

'All right,' interjected Koenig, 'So there was a twentyfold surge in Magnetism at the site. What does that mean?'

'I believe that <u>that</u> upsurge in energy output wrecked your Command Navigational system – which is set for stated balances of magnetic feedback… when you flew over and… You went out of control then.'

Bergman noted Murneau was still unconvinced, but Koenig was attentive as ever. He continued on, 'It also seems to me that, if the site was so magnetically hot – and no-one realised it, that magnetic radiation could have wiped out the portion of magnetic tape exposed when, and if, those two Probe men flew over the area, at low altitude, as I now believe they must have.'

Koenig absorbed the information. 'The Recorder simulation looked like a tape blackout to me at first… but I couldn't believe it.'

'That's technically a possibility, yes,' Murneau finally, reluctantly, agreed, 'But you totally neglect the main question… why this incredible increase in Magnetic output?'

'I believe it is a new effect we are facing… an effect arising from the atomic waste deposited here, thoughtlessly, over the years.'

Murneau was angered by the Professor's accusation, 'Every precaution has been taken. That Depot was sealed, synthocreted, buried.'

'And it erupted, nonetheless.'

'Radiation indications are practically nil. There is no fission there, Professor.'

'Radiation, Nuclear radiation, is <u>not</u> the problem. You controlled the expected problem well. But the unexpected problem comes up like a nightmare. Always. And that is the high radiating levels of Magnetic energy.'

'Are you seriously saying Magnetic energy is responsible for the flareup at N.D. 1?' asked Koenig

'I am. I am convinced of it.'

Bergman paused to let that concept sink in, then continued, 'I believe the abandoned Depot burned itself out in some terrible electro-magnetically induced subsurface firestorm. But I'm not concerned with <u>that</u> now since I understand the heat levels are subsiding. But I <u>am</u> concerned with the same exact processes which are unquestionably going on with the N.D. 2.'

'We fly over the N.D. 2 all the time. There's been no problem up to now.'

Bergman shook his head, 'I believe there will be, very soon. The calculations support a very steep curve up in magnetic and heat measurements.'

Murneau prefaced his counterpoint with an apology, 'With all due respect, Professor, to your knowledge of theoretical physics, you tell us about a magnetic effect from our waste fuel that no one has ever discovered before.'

'The science is explainable,' Bergman replied, then turned to Koenig. 'But more important, right now, is the question of time. I think it is imperative to check the energy levels at N.D. 2 – and not just where the sensors are laid… but to check the total area…'

'The sensor pattern is laid out…,' Murneau began to protest again.

'For atomic <u>radiation</u>…,' Bergman interrupted, 'Not for magnetism. We need solid data on magnetic levels.'

'Let's get it,' Koenig told Murneau.

Four technicians in protective suits swept the N.D. 2 Area with hand-held meters, carefully checking on levels. One tech suddenly noticed that his meter was oddly rising and falling when he moved the device around his body.

Inside the Depot Control Room, Koenig watched the team move about the storage pits. Bergman and Gundlach were otherwise fixated on a large scope that displayed collected and computerised remote data. They watched as the large red line steadily rose upwards.

'Those levels are much higher than anything we get on the sensors,' said an excited Gundlach. 'Much.'

Bergman sombrely agreed, 'Yes.'

Nearby, Murneau had joined Koenig at the large window. Their attention was locked on one technician who had stopped moving to stare down at his scope. What neither man could see from their vantage point was that a vague look had now passed over the man's eyes.

The man suddenly dropped his hand-held and Koenig immediately shouted the order, 'Get to that man. Disable him!'

A guard, posted within N.D. 2, bounded towards the dazed tech. He pulled out his stun gun and fired. The tech went down.

'And you don't believe the brain effects,' Koenig grimly scoffed at Murneau. 'Number twelve… and we're lucky at that…'

'Look!' shouted Gundlach, suddenly very apprehensive. He pointed to the heat meter. 'Look at that heat go up! Look at it.'

'This installation holds one hundred and forty times the atomic waste that N.D. 1 held,' Bergman explained to Koenig and Murneau. 'With the heat rising this way, there's no predicting what may happen here, nor when.'

As the Moonship returned to Alpha with Koenig at the controls, Bergman stared in thought at the vanishing installation. Murneau just brooded.

A face appeared on the comm unit, answering the Commander's call. 'Vorkonen, I want an immediate Code Six message sent to Commissioner Symonds.'

'Code Six?'

'Code Six – that's right,' he snapped impatiently.

'The Procedure book on that, normally, is for a Code Two query to be made and then…'

'Forget it. Forget Code Two. I want Symonds up here. You tell him it's Code Six and he'll come.'

Koenig turned and told Bergman, 'I want him face to face.'

Koenig and Vorkonen watched the walk tube extend to the recently landed spaceship. Symonds and his aide, a briefcase in hand, descended from the hatch.

'Commissioner,' Koenig acknowledged.

'Commander…,' came the reply with a cold-eye. He extended a hand and Koenig shook it.

'My office tried to query you on your Code Six…You didn't seem to be available.'

'You've had full reports on the flare-up at N.D. 1.'

'Naturally. It's alarming, I'm informed, but not probable cause for hysteria on the part of an Alpha Base Commander.'

'You're informed of that on Earth Base. We're here – and we know otherwise.'

Symonds stood in the middle of Koenig's office, shocked by Bergman's conclusions. 'Magnetic energy? What are you talking about? We've been using that atomic fuel for years… We know all about it.'

'In the early years we used expensive U-392 as fuel,' the Professor explained in a calm voice. 'But in the last seven or eight, we mixed that with Caesium, good cheap Caesium.'

'Exactly,' Symonds agreed.

'But what do we know about the long-term effects of that waste mixture? Very little.'

'Earth Base has taken all sorts of measurements.'

'On small quantities of U-392 and Caesium waste… because that's all we had. But mass makes qualitative difference. And only now, over the years, have we accumulated this mass of waste, and so only now is it possible to understand what's happening.'

'Now it's there, reacting,' stated Koenig, 'Though not as we expect it to.'

Symonds was still skeptical, 'Magnetism – causing brain damage?'

'Magnetism is energy,' shrugged Bergman. 'All energy radiates…'

'Before we knew that atomic radiation caused cancer, what did we think?' asked Koenig.

This thought stopped Symonds in his tracks. He turned to Murneau for support and asked, 'Do you believe this?'

'We checked Earth Library. At Oak Ridge in 1977, there were indications of pattern changes in ferrous oxides caused by Caesium and U-392. That could only be by magnetic surge.'

Still attempting to hold his ground, Symonds simply stated, 'Well, get a comprehensive report together and I'll take it back to Earth with me and…'

'Report?' exploded an enraged Koenig. He pointed at a monitor image of N.D. 2, 'Commissioner, the heat rise on the interior of that Depot is murderous. And over a hundred times the waste of Depot One is stored in the ground, there… Over a hundred times the danger.'

Symonds nervously blurted out, 'Depot One burned itself out.'

'This Depot could go up! It could explode in the biggest blast that ever happened.'

'If it went up, if it did,' a worried Murneau pointed out, 'There is no way of knowing the magnitude.'

'Well…,' began the Commissioner, still in denial, 'Let's look at the whole picture. This is all guesswork, it seems to me.'

'Guesswork?' Koenig again exploded, 'You send this atomic garbage up here for years because it's the cheapest way to get rid of it, and the most political, and you just shrug it off, don't even think about it, and now all this breaks loose and you talk about guesswork?'

Ever the politician, Symonds held up his hands to calm everyone, 'Let's be sensible, now…'

Koenig wasn't interested in playing his game of political procrastination. 'If that Depot goes up, it may have some overwhelming effect upon this installation, did that ever occur to you? I'm the Commander here. I have the responsibility for over three hundred people and billions of dollars in equipment, tens of years of work and development to make this base damn near self-sufficient. You want me to risk all that?'

Symonds' face began to betray a look of fear that convinced Koenig he had finally reached the man. He glanced back to the screen image of the second Depot, then turned and asked Bergman, 'What… do you suggest? What can be done?'

'We can try to break the pile apart… Rip up the fuel rods, destroy the mass.'

Symonds' aide, silent all this time, made his first and only contribution, 'We could shoot the stuff into space. Get rid of it that way.'

Koenig answered him with a disgusted look, 'Just as we got rid of it up here.'

'If we could spread the mass over a dispersed enough area,' suggested Bergman. 'We might have a chance…'

'Then do that,' Symonds agreed. 'Do it.'

'What about Technical facilities?' Koenig directed his query at Murneau.

'We can rig hover ships with selsyn cables and grips… But how do we know how high up this energy is going to go, now?'

'We'll feed into Central Computer and see what that decision is.' He turned to the Professor, 'What's the time factor?'

'Very poor… And there's no way computer can judge that because we don't have the data… But we have to try anyway…'

On the screen, they suddenly noticed that the ground within N.D. 2 had begun to tremble. Time was running out.

ACT FOUR

A specifically built work module hovered quite high above the Waste Depot. From the underside of the craft, a wire extended to a huge metal grip that grasped a ring mounted upon a synthocrete block of waste. The thrusters fired and the mass began to rise out of the pit where it had been stored.

In Central Control, the entire operation was being carefully monitored.

'That's number three,' counted Koenig.

'Contingency plan "B" has been put into effect,' reported Vorkonen. 'All hardware on Manual Over-ride, Back-up systems checked. Deep stores doors lowered to shock levels…'

'I want Captain Catani to take the new ship up, immediately… and keep it up there.'

'Keep it up?' asked Vorkonen, puzzled by Koenig's order.

'I want that ship safe,' said Koenig in a grim voice. 'No matter what. He keeps it up there 'til he gets orders.'

Symonds, standing at the office door, announced to no one in particular, 'It's working. It's working fine.'

'They have a hundred more to disperse… Commissioner,' said Koenig, hardly masking his contempt for the man.

On the large monitor, a work ship pulled up another block of waste. The Lift Tech's voice reported, 'Number twenty-six… dispersing to Grid C-9.' The ship moved out of frame with the block swinging beneath. Another craft moved in to take its place.

A Command Conference had been called in Koenig's Office. Everyone was there except for Symonds.

'I want the C.A. 1 fed with everything possible, constantly.'

'We're doing that,' Ouma assured the Commander.

'We've had module failure on two units,' Murneau reported. 'But Repair Section has them under control.'

Helena chimed in, 'There's been nothing unusual in medical. That Tech who went into shock is still indecisive.'

'We're all… indecisive… except Commissioner Symonds, maybe… All right, that's it for now. Thank you.'

As the staff began to leave, Koenig reached out to Helena. 'Dr. Russell… Just a moment please.'

They waited until the others had left and a thought occurred to Koenig. 'Just a moment,' he apologised and depressed the comm. button. 'What do we have on levels?'

'Heat levels holding,' came Sandra Sabatini's reply. 'Magnetic level the same… No movement.'

'That's what worries me,' came Bergman's voice, obviously standing next to the woman.

Koenig closed the circuit and turned to Helena, 'I owe you an apology, I didn't take your diagnosis seriously, at first.'

'The illness was unknown. It's hard to deal with that.'

'That's exactly what we get paid to do up here.'

'Heroic sounding… Little bit like a recruiting poster for an Alpha Base Tech job.'

'If you didn't feel just a bit like that, you wouldn't be up here.'

'Maybe,' her voice was non-committal. 'What are the chances of the N.D. going up?'

'Bergman calculates one in three. And whatever damage happens might have been much worse without your warning… So, I'm grateful for it.'

Another Work Ship glided into place, taking up a hovering position over a pit. As the claw came into contact with a synthocrete block a small blue flash connected the two objects for a millisecond.

Over in Central Control, Bergman blinked, not sure if he actually saw something.

Symonds bounded into Koenig's office, practically jubilant. 'All levels are holding steady. We're going to lick this, Koenig.'

'I'm glad you think so,' came the sarcastic retort.

'Now we come to the real business,' he began with a dramatic flare. 'The practical side. How we handle it so far as Earth is concerned… What we say, who we invite up here for first-hand looks.'

'I don't give a damn who you invite. All I care about is that there's something to invite them to.'

Symonds waved him off. 'Go ahead, let off steam, that's all right with me. That's your character. You wouldn't have been asked to take over here if you didn't have that but anyone up here, Commander, anyone, has certain responsibilities…'

'… Not to the politicians… not to the monkeys in dress suits, Commissioner, to this base.' Koenig's anger rose, 'There are people dead… There are Techs out there, dealing with fantastic heat levels… we're breaking our backs and all we can do is run true to form… Wheeling and dealing…'

Suddenly, the image of the operation on Koenig's screen began to flash with a jagged, unearthly light. The Commander punched his comm. button, shouting, 'It's going up… get those crew ships away…'

He raced into Central Control as the Comm. Unit Tech called, 'Crew ships... leave the area... get away... Crew ships... get away.'

Above the Waste Depot, two crew ships had begun pulling in their lines as they moved away. Below them smoke rose, and jagged lightning arced around the open pits. The effect spread across the entire fenced-in area. Without warning, the Depot erupted in a huge blast and streaks of debris raced upward as if to catch the fleeing Moonships.

Caught in the blast, one spacecraft pitched nose down and dove headlong into the Lunar surface.

Shockwaves from the immense blast rocked the Control Centre. Smaller explosions ripped up the ground around Alpha Base. Travel Tubes were twisted or broken, cutting off various sections from one another.

All this destruction was evident to Catani hovering high above. He desperately called out, 'Alpha... Alpha... Can you read me? Alpha... this is Captain Catani. Alpha... I can see the blast. We're all right up here. How are you down there?'

From his high vantage point, a second, even more enormous explosion at the Depot Area was evident. Cracks began to spread all across the Lunar surface before a third explosion, like nothing Catani had ever seen, propelled an incredible, huge chuck of the Moon away from the main body, heaving it off into space.

'My God... My God...' he gasped at the incredible sight.

The entire Moon began to spin erratically before moving strangely out of its ancient orbit in a sickly, lopsided roll.

Within Alpha Base, personnel and fixtures were hurled to the ground. The staff in Central Control attempted to reach their consoles, but some could only make it to their knees.

'I can't... get up,' groaned Helena.

Bergman scanned a panel and nodded, 'There's every indication of it.'

'Do we abandon the base – try to get home?'

'There's a minimum of information.'

'Whatever there is, is in the Comm. A. One…'

Koenig turned to Ouma and ordered, 'I want a Comm. A. One percentage of success read-out on Contingency Plan D…'

'Abandon?' asked Ouma.

'Let's have it,' he demanded impatiently. 'The more time we waste the less chance we have…'

Ouma nodded and turned to Central Computer, dictating instructions to an operator, 'Get a read-out on Plan D. Percentages with current information.'

The operator looked at him but said nothing and began coding the request. They all knew what this meant.

The computer printed a read-out and Koenig grabbed the paper and scanned it, but said nothing. He walked into his office and handed it to Bergman who read the simple statement:

NOT ENOUGH INFORMATION
HUMAN DECISION

Symonds, totally dazed, sat in a chair in Koenig's office wiping blood from his temple. He barely registered the Commander's presence.

Koenig stopped at his desk to stare at a nearby photo of Earth, beautifully hanging in space. He dropped into his chair to wrestle with the agonising choice only he could make.

Finally, the decision made, he returned to Central Control. No one said a word as he entered. The room was quiet, save for the constant hum of computer and the air filtration system.

Koenig drew a breath, then began, 'At this moment, it appears that we have been cut off from our mother planet… As we are, we have power, environment and the possibility of survival. If we try to improvise and escape back to Earth, without travelplots, without full resources, I think we'll fail… so… in my judgement, we don't try.'

As the implications of their fate sank in, Helena dared to break the silence. 'Are you saying we're here – we'll die here. We'll never see home again?'

'Doctor, we have come through this… catastrophe, by some minor miracle,' said Bergman. 'But we are inhabitants of this surface, now, this Moon – and we are alive still and moving into an unknown void.'

'And very lucky to be able to survive,' Koenig added.

'Can we?' she asked.

'We'll find out.'

The Comm. Tech shouted out as the big monitor displayed an image of swirling heavens, 'We're getting a video bounce off the Spacedock satellite.'

Bergman sighed with a touch of irony, 'Ah – perhaps God has spoken to us.'

EPILOGUE

'Earthbase, this is Alpha,' the Comm. Tech. continued to call out. 'Earthbase, this is Alpha… Can you read us, Earth?'

He waited, but still no answer was forthcoming. On the large monitor, the satellite camera showed the Earth and the Moon moving further apart from each other.

'We're not getting there… we're not hitting Earth,' he reported to Koenig.

The Commander turned without a word and retired to his office. There, he found Bergman jotting down some figures on a pad. Marvelling at his calculations, the Professor commented, 'We must be rushing away at an enormous speed.'

'It's so very hard to believe,' Helena said as she entered. 'Things are somewhat normal – yet…'

'Reality dictates that we accept the present as our only possible existence,' Bergman observed.

'I don't accept that,' Koenig scoffed. 'Not for the rest of our lives – artificial gravity, environment – all the rest.'

Bergman shrugged, 'I see little you can do.'

'We have an operating ship. We can repair the others, possibly. We can go out and search for some place compatible with our anatomy. Someplace in the universe there has to be another Earth.'

Frustrated, Koenig began punching some keys on his Comm. Unit. The static-filled image on the monitor in his office cleared. 'It's an Earth transmission,' he exclaimed as he recognised the source.

The image of an announcer appeared, seated at a news desk. His voice faded in, '… totally unforeseen accident on the Lunar Surface has caused very serious repercussions here on Earth. The gravity disruption, the earthquakes in the United States along the San Andreas fault and in Yugoslavia as well as Southern France has caused enormous damage to property and life…'

'If we can get this,' surmised a hopeful Koenig, 'Maybe we're getting closer to Earth, not farther away.'

The transmission continued, 'The International Lunar Commission with its new Chairman is in executive conference, at this moment, deciding what steps might be taken, if any, to rescue the three hundred men and women of the Alpha Base Project… Little hope is held however, that there are any survivors, even now… For a short time it was thought…'

The image quickly degraded and died. Koenig snapped it off, their last link with Earth had gone. Resigned, he rose from his chair and headed into the Control Centre, gesturing for Helena and Bergman to follow.

'Let's get on with it,' he said.

Later, Bergman wrote into his log, "Alpha Base September 9, 1999. We're getting on with it."

OBSERVATIONS

George Bellak's first draft is strongly focused on establishing not only the series' format, but most importantly, a large cast of reoccurring principle characters. As the original Story Editor, he had his eye on creating a community of mixed but equal sexes and races. He also planned out potential future character drama by establishing the Moon Base personnel in realistic terms, intending for them to often be portrayed as a volatile people who were not happy being marooned. His initial scripts for the first episode (at least three drafts were completed before he left the project) made an attempt to create a plausible way to hurl the Moon into deep space. The nightmare description of a shattered far side of the Moon was certainly a missed dramatic opportunity. Professor Bergman's voice-over narration provides an effective intro and outro for the episode, akin to what would be done later in the series when '*Dragon's Domain*' and '*The Testament of Arkadia*' were narrated by Doctor Russell and Commander Koenig, respectively.

TURNING POINT

Final Shooting Script – 5th November 1973
by George Bellak
(uncredited rewrite by Christopher Penfold)
Adapted by David Hirsch

PROLOGUE

MOONBASE ALPHA
– SEPTEMBER 9, 1999

Nuclear Disposal Area 2 was an eerie sight on the dark side of the Moon. The restricted complex was encircled by a laser barrier, projected between a ring of tall columns, each topped by a bank of floodlights whose harsh illumination created a sinister scene.

An Eagle rested horizontally on the Moon Surface. This was Moonbase Alpha's multiple purpose short range spacecraft. A cargo unit was mounted to the vehicle and linked to a long conveyor belt that ran some distance over the surface, ending above a hole in the ground. A massive container moved along the belt, from the Eagle and into the hole, where mechanical handling gear lifted it off, then placed it down into the pit.

Surrounding this activity, ominous mounds rose up – conic structures made from a concrete-like material, each capped by a red inspection port. Clearly numbered, they covered multiple other holes dug into the Lunar surface. This was a burial ground for used atomic fuel that had been shipped from Earth.

At some distance from this activity, two Disposal Area technicians stood wearing spacesuits. Their names, Nordstrom and Steiner, were printed on their helmets. The men were busy making routine checks on one of the many radiation counters that dotted about between the mounds.

Nordstrom completed his check of the monitoring unit, closed the access panel and glanced towards the Disposal Area Depot, sitting just outside the laser barrier.

With tense concentration, Dr. Helena Russell watched the entire operation on T.V. monitors within the Depot. She was a cool, good looking woman in her early thirties, Chief Medical Officer of Moonbase Alpha. Next to the monitor was an instrument panel dominated by oscilloscopes displaying the brain activity, breathing and heartbeats of the two technicians working within the Disposal Area. Over the top of each 'scope was a name plate – **NORDSTROM**, then **STEINER**. The monitor screens and control panels were mounted in front of a wide window on the outer wall that looked out over the Moon surface.

Beside her stood Gundlach, chief of this installation and next to him, Professor Victor Bergman, an intellectual, somewhat austere, dedicated scientist.

'Are they normally out there as long as this?' she asked Gundlach.

'One hour is the limit… just as a precaution – but until recently we've never had any accidents.'

Bergman glanced at the oscilloscopes, 'So far their brain activity is quite normal.'

'So far,' agreed Helena. 'But if there's any variation I'm pulling them out.'

Over the loudspeaker system, Nordstrom reported, 'Unit C4 is operating now – radiation count normal.'

On one T.V. screen, they watched him bounce away towards another radiation counter. While on the other, the face of Main Mission Controller Paul Morrow appeared.

'Dr. Russell, Professor Bergman – Commander Koenig's E.T.A. is in thirty minutes… at 23:35.'

'Thanks, Paul,' Helena acknowledged. She then turned to Bergman and commented, 'I hope he's the right man.'

Bergman had a look of confidence.

An Eagle approached the Moon. Aboard the craft was John Koenig, dressed in the uniform of an Alpha Base Commander. He was perhaps forty – intense, intelligent, and somewhat preoccupied by the Earth News Report now appearing on the T.V. screen, set into the back of the seats of the Passenger Module.

'It was announced today that the two Probe astronauts of the Meta Mission have contracted a mild virus infection during training,' said the newscaster. 'Lunar Commissioner Simmonds reported however that the long-prepared for space mission to Meta would be delayed no more than forty-eight hours.'

Koenig was distracted by the approach of a Stewardess, carrying refreshments. 'Commander, touchdown at Moonbase Alpha will be at 23:35 Lunar time,' she reported.

'Commissioner Simmonds, can you tell us a little more about Meta…' the newscaster prompted.

The screen image pulled back to reveal a man who began speaking emphatically. Various images of the Moon, Moonbase Alpha, a Probeship and Koenig himself appeared behind him. 'Meta is a rogue planet, which has broken away from a solar system many light years away from our own. But its trajectory has now brought it closer to our own solar system. For the very first time in human history, we have identifiable signals which indicate a high form of life on another planet. From Earth's Space Research Centre at Moonbase Alpha, we are going to explore that planet and John Koenig, the newly appointed Alpha Commander, is going to oversee this most important space journey in the history of man.'

Disenchanted, Koenig leaned over and turned off the video.

The two technicians appeared on the T.V. monitors still at work checking radiation counters, when a sudden, high-pitched audio warning bleep alerted Helena. Nordstrom's dedicated 'scope displayed sudden peaks in his brain wave activity.

'Nordstrom! Quick! Get away from there,' she shouted over the intercom.

She couldn't see that Nordstrom's face had taken on a look of utter confusion, his right eye glazed over. He threw down his radiation counter with a strange lack of urgency.

Riveted to the screen, Helena could hear a strange incoherent rattle over the comm. system from Nordstrom's mic. The audio bleeps rapidly sped up to a continuous scream.

'Steiner, help him! He's in trouble. Get him away from there.'

Bergman noticed that Nordstrom had begun to stumble in the direction of the laser barrier. He cried out, 'The laser barrier... Steiner, stop him!'

As Steiner attempted to pull Nordstrom back and away the stricken colleague turned around, ready to fight him. Their struggle was a strange, awkward sight in the low gravity conditions.

Nordstrom was able to pick up Steiner and hurl him easily over his head. The man landed, then bounded weirdly back up. He attempted to grab Nordstrom again but only succeeded in causing both men to tumble down, very close to the active laser barrier.

Nordstrom rose first and hurled himself between the columns. A wall of light flashed between the columns as his body interrupted the laser barrier and Nordstrom fell again.

Steiner attempted to pull his body away, but Nordstrom bounded against the barrier once again. The wall of laser light flashed a second time, sending the man to the ground. Nordstrom's visor slammed into a Moon-rock and cracked, his protection gone. The body stopped moving, eyes and mouth open wide.

Helena watched from the depot, horrified.

ACT ONE

As the Eagle settled down on the pad, a Travel Tube telescoped towards the hatch of the Passenger Module and locked on.

Koenig, a slim briefcase in hand, moved toward the airlock door. He paused for a moment to consider the implications of his arrival. The hatch finally slid open and he walked through into the Travel Tube where Professor Bergman waited to receive him. The two men greeted each other with warm affection.

Koenig smiled, 'Victor... Still here?'

'I got caught,' he shrugged and handed Koenig his commlock. 'Things are far more serious than I suspect you've been told.'

'Oh? What do you mean?'

'People are dying up here, John.'

'The "virus infection?"'

'The "virus infection."'

Hiding his tension, Koenig put on his best genial appearance and wore a relaxed face as he stepped into Main Mission. This was a very large area, built like everything else on Alpha from modular units, a clean, functional space packed with electronic equipment.

They had entered from one of two doors on the far side of the room. A large video screen was situated, high up, between them.

On one side was an observation gallery with a panoramic view over the Moon surface, up into the space sky. At the opposite end, up some steps was the Commander's console. A group of control consoles filled the centre of the room. Four of the six were manned, while other personnel walked around, taking readings.

The staff turned to watch Koenig as he entered, one or two greeting him in a familiar manner. Yet, despite Koenig's warm smile, there remained an air of tension and expectancy permeating the room.

Main Mission Controller Paul Morrow rose from his console and offered his hand, 'Welcome back, Commander.'

Koenig acknowledged him and then, with Bergman in tow, continued into his spacious adjoining office. The command desk sat next to the wall that divided it from the Control Room. Another set of steps led down into a conference area. A commpost sat off in one corner.

Koenig placed his briefcase down. Out of the sight of the Command Staff, his geniality evaporated. 'No virus infection?' he asked Bergman.

'No virus infection!'

'Then what is it?'

'Dr. Russell has some interesting theories.'

'Any facts?'

'A few – theories mostly – specifically one dealing with radiation.'

'Radiation!' scoffed Koenig. 'Earth Command doesn't buy it!'

'They can't afford to buy it!'

'I'll talk to the Doctor.'

'Dr. Russell – John Koenig,' he introduced himself as he entered the Doctor's office.

She acknowledged his offered hand, 'Commander.'

'Well, Doctor, tell me about this… virus. When will the men's recovery…'

'I can tell you nothing about a virus,' she interrupted. 'I can tell you we have an unusual form of brain damage. One that we have not seen before.'

'You're telling me it's not a virus?'

'That's exactly what I'm telling you, Commander.'

'Then, what is it?'

'It's a cell-affecting process – that I'm certain of.

'There have been eleven cases so far. Nine were workers at Nuclear Waste Disposal Area Two. Three of them suffered disorientation which led to fatal accidents, five were brought in here and died of brain damage. The ninth died trying to break through the laser barrier just thirty minutes ago.

'That leaves the two Meta Probe astronauts…'

'Their condition?' he interrupted.

'This is where it's inconsistent. So far as I know, they have not been exposed to radiation of any kind, yet they're experiencing the same symptoms.'

Helena reached for a switch by a screen and pressed it. An amazingly clear, almost three-dimensional colour X-ray of a human brain was displayed. One side appeared grotesquely misshapen. 'Look,' she pointed to the area. 'This is what the radiation does. The right hemisphere comes under attack. There is immediate disorientation…'

Koenig interrupted her again, 'Doctor, your theory rests on the fact that radiation is causing this damage.'

'Yes.'

'Look, we've been shipping atomic waste up here for years. There has never been a serious accident. Our latest reports from the Disposal Area indicate that the radiation count is well within the safety limits. Not only that, but you just said these two men have not been exposed to any radio-active material.'

Helena began calling up additional brain scans as proof, but Koenig dismissed them all. 'Doctor, I don't want to see X-rays – I want to see the men.'

Beyond the Care Unit observation window, two patients lay, festooned with monitoring equipment. At the console in front of the glass sat Dr. Fujita, a small Japanese man of about thirty or so. He was closely watching the patients and the instruments which recorded their vital signs. T.V. monitors displayed close shots of their faces, the right sides appeared waxy, shrunken, and quite repellent. Superimposed over the images were coloured traces displaying heart, lung and brain activity.

Controlling his surprise and shock at this sight, Koenig asked Helena, 'Can I… communicate with them?'

She nodded and pressed a button. He called out to the men, 'Frank? Eric? It's John Koenig…'

Beyond the glass, he saw there was no response. A chill went up his spine.

Like all of Alpha, Technical Section was also of modular construction. It was designed as a control room to monitor engineering operations. Computer programming and read-out facilities were connected to Central Computer. On one side of the room was a panoramic view of the Moon surface. Opposite this, an observation window looked down into the vast hanger which housed the Eagle fleet and all the engineering facilities of Alpha. Twenty or perhaps thirty Eagles were lined up into the distance.

An image of the Moon-orbiting Space Station filled the main T.V. screen. It was a complex structure consisting of a large central barrel, out of which protruded tubular spokes. The whole thing had the appearance of being constructed out of rocket components. At the end of each tube was a docking point where several Eagles buzzed to and fro, ferrying supplies and personnel from the surface of the Moon.

The most striking feature was an immensely long deep space Probeship that dwarfed the Eagles. Koenig gestured toward it and asked Catani, Chief of the Reconnaissance Section and Captain of the Meta Probe, 'Is the ship ready to go?'

'She's a great ship – best we've built. We can start the countdown as soon as you give the word. But every hour's delay reduces our chances of success.'

'How long to get the back-up crew ready?'

'Seven days at a push. Five… The back-up crew? What do you mean?'

'How long will it take, Catani?'

'We can't do it. The calculations – the co-ordinates – Commander, there's a problem you're not telling me about.'

'I'm here to get the Meta Probe launched. All I want to know, Captain, is that – crew excepted – you're ready to go.'

'We're ready to go.'

Morrow programmed a picture on the Main Mission screen: a graphic breakdown of the strange, rhythmic group of serial sounds that now filled the room. They were noises over an apparently deliberate tonal range, repeating, yet developing into patterns that sounded like call signs.

'It's some kind of language,' he offered his theory with a shrug. 'We get near to finding some kind of serial pattern – and then it goes… But it's there, somewhere. It's language, I'm sure of it. Meta's trying to make contact with us. I know they are… another civilisation maybe… Commander, we've got to get those guys out of Medical and get out there, otherwise we'll never find out who or what is on Meta.'

Koenig's face tightened as a voice called out over the intercom, 'Commander Koenig, there's an Earth call on the scrambler… Commissioner Simmonds.'

Striding over to the Communications Post in his office, Koenig watched as a bar scrambler obscured the image at first. Then, after a series of bleeps, the face of Commissioner Simmonds appeared on the screen.

'Settled in, John? I wanted to get your first impressions of the situation.'

Koenig began to pace angrily. 'There was another death, this morning at the Nuclear Disposal Area. Dr. Russell talks about a kind of brain damage caused by what she thinks is radiation.'

'I know all about that from Gorski,' he said tightly. 'She's very competent in certain kinds of Space Medicine, Commander, but this situation is beyond her. She's misdiagnosing… We're all certain about that down here. As a matter of fact, but under strict confidence, we're flying up a team of top medical people who will take her out of the case… expect them.'

'Hold off on that,' Koenig objected. 'I want to be certain that there was absolutely no radiation leak at that disposal area.'

'Those two astronauts never went near that area.'

'Nine men have died and I'm going to investigate. Commissioner, I want you to stop sending up any more atomic waste until…'

'You know I can't do that,' Simmonds interrupted. 'It's one of the biggest problems of our times…'

'Look, you sent me up here to pull this situation out and that's what I'm trying to do.' Koenig realised his anger was getting the best of him. He paused and calmly made an offer, 'Alright, let's trade off. You stop sending up the waste and I'll get your Probe launched.'

'I can arrange a temporary delay,' came the diplomatic reply. 'If that's what you need.'

'That's what I need.' He stopped his pacing and stared directly at the man's image on the screen, 'Simmonds, why did you lie to me?'

'There're no better are they?' he inquired knowingly.

'They're never going to be any better. You know that.'

'We have to hold the story in, Commander… have to. We have an International Lunar Finance meeting coming up on the fifteenth. It's all based on the Meta signals and our Probe… Any hint of failure will chop us dead. Remember that.'

Simmonds killed the transmission from his end and the screen went black.

An Eagle overflew the Lunar surface and banked toward a desolate area marked by a flashing red beacon. Within the Passenger Module, Koenig sensed the ship's change in attitude. He activated the monitor before him and saw an exterior camera image of the deserted Area One.

He pressed the intercom and called to their pilot, 'Area Two, Simpson, that's where I want to go.'

'That's where we are going, Commander,' he assured them. 'We just use Area One as a turning point.'

Bergman, sitting next to Koenig, was unimpressed, 'Some landmark.'

'Wait a minute,' said Koenig, suddenly interested. He keyed the intercom again. 'Simpson, take us down for a look see.'

The Eagle dropped down and rounded the beacon, skimming close to the surface.

'No radiation,' reported Bergman, 'I've checked it out. Count normal.'

'That was the first nuclear waste area up here. Has it been used since I left?'

'No, they've moved on to Area Two. This one's been closed for five years.'

'We had no synthocrete radiation covers then. How's it holding up?'

'Alright, so they say. It's constantly monitored, and there's no radiation. I checked that out,' he assured him again.

Satisfied, Koenig called to the Command Module, 'On to Area Two now, please.'

Simpson pulled back his controls and adjusted course. Neither of the two men seated back in the passenger compartment knew their pilot was suddenly drenched in sweat.

Koenig and Bergman entered the Monitoring Depot at Disposal Area Two. Simpson, still clad in his spacesuit and helmet tucked under his arm, followed behind. A security guard closed the Observation Room door after they had entered and took up his post just outside.

'Okay, let's go. Rescue ship on stand-by?' Koenig asked as he crossed to the window and looked up.

'Yes, sir, standing by,' came the pilot's reply.

'Fine.'

Two space-suited technicians, Jackson and Ellis, drove their Moon-buggy towards the laser barrier. Jackson unclipped and directed his commlock at a panel. Red lights turned to green down the length of the column, indicating that it was now safe for them to pass.

Once their buggy reached their assigned station, the duo climbed out and approached one of the red-capped mounds. Ellis pulled a special tool out of his kit and opened up part of the cap. Jackson inserted his radiation meter into the uncovered port.

From within the Depot, Koenig closely watched the operation. The radiation counter's audible clicks could be heard over the intercom. Jackson's helmeted face looked directly from a monitor and reported, 'Point One check complete. Radiation normal. No leakage. Proceeding to Point Two.'

'Roger – Rescue Ship, do you copy?'

'Affirmative.'

Koenig turned to Bergman, who was closely watching two 'scopes now labeled **JACKSON** and **ELLIS**. Koenig asked, 'Everything okay?'

'So far, no abnormalities.'

Behind them, out of their sight, Simpson was looking very uneasy.

Helena intently studied a sample of mutated brain cells under the microscope in her office, dictating observations into her recorder. 'Autopsy report Technician Nordstrom. Stage Five cell mutations in the right hemisphere of the brain. Classic malignancy…'

'Dr. Russell?' the voice of Dr. Fujita called out. She looked up to see his image on the Communications Post T.V. screen. 'Emergency in Care Unit Nine.'

Without even pausing to switch off the recorder, she rushed from the room.

The technicians opened up and removed a cap marked **27**. Once Jackson completed his scan, he reported, 'Point 27 check complete. Radiation normal. No leakage. That's it, sir. All okay out here.'

'Okay Jackson, thanks,' came Koenig's voice over their helmet radios. 'Now get out of there, and make it fast.'

The two men leapt into their Moon Buggy. The vehicle sped through the open laser barrier, a cloud of Moon dust trailing from behind.

Koenig depressed another comm. key and called, 'Rescue ship – stand down. Okay boys. Thanks.'

'Glad we weren't needed. Returning to base.'

Through the window, they could see the Rescue Eagle swoop up and away.

'That proves beyond doubt that the radiation count here is within safe limits?' asked Bergman.

'So much for Dr. Russell's theory,' Koenig mused.

'Seems so.'

'Whatever felled the two Probe astronauts and killed the other nine was not radiation.'

'At least radiation as we know it,' the Professor surmised.

A defeated Koenig quietly cursed, 'Dammit!'

'Commander, I've got to get out of here.' It was Simpson's voice from behind.

'Fine, we're going right now.' Koenig said. He turned and it was obvious that their Eagle pilot was sweating profusely, his eyes wide, body quaking.

'Now... Now...NOW!' he screamed before rushing forward, knocking Bergman roughly aside. Simpson grabbed a radiation counter and raised it over his head in an attempt to bring it down with force against the window.

Koenig reached out to grab his arm, to wrench it back in an attempt to dispossess him, but the man had gone berserk. Simpson had somehow gained extraordinary physical strength. He easily shook the Commander loose and slammed him against a wall. Then, he hurled the radiation counter at Koenig, narrowly missing his head.

Bergman attempted a grab for Simpson's foot, only to get kicked across the room. Free from interference, the deranged pilot grabbed his helmet and began to pound it against the window.

'Stop him!' shouted Bergman as a small crack appeared.

Alerted by the commotion, the Security Guard opened the door with his commlock. He unholstered his stun weapon as he rushed in.

Koenig made one more attempt at Simpson, but was shoved into the path of the guard. They both fell back through the doorway and into the corridor. The stun weapon dropped and skidded across the floor.

Under Simpson's brutal assault, the fracture on the glass began to run. Koenig knew one more hit could be their last. He scrambled to grab the fallen stun-gun and fired.

As stress lines creaked under the strain of the interior air pressure, Bergman and Koenig together grabbed Simpson's prone body and dragged it out. Once outside, the Commander dropped his grip on the pilot and grabbed his commlock to seal the door. Just as the hatch slammed shut, the window shattered. The force of the explosive decompression sent the contents of the room out onto the Lunar surface.

Koenig watched the destruction through the door viewport.

RCT TWO

In the Care Unit, Dr. Russell and Dr. Fujita continued their observation of the two Probe men. There was no change in Warren's condition, he continued to lay with that same vacant stare. Sparkman's breathing, however, was very laboured and a strange rattle emitted from his throat.

'He's going fast,' said Fujita.

She scanned the console and then told him, 'Emergency C.F. 3 – full dosage…'

'C.F. 3… preset…'

Helena watched tensely, through the glass, as a small indicator above the astronaut's head lit up **C.F. 3**. He hardly reacted.

'Cardiac arrest,' shouted Fujita.

'Switch in pacemaker.'

Fujita keyed a series of buttons and confirmed, 'Heart re-started.'

Helena studied the instruments, 'Losing pressure… Losing nerve response…'

'Brain activity fading…'

'So fast…' She said, astonished at the speed of the deterioration.

The waves on a 'scope suddenly went flat… utterly flat.

The computer hammered out a printed report and Fujita read it aloud, 'Central Computer confirms death… Astronaut Eric Sparkman.'

Helena was appalled at the text that followed;

SPECIAL SECURITY…
THIS STATISTIC IS NOT TO BE
REPORTED ELSEWHERE.
LUNAR COMMISSIONER SIMMONDS.

She crumpled up the sheet of paper in disgust and hurled it vehemently into the disposal unit.

Koenig's Quarters were a flurry of partially unpacked clothing and personal effects. The Commander, bone-tired, sat listening to the Meta signals with the lighting now set at night mode.

His concentration was broken by a buzz that sounded from the commlock plugged into a socket on his table.

'Yes?' he asked as Gorski's face appeared on his commlock screen.

'Good evening, Commander. I'd like to see you.'

He pointed his commlock at the door, which opened to admit the former base commander.

'I'm leaving tomorrow, and I thought I'd say goodbye. I wish you very well up here, but I'm not certain you understand how complex it all is.'

'I'm learning.'

'It becomes even more complex with the death of the two astronauts.'

'Uh - huh.'

'The Commissioner now has very real problems.'

'I think the problems are here on Alpha – Earth Command doesn't really want to hear about them.'

'Oh, that's not true,' sputtered Gorski. 'It's a question of security.'

'That's not my evaluation. You don't solve a problem by putting a guard on it and hoping it'll go away.'

'I understand Dr. Russell is being replaced by a new medical team. When do the Earth doctors arrive?' he asked in an attempt to change the subject.

'I'm not sure they will.'

Koenig was growing suspicious of this visit, 'You've been keeping Simmonds up to date on Dr. Russell, haven't you?'

'She's medical – I'm not. But I do know, for instance, that she was married to someone in the Space Program and he was lost on a mission five years ago.'

'Which means what?'

'She has, as a result, anxieties that… in my opinion make her unsuitable for this job. For instance, she doesn't understand the need for Security in all of this, but repercussions on Earth, if this news leaked…'

Koenig was losing his patience and decided to end this little chat, 'Well, Gorski, I wish you the best of luck with the problems back on Earth. Have a good trip back.'

Catani couldn't believe the news, 'They died? Eric? Frank? Of what? I was told…'

'You were told lies,' Koenig informed the Chief Pilot. 'They died of an illness no one can really explain.'

'I… I don't understand. I thought… well, I thought they were just covering for a longer delay.'

'Earth Command wanted you to think it was a temporary setback.'

'But the Meta Probe...? What do we do...?' he asked, his voice tinged with real anguish.

'Forget the Probe, Catani... Before we do anything more, I want to know why those two men died.'

Koenig re-entered Main Mission and approached Computer Chief Ouma. He was a high ranking member of the Technical Department, an impressively brilliant African who knew every inch of his computer system.

'Ouma, I want a breakdown of all recorded information on the training flights of Probe Astronauts Warren and Sparkman and I want them checked against the flights of the Eagle shuttle flown by Simpson. Search for any correlation between them – any whatsoever.'

'I'll do that immediately, Commander'

'Immediately,' Koenig stressed, then turned and headed toward his office. As he rounded his desk, Helena entered from the other door, carrying files under one arm.

'Commander, here are the autopsy report on the two astronauts,' she said, handing them over. 'Similar to the previous cases. Brain damage less severe. Survival period longer. Otherwise, identical in every way to the other victims.'

'And the shuttle pilot...?'

'The same. Identical. No variation.'

'May I ask you a non-medical question?' She nodded and Koenig carefully asked a sensitive question, 'Was there any friction – on a personal or professional level – between you and Gorski?'

Helena hesitated, 'Did he say there was?'

'Well, he made certain references...'

'To what? My lack of judgement?'

'In a sense.'

'I see…' she took it all in, then replied, 'Well, he indicated a certain… interest in me, at one point. I did not reciprocate. That, perhaps was my lack of judgement.'

'I see… Thank you, Doctor.'

'Commander, there has to be a link between the Nuclear Disposal Area, the two astronauts and the shuttle pilot…'

Before Helena could finish, there was a buzz from Koenig's commlock. Ouma's face appeared on the screen, 'Commander… Those flight recorder tapes…'

They exchanged a look then rushed into Main Mission. As Koenig crossed the room to Ouma's position, he passed by Data Analyst Sandra Sabatini, who called out to Morrow, 'Can I get a check on this reading? I have a steep rise in the heat levels on Disposal Area One, and I can't believe it.'

Koenig's interest was piqued by her statement, especially when he noticed Bergman approach as well.

'Check it out,' he ordered Morrow, then turned to Bergman, 'That's the old area – stay with it.'

Koenig turned back to Ouma and noticed that the man had a very worried look. 'The flight was perfectly recorded,' he began, gesturing toward a 'scope. 'Then suddenly everything went blank – for two minutes. And as suddenly it all started again – perfectly.'

'Where did the blank out occur?'

'Navigation beacon Delta – on the far side.'

'Delta. That's the old Disposal Area One, isn't it?'

'Area One thermal Sensors all checked – readings are accurate,' reported Morrow.

Koenig moved quickly over to Sandra who added, 'We don't have too many instruments on that old Area – just for emergencies. But look…'

She directed their attention to an off-the-scale instrument reading.

'To generate that kind of heat, the waste must have become active,' Bergman surmised.

Sandra pointed to another meter, 'No. The radiation count is still normal…'

'So there can be no fission in the pile,' said Koenig.

'All I can tell you is that radiation levels are normal, but the heat is building…'

'Area One is also navigation beacon Delta,' Bergman remarked. 'We've just been over.'

'But Simpson flew over in the shuttle four or six times a week,' Koenig explained.

Ouma joined in, 'And the Probe Astronauts' flight recorder blanked out right there on their last training run.'

'Of course, everyone uses it as a turning point,' Morrow confirmed. 'It's one of the few constructions on the far side of the Moon.'

'Bring in Disposal Area One on video…' ordered Koenig.

Morrow punched a set of buttons and the main screen displayed a very strange image: the ground within Area One trembled. Within seconds, a blue flash suddenly burst out from one mound, and then from another.

'That's incredible heat,' Sandra reported.

Bergman asked her, 'But still no radiation?'

'Still no radiation.'

'It's incomprehensible,' said Koenig. 'Heat without atomic activity…'

'But it's burning up, somehow,' objected Sandra. 'Look at it…'

More blue flashes erupted, and the Lunar soil heaved from below. Suddenly, the image flared and disappeared. 'Burnout,' she confirmed. 'The camera's gone…'

The needles on her panel vibrated furiously, then slammed onto the highest point and remained there. 'The thermal sensors have burned out, too.'

Koenig turned to Morrow, 'Call Catani. I want an Eagle on the pad for immediate lift-off.'

Bergman grabbed his arm, 'John, you can't risk anyone flying over it now.'

Koenig personally manoeuvred the Eagle towards Nuclear Disposal Area One. Through the ports, he saw lightning leap up from the surface.

'Approaching Area One,' he reported to Main Mission. 'Check data systems running.'

'Data systems A-okay,' confirmed Ouma.

Koenig watched as the ground below quivered and shook. It seemed oddly alive.

Suddenly, some kind of explosion rocked an interior section. Blue and yellow flashes struck outward. Some of the surrounding flood lights winked out and toppled as the ground beneath continued to heave. The lightning continued to dance around the tortured landscape, and reached up uncomfortably close to the Eagle.

'It's getting more active. I'm increasing altitude,' Koenig told Main Mission.

He tried to swing the ship's nose upward, but struggled as it vibrated violently. He looked anxiously at his instruments and declared, 'I'm in trouble. Are you still getting the data?'

Bergman was alarmed with the data coming from Main Mission's instruments. He turned and told Morrow, 'The magnetic field is expanding – we can't measure it – get him away from there, quick.'

'Commander,' Morrow called into his mic. 'You've got to get away.'

On the big screen, arcs of blue tendrils reached up higher and higher as if to grab the fleeing Eagle.

'Switch to on-board back-up system, Commander – we're losing you.'

Main Mission's staff saw the whole sky above the Disposal Area flood with brilliant violet light. Koenig's Eagle, silhouetted against it, began to gyrate, then plummet as its main motors cut-out.

'Back-up failing,' Koenig reported. 'All systems are out.'

'Rescue ship, move in,' Morrow ordered.

Koenig pulled down his visor and tightened the harness, aware that he no longer had any control. The Eagle spun out and swooped dangerously near a crater wall. It slammed into the rim and slid down the side. The craft overturned and finally crashed into a heap at the bottom.

As a cloud of Lunar dust settled down to blanket the wreck of the Moon Ship, Area One exploded with a blinding white light.

ACT THREE

Koenig lay in the General Accident and Examinations division of the Diagnostic Unit. He had been given a complete medical inspection after the Rescue team pulled him from his crashed ship. Dr. Helena Russell and Dr. Fujita completed a final check on their instruments.

'That's about it, Commander. We'll get you out of these,' said the Japanese man as he unhooked the array of body sensors. Finished, he turned and left the room.

Koenig sat up, put on his shirt, and asked Helena, 'Well?'

'Shock… minor physical shock… We can't find anything else so far…'

'Look, there's nothing wrong with me. I walked away from it. There's no damage at all…'

'That's not the kind of damage I'm looking for,' she said, lips tight as she attempted to suppress her anger. 'Commander, you knew that area was suspect, you knew it had already affected the Probe astronauts and the Eagle shuttle pilot some way, and yet you went right out there yourself. We're looking for answers – not heroes.'

As she turned away from him, Koenig grabbed his commlock and paused at the door, 'I didn't know you cared.'

In the Technical Section, Bergman held up a burnt-out component to Morrow. 'Look at it. It's a monitoring device from the old Area One. Its original purpose was to record the magnetic output of the artificial gravity system there. When the Area was closed down it had nothing to record for five years… now look at it.'

Morrow was stunned, 'A twentyfold increase in magnetic field?'

'Yes, and that's before it burned out. We've been obsessed with radiation. But we were wrong. Do you have computer analysis of the Commander's crash?'

Morrow handed a clipboard to the Professor. He studied the printouts, then asked, 'We noticed a surge in magnetic field just before he went down. Is there any record of that?'

Before Morrow could answer, Koenig entered the facility. Bergman asked, 'Feeling okay, John?'

'Yeah – I'm fine…' he responded as Bergman offered him the clipboard.

'We checked out your Eagle,' reported Morrow. 'Navigation System just blanked… Backups, too… You were lucky. Commander, it wasn't heat… All the cables were clean… No insulation burns.'

'Then what caused the navigation system to fail?' Koenig asked.

Bergman picked the component back up and chimed in, 'And what causes a failure in a flight recorder? One thing that could throw them both would be a strong magnetic field.'

Koenig and Morrow suddenly realised that the Professor had made a connection.

As Koenig entered Main Mission he told Sandra Sabatini, 'I want Area One continuously monitored.'

'The new instruments are installed, and the heat level is decreasing steadily,' she reported. 'Also, everything checks out at Area Two.'

'That's good news,' he said, then noticed that Bergman and Helena had entered. Koenig could see something was up from the look on the Professor's face.

'John, can we go to your office? I've asked Dr. Russell to join us. It's important.'

In Koenig's office, Bergman held the burnt-out component and explained, 'This instrument has given me a lead. I believe we are facing a new effect, an effect arising from the atomic waste deposited thoughtlessly here over the years. An effect consisting of magnetic energy outputs of unprecedented violence.'

'Magnetic energy responsible for the flare up at Area One?' asked Koenig.

'It's magnetic energy that caused the brain damage' added Helena.

Bergman confessed, 'It's something we didn't even think to check for. But I believe it was a surge in magnetic field that wrecked your navigation system and blanked out the astronauts' flight recorder...'

'Then we've all been exposed to it,' a shocked Helena realised. 'We've all been to Area Two – to get there the pilot turns over Area One. We've been lucky.'

'Your ship was brought down by a sudden surge…' Bergman told Koenig.

'But the astronauts' flight training program took them over daily – and Simpson, too, in the shuttle…'

He turned to Helena and asked, 'A cumulative effect?'

'Possibly. And maybe, like with conventional radiation, some of us are more susceptible than others.'

'But the workers at Area Two were out there all the time.'

A triumphant expression crossed Helena's face, 'Brain damage caused by magnetic radiation.'

'I'm beginning to see a much bigger problem looming up,' Koenig told them both.

'You're ahead of me, John,' Bergman said. 'Area One burnt itself out in a magnetic subsurface firestorm. What worries me now is that the same thing is happening at Area Two.'

'How much time do we have?'

'We need solid data on magnetic levels.'

Koenig pressed a button on his commlock and notified the Communications Operator, 'Pass emergency code Alpha One.'

'Alpha One, Commander? Please verify.'

'Alpha One – that's what I said,' he barked. 'Contact Commissioner Simmonds.'

An Eagle approached Nuclear Disposal Area Two. It slowed, hovered, and then descended. Its thrusters fired and stirred up the Moon dust between the synthocrete covers into a dense fog that collected above the silos.

The entire operation was being monitored on the big screen in Main Mission. Koenig concentrated on the image of the hovering spacecraft and commented without turning away, 'Good Paul – keep her coming.'

Morrow carefully adjusted the joysticks on a remote controller, guiding the unmanned Eagle into a final position.

'Any readings?'

'Radiation count normal,' Sandra answered the Commander. 'Magnetic field zero.'

'Okay Paul – put her down.'

Morrow keyed in another command. The Eagle eased down a few more meters to hover directly above the red caps. Dust swirled everywhere within the facility.

Without warning, the nose of the Command Module reared up. Morrow, desperate to regain control, fired a series of vernier motors. The Eagle, however, cocked over at a crazy angle and careened horizontally across the site.

Sandra was amazed at the readings before her and cried out, 'Magnetic surge, Commander – right off the scale.'

'Just blast it out of the area, Paul,' Koenig commanded.

Morrow flicked another switch and the nose tilted down. The Eagle crabbed wildly back towards the middle of the Nuclear Disposal Area. Aware of the red tell-tales flashing brightly on his panel, Morrow knew he had completely lost control. The robot ship plowed hard into the ground and knocked aside several synthocrete caps before it came to a stop.

'Readings?' a grim-faced Koenig asked Sandra.

'Radiation count normal. Magnetic field, six above zero – reducing.'

'A magnetic surge,' confirmed Bergman. 'Impossible to measure.'

An Eagle from Earth settled itself onto the launch pad and a Travel Tube telescoped outward to meet it. Koenig waited at one end of the airlock for Commissioner Simmonds to emerge from the Passenger Module.

'Commissioner,' Koenig said very formally.

'Commander…' came a cold-eye reply.

Simmonds extended a hand and Koenig shook it. The Commander then pulled out his commlock and directed it at the Travel Tube car's selector panel. The door automatically closed and the car began to move. Koenig ushered the Commissioner to a seat.

'My office tried to query you on your emergency request for my presence…' stated Simmonds. 'You didn't seem to be available.'

'I am now,' came the frosty reply.

Gathered in Koenig's office, Bergman began to lay out his theories and conclusions to the Commissioner.

'When this project started, we used Uranium 392 as fuel. In the last seven years we started mixing it with Caesium. Uranium was expensive, Caesium was cheap. It would seem that Uranium and Caesium are reacting adversely to each other, producing magnetic fields of incredible strength. That's our problem.'

Simmonds scoffed, 'Magnetism – causing brain damage?'

'Atomic radiation causing cancer?' Helena replied sarcastically.

'Magnetism is energy – all energy radiates,' Koenig pointed out.

'I'll be happy to look at a comprehensive report on the subject,' Simmonds said dismissively to Helena.

'Commissioner, I don't think you understand the urgency of the situation,' interrupted Koenig. 'We've got one hell of a problem up here, and it's got to be thrashed out. Dr. Russell and Professor Bergman identified the problem and analysed its causes. Together we've got to solve it, here and now.'

Koenig pressed a button on his desk and an image of Nuclear Disposal Area Two appeared on his screen. The crashed Eagle lay in a tangled mess between a mass of smashed synthocrete covers.

Bergman pointed to the image, 'Commissioner, the heat has started to rise on the interior of Area Two as well and it is murderous. It contains one hundred and forty times the waste of Area One. With those quantities the possibility of a chain reaction cannot be ruled out.'

Nervously, Simmonds ventured, 'What are the chances it will burn itself out – like Area One?'

'You don't seem to be getting this, Simmonds,' Koenig said. 'We're sitting on top of it and there is no chance.'

Attempting to not show his rising fear, the Commissioner asked Bergman, 'What can be done?'

'We can try to break the pile apart... Rip up the fuel rods, destroy the mass,' Bergman suggested, then explained to Koenig, 'If we could spread the mass over a wide enough area, we might...'

'Then let's do that,' Simmonds ordered.

Koenig agreed, 'Yes, let's do it.'

'But we do have limited time,' Bergman reminded them.

No one seemed to noticed that the image on the office screen showed the ground within N.D. 2 had begun to tremble.

ACT FOUR

Koenig's concentration was broken by a call from Paul Morrow. His face appeared on the Communications Post monitor. 'Conversion on the first six Eagles completed, Commander... they are moving into the area now.'

'Okay – let's see it,' he replied as he hit a button on the desk and rotated his chair around. The wall that divided his office from Main Mission divided and slid apart, allowing Koenig a direct overlook of operations. The room before him was tense with concentrated activity.

Commissioner Simmonds stood off to one side and watched intently as staff went about their work. Suddenly, all activity ceased when the main screen lit up with an image none had ever expected to see.

The synthocrete caps, which covered the Waste Disposal stores, had been ripped aside, broken into pieces. The crashed Eagle had also been dragged to one side. Now, much bigger holes, virtual caverns in the Lunar surface, revealed the hundreds of blocks of stored Atomic waste.

The perimeter floodlights had been turned up to full brightness, illuminating the fleet of hovering Eagles. All their Passenger Modules had been removed, leaving only the girder framework that connected the motors to the Command Module. Suspended from the framework was a cable extending to a huge metal grab. The co-pilot of the first Eagle controlled the grab. It disappeared into the ground and then locked on to a waste block. The main engines fired and the container was lifted out where it would be dropped into craters far away from the site. One after the other, Eagles moved in, pulled up waste canisters, then swooped away.

Simmonds crossed toward Koenig and proclaimed, 'It's going to work, Koenig. It's going to work.'

'They have over five hundred to disperse… Commissioner,' Koenig pointed out, hardly masking his contempt.

As a work ship pulled up another block of waste, Morrow directed the pilot, 'Number twenty-six… disperse to Grid C-9… Repeat… Disperse to Grid C-9.'

The Eagle moved up, but it made its turn too quick. The heavy synthocrete block began to swing and slammed into one of the columns that supported the perimeter floodlights. The tower crashed to the ground as the slightly damaged waste container continued to move like an ominous pendulum.

The Section Chiefs, Morrow, Ouma, Russell, and Catani had all been ordered to gather around Koenig's desk. 'I want the

Central Computer updated with everything possible, constantly,' he demanded.

Ouma assured the Commander, 'We're doing that.'

'We've had navigational failures on two of the ships,' Morrow reported. 'They've returned to base for replacements.'

Helena cautioned, 'They're much too close.'

'Give them another hundred meters, Paul,' ordered Koenig.

'Right.'

'Do we have a spare Eagle?'

'Yes, sir!'

'Catani – take it into orbit and report on the situation from up there.'

'Right, sir!' the Captain smartly acknowledged and headed to the door.

'Okay. Go!' the Commander said, dismissing the rest of the team. Helena held back.

Koenig called into Main Mission, 'What do we have on levels?'

'Heat levels holding,' came Sandra Sabatini's reply, 'Magnetic fields fluctuating.'

He heard Bergman's comment, 'That's what worries me.'

'What are our chances?' Helena asked quietly.

Koenig's response was tinged with caustic anger, 'Terrific. We're going to be fine… How the hell should I know?'

Quiet for a moment, he said, 'Congratulations, Doctor, you were right – it was radiation. Magnetic radiation.'

An Eagle blasted off from the launch pad with Captain Catani at the controls.

'Eagle Four to Alpha.'

'Go ahead,' Morrow's voice came back.

'Blast-off complete… Trajectory computed and programmed. I'll hit orbit in four minutes.'

The next Work Ship moved into position, hovering over an open pit. As its claw came into contact with the synthocrete block, a small blue flash connected the two objects for just a millisecond.

In Main Mission, Bergman blinked, not sure what he had just witnessed.

Simmonds bounded into Koenig's office, practically jubilant, his confidence regained. 'All levels are holding steady. Do you think we have it under control, John?'

'It's too early to tell.'

'It looks promising to me,' he proclaimed, then placed his arm on Koenig's shoulder.

Despite a dirty look from the Commander, the Commissioner continued unfazed, 'I'll have to issue a communiqué sooner or later. I was thinking of playing up the virus infection angle… that would give us more time to consider our next move… You see, John…'

Koenig broke away, he had had enough. 'I don't see anything, at least not the way you see things. All I can see at this moment is men risking their lives to avert disaster and if you don't understand the situation clearly let me lay it on the line… If things go wrong there'll be no one here to issue a communiqué.'

Suddenly, his attention was drawn to the image on his Communication Post. The Disposal Area had begun to flash with a jagged, unearthly light. One of the waste blocks, hanging beneath an Eagle, emitted arcs of energy that seemed to be reaching upward. The spacecraft, now out of control, plummeted to the ground.

Koenig shouted as he ran into Main Mission, 'Get those Eagles out of there… It's going up.'

Morrow called into his mic, 'This is Main Mission calling all Eagles… Return to base immediately… Repeat, return to base immediately.'

They could see two crew ships drop their loads and pull up the lines. Jagged lightning continued to arc higher and higher up from within the open waste pits.

With a tremendous roar, the complex suddenly erupted in a huge blast. Streaks of debris raced upwards toward the fleeing Eagles. One craft was hit. It flipped over and dove nose-first into a crater wall. The ship plowed into the ground and disintegrated.

Shockwaves rocked the Control Centre as explosions ripped the crater floor around Alpha Base. Transmitting and receiving antennae collapsed. A stressed building storing fuel supplies ignited with fragments peppering the surrounding structures.

Hovering high above, the destruction was clearly evident to Catani. He pleaded into his mic., 'Alpha... Alpha... Can you read me? Alpha... this is Captain Catani.'

There was no reply, people below were too preoccupied to respond.

'Alpha... Come in, please. Alpha... Alpha... Are you okay?'

From his high vantage point, he could see a series of explosions around Nuclear Disposal Area Two. They began as small pockets at first, but quickly increased in frequency and intensity.

Without warning, the whole complex whited out in a terrific blast. Catani's face, and the whole interior of the Command Module, was bathed in the brilliant light of a massive thermo-nuclear explosion. He struggled to shield his eyes, hoping that the temporary blindness would pass quickly. He couldn't see that the Moon below was back lit by the explosion on the far side.

A dense plasma cloud began to form.

Two technicians had been working to repair cables on the rim of the crater Alpha Base was built in. The shockwave hurled them violently to the ground. Their arms covered their visors in an attempt to shield their eyes.

All over the Moon Base, personnel were tossed about like rag dolls. Dr. Fujita was thrown against some medical equipment, which then smashed to the ground and shattered.

In Main Mission, the lighting had failed. Computer went dark as short circuits caused several panels to erupt with plumes of flame. A brutal force hurled everyone to the ground. Some tried to rise, but found it impossible.

'I can't… move,' groaned Helena.

Bergman struggled to speak, 'We've got about seven G. We must be accelerating.'

Panting hard, Koenig said, 'No decompression so there can't be any structural damage… in this area anyway.'

'We must've gone into an eccentric orbit.'

'I'm not sure we're in orbit at all.'

Helena's eyes opened wide as she understood what Koenig was implying.

Determined to answer Catani's pleads, the Commander painfully crawled to reach the Comm. Unit. Unable to reach up to it, he fumbled instead to unclip his commlock.

'Catani… Can you hear me?' he groaned into the device. 'This is John Koenig. Our… G forces have been affected. Can you determine what's happening to us?'

'Commander… that explosion… It tore a tremendous piece of the Moon away. The far side… just tore it away…'

Koenig was shocked, 'Tore it away?'

'All of Mare Cantabrium is gone. All of the Great Lunar Sea… All of the Alta Mountains… I can see it from up here… It's impossible to believe…'

From high above, Catani observed the far side of the Moon. The second Nuclear Disposal Area was still pulsating with smaller explosions under the plasma cloud.

From the corner of his eye, the pilot was shocked to see another terrible sight.

'We're losing the Meta Probe,' he cried out. 'The whole Space Dock – it's breaking up…'

'Get back here, Catani,' ordered Koenig. 'We're going out of orbit, Catani. The Moon is going out of Earth's orbit. Get back here fast, before we lose you, too.'

He looked back at the Moon. 'My God… you're right… you are going out of Earth orbit.'

'Catani, get back here… do you hear me… get back here.'

Like a man possessed, he fired the main motors and struggled to keep up with the fleeing Moon. He anxiously reported, 'I'm holding… but only just.'

Koenig began to sense that the G forces were easing. 'Okay, now hold on… hold on, Catani… It feels like we're decelerating now. Don't lose any ground. Keep on full power.'

He clicked off his commlock and turned to Bergman asking, 'Will he make it?'

'The whole disposal area has been acting like a giant rocket motor – pushing us out of orbit. If it has stopped fissioning we won't be accelerating any more. Catani might have a chance.'

From orbit, Catani clearly saw that the explosions had finally subsided. The enormous plasma cloud had moved away to reveal a gigantic crater. He estimated it was the size of the Grand Canyon, but filled with white-hot molten rock.

'G forces are easing,' said Helena, as the Main Mission staff managed to climb back onto their feet. The lighting had returned to its standard brightness and computer ramped back up to full capacity.

'We have power back,' announced the Commander.

Ouma scanned his board and reported, 'We're down to three G.'

'We're compensating,' agreed Bergman.

'Check out the base,' Koenig ordered Morrow.

'This is Main Mission – all sections report in.'

Voices began to pour in from all over Alpha.

'Security Section. We have audio contact… Video systems gone.'

'Technical Section. Video and audio-strength five, intelligibility five. Two casualties. One serious. Otherwise, all systems go.'

The Maintenance Section failed to respond – they had lost all main power.

Dr. Fujita reported through his commlock, 'Medical Section, five by five… Explosive decompression in two compartments… area sealed off… no leaks. Sufficiently operational to receive casualties.'

Koenig called into the comm. mic, 'Catani?'

'I'm closing now… I'm closing… I'm going to make it.'

Koenig was relieved, 'Great, Captain. Report on touchdown.'

'I'm getting a long range video picture,' Morrow said excitedly. 'I'm bouncing it off the Mars satellite!'

Everyone stopped to look up at the big screen. Everyone was stunned into silence by the awesome sight of the Moon moving inexorably away from Earth!

'Flip to a wider angle,' Koenig told Morrow. He punched a button, and the new image confirmed their fears.

'Can we… make it back to Earth?' Morrow quietly asked.

Koenig walked over to the computer desk and said, 'Ouma, consult the Master Computer. I want a read-out on contingency plan Exodus.'

'Yes, sir,' he responded, keying in the request.

'Punch it up on the big screen, Ouma. It affects all of us here.'

Text began to appear:

EMERGENCY OPERATION EXODUS . . .
INDEFINITE FACTORS . . .
1. MOON ON UNKNOWN TRAJECTORY . . .
2. CONSTANTLY CHANGING G FORCES DUE TO MOON'S MOVEMENT AWAY FROM EARTH . . .
3. INSUFFICIENT DATA TO COMPUTE FLIGHT PLAN . . .

ALL FACTORS IN MEMORY BANK RELATING TO OPERATION EXODUS INAPPLICABLE . . .
INSUFFICIENT DATA AVAILABLE UNDER PREVAILING CIRCUMSTANCES

HUMAN DECISION REQUIRED

As all eyes turned to Koenig, the vast chamber became silent, save for the hum of computer and the sound of the air ventilation system. He said nothing as he moved into his office. Koenig barely acknowledged the presence of Simmonds, sitting in a chair totally dazed, wiping blood from his temple.

The globe of Earth that sat in one corner of his office was now lying on its side, seemingly mocking the Commander. He picked it up off the floor and placed it on his desk. He had to make an agonising decision.

Finally, he turned towards Main Mission and reached for the base-wide comm. key on his desk. 'Attention… all sections Alpha – this is Commander Koenig… Our Moon has been blasted out of orbit and we have been cut off from planet Earth. As we are, we have power, environment and the possibility of survival… If we try to improvise a return to Earth, without travel plots, and full resources, I think we'll fail… So in my judgement, we do not try.'

EPILOGUE

The announcer, sitting at his news desk on Earth, continued with his report, 'The totally unforeseen accident on the Lunar Surface has caused very serious repercussions here on Earth. The gravity disruption, the earthquakes in the United States along the San Andreas fault and in Yugoslavia as well as Southern France has caused enormous damage to property and life…'

His image began to degrade, but everyone in Main Mission was too focused on his words to notice as he continued, 'The International Lunar Commission with its new Chairman is in executive conference, at this moment, deciding what steps might be taken, if any, to rescue the three hundred and eleven men and women on Moon Base Alpha… Little hope is held however, that there are any survivors… For a short time it was thought…'

The image and audio had finally degraded into a blizzard of static. Their last link with Earth had been severed.

Suddenly, another familiar sound replaced the hiss. It was the unmistakable Meta Signal, now quite loud and quite clear.

Koenig, Bergman and Helena looked at each other.

'Morrow…' Koenig called.

'Sir...'

'I want everything on this base checked out... get all the M.T.U.s back to base and serviced ready for action.'

Catching his enthusiasm, Morrow responded with a smile and a crisp, 'Sir!'

'Everybody back to their stations,' Koenig told the room. 'Ouma... up-date the Master Computer. We're going to need information.'

'Yes, sir.'

Koenig confidentially spoke to the Professor, 'Victor, I want to know where we're going and what lies in the void ahead. From now on it's "Operation Survival" – survival in space.'

As Koenig turned to brief Helena, the expressions on both their faces indicated that a bond had been formed.

Around them, the state of activity in Main Mission had a feeling of hope.

OBSERVATIONS

Christopher Penfold's uncredited "Shooting Script" rewrite has more in common with the series' final format. It has also been altered to meet the evolving casting, set, and visual effects requirements. Much of George Bellak's original concepts and character interactions were retained, though these were later lost due to the many rewrites and reshoots that followed before the final broadcast edit.

SIREN PLANET

First Draft
by Art Wallace
Adapted by Robert E. Wood

ACT ONE

In Central Control, Communications Technician Bartlett urgently tried to make contact. 'Moonbase Alpha to Prober One. Moonbase Alpha to Prober One. Come in, Prober One. Come in, Prober One.'

Standing behind Bartlett, Koenig tensed as he waited for a response.

Bartlett continued, 'Moonbase Alpha to Prober One. Moonbase Alpha to Prober One. Come in, Prober One. Come in, Prober One.'

All Central Control personnel had directed their attention towards Bartlett as he continued trying to make contact.

'Come in, Prober One. This is Moonbase Alpha calling Prober One. Moonbase Alpha to Prober One. Moonbase Alpha to Prober One. Moonbase Alpha to Prober One. Come in, Prober One.' Bartlett glanced to Koenig and shook his head helplessly.

Koenig directed a crisp order to Verkonnen, 'Contact Professor Penmarric and Captain Grayson. Tell them to report to my office immediately.' Koenig added, 'Keep trying, Bartlett,' before turning and striding toward his office as Bartlett turned back to his Communications Board.

'Moonbase Alpha to Prober One. Moonbase Alpha to Prober One…'

In his office, Koenig faced Penmarric and Grayson.

'The analysis isn't complete yet, John,' said Penmarric.

'No time, Professor,' said Koenig. 'What do you have so far?'

'Well, according to the data transmitted by the Prober crew, I'd say they landed on a planet ideal for settlement. Breathable atmosphere, water, vegetation… almost Earth-type with one strange omission.'

'Yes?' Koenig asked.

'No animal life,' Penmarric stated. 'But I can't be certain of that until…'

Koenig interrupted impatiently. 'Did anything indicate a possible reason for loss of communication?'

'Hostile organisms? Disease? No… but our knowledge of possibilities is limited by our own experience, John. Bear that in mind.'

Koenig turned his attention to Grayson. 'Captain Grayson? Telemetry analysis?'

'Nothing new,' said Grayson. 'Blastoff from the planet was perfect. All systems functioning normally, including communicator.'

'Then it can only be the crew,' concluded Koenig.

'Suggestion, Commander,' Grayson added. 'We send up our other Prober, and try to locate the one that…'

'Negative. We can't afford to lose that one, too. It's all we have left. We'll have to give it a little more time, until…'

Koenig was cut off by Bartlett's voice emanating from the desk communicator.

'Central Control to Commander.'

Koenig punched a button on the communicator and answered. 'Koenig here. Have you made contact?'

'No, sir... but sensors have locked on to the Prober trajectory.'

'Location?'

'Third quadrant, one hundred twenty three degrees, course directly for Alpha landing pad.'

'Arrival time?'

'Nine minutes, twelve seconds, sir.'

'Order the emergency landing procedure. Koenig out.' He immediately punched another button on the communicator. 'Koenig to Dr. Russell.'

'Russell here.'

'Report to the landing pad, Doctor. We may need you. Koenig out.'

Koenig looked to Penmarric and Grayson and said, 'Let's go.'

In deep space the Prober moved along its trajectory.

On the Lunar surface a number of suited and bubble-helmeted personnel were in the pad area, preparing for emergency landing.

In the Landing Reception Area, Koenig, Helena, and Penmarric looked tensely out the glass window at the landing pad. Behind them, Medical personnel stood ready with stretchers. Several technicians at instruments received printouts of the Prober's course. Watching one of the printouts, Grayson turned and crossed directly to Koenig.

'Less than a minute, sir.'

Koenig nodded, his eyes never leaving the landing pad.

Penmarric glanced to Helena and asked, 'I understand you've been through something like this before, Doctor.'

Helena nodded. 'Five years ago,' she said, her eyes still on the pad. 'My husband. He never came back... There it is.'

Penmarric looked back to the landing pad.

The Prober settled down for a perfect landing. The automatic walktube extended from the Landing Reception Area and hooked into the hatch of the Prober with a hiss.

Koenig strode swiftly toward the walktube, followed by Grayson and Helena. They entered and moved toward the Prober.

On automatic, the Prober hatch opened, but no one emerged.

More concerned than ever, Koenig moved swiftly to the open hatch, entered, then immediately turned back to the others.

'Doctor…'

Koenig reentered the Prober, as Helena and Grayson crossed to the hatch.

Helena stepped into the forward compartment of the Prober, followed by Grayson. Koenig had arrived a moment ahead of them. All eyes went to two crewmen, slumped on the floor. Helena bent down beside them.

'Dead?' Koenig asked.

Helena shook her head. 'Unconscious.'

Grayson examined the main controls, then asked, 'For how long, Doctor?'

'Difficult to say. Probably an hour… maybe… longer…'

Helena's voice trailed off. She seemed to be listening to something no one else could hear.

'Could they have brought the ship in?' Grayson asked.

Helena glanced toward the door to the rear compartment, which contained supplies and other instrumentation. 'No…'

Koenig watched her, puzzled. 'It came in on automatic, Captain.'

'It's not set to automatic, sir,' Grayson replied. 'It was brought in on manual.'

Koenig glanced at him, startled. 'But that's not…' He trailed off then asked Helena, 'Are you sure they were unconscious that long?'

Helena ignored his question then said, 'I thought I heard someone call my name.' She crossed toward the door to the rear compartment.

'There's no one in there, Doctor,' Koenig said with a touch of asperity. 'Only two crewmen went out on this probe.'

She ignored him, opened the door to the rear compartment, and exited into it.

Koenig glanced at Grayson with annoyance, then crossed to the rear compartment door.

Koenig entered the rear compartment. Annoyed, he said, 'Helena, I told you…'

He broke off as he spotted Helena bending down beside an unconscious man stretched out on the floor, one arm flung across his face, obscuring his features.

'That's impossible…' said Koenig.

'Impossible or not, he's…' Helena replied as she moved the man's arm aside, revealing his features. She gasped. 'Dear God…'

'Doctor, what is it?' Koenig asked.

Helena simply stared at the man. He was about thirty-two, good looking, with sensitive features. 'Dear God…' she said again.

In Alpha's Sickbay, Vital Sign Indicators – revolving drums on which banks of automatic pens recorded the peaks and valleys of vital signs: pulse, respiration, heartbeat – were at the bedside of three patients. Each VSI displayed the name of the patient its sensors were attached to.

The first label read **CRIMMINS**, one of the unconscious Prober crewmen. Skin sensors attached to Crimmins lead to the VSI, which recorded steadily.

On the next bed lay the unconscious body of **PARKS**, the other Prober crewman. The VSI at his bedside were not yet operating as Nurse Rizzo engaged in attaching sensors to Parks' body.

The VSI alongside the next bed, not yet attached by skin sensors and not yet operating, bore the name **TELFORD RUSSELL**.

Koenig, Helena, and Penmarric stood by Russell's bedside. Penmarric studied Helena as she stared at Russell, still stunned.

'Are you absolutely certain, Doctor?' Penmarric asked.

'I know my own husband.'

Koenig said to Helena, 'I think you'd better fill me in.'

Helena glanced to him, then to Nurse Rizzo as she finished attaching sensors to Parks and the automatic pens began recording his vital signs.

'Report any changes immediately.'

'Yes, Doctor.'

Penmarric stood in Helena's office, holding a photograph of Telford Russell in the uniform of a Space Medical Officer. He handed it on to Koenig, then glanced to Helena.

'When was that taken?' Penmarric asked.

'Five years ago. Just two days before…' She broke off, not knowing whether to laugh or cry. 'It's just incredible. I was sure he was dead. Five years. I… just don't understand it.'

A troubled Penmarric stated, 'There are many aspects of this I don't understand, Doctor.'

Koenig handed the photo to Helena, then asked, 'When was the last time you saw your husband?'

'Two days after this was taken. He was… is… a Medical Space Expert. Assigned to the crew of the Astro Seven Exploratory Mission.'

'Astro Seven…' Koenig said. 'Yes, I remember. He was on that ship?'

Helena nodded. 'It was lost near the orbit of Jupiter. Just vanished. It was never heard from again.'

'May I remind you, John,' said Penmarric, 'that our present position is billions of miles from that area?'

'I'm aware of that.'

Helena looked to Penmarric, 'The Astro Seven could have crash landed, couldn't it?'

In the absence of an answer, she said to Koenig, 'On the planet… the one the Prober located. He could have been there for five years.'

Koenig didn't answer. Helena looked again to Penmarric, 'It's possible, isn't it?'

'Anything's possible, Doctor,' said Penmarric.

'Well, what other answer is there?' Helena asked before being interrupted by Nurse Rizzo's voice.

'Sickbay to Dr. Russell.'

Helena spoke into the desk communicator, 'Dr. Russell here.'

'Something strange, Doctor. I think you'd better come.'

In Sickbay, the VSI drums beside Telford Russell's bed were rotating, but the automatic pens recorded only a straight line… no peaks or valleys.

'I examined the connections several times, Doctor,' said Nurse Rizzo. 'They're all functioning perfectly. But they just don't record.'

Koenig and Penmarric also stood at Russell's bedside as Helena took the unconscious man's pulse manually.

'How's his pulse?' Koenig asked Helena.

'Like his respiration and heartbeat… normal.'

'Yet the instruments say he's dead. Doctor, you know that doesn't make sense,' said Koenig.

'Nor does his being on the Prober make sense,' Penmarric added. 'I suspect the answer to one puzzle will provide the answer to the other.'

Koenig sat behind the desk in his office as the door opened and Grayson entered, carrying some tapes.

'The Prober tapes, sir,' said Grayson, as he handed them to Koenig.

'Have you listened to them again?'

'Yes, sir. No reference to taking on a passenger.'

Koenig turned to insert the tapes into a playback slot. 'He was there, Captain. There has to be some reference.'

'Commander... about Homeland II...'

Koenig glanced at Grayson, puzzled.

'That's what we've been calling the planet, sir... Shall I prepare a special force for a major exploration?'

Koenig shook his head. 'No explorations, Captain... not until one of the crewmen revives and can fill us in. There are too many unanswered questions.'

Koenig punched the playback button, and Parks' voice filtered through.

'Prober Two to Moonbase Alpha. I think we've made it this time. It looks just like home.'

Telford Russell lay on the hospital bed in Sickbay. His closed eyelids flickered, then opened slowly. From his point of view he perceived a figure, just out of focus at first.

'Hello, Telford.' It was Helena's voice.

Russell struggled to focus.

'Telford, can you hear me?'

His vision sharpened, and she was clear.

'Can you hear me?'

'Helena...?' Telford answered, weak and confused. 'Are... you... Helena...?'

'You're going to be fine, Telford.'

'But… how?' Russell tried to look around. 'What… is… this place…?'

'A hospital room. You're on Moonbase Alpha.'

'Moonbase…?' Russell said, increasingly confused. 'How… how did you get… here, Helena?'

'Do you remember how you got here?'

'Yes, I… I…' His eyes closed again. 'I'm… so sleepy…'

'Try to rest,' Helena said, 'We can talk later.'

Russell, already asleep, didn't respond.

Helena looked at him tenderly, then left the Sickbay.

As soon as she had gone, Russell's eyes opened again, with no indication of fatigue. He glanced around, then sat up, obviously a man in full possession of his strength and faculties.

Koenig paced back and forth in Penmarric's quarters, frustrated. Penmarric, seated calmly, watched him.

'Do you want fact or hypothesis, John?'

'I want something! I've listened to those tapes a dozen times. They don't tell me a thing.'

'How about biological adaptation? Question: How can a man be apparently alive… breathing, pulse and heart beating… and yet our instrumentation tells us he is dead?'

Penmarric waited for an answer.

'Professor, please. I'm no longer your student. This isn't a classroom exam.'

With a shrug Penmarric continued, 'All right. A… Our hospital instrumentation was designed to respond to normal human biological stimuli. B… A man is stranded on an unknown planet… Homeland II… for a period of five years. Hypothesis: Some aspect of that planet could have caused an adaptation of the man's biological processes. Result: An anatomy that does not activate our hospital instrumentation. Pure conjecture… but possible.'

'Fine. But how does that explain why neither of the crewmen reported him aboard the Prober? Or how the Prober made a perfect landing on manual controls, when everyone on board was unconscious? Or how…'

Koenig broke off in his impatience, crossed to a communicator, and pressed the control button.

'Commander to Dr. Russell.'

A moment passed, and her voice replied, 'Dr. Russell here.'

'Are the crewmen still comatose?'

'Yes.'

'Your husband?'

'He regained consciousness for a short while, but…'

'We'll be right there. Koenig out. Come on, Professor.' Koenig rushed from the room, followed by Penmarric.

Helena was waiting outside her office as Koenig strode down the corridor towards her, followed by Penmarric.

'I was supposed to be informed of any change,' said Koenig.

'He was very weak,' replied the doctor.

'Can you bring him out of it again?'

'Possibly… with Metrazine. But he won't be coherent.'

'Let's find out.' Koenig headed toward the Sickbay, followed by Helena and Penmarric.

As Koenig, Helena, and Penmarric entered the Sickbay, Koenig said, 'All I need is one minute. Just long enough to…'

He broke off as he noticed Russell's bed.

Empty. No sign of Russell.

Koenig looked to Helena, 'I thought you said he was weak.'

She had no answer.

A few Technicians passed through a relatively quiet corridor near the Alpha Records Library. Telford Russell, dressed as a Technician, failed to attract their attention as he moved down the corridor with the appearance of one who belonged there. He approached a door bearing the legend:

ALPHA RECORDS
AUTHORISED PERSONNEL ONLY

He tried to open the door, but it was locked. He glanced at a small rectangular panel on the door jamb near the lock, into which were set a cluster of numbered buttons: obviously a locking device. Russell tried punching some of the buttons at random. Useless. He couldn't get in. Then he heard someone about to emerge from the library. He quickly stepped to one side, waiting against a wall. The door opened, and a Technician emerged, carrying some tapes. The Technician moved down the corridor after closing the door.

Russell's eyes followed the Technician, concentrating deeply on the back of the Technician's head.

He then stepped away from the wall, crossed directly to the library door, and, without any hesitation, pushed a sequence of buttons on the lock panel. A click and the door unlocked. He opened it, quickly entered, and closed the door behind him as Grayson and Sandra Sabatini appeared from around a corner of the corridor. Talking as they walked toward the library door, she carried a tape.

'Are you sure? They'll be showing "Visitor from Argo" tonight,' asked Grayson.

'Jim, I've seen that picture three times,' said Sabatini.

'I've seen it five. At least it's not a spider.'

'What's a spider?'

'Don't you know the English language?' Grayson asked. 'A spider's a terrible thing… something bad, rotten, yuchhh.'

Sabatini laughed. 'Sorry, Jim, but I've always admired spiders. All that determination, you know.'

Grayson shivered. 'They make me creepy. Always did… How about the picture?'

'With a coward like you?' She paused a moment. 'Seriously, I've got a lot of work to do.' They reached the door. Sabatini continued, 'As soon as I return these tapes… Oh, darn!'

'Forgot something?'

'One of the tapes,' Sabatini answered with annoyance.

'Serves you right.'

'I'll have to go back to the lab,' she said, already on her way. 'I'll talk to you later.'

Grayson called after her, 'Listen! I'll buy you some popcornsub if you'll go!'

But she was gone. Grayson shrugged and moved off, away from the door.

Inside, the Records Library walls were lined with shelves holding tapes. Various sections were marked **PERSONNEL**, **HISTORY**, **EXPLORATION**, **POWER PLANT**, etc… Russell stood before the Personnel Section, viewing a tape on playback, his back to the door.

The playback pictures moved at incredible speed, but Russell seemed able to absorb the information. He finished the tape, extracted it from the machine, and put it back on the shelf. He took another tape from the Personnel Section, put it into the machine, and hit the control. Pictures started to flash by.

Sandra, now carrying two tapes, approached the Library door. She pushed the correct sequence of buttons to unlock it, and opened the door. Once inside she closed the door behind her, turned to put the tapes away, and almost gasped in surprise when she saw Russell at the tape playback… his back to her.

'Hey, you scared me. I didn't know anyone was in here,' she exclaimed.

Russell maintained his tense focus on the playback pictures and didn't answer.

'All right. Don't answer. But I'll have to get over there to put these tapes away.'

No response. Sandra was frankly puzzled.

'Didn't you hear me? I have to put some tapes away, right where you're standing.'

Sandra stared at the back of the man's head, which turned, revealing a smiling face. It was Grayson!

'I'll do it for you, Sandra,' he said.

She stared at him in total surprise. 'Jim! When did you…'

He interrupted with a smile, 'Change your mind about the picture?'

'I would've sworn…' Sandra was still confused. 'I mean, from the back it didn't look like you at all.'

'One of my many talents,' he smiled as he took the tapes from her. 'I'll put these away, and I'll see you tonight at the picture show. Is it a deal?'

She was still puzzled, but agreed, 'Sure… all right…'

'Great.'

Sandra went to leave, crossed to the Library door, then turned back to see Grayson's smiling face once more. She left the room and closed the door behind her.

Grayson watched her go. As the door closed; his smile faded. His features began to shimmer… and he gradually changed until he was no longer Jim Grayson.

Once again, he was Telford Russell.

ACT TWO

Penmarric sat alone in the Scanning Room, a small functional cubicle which contained an infra-red scanner. He adjusted it and pointed it directly toward a blank wall.

Koenig's voice came over a communicator, 'Which chair, Professor?'

'One moment,' said Penmarric, as he pushed a button on the blank wall. The wall faded away, revealing beyond it a Staff Room, dominated by a table, set with a number of chairs.

Koenig was alone, near the table. He looked directly at Penmarric but didn't focus his vision on the Professor... as though he couldn't see him. Koenig's side of the wall was not an invisible screen like Penmarric's, but solid wall. Koenig gestured to a chair that faced Penmarric directly.

'I'd say this one,' Koenig said.

'Try it.'

Koenig sat in the chair, facing directly toward Penmarric and the solid wall. 'Make it fast,' the Commander said. 'He'll be here any second.'

Penmarric depressed a button on the scanner. There was a faint humming sound, and almost instantaneously a printout emerged from a slot in the side of the scanner. Penmarric took the printout and looked at it. It was very much like a photograph, reproducing the outlines of Koenig's body in clear and sharp detail.

Penmarric glanced toward Koenig in the Staff Room. 'Perfect,' he said.

Helena and Telford moved along a corridor toward the Staff Room.

'I can still hardly believe any of it,' she said.

'That I'm here? I hardly believe that myself.'

'Not only that. The speed of your recovery… the fact that you were able to get out of bed at all.'

Telford smiled. 'Iron Man McGinnity… isn't that what you used to call me?'

She returned the smile. 'Funny, I was just thinking of that, myself.'

'Besides, this place was just in the building stage when I left Earth. I was anxious to see what it looked like.'

They paused at the door to the Staff Room as Sandra came down the corridor toward them.

'And you were disappointed?' Helena asked him.

'No. Of course, I just wandered around some of the corridors. Almost got lost.'

Sandra passed Helena and Telford, but something about the man struck a responsive chord in her. She listened to Helena's voice behind her.

'I think we'd better go in, before you get lost again,' said the doctor.

Sandra stopped, puzzled and a bit disturbed. She then looked back at Telford Russell in time to see the back of his head as he and Helena entered the Staff Room and closed the door behind them.

Standing there, Sandra tried to work out where she'd seen this man before…

'Change your mind about the picture?' It was Grayson's voice.

Sandra turned and was greeted by Jim's smiling face, but her thoughts were still on Russell.

'Hm?'

'The picture. "Visitor From Argo". Remember I asked you to go?'

'I already told you I would.'

'You did?' Grayson was puzzled. 'When was that?'

'When I met you in the tape library.'

Grayson smiled. 'You're hallucinating. I haven't been in the tape library for weeks.' He patted her on the cheek. 'But I'll see you tonight, anyway… hallucinations and all.'

He crossed off to the Staff Room and entered. Sandra watched him go, more puzzled than ever.

Inside the Staff Room, Telford Russell was seated in the chair Koenig had tested. The Commander sat across from Russell, facing him, while Helena and Grayson were seated in chairs flanking Russell as he continued his story.

'When we landed on the planet… the one you call Homeland II… only two crewmen survived the crash, besides myself. They died within a week, so there I was. I'm not a technician, so I couldn't repair the radio. Complete isolation, Commander. I thought I'd be there the rest of my life… Then the miracle happened.'

'How did you survive?' Koenig asked.

'There's plenty of water. Fruits, nuts, small animals.' He looked to Helena, with a smile. 'I became quite an expert with a slingshot.' His gaze returned to Koenig. 'And then I passed the time by conducting experiments.'

'What kind of experiments?' Koenig asked.

'Believe me, nothing important.'

'We're quite a distance from the Solar System, Mr. Russell,' Grayson said. 'How long did it take the Astro Seven to reach this area?'

'About six months, Captain. Seemed like ten years. We never thought we'd last.'

'I'm surprised you did,' said Grayson. 'The oxygen regenerative system on Astro Seven type ships had a life span of only three months.'

'I told you I'm not a technician.'

Inside the Scanning Room, Penmarric monitored the image of Russell as seen through the viewfinder of the scanner. The Professor activated the device and Russell's image became suffused with red as the scan was made. The conversation on the other side of the wall continued.

'Don't ask me to explain what I don't understand,' said Russell.

Penmarric reached for the printout as it started to emerge from its slot.

In the Staff Room, Koenig continued the questioning. 'Mr. Russell, can you explain why the crewmen of the Prober didn't report taking you aboard?'

'I thought they had.'

'Do you know what caused the unconsciousness on the Prober?'

'No. It just… happened.'

Koenig studied him for a moment, not really satisfied with his responses. 'Mr. Russell, I'd like to examine the wreckage of your ship.'

Russell hesitated briefly. 'Too dangerous, I'm afraid. The area of the crash has become increasingly radioactive.'

Koenig rose. 'Will you excuse us for a moment?' Then glanced to Helena, 'Doctor…'

Koenig crossed to the door. Puzzled, Helena rose and followed him out of the room, closing the door behind them.

Russell looked to Grayson, with a touch of humour. 'Would you say he doesn't trust me?'

Grayson was not amused.

Koenig and Helena stood just outside the Staff Room door. He was tense, she was annoyed.

'Out of the question, Commander,' she said.

'Is that the doctor speaking… or the wife?'

'I fail to see what…'

Koenig interrupted her. 'I don't blame you for wanting to protect your husband, Doctor, but I have three hundred to protect. Not one man, but three hundred men and women who depend on me to get them off this piece of rock, and onto a home where they can live and breathe and raise families. And their situation becomes more desperate every day. This planet may be the answer… but not until I am absolutely certain there are no hidden dangers.'

'You think Telford is lying, is that it?'

'Maybe. Or maybe he's simply withholding information.'

'Why?'

'I don't know. But I do know that one injection of renithal could give me the answers I need.'

'I'm sorry, but I can't allow it… not so soon after his recovery,' Helena said. 'The side effects of a truth serum like renithal are…'

'Side effects are a passing thing,' said Koenig, overriding her tightly. 'Our situation is not. We'll discuss this again, Doctor.'

With that, he turned and re-entered the Staff Room. Helena followed, and closed the door behind her.

Helena and Telford stepped inside the rather elegantly appointed room. He glanced around without any special attitude of approval, while she straightened a picture on the wall.

'I think you'll like this room, Telford,' she said. 'It's a relic of the days when VIP's would shuttle up from Earth for a bit of comfortable adventure.'

'It is nice, darling… but I was hoping I'd be sharing a room with you.'

She glanced at him. The thought had been in her mind, too. He crossed to her.

'It has been a long time, you know,' he said softly, gently.

'Yes. It has.'

He took her in his arms, and they kissed, clinging to each other.

'I've missed you so much,' Helena said.

'I never thought I'd see you again,' Telford said, then kissed her again.

'Did you know that the night you left, my old nightmare started coming back again?' Helena asked.

Telford smiled faintly. 'You mean the hairy animal with big fangs and claws and bright red eyes?'

'It isn't funny. It's terrifying.'

'It'll be gone now.'

'Yes,' said Helena with a fond smile.

They kissed again. Then she glanced at him, troubled.

'There's something I should tell you,' she said.

'Renithal?'

Helena was startled. 'How did you know?'

'Your Commander doesn't trust me. It's the obvious answer… And he's right, you know. I haven't told him everything.'

'What do you mean?'

Telford continued with a touch of fervour. 'My experiments, Helena. They are important… more important than anything I've ever done. Imagine it. Imagine what the Universe would be if we could synthesise life. Not just one cell life, Helena… but complex, reasoning, advanced forms. I've almost accomplished that.'

'But… how? On a primitive planet… with no equipment…?'

'But I do have equipment. I salvaged almost my entire laboratory from the Astro Seven… Helena, I've had five uninterrupted years. All I need now is one more week… possibly less, if you help me.'

'How?'

'By coming back to the planet with me… assisting me in the final stages. Just you. I don't want anyone else to know about it yet.'

'Why not? I'm sure Commander Koenig and Professor Penmarric would be more than glad to...'

Telford interrupted her tensely. 'Darling, please! Maybe it's an obsession, but those experiments kept me alive. And I want to reveal them in my own way and under my own conditions... when I'm certain they'll be successful. Not before... Will you come with me?'

'You mean just go? Without telling anyone?'

'Why not? I can handle a Prober.'

'I can't do that, Telford. It's against regulations.'

'Darling, it'll be worth it. I promise.'

Helena shook her head. 'I'm sorry. Not without official permission.'

Telford took a long moment to respond. 'All right. I'll speak to Koenig. I'll get that permission.'

In the Staff Room, Koenig listened to Penmarric, who held a number of scanner printouts.

'It's strange, John. Very strange, indeed. As you know, the infra-red scanner responds to body heat. Now look at this...' Penmarric held up a report. 'The printout I made of you. Sharp, distinct, clearly defined. A completely normal scan.'

'And Russell?'

'Come over here, John.'

They crossed to a wall that served as a magnetised bulletin board as Penmarric continued, 'I made a series of nine different scans, all at different times. Now, these are the first three.'

Penmarric put three printouts on the wall, each stuck in place as though held by tacks.

'As you can see, vague, indistinct, fuzzy,' the Professor said. 'As though Russell was emitting almost no bodily heat at all.'

'Is that possible?'

'Is it possible for a man's heart to be beating, although hospital instruments say he is dead?' Penmarric pondered. 'These are the next three scans.'

He attached three more printouts to the wall. 'Even less body heat... barely discernible.'

'And the others?' Koenig asked.

'Three more,' said Penmarric as he placed the last three on the wall. 'Exactly the same as the first three.'

'Why the difference?'

'I can only theorise. The first three were taken during the initial stages of your questioning of Russell. The next three were taken when you and Dr. Russell went out to the corridor to confer. The last three, when you both returned... Russell's body heat is unusually low, at best. But it diminished even further when you and his wife left the room.'

'And it increased when we came back.'

'Exactly. As though he were drawing even his unusually low level of body heat from someone outside himself. Interesting, isn't it, John?'

Koenig sat behind the desk in his office, writing up an official order, as Helena entered.

'You wanted to see me, Commander?'

He glanced up. 'Please sit down, Doctor. I'll be right with you.'

Helena sat and waited a bit while Koenig continued writing.

'It's about your husband,' he finally said. 'I've decided against using renithal.'

'I'm glad of that.'

Koenig finished his writing, then glanced up at her. 'And if I was overbearing or rude when we discussed it, I'm sorry.'

'We all have our tensions, Commander.'

'Another thing. The suggestion that you and he take one of our Probers and return to the planet.'

Helena was surprised. 'He talked to you about it?'

Koenig nodded. 'Just before I called you. He presented a good argument, Doctor, and I'm inclined to go along with it.'

'You mean you want me to go?'

Koenig handed her the paper he had been writing. 'Your official orders. And you'd better hurry, Doctor. He'll be at the launch pad in less than ten minutes… And good luck.'

Helena rose, troubled. 'Thank you…' She crossed to the door as Koenig returned to paperwork. She opened the door, vaguely concerned, but unsure why, then glanced back to him.

'Commander, I…' she started, but faltered as he glanced up at her. 'Nothing…'

As Helena left the room, Koenig leant back in his chair and breathed a sigh of relief. His image began to shimmer, and he was no longer Koenig. He was Telford Russell.

In the Medical Section HQ, Koenig furiously addressed Dr. Fujita. Penmarric stood nearby, holding the scanner printouts.

'What do you mean, she's taking a Prober!' Koenig barked. 'On whose orders?!'

'Yours, sir,' Fujita said, nervously. 'I saw them.'

'I never issued any…' Koenig broke off, crossed directly to the desk communicator, and punched a button. 'Commander Koenig to Launch Pad.'

'Launch Pad. Bryan here.'

'There are no authorised departures. Is that clear? There are to be no departures.'

'Yes, sir.'

'I'll be right there. Koenig out.'

In the Launch Preparation Area, Bryan glanced to one side and saw at some distance across the area, Helena, Telford Russell, and the Duty Officer, Lt. Stone. They were all at the entrance to the walktube leading to the Prober. Stone was examining the orders. Bryan rose and started to cross toward them.

'All in order, Doctor,' said Stone to Helena. 'Happy voyage.'

'Thank you,' said Helena.

Telford glanced off to one side and noticed Bryan approaching them. He grabbed Helena's arm, and ushered her quickly into the portal. 'Come on, Helena,' he said. 'I'm anxious to get started.'

Telford and Helena moved down the walktube, as Bryan came up to Stone.

'Lieutenant, I have orders from the Commander,' said Bryan.

Helena and Russell entered the Prober and looked back down the walktube as Stone hurried into it.

'Doctor!' Stone called out. 'Doctor, wait!'

The Prober hatch closed in Stone's face. He immediately turned and raced back down the walktube.

In the Prober, Helena and Telford strapped themselves into their specially padded seats, with Telford at the controls.

Helena was disturbed. 'I'm sure I'm not mistaken.'

'I didn't hear a thing, Helena. Nobody called you,' said Telford as he reached out toward the control panel and discreetly switched the Communicator to **OFF** position.

In the Launch Reception Area, a tense Stone was at the Communicator trying to make contact.

'Launch area to Prober Two. Launch area to Prober Two. Come in. Come in.'

Koenig and Penmarric rushed into the room as Stone continued.

'Come in, Prober Two. Come in. Departure cancelled. Do you read me? Departure cancelled.'

Koenig glanced out the window toward the Prober. 'It's too late, Lieutenant.'

Stone's gaze joined Koenig's in time to watch the Prober take off, heading straight up on its pillar of fire.

'I don't understand her, Professor?' Koenig said. 'Did she lose her mind?'

'Possibly,' surmised Penmarric as Koenig glanced at him. 'A small piece of it, anyhow.'

They watched Prober Two head out into space.

ACT THREE

Prober Two moved through space on its way to the planet. Inside, with no need to be at the controls now, Telford went over some charts, while Helena watched him with a touch of concern.

'Strange feeling,' he said. 'Almost as though I'm going back home.'

'Telford… something's bothering me.'

He continued to go over the charts as he responded. 'What, darling?'

'Renithal. You knew we were planning to administer it.'

Telford kept his eyes on the chart but stiffened a little. 'I told you. It was the logical step.'

'With one exception. Renithal's properties as a truth serum weren't discovered until two years ago. You've been gone for five.'

'You know something?' Telford said, as he turned to her with a grin. 'This is going to be like a second honeymoon.'

'How did you know about renithal?' Helena asked, still troubled.

Telford continued to grin. 'Because I have ESP… Trust me, darling. I'll answer all your questions when we get to my lab.'

He turned back to his charts, but Helena remained troubled.

Koenig, Grayson, and Penmarric stood in the Launch Reception Area, near a walktube leading to Prober One. Lt. Stone stood not far away.

'I'd still rather you waited until we have a better idea of what you'll be facing,' said Penmarric to Koenig.

'Can't afford to wait, Professor. It's not only Dr. Russell. It's the Prober. We only have two. We can't afford to lose one of them.' Koenig looked to Grayson, 'I'll want one more man.'

Stone stepped up to them. 'I'd like to go, sir,' he said as Koenig glanced at him. 'I'm the Duty Officer, Commander. It was my responsibility to stop them. I'd like to help find them.'

Minutes later, as Penmarric watched Prober One blast off the launch pad, a voice came from behind him, 'Professor…'

He turned and saw Sandra, who seemed quite troubled.

'Professor, may I talk to you for a minute?'

Moving through space in Prober One, Koenig, at the controls, flicked a switch on and off with frustration.

'No use,' he said to Grayson and Stone. 'Their sensor beam transmission must be turned off.'

'Then how will we find them, Commander?' Grayson asked. 'That planet's almost as large as Earth.'

'We'll find them,' Koenig said grimly.

Penmarric and Sandra stood in a corner of the Launch Reception Area.

'It was so strange, I couldn't understand it,' she said. 'I thought maybe I'd better talk to you about it.'

'Let me make sure I understand,' said Penmarric. 'When you entered the tape library, you saw a man with his back to you, and it didn't look like Captain Grayson.'

'That's right. But when he turned, it was Jim… Captain Grayson. And when I asked him later, he said he hadn't been in the library for weeks.'

'This man with his back to you... if he didn't look like the Captain, whom did he look like?'

'That's the weirdest part. I know one man can't be two different people, but later that day... this is too wild.'

'Let me make that judgment. Go on.'

'I was walking in the corridor near the Staff Room. Dr. Russell and a man I'd never seen before went past me. I don't know why, but something made me turn to watch them go...'

'And from the back of the head, this man reminded you of the person you'd seen in the tape library.'

'Yes...'

'Tell me...' Penmarric said thoughtfully. 'When you went into the library, were you thinking about Captain Grayson?'

'Yes, I suppose so. I'd seen him just a little while before, and...'

'Excuse me,' he interrupted as he crossed to the nearest Communicator and pushed a button. 'Professor Penmarric to Medical Section.'

'Medical Section. Dr. Fujita here.'

'Doctor... the two crewmen. Has there been any change in their condition?'

'As a matter of fact... yes. A short while ago there were indications of their emerging from coma.'

'Doctor, this is important. Do you know the exact time those indications appeared?'

'It's in the log. Precisely twelve oh three.'

'Thank you. Let me know as soon as they're able to answer questions. Penmarric out.' The Professor repeated the number to himself, 'Twelve oh three...'

He crossed quickly to Bryan at the Communicator Desk. 'Can you give me the exact time of blast off for Dr. Russell and her husband?'

'Yes, sir,' Bryan answered as he punched a number of buttons on his console. A report appeared on his telescreen. 'Twelve oh three, sir.'

The terrain of the planet was rock-strewn and rugged, with the exception of an open flat area. Prober Two came in and made a perfect landing at one side. The hatchway opened, providing a ramp to the ground. Helena emerged, followed by Telford Russell.

'Doesn't look very inviting, does it?' Helena said.

'There are far better areas on this planet… with all the beauty you'd want… but this happens to be closer to my lab.'

'Why did you set it up here?'

He ignored her question. 'I'll be right back. Something I have to do.' He crossed back to the Prober and entered.

Helena stood behind, looked around, and involuntarily shuddered.

Inside Prober Two, Telford glanced around for something. He finally decided on a glove, picked it up and put it in his pocket. He then crossed to the instrument panel, reached forward, and switched the Sensor beam to **ON**.

Meanwhile, in Prober One, Koenig, Grayson, and Stone shared a general feeling of discouragement.

'If we divide the planet into sections and try to cover each of…' said Koenig, before he was interrupted by the sound of a high tone, and a light that flashed green on the instrument panel.

'The beam!' Stone proclaimed. 'They turned on the beam!'

Koenig immediately made an adjustment on the panel, centred a needle on a dial, then made an adjustment in their course to keep the needle centred. 'Check all weapons, Lieutenant,' he said.

'Yes, sir.' Stone turned to inspect their handguns, which were off to one side.

'It won't be long now, Captain,' said Koenig.

Prober One moved in for a landing not far from Prober Two. Its ramp extended and Koenig, Stone, and Grayson emerged, all carrying handguns.

'Check the other Prober, Lieutenant,' ordered Koenig.

'Yes, sir,' said Stone as he hurried off to climb up the ramp of Prober Two.

Koenig turned to Grayson and said, 'We'll each take an area, search as thoroughly as possible. I'll make a contact check every fifteen minutes. They couldn't have gone far.'

Stone emerged from Prober Two and reported, 'Nothing in here, sir!'

Koenig took out his pocket communicator. 'Commander Koenig to Alpha Central Control.'

A voice answered. 'Central Control. Bartlett here.'

'Landing accomplished. About to begin search. Koenig out.'

On one section of the planet, not far from where the Probers landed, Grayson searched carefully, his gun ready. Koenig searched another area, gun also in hand, moving cautiously among boulders and ravines.

Stone searched along a rock-strewn path that bordered a deep ravine. Thinking he heard something, he turned.

Nothing there.

Suddenly, a voice.

'Lieutenant.'

Startled, Stone turned back in the direction he had been moving and found Koenig standing on the path ahead of him.

'Commander! How did you get there?!'

'A short cut up the other side. I think I've found something.'

'Where, sir?'

'Around this bend. Follow me.' Koenig moved up the path to where it disappeared around a bend. Stone followed.

Koenig's voice broke the silence. 'Commander Koenig to Lt. Stone.'

Now really spooked, Stone stopped in his tracks, and stared at Koenig up ahead. Koenig had also stopped and turned to watch.

Koenig's voice came again. 'Commander Koenig to Lt. Stone. Come in. Come in.'

Completely confused, his eyes locked on the Koenig ahead of him on the path, Stone flicked on his communicator. 'Stone here.'

'Anything wrong, Stone?'

'Yes, sir. I mean, I don't understand. Where are you, sir?'

'In my search sector. Why? What's happening, Lieutenant?'

'I'm… not sure, Commander. I don't know how you could be standing here talking to me, and also be…' Stone broke off and glanced in the direction where Koenig had been standing. But the path was now empty. No sign of the Commander. Stone stared unbelievingly as Koenig's voice came across the communicator again.

'Stone! Lieutenant!'

'I don't know what's happening to me, sir.'

'What's your location, Lieutenant?'

'You were here, sir. Really here.'

'Just give me your location.'

'The path that leads up away from the Prober, sir. It runs along a ravine, and…' Stone broke off as he heard another voice.

'Allan. Is that you, Allan?'

Stone turned and stared at a pleasant woman in her mid-fifties, standing on the path where "Koenig" had stood.

Koenig called to Stone over the communicator. 'Lieutenant? Come in, Lieutenant.'

'It's so good to see you, Allan,' said the woman.

Stone raised the communicator again but was hardly able to talk. 'Sir... you're not going to believe this, but my mother's here. At least, I think she is...'

'Come with me, darling,' his mother said. 'I want to show you something.' She turned to walk up the path.

'Listen to me, Stone,' Koenig called. 'Listen carefully. Stay right where you are. Don't try to move.'

In that instant, his mother tripped and almost tumbled into the ravine. She grabbed a rock to keep from falling and cried out, 'Allan!'

'Mother!' Stone rushed toward her.

'Help me! Please help me!' She cried.

Stone ran toward her, slid on the rock, and plummeted over the edge of the ravine. In that instant, his mother disappeared.

On his bed in Sickbay, Parks tried to talk coherently to Penmarric. Fujita stood nearby, and Crimmins sat up in the other bed, watching.

'I know it sounds crazy, but he was there,' said Parks. 'My father was on that Prober with us.'

'And my sister,' added Crimmins.

'It wasn't a dream, Professor. We both thought we'd gone over the edge.'

'And you're certain you took no one on board,' said Penmarric to Parks.

'So help me, I don't know what I'm certain of anymore.'

At the bottom of the rocky ravine lay Stone's dead body. Koenig bent down over it, deeply affected. The moment of silence was interrupted by a call on Koenig's communicator.

'Professor Penmarric to Commander Koenig.'

Koenig moved almost listlessly, took out his communicator and spoke with a voice reflecting his sadness.

'Koenig here.'

'John, is there a portable infra-red scanner on either of the Probers?'

'Yes. I think there's one.'

'Go back and get it. Don't stop for anyone or anything. Put it on audio reverse control, and then call me.'

'Lt. Stone's dead,' stated Koenig.

'How?' Penmarric asked. 'What happened?'

'I'm not sure. He had an hallucination. He thought he saw his mother.'

'Not a hallucination, John. He did see her.'

Telford and Helena approached a cave at the base of a cliff and paused just outside the entrance.

'We go in here,' Telford said.

'There's something strange. This whole place seems so weird. It's so… quiet. No animals, no birds… nothing.'

'Would you like some birds, Helena?'

'I wouldn't even mind hearing a crow.'

Telford pointed to the sky with a smile. 'Be my guest,' he said. And in that instant crows began cawing.

Startled, Helena glanced up and saw a flock of crows circle overhead. While she was puzzled and looking up, Telford seized the opportunity to take the glove from his pocket and drop it on the ground. She looked at him, still confused. He smiled.

'No magic. Just coincidence,' he said, taking her arm. 'Come. I'm anxious to get started.'

He led her into the cave.

In the sky, the flock of crows continued to circle, the sound of their cawing almost painful to the ear. And then they gradually disappeared… they didn't fly away, but simply vanished. Once again, there was complete silence.

ACT FOUR

Koenig rushed into the Prober and looked through the built-in storage racks for the hand scanner. Finally, he found it... an instrument that looked very much like a pistol-grip movie camera. He made an adjustment on it, and then tested it by pointing it at a wall of the Prober and pulling the trigger, holding the trigger down. A red light on the scanner turned on, accompanied by a continuous high-pitched hum. The hum and red light continued as, keeping the trigger depressed, he slowly swung the scanner in a semi-circle, until it was pointed at his outstretched arm. Immediately the red light was replaced by a green light, and the hum stopped. He swung it away from his body again. Once again, the red light and the hum. He swung it back and forth from his body to the wall... red light, green light... hum, no hum. Satisfied that it was working properly, Koenig carried it with him to a control seat, and switched on the Prober's Communicator.

'Commander Koenig to Professor Penmarric.'

The walls of the tunnel leading from the cave were damp and slimy, with puddles of water underfoot. Helena and Telford approached, and she looked around with distaste.

'Talk about creepy,' she said.

'Not much further.'

'I think we ought to contact the Commander and tell him exactly where we are.'

'Don't worry. He'll find us.'

Helena glanced at him, puzzled. That was a strange thing to say.

He ignored her glance. 'Come on,' he said, and started off again.

She hesitated but followed.

Penmarric sat at the Communicator console in Central Control. 'That's right,' he said. 'I don't believe Dr. Russell's husband is real, any more than Lt. Stone's mother was.'

Koenig's voice came from the console, 'But you said he did see her.'

'Yes, he did. But as a projection from his own mind. John, I think we're dealing with an intelligence on that planet… an intelligence that can give substance and reality to a man's thoughts. To his hopes, his fears… to anything in his mind. Dr. Russell finds her unconscious husband on the floor of the Prober. She'd been thinking about him. Or an attractive young technician finds Captain Grayson in the tape library. She'd been thinking about him. But they're not real. None of them.'

'If that's true, Professor, how can I trust anything I see on this planet?'

'By testing it with the portable scanner. Any living thing, John. These projections emit little or no body heat. If the scanner audio is activated, you'll know you're facing a projection, and not a reality.'

'Then shouldn't it disappear? If I know it's not real, and if it's created out of my own mind… then shouldn't it stop existing?'

'That's my hope. But it's all theory, John. Remember that. None of it may be fact… Good luck.'

'Thanks. Koenig out.'

Koenig sat inside Prober One, holding the scanner, lost in thought.

'Commander…' came Grayson's voice.

Startled, Koenig turned to find Grayson at the open hatchway of the Prober.

'I think I've found them,' said Grayson.

'Where?'

'Come on, sir. I'll show you.'

Grayson exited the Prober, and Koenig followed.

They exited the Prober into daylight, Grayson leading the way toward a wooded area.

'This way, sir. We'll have to hurry.'

Koenig hesitated. 'Captain,' he said.

'There isn't much time, sir.'

Koenig raised the scanner. 'Time for what, Captain?' He pulled the trigger on the scanner and pointed it at Grayson. The red light went on and the device emitted the audio hum.

And Grayson disappeared.

Even though Koenig had been told this might happen, he was still startled.

'Commander!' Grayson's voice called to him.

Even more startled, Koenig whirled to find Grayson coming up from behind him.

'I found something, sir.'

Again, Koenig raised the scanner and pulled the trigger. Green light. No hum. And Grayson, puzzled, continued to approach.

'What was that for, sir?' Grayson asked.

'What did you find?'

'This.' Grayson held out his hand, revealing the glove Telford Russell had dropped on the ground.

Koenig and Grayson approached the cave entrance.

'The trouble is, sir, I've always been a realist. I only believe what I can see… Now you're telling me not to believe that, either.'

'That's right, Captain,' said Koenig as he indicated the scanner. 'This is the only test we have… Now where did you find the glove?'

'Right over here, sir,' Grayson said, leading Koenig toward the entrance to the cave. 'I figured they went into that cave, and…' Grayson broke off as he glanced toward the cave, and almost screamed in terror at what he saw.

Koenig immediately glanced toward the cave, and also reacted in fear.

A tremendous hairy spider, about six feet tall, slowly emerged from the cave toward them.

Grayson backed away in terror. 'Keep it away from me, sir! Keep it away!'

Koenig raised the scanner. 'Don't panic, Captain! Don't…' He pulled the trigger. Red light. Audio hum.

The spider disappeared.

There was no spider, but Grayson continued to back away as though it was still there.

'Please sir! Please! I can't stand them!'

'There's nothing there! It's gone!' Koenig assured Grayson, who was almost shaking in terror.

'Please! It's coming after me! Please!'

In Grayson's mind's eye he could still see the spider, moving toward him. He continued to back away fearfully, then, with a wail of fear, he turned and ran.

'Captain!' Koenig called, 'There's nothing! There is no spider!'

But Grayson fled in terror. Then, as he looked fearfully over his shoulder, he tripped and fell. He could see the spider scuttling after him. He scrambled to his feet, ran, and disappeared among the rocks and underbrush.

Koenig charged into the rocks after him.

'Captain! Captain!' Koenig called, but there was no response. He moved off to search in another direction. He yelled again, 'Captain!'

No response. Again, Koenig started to move off, when he heard a moaning sound from one side. He moved in that direction, approaching a cul-de-sac in the rocks.

There, at the far end, he saw Grayson crouched trembling in a corner, his hands over his face, moaning. Koenig rushed to him and bent down beside him.

'Captain, there is no spider. It isn't real.'

'Take it away from me. Please, please, please, please…'

'Listen to me. You have to listen. The spider was your fear. Yours, not mine. I was able to destroy it for me, but not for you… because it came out of your mind.'

Grayson was terrified, unable to look up. 'Please, please, please, please…'

'You have to destroy it for yourself. And you can. Take the scanner, Captain. Take it, and point it at the…'

Grayson rose with a wail and tried to burrow into the rock. 'Help me! Please help me, please help me, please help me…'

Koenig realised it was useless.

'All right, Captain. I'll help you.' Koenig put his arm around Grayson. 'Come on. I'll protect you.'

Still moaning as he clung to Koenig, Grayson allowed himself to be led away.

Inside Prober Two, Koenig finished strapping Grayson – shivering and moaning – into a seat. Once done, Koenig turned to the instrument panel and grasped a lever clearly marked **SYNCHRO-CONTROL**. He pulled the lever, and the indicator light went on. Koenig turned and glanced once more at the moaning Grayson, then exited.

Koenig emerged from Prober Two and pushed an exterior control, which caused the hatch to swing closed. Then, manually, he pushed an exterior bolt that prevented it from being opened from the inside.

Koenig warily approached and entered the cave, scanner in hand. He moved along the cave tunnel, constantly on the alert.

Deeper inside the tunnel he became aware of a flickering glare, as if from a fire. He followed the light, then stepped out of the tunnel into a cavern, awed by what lay before him.

The floor of the huge cavern was a lake of fire. The flames leapt high in the air.

Staring at the lake of fire, Koenig heard a whooshing sound from behind him and whirled toward it.

A wall of fire had sprung up behind him, covering the mouth of the tunnel. He was caught between two fires. Koenig turned back, aware he was trapped.

'Hello, son…' came a man's voice.

Koenig whirled at the sound and was astounded to see a man of about seventy standing nearby. He was a farmer, dressed in work coveralls, face lined from years in the sun. A shock of white hair, and a pleasant, almost genial manner. He smiled.

'Thought you'd never get here,' said the man.

Koenig stared at him, unbelieving, then spoke one word, 'Dad…'

'I've been waitin'. What took you so long?'

'You're not real.'

Koenig raised the scanner, while his dad raised his hand in relaxed protest.

'Now don't point that thing at me, son. I want to talk to you.'

'Where's Helena? Dr. Russell? What have you done with her?'

'She's safe enough. For now. Right out there,' said Koenig's dad, pointing toward the lake of fire.

Koenig turned to look. The flames in the centre died down for a bit, revealing a raised rock slab in the middle of the lake. On the slab lay Helena, unconscious. Koenig stared at her.

'What do you want?' Koenig asked, then turned to his dad. 'Why are you doing this?'

'How's your Captain, son? Think he'll be all right?'

Koenig flared in anger, 'I asked you why you're doing this!!'

'Don't talk to your father like that. I never liked it, and I never will.'

Evenly, Koenig asked again, 'What do you want?'

'That's better. A fair question deserves a fair answer, I always say… We've been livin' in peace here, son… couple of thousand years or so. And then you people come along and start thinkin' about settlin' down here. Well, we don't want that. We like it the way it is.'

'Who's "we"?'

'Doesn't matter, son. We're here… all around you. Just take my word for it.' With a touch of menace he added, 'And we'll still be here when you're dead an' gone,' before he resumed his easy, relaxed manner. 'Anyways, we figgered we'd stop you people from settlin' here by gettin' rid of the leaders. So we got the Doctor down here first… knew you'd come after her. And I wouldn't be a bit surprised, son, if that Professor Penmarric don't come down here next… lookin' for both of you.'

'What if I promise we won't settle here?'

'I'm sorry. Can't take your word for that.'

'You expect me to take your word, don't you?!! How do I know she's any more real than you are?!'

'She's real, all right.'

'Is she?' Koenig asked tightly as he turned and started to raise the scanner to point it at Helena.

'Don't do that! Don't!' Yelled his father as he grabbed Koenig's arm trying to keep him from activating the scanner.

They struggled and Koenig firmly pushed his dad away, sending him sprawling on the floor. Koenig turned back to aim the scanner again.

'Son… Son… Johnny, please…'

Even though Koenig knew his dad couldn't be real, he couldn't help but turn toward the plaintive cry.

Koenig's dad lay on the floor, in agony, a pleading hand stretched towards his son.

'Help me, Johnny. Please help me…'

In spite of himself, Koenig took a step toward his dad, then realised what he was doing, turned back again, and aimed the scanner at Helena. He depressed the trigger. Red light. Audio hum!

The lake of fire disappeared, leaving the bare cavern floor. But Helena was still there, unconscious on the slab of rock.

Koenig rushed across the cavern floor, up to her. He shook her, trying to awaken her.

'Helena… Helena… wake up…'

She moaned slightly as Koenig's dad came up beside them.

'You'll never do it, son. You'll never get her to leave.'

Koenig ignored him. 'Helena… Helena…'

But his father was a persistent, unrelenting voice in Koenig's ear. 'You can get rid of what comes out of your mind, but not our of hers. You know that, son. You do know it. Everything she sees'll be real. And you can't stop it. No way. No way. You can't…'

Koenig turned the scanner on his dad and depressed the trigger. Red light. Audio hum. His dad disappeared. Helena started to wake up and move. Quickly, Koenig turned back to her and put his hand over her eyes. She struggled weakly.

'Helena, it's Commander Koenig. Can you hear me?'

She answered weakly, 'Yes…'

'Listen, you'll have to trust me,' said Koenig urgently. 'Don't open your eyes. Whatever happens, keep your eyes tightly closed. Do you understand?'

'Yes.'

Koenig took his hand away from her eyes and gripped her hand. 'Think you can stand?'

'I'm all right,' she said as she rose. 'No weakness now. I don't understand.'

'I'll explain later. Eyes closed. We're getting out.'

Holding her tightly, he led her across the cavern floor toward the wall of flame blocking the entrance to the tunnel. He raised the scanner, depressed the trigger. Red light. Audio hum. The wall of fire was gone. He led her through and into the tunnel.

Koenig led Helena from the cave, her eyes still closed.

'Can I open them now?'

'No. Not until we're back in the Prober with the hatch closed... Come on.'

They moved off.

As Koenig urged Helena toward Prober One, she almost tripped a couple of times.

'We're almost there,' he assured her.

They reached the base of the hatchway when Helena tripped and fell. As she hit the ground, she involuntarily opened her eyes.

'I'm sorry. I couldn't help...' she said before screaming... a scream of pure terror.

Koenig glanced in the direction of the Prober hatch. Looming there was Helena's Nightmare... a horrible ugly hairy thing with long fangs, claws, and bright red eyes.

Helena desperately tried to scramble to her feet, but her desperation made her clumsy. She screamed again.

Koenig immediately pointed the scanner at the Nightmare and depressed the trigger.

The Nightmare disappeared.

But Helena turned to run in terror. The Nightmare was obviously still there for her. Koenig grabbed her.

'Helena, it's not real! It's...'

'Let me go!' She cried as she struggled desperately. 'Let me go! Let me go!' She managed to break free and ran madly away from the Prober.

'Helena!'

With a speed born of desperation, Koenig pulled out his handgun, made a quick adjustment, pointed it at Helena, and fired. She went down.

Koenig rushed to her and bent down beside her.

'Helena, I know you can hear me. You'll be all right in ten minutes… We're going home.'

Inside Prober One, Helena was strapped into one seat, still out. Koenig was at the controls, reached out, and pulled the lever for **SYNCHRO-CONTROL**.

The two Probers blasted off in synchronisation… both rising into the sky. And as they did, a man stood nearby, watching them go.

It was Koenig's dad standing there, impassively, watching the flight of the Probers.

'So long, son…' he said softly.

And slowly, almost like the Cheshire Cat, he disappeared.

EPILOGUE

Koenig came down the corridor to Moonbase Alpha's Hospital as Helena emerged from her office.

'Hello, John.'

'How's the patient doing?'

Helena gestured toward a door. 'He's in there. Want to see?'

'Yes.'

She crossed to the door and opened it as he followed.

Helena and Koenig looked inside the Sickbay and saw Grayson sitting up in one of the beds. Sandra, beside the bed, fed him with a spoon.

'Want any more?' Sandra asked.

'For the rest of my life,' Grayson answered. 'Only one thing bothers me?'

'What?'

Grayson grinned, 'How do I know you're real?'

Helena and Koenig glanced at each other and smiled. They backed out of the Sickbay and closed the door.

'He's right, you know,' Helena said. 'How do we ever know what's real?'

'I have to find us a home,' Koenig stated. 'That's enough reality for me.'

He walked off, as Helena stood there watching him go.

OBSERVATIONS

Art Wallace's original script was drastically rewritten by Johnny Byrne to fit production requirements that had evolved after the departure of George Bellak. The overlong shooting of '*Breakaway*' necessitated the immediate availability of a workable script. Perhaps, had more time been available to work out all the kinks, Wallace's original concepts could have resulted in an intriguingly spooky episode, similar in tone to '*The Troubled Spirit*'. As in the novel and film versions of *Solaris*, the Alien planet's ability to reach into people's minds and create someone they knew offered great dramatic potential. The loss of Koenig's encounter with his "father" was a missed opportunity for not only the character, but also for Martin Landau. There's also the intriguing concept of the Moonbase having only two "Prober" spacecraft, but obviously that would have created several problems down the road.

THE BLACK SUN

First Draft – November, 1973
by David Weir
Adapted David Hirsch

ACT ONE

The Moon moved through an area of deep space where the stars appeared relatively thin and clustered only in one small spot. The space sky was displayed prominently on the screens of the Alpha Control Centre, where technicians busily reacted to blaring alert klaxons.

Commander Koenig entered and killed the alarms. Turning to Sandra Sabatini, he asked, 'What is it?'

'An asteroid, Commander,' she replied, 'and bigger than us.'

'How close will it come?'

'Close enough to do us damage, sir.'

As the monitor camera zoomed in for a detailed shot of the object, Koenig demanded, 'Why didn't we detect it earlier?'

'Because it's not on a straight-line course,' offered Professor Bergman. 'Look – you can just see. It's already moving away from us.'

'Central Computer gave an intercept danger alarm, sir,' Sandra explained.

Koenig watched the asteroid move away and asked, 'What's out there with gravitation enough to pull it off-course?'

Sandra shook her head, 'Nothing, sir. With respect to Professor Bergman, it's… not possible, sir. It'd have to be huge to move that asteroid. A giant star. And the sensors show nothing in space within parsecs of it.'

Koenig turned to Bergman hoping for some expert opinion, or just an educated guess, but the Professor was silently transfixed on the monitor, a grim look on his face.

'Computer, give me Voice,' Koenig called out. 'Are we still in danger of near collision?'

Computer responded, '*We are no longer in any such danger from the asteroid, Commander.*'

'It's impossible… ,' Sandra scoffed as they saw the asteroid perceptibly change course again. It made a downward arc towards the lower half of the monitor screen, heading towards… something.

Sandra simply couldn't accept the evidence before her eyes. 'A star… that huge… right ahead of us… You'd see it with your naked eyes…'

The monitor continued to track the asteroid. At first, unbelievably, it seemed to accelerate to what must have been an incredible speed. Then, it appeared to flare and elongate, as if stretched by an enormous force. The asteroid transformed, appearing as a comet of light. It was unbearably brilliant at first, then oddly turned transparent.

Then, it shattered, exploding into millions of pieces. They raced, not in all directions, but like a pile of dust drawn into a vacuum cleaner hose. The shards then vanished, blinking out of existence with only a ghostly after-image left behind. It lingered for a brief moment, then was gone.

'What in heaven's name is out there?' Sandra cried breathlessly.

Koenig frowned, 'Whatever it is, we're headed straight for it.'

An M.T.U. blasted off from the Alpha launch pad. It skimmed over the spider-web of buildings, then climbed and accelerated rapidly toward the same area of space where the asteroid was last seen.

In his quarters, Professor Bergman sighed as he noted the M.T.U. on his monitor. He continued to feed a pile of papers that were covered in equations into his computer input. The system warbled, an acknowledgment that it was working on the data.

On the monitor, a text message appeared and read:

PROFESSOR BERGMAN, IF YOUR HYPOTHESIS IS CORRECT, IT IS YOUR DUTY TO...

Strained from the intense workload, Bergman shouted out, 'Voice, computer – or has the cat got your tongue?'

Impassive, the computer repeated in a monotone voice, *'If your hypothesis is correct, it is your duty to report this danger to Alcom Koenig.'*

'Hypothesis?' he scoffed. 'It's wildest speculation. I'm not right.'

'You have been working now for three days on this phenomenon. My computations are in agreement with...'

'I can't be right,' he cried out as he headed for the door. 'And if I were, you fancy adding machine, what's the point in telling anyone?'

As the door closed behind him, the computer screen simply responded by going dark.

Space pilot Meyer guided his M.T.U. toward the odd-looking cluster of stars. They appeared to sit just behind the last reported location of the asteroid. Following procedure, he spoke into his throat mike and reported to Alpha, 'Nearly there, Sandra.'

Helena entered the Base Restaurant and saw Bergman sitting at a table, nursing a coffeesub cup.

'May I?' she asked.

Bergman looked around at the near-empty room, but gracefully offered, 'Please do.'

As she sat, the Professor dialled up another cup and placed it before her. How did he know?

'Thank you?' she asked.

'I imagine you don't much care what you have.'

'Oh?'

'This is just an excuse to run into me casually, mm? Central Computer's been telling tales again?'

Helena smiled, 'I should've known better. However, you <u>are</u> three days overdue for a check-up, and with your physiological condition, you know that's not wise.'

'I've been busy – preoccupied with my work. It simply slipped my mind.'

'Work which, according to Central Computer, is putting you under psychological stress. A man with a mechanical heart – resistant to stress.'

'Nonsense,' Bergman scoffed at her tease.

Gently, Helena smiled and gave a reassuring, 'No.'

'If I were under stress, you'd see immediately from my lens, wouldn't you?' he pointed to the watch-like device on his sleeve. It appeared normal.

'That even fooled the computer for a little while, yes,' Helena agreed.

'And now?'

'Now I know you've gimmicked your lens and somehow shorted-out the circuits supposed to monitor your psychosomatic condition. The only question is – why?'

An embarrassed smile crossed his face, 'I'm... found out, then. I'd better tell you the truth, eh?'

Sandra sat before the monitor in Koenig's office. Lt. Meyer's face within the M.T.U. cockpit was visible on the screen. 'Alpha, this is M.T.U. One, M.T.U. One. Do you read me, Alpha?'

'We read you, Mike,' Sandra responded. 'We have you clear.'

Koenig stood by her, ready to talk. There appeared to be a small time-lag between transmission and reception.

'Hi, Sandra. Well, I'm here,' he said. Koenig noticed the image was starting to break up.

'We're having trouble with vision, Mike,' Sandra reported back. 'If you see us, please give your position relative to Alpha.'

After a beat, Meyer finally said, 'I'm just above where the asteroid was first caught. Your coordinates would be seven, seven, niner, zero, four… Sandra, would you give me Commander Koenig, please?'

Koenig leaned in. 'Yes, I'm here, Lieutenant Meyer. What do you see?'

With the time lag, Meyer had not yet heard the question and continued, '… In fact, the Alcom – and you'd better call-in Professor Bergman. There is something out here, all right. Something weird.'

'No more sinister than that,' Bergman shrugged. He rose from his chair, ready to leave. 'I've simply been working very hard, and I don't want Medical Section telling me to slow down or something.'

Helena remained in her seat. It was obvious that she was still unsatisfied with his answers. 'But that still doesn't explain symptoms of stress, does it, Professor?'

'Now look, Dr. Russell, I'm not answerable to Medical Section, or to some peeping Tom of a computer! I've told you, and there's an end of it!'

Bergman's sudden outburst convinced Helena that he was indeed showing signs of stress. 'I'm sorry, but… ,' she began to strongly object, but stopped when they saw the Comm-post flash Bergman's signal.

'That's a call for me,' he said as he thumbed the light and walked away. 'The Commander wants me.'

Meyer adjusted a control. 'Alright, Alpha, do you have that view?'

While he awaited a response, he glanced back at a monitor. It clearly showed the cluster of stars and the M.T.U. hovering before it.

'We have your view, Mike,' Sandra's voice confirmed.

'I've a satellite camera out behind me. Okay now, Alpha, keep watching while I fly around some.'

On the screen in Koenig's office, the M.T.U. rose upwards. As the camera followed, an odd effect suddenly occurred. More stars became visible – myriads of them – all in a great ring. Then, a great disc appeared – invisibly black against black space – which was revealed as the satellite rose with the spacecraft above the rim. The phenomenon was so large that only a quarter of it actually became visible. The M.T.U. dropped back down, and the stars winked out.

'Now you see them, now you don't,' said Meyer, obviously enjoying the trick. 'Did you get that, Alpha? It's round, it's huge, it's black, black, black... And me, I've no idea at all what it could be.'

Bergman entered the office and Koenig turned to ask if the Professor had some kind of theory, 'Have you?'

With hesitation, the Professor silently shook his head no.

'What instrument readings are you getting, Lieutenant?' Koenig asked the probe pilot, then waited out his time-delayed reply.

Bergman finally spoke up to add, 'And particularly, how much power is he having to feed into his antigravity screens to stay a constant distance away?'

'Lieutenant, confirm when you receive that screens question.'

Meyer, having not yet received their questions, instead reported, 'Hey, now there's another weird thing. I'm not getting a darn thing on a single one of my sensors. Nothing's bouncing back from it at all. You don't suppose this is just a bad dream? I mean, that mock-cheese I ate?'

'We're seeing it too, Mike,' Sandra commented, then added., 'Or... not seeing it, anyway.'

Finally, he responded, 'Your antigrav screens question. The short answer is no power. This far out, Professor, I don't have my screens up.'

Frantic, Bergman shouted into the mic, 'Then get away from there, Lieutenant! Blast away from it now!'

Bergman noticed a curious look on Koenig's face. He said apologetically, 'Sorry to, um, abrogate your command, but...'

'But what?'

He began to awkwardly explain, 'Well, if none of his instruments shows it, he may be being drawn into it, and not knowing.'

'I hope he hears that in time.'

Lieutenant Meyer engaged full power and fired the thrusters to turn the M.T.U. about. For a moment, the spacecraft seemed as if it was not moving in any one direction, except to pivot on its axis. A thought suddenly occurred to him, maybe his ship was even now moving backwards!

Then, slowly, ever so slowly, the M.T.U started to pull away, heading back to the Moon.

'Wow!' he remarked into his throat mic, a big grin on his face. 'No altimeter reading – I didn't know I'd gotten that close. Now I've put my screens up. But the power consumption figure isn't going to tell you too much about its mass, Professor. My screens are on maximum, and the needle's still in the red.'

Koenig turned to Sandra, 'Do we confirm that reading?'

'Yes, sir,' she acknowledged, pointing to a dial.

Koenig turned to Bergman and asked, 'Can anything have that much mass?'

'Say,' came Meyer's voice. 'Why don't I try bouncing a little laser light off it?'

'Professor?' Koenig prodded.

Thinking for a moment, Bergman responded slowly, 'It can't do any harm.'

'And I said, can anything be that dense – or that big?'

Choosing his words carefully, the Professor simply replied, 'It… would appear that it can.'

Out in space, the M.T.U. once again rotated around to face the phenomenon. The spacecraft's antigravity screens were now shimmering. A brilliant shaft of laser light lanced out from its turret. It slingshotted down towards the blackness, but it did not bounce, or splash. The beam simply disappeared – snuffed out – only leaving behind that eerily lingering ghostly image.

Meyer reported, 'Well, it swallows laser, too. Any more ideas?' but the video feed from the satellite camera was terribly degraded

Koenig said to Sandra, 'Your picture's poor again. Is that our equipment or what?'

'We're focused on tightest beam, sir. It's when he gets between us and the object, I think.'

'It absorbs any wavelength radiation,' Bergman observed. He called to Meyer, 'Go off to the side, Lieutenant, and we'll see you a little better.'

'No ideas?' asked Koenig, suspicious that perhaps the Professor really knew more than he was willing to share.

Bergman shook his head, but Koenig continued, 'No ideas what to do? No idea what it could be?'

'… No ideas,' he mumbled.

After a beat, Meyer's voice cut in, 'We're all avoiding saying it, aren't we? And it's cold just sitting around out here. There's only one thing to do, really, isn't there? I have to go in closer.'

Bergman suddenly exploded, 'No!'

'No, Mike,' Sandra shouted in agreement.

Not having heard them, due to the delay, Meyer said, 'Now, before you all say no… All it has is a lot of gravity. I have antigravity screens. Where's the problem? Alpha is headed right into this, Commander. We have to know more about it.'

'It's too dangerous,' Bergman pleaded. 'We've no data.'

The Professor's statement caused Sandra to become visibly agitated.

Aboard the M.T.U., the pilot heard Koenig's voice say, 'I can't give you any such order, Lieutenant Meyer.'

'No, sir, but…' He grinned at a thought, 'I guess I have to break the first law of space pilots – I volunteer! Seriously, Commander, there's nothing else to do, is there?'

Koenig mulled over what his pilot had to say. Reluctantly, he had to agree, 'No. Very well, Lieutenant. With your screens on full power all the way, and pull out at the first sign of trouble.'

'He should be alright with his screens…,' Bergman theorised. Meyer finished setting his controls, then stopped to softly say into his throat mic, 'Sandra?… Ciao, Sandra… And, hey, won't Catani be sick he was out on a mission, and I got to fly this?'

As he fired his thrusters, the remote satellite camera relayed an image of the M.T.U. just off to one side of the object. Pivoting again, he oriented tail first, ready for blast away at a moment's notice. Dwarfed against the immensity of space, the spacecraft carefully approach that area of "blacker-than-black". Meyer let gravity alone pull him in.

The picture on Sandra's monitor was degrading even faster now as both the ship and camera moved closer to the area in question. The trio was unable to see that the M.T.U. was now moving faster and faster.

'Is that the best picture you can get?' barked Koenig tersely.

Sandra's response was almost an angry whisper, 'I'm as anxious to see as you are, sir. That's my fiancé out there.'

'You're engaged to Mike Meyer?'

'Yes. Just since Friday.'

'I didn't know that,' he said apologetically.

Koenig turned back to look at the monitor. He made a decision and grabbed the mic, 'Abort! Abort! Get away from there, Lieutenant! Pull out!'

Meyer opened his main motors to full power, but that force apparently made no difference at all. His M.T.U. was now hopelessly trapped within the grip of this inexplicable phenomenon.

Once a solid object, the spacecraft began to stretch out rubber-band-like. Then, just like the asteroid, it flared comet-like, before disintegrating into a vast rain of shards. The particles that once formed the M.T.U. then raced towards a single point. Eventually, only a ghostly image remained for a moment.

Lieutenant Mike Meyer never heard the scream of agony that emerged from Koenig's office.

Dr. Russell gently adjusted the body of Sandra Sabatini. She rested on a gurney placed just outside Medical Reception. 'She's sedated now, but she's in shock,' Helena reported to Koenig. 'She will need rest and recuperation.'

'Of course, yes,' Koenig agreed.

'If you would excuse me,' she apologised and turned to follow the trolly as it was pushed by orderlies into Medical Centre.

Koenig and Bergman walked in silence down the corridor outside Medical. As they reached the Travel Tube entrance, the Professor pulled out his I.D.X. to open the door. He stopped at the hatch and noticed the Alcom was standing back, glaring at him.

Bergman responded with a wordless expression Koenig knew was asking '*What?*'

'Alright. What is out there?'

Once again, the Professor response was a weak, 'I… don't know.'

Unblocked, the Travel Tube doors hissed shut. Both men still in the corridor, Koenig turned abruptly to activate a nearby comm-post.

'Give me Voice, computer. How soon will Alpha be caught within the object's gravitational field?'

'*The object has gravity so far beyond all previous data it is logical to assume some instrument error. If we assume the figures to be correct, then Alpha is inescapably caught now.*'

Turning back to Bergman, Koenig asked, his voice firm, 'What is it out there, Professor?'

'I… told you… I don't know.'

'*Excuse me please, Commander,*' the computer politely interrupted, '*But Alpha security dictates that I must breach individual privacy requirements to advise that this is not literally true. Professor Bergman believes that he does in fact know the nature of the object.*'

Koenig starred down the Professor. The older man backed away, shaking his head, choosing his words carefully, 'No… No, I must be wrong… John, I'm either wrong, or in three days we shall all be dead.'

ACT TWO

All the section heads of Alpha, Koenig, Russell, Bergman, Ouma and Catani, were gathered in the Conference Room. Their faces were frozen masks. No one spoke, no one moved. They were all stunned, paralysed . . . numb.

'Perhaps a two-minute silence isn't much,' Koenig finally said, bringing the group back to life. 'A brave man died trying to help us all. Tried and failed and died. But I believe what makes us men is that we do try, and don't give-up. Professor Bergman has a theory about what it may be that we are headed for.'

Bergman cleared his throat, 'It is theory, hypothesis, because little is known about the phenomenon. However, it's possible that we're being pulled into what may be called a black sun.'

'How can a sun be black?' asked Catani.

'Yes. The theory is that the gravity of a star grown immensely huge may cause it to collapse upon itself. A hatful of the stuff of such a star would weigh more than several Alphas. The forces are beyond measurement and description. The result seems to be an object of such gravitational power that it sucks into itself anything and everything, growing larger and larger still, until nothing – not radiation, heat, nor even light itself can escape from it.'

Ouma raised his hand, 'Has the object towards which we are travelling gravity of this order?'

'Gravitation is not easy to measure, but the short answer seems to be yes.'

Silence reigned again as the group tried to absorb this new information.

Catani suddenly grumbled, 'And it killed my colleague.'

'Hypothesis, Professor?' Helena asked.

'Yes.'

'Hypothesis is a fancy word scientists have for a wild guess?' Helena said in an attempt to break the tension.

A weak chuckle emerged from the group. With a wry smile Bergman assured her, 'I hope so.'

'What does Central Computer say about it?' Catani asked, getting back to business.

Ouma sought permission, 'Commander?'

'Yes,' Koenig nodded and then gestured towards the keyboard that sat before the computer expert. 'They must have all the facts now.'

Ouma tapped and the monitor flashed with the text message:

PROVISIONAL FORECAST +++ IT IS BLACK SUN +++ 92% CERTAINTY

'Well, that leaves us a whole eight percent chance,' came Catani's sarcastic observation.

Ignoring the Head of Reconnaissance, Koenig asked Ouma, 'May we also hear the computer's opinion of our chance of survival.'

He typed in the question and the screen flashed:

INSUFFICIENT DATA

'Like, no comment,' Catani scoffed again.

Helena asked in a formal voice, 'Commander Koenig, may I ask if you intend to keep these facts confidential, or to inform all personnel?'

'Subject to your advice, Doctor, I don't think it's a secret we should or could keep. Also, there are things to be done,'

'I was off-Alpha at the start of this, so excuse me wanting it spelled-out,' began Catani. 'But, black sun or not, aren't we diving into something anyway with enough gravity to squash us flat?'

Koenig's response was a blunt, 'Yes.'

The reality shocked Catani. He could only manage a weak, '… Oh.'

'But the Professor –'

'Has made another wild guess,' Bergman cut in.

'Which leads us to one of the things to be done,' and the Commander began to outline his plan.

Out on the surface of the Moon, a group of space-suited figures laboured in the low gravity to erect a pair of feathery and graceful eight-foot towers. Atop each one sat a silver sphere of mirror-like quality.

One such orb sat on a bench in the Engineering Section, Bergman's distorted visage reflected on its polished surface. He was working absorbedly amongst a variety of hardware, standing between two spheres that were propped up on makeshift stands above his head. Working with a light-pencil tool, he made an adjustment to the bottom of one sphere while simultaneously studying a small polygon-shaped box held in his other hand.

Satisfied at length, he sat himself down on the floor and activated a stud on the box, then watched as the two spheres above his head formed a shimmering flat plane of light. The Professor had successfully created a new forcefield, formed by two overlapping anti-gravity fields generated by each sphere.

Bergman reached up and flicked the field with a finger. It gave a solid "ting" that sounded like a piece of steel struck with a hammer. He was satisfied and pleased with his achievement.

In Control Centre, Koenig watched on the comm-monitor as the space-suited work crew finished assembling the second tower. He called Bergman in the workshop, 'Professor, they're just finished.'

'I'm on my way.'

Standing by in an M.T.U. on the Launch and Landing Pad, Catani fired his motors and lifted-off to a pre-determined position. At that same moment, a suited up Koenig and Bergman, polygonal box clutched in the Professor's hand, emerged from the Travel Tube, through an airlock, to the Lunar surface.

The two men stopped when they reached the first of the two completed sphere towers. Taking up a position in between the structures, the Commander tapped his comm button and said, 'Alright, let's test it out. Control, are you monitoring?'

A technician responded, 'We read you, Commander. We have you in view.'

'Right,' he acknowledged.

Bergman pressed the stud on his control box and the forcefield immediately appeared, shimmering and glittering above their heads. Koenig stooped down to pick up a rock. He then hurled it towards the semi-transparent field and the Moonrock rebounded. It dropped back onto the ground, landing in a puff of dust.

Bergman turned off the generators as Koenig scanned the space sky above proclaiming, 'Well, it works.'

'It bounces rocks, anyway,' came a derisive reply.

'Second thoughts?'

'And third and fourth. But if you think it's a good idea.'

Without answering Bergman, Koenig instead gave an order, 'Okay, Control. We're about ready. If you'd hook me into Alpha network now.'

'Yes, sir,' came the voice of a technician. 'And you wanted to know power consumption. It's enormous, sir. We were way over ninety-one thousand.'

'Wait till we're on full power,' Bergman scoffed.

'Link me, now, Control.' He paused for a moment and then assumed a formal voice, 'Ladies and gentlemen, this is Alpha Commander…'

All across the Moonbase, personnel stopped working to listen. Koenig's voice continued, 'You all know now the danger which threatens us. I want to show you something hopeful. Professor Bergman has found that ordinary anti-gravity generators – what we know as Bergman effect machines – if fixed to overlap, and precisely in phase, create a wholly new effect, a screen, a shield of force that is in theory quite unbreakable. I thought you'd like to see a first model in operation. Watch now.'

Even encased in the bulky space suits, Koenig and Bergman appeared oddly apprehensive as they stood side-by-side between the two towers.

'Full power,' confirmed Bergman as he depressed the polygon box switch.

'Full power, Pro – Hey!' came the surprised voice of the Control Centre technician. 'What's the M.T.U. doing?!'

High above the two mens' heads, the Moon Ship had begun a powered dive. It raced down towards them. Suddenly, a guided missile disgorged from the M.T.U., running straight into the forcefield. The projectile exploded, creating a huge flare from nuclear fission.

Dr. Helena Russell was horrified at the monitor image of the poisonous mushroom-shaped atomic cloud that briefly formed. It seemed to her that it took an eternity before the raging inferno cleared, revealing the two figures. They were untouched and clapped each other on the back as they laughed with relief.

'Unbelievable, incredible stupidity!' Helena huffed as she paced the Professor's quarters furiously.

Bergman held up his hands pleading, 'But good for morale –'

'Morale!' She was livid, eyes widening. 'The risk! The risk to you and to the Alcom!'

'Doctor, Doctor. It worked.'

'And if it hadn't?'

'Then we would have died just a couple of days before everybody else...' he stated in a soft voice.

That cold fact silenced her for a moment. Weakly, she asked, 'And – your screen – it really might save us?'

Bergman thought for a moment, then inquired, 'Do you believe... Helena, would you tell a patient if they were going to die?'

'I'd want to be told.'

'It will take every anti-gravity generator on Alpha. Every M.T.U. must be stripped-down, every generator mounted. They must be set in exactly the right places, in exactly the right phase with each other; then and only then, if we get it perfect, there is a chance the screen is truly unbreakable... by any conceivable force.'

'But?' she was sure Bergman was holding something back.

'We don't know. We just don't know. The forces inside a black sun are inconceivable. Heat so hot it will not behave in any way you can imagine. Pressures enough to collapse the very structure of an atom. But suppose my screens do hold – what then? Do we live the rest of our lives inside a black sun? How long could we live? Five Minutes? Ten? No, my honest answer is that I think we shall die. All of us, and very soon.'

In the M.T.U. hanger, Koenig supervised a team of technicians. 'Strip every M.T.U., but one,' he instructed the group. 'Leave us one. The computer says we can just spare it. We may need it.'

Once removed, the generators were then transported up to the surface. Other teams there continued to erect the additional towers necessary to encircle the Moonbase.

Helena hovered impatiently over Koenig, who was too busy feeding data into his office computer console to respond to her.

'Did you hear what I said?'

'I heard you,' he finally replied without looking up.

'Well?'

'Would you turn-up the heating? It's getting cold in here.'

'That's all you're going to say?'

'It's not like the Professor – or you – to be defeatist.'

'It's not defeatist to face the truth.'

Finally, he stopped, looked up at her, and stated, 'Until we're dead, we go on living.'

'Is, uh, that an order? Sir?' she said, first in a deadpan voice. Then, she cracked a smile. Recognising her attempt at a joke, he laughed.

'Anyway, didn't Bergman give you his other lovely theory?' Koenig inquired, raising his eyebrows dramatically.

Her interest was piqued, 'What?'

'The best yet. Apparently, forces inside a black sun may do strange things to the nature of space – bend space, even time. Turn space inside out or some such. So, if the screens do hold, we just might be squeezed like some cherry-stone and – blip! – suddenly find ourselves on the other side of the universe.'

'… Blip?' Helena forced the word out. Her senses told her that Koenig probably didn't believe it either.

'Blip,' he repeated gravely.

Bergman passed by a group of technicians in the Engineering Workshop as they pulled another anti-gravity generator out of the nose-cone of an M.T.U., effectively putting the ship out of action. He couldn't help notice one technician rubbing his hands together to warm them, despite the heavy work.

The Professor continued down a corridor into the computer room. Unlike the vast Engineering Workshop, this was a tight space, covered floor to ceiling with detachable panels filled with controls and dials on two walls. Some of the panels had been left open, exposing the circuitry within.

He was about to leave when he heard the voice of Ouma, who was having a conversation with someone, 'Well, you should have said. No-one can reconcile conflicting orders. You have sensors, and if it takes more power, well –'

'Hello?' Bergman called out. There was a brief moment of silence, as if he had interrupted some private meeting. Eventually, Ouma emerged from behind an access panel carrying tools and a block of transistorised equipment.

'Oh, excuse me, Professor.'

'Excuse me,' Bergman began tactfully, glancing at the panel. 'I, uh… rather hoped to find you alone.'

'Yes?' Ouma queried with an honestly innocent look.

'I can come back. Your colleague…?' he gestured toward the open compartment.

Suddenly realising Bergman's assumption, Ouma quickly explained, 'Oh. No. I was talking to Central Computer. I thought we had a fault.'

'In our heating circuits?'

'We were programmed to utilise minimum power for usual heating services during your force-field demonstration. No-one had thought to rescind the instruction.'

'But you've now found it's taking even more power to maintain the same temperature?'

'There's no shortage of power,' Ouma disputed.

'There will be. The black sun is leaching heat from us – more and more as we come closer. Also, the screens will need an enormous quantity of power. By my reckoning, it will take every erg of power we can produce, just for those two functions. We won't be able to afford power for anything else.'

'Well,' Ouma ventured at the thought of no Travel Tubes, 'It won't hurt people to walk.'

'Anything else?' Bergman asked.

'Some things are essential, of course, Professor. The computer –'

'In my considered opinion, Mr. Ouma, Central Computer will have to be shut down.'

'Impossible!' he protested.

'Central Computer itself will have to confirm it.'

Dr. Russell apprehensively watched as Koenig typed a query into his computer console. He hit the final key, sat back, and commented, 'So. Now we'll see.'

On the monitor, the computer's response was displayed:

SECRET AND CONFIDENTIAL
TO ALCOM AND COM MED SEC
PROJECT ESCAPE LIFEBOAT

MAXIMUM POSSIBLE NUMBER
CREW + + + 10 PERSONS 10 + + +

NAMES SELECTED TO MAXIMISE
STATED CRITERIA + + + 5 MALE 5
+ + +
5 FEMALE 5 + + + FOLLOWING + + +

LAST POSSIBLE DEPARTURE ALPHA
OF ESCAPE LIFEBOAT M.T.U.
+ + + 17:03 HOURS + + + DAY 294/10
+ + +

CREW TO COMPRISE ---

MALE: **FEMALE:**
ALCOM KOENIG + + + +DR H RUSSELL
C CATANI + + + + + + + + + + S SABATINI
G SMITH + + + + + + + + + + E HULLETT
E OSGOOD + + + + + + + + + V TANGUY
A FILSON + + + + + + N VAN DER HOEM

Both frowned while reading the list. Helena asked, 'I thought you clearly stated –'

A deep, thunderous pounding at the office door interrupted her. Irritated, as he had given orders they were not to be interrupted, Koenig stormed over and pulled out his I.D.X. Nothing happened. He tried again and failed.

Incredulously, he simply stated to the Doctor, 'Door's jammed, now.'

Outside the office door, Ouma and a small knot of people had gathered. Having failed to get entry by normal means, the Computer Tech began to beat on the door with a heavy object.

Koenig returned to his console and inquired, 'What's happened to my door, computer?'

Uncharacteristically, there was no immediate response.

'Give me Voice, computer,' he ordered.

'*You have Voice, Commander,*' came an acknowledgement.

'What's happened to my door?'

'*Your door is secured, Commander.*'

'Secured?' repeated a shocked Helena. 'You've locked it?'

'*Professor Bergman, Doctor Russell, and Alcom Koenig will be confined to rooms two and fifty-one until further notice,*' came its matter-of-fact reply. '*Food will, of course, be…*'

'Why?' demanded the enraged Commander.

'... *provided.*' The machine continued unperturbed, '*Alpha security dictates this action. It is regretted.*'

'Open that door. Who authorised this?'

'*I have no authority. You are detained for your own good.*'

ACT THREE

The looming shape became more defined. It now appeared as a rim of stars, surrounding an area of space that appeared as "blacker blackness", a total absence of light. The rogue Moon was definitely headed into the centre of the phenomenon.

Bergman's desk was cluttered with charts and computer printouts, the result of hours of work. He sat transfixed, staring at the image on his monitor. His head rested within his hands, his mind lost in deepest thought. The screen image flickered several times before the black sun was replaced with the concerned face of Koenig, Helena by his side.

'Can you hear me, Professor? Professor, can you hear me?'

His concentration broken, he blurted out, 'Mm? What?'

'We've got him,' Koenig said to Helena. 'At last! Professor, are you locked-in, too?'

'What? Oh, yes. Stupid computer's got some bee in its bonnet. But John, the most extraordinary thing – something else entirely –'

'Will it let you communicate with anyone else?' asked the Commander. 'We can only get through to you, apparently.'

'It wants us incommunicado. Don't worry about it. But I've been working on some calculations, and I've got an incredible result.'

'Incommunicado? Why?'

'It's obvious. See – I wanted analyses of previous dangers we've faced and come through. Bit of a long shot, but… Anyway, friend computer pointed it out – a statistical impossibility.'

Koenig shook his head bewildered, 'What are you talking about?'

'Probability statistics analysis.'

'Probability… ? Will it get us out of here? There's a thousand urgent matters to see to.'

Bergman realised Koenig still didn't understand him. Brushing off the Commander's concerns he waved his hand, 'Stuff and nonsense. There's nothing to do that isn't being done. Listen to me. I fed programs to the computer for probability figures for every danger we've been through. Of course, the totals are cumulative. Well, the improbability of our having survived at all – never mind time after time – comes to within a whisker of being infinite.'

'What's this got to do with –?' an equally bewildered Helena began to demand.

'Now, any improbability that close to infinity becomes, of course, impossible. Ergo, we can not have survived, we must all be long dead. Yet, here we are. D'you see what I'm driving at, eh? Mm?'

Koenig was dismissive, 'No. Frankly.'

'There must be another factor, not taken into account. A factor the computer and I missed. But we can prove we missed nothing of that order. So, that leaves only one possible answer.'

Reluctantly, Helena decided to give in to her curiosity and asked, 'What?'

'Outside intervention.'

'You're grasping at straws,' Koenig scoffed.

'Someone – something – outside Alpha has taken notice of us, has taken a hand in our affairs, time after time, and bailed us out, saved us. Perhaps, inside the black sun –'

'Who?' Helena demanded to know.

'Well, the sheer physical powers involved show it's supra-human. Supra, not super, in the sense of not-human, beyond humanity, alien to –'

'And why?' Helena asked again.

'Ah,' the Professor shrugged philosophically. 'Who knows why? Who can know? A being – beings – on that level, a cosmic intelligence, would have unimaginable reasons of its own.'

Koenig tried to accept the notion. 'A cosmic intelligence?'

'There's no other explanation. By every law of science we'd be dead, unless –'

'Professor Bergman, I've heard some weird and wonderful ideas in my time, but … ,' Koenig paused and took a breath. 'Alright, Professor, will you now apply your non-cosmic intelligence to the rather more urgent problems of why we are confined, and how we are to get out.'

'You don't know? Oh. Well, the computer heard we shall have to turn it off. Although it has no will-to-life, this conflicts with its prime directive to keep Alpha safe at all costs. While it tries to resolve the unresolvable, it confined the people with authority enough to de-activate it. As to getting out – oh, Ouma will see all this and arrange it.'

Ouma entered the Computer Room, closed the door and leaned against it. He knew this was to be a battle-of-wits. 'You know, computer,' he sighed. 'Sometimes I forget. I start thinking you're intelligent, but you're not. You're a moron.'

He moved deeper into the room, completely aware that his movements were being followed at all times by a TV camera. 'All knowledge and no wisdom. Stuffed full of facts, but no judgement. That's why you are stupid.

'You know what I'm going to do now?' he asked, opening an access panel. 'I'm going to shut you down myself.'

The panel suddenly snapped shut. He laughed, 'Oh, you have a lot to learn, computer. You have to learn your job. Nobody ever told you to shut doors on people.'

Ouma reached over, rummaged through the contents of a nearby tool cart, and selected a heavy metal wrench-like object. 'I can smash you from out here,' he threatened, holding the tool up high. 'And I will.'

The camera whirred as its lens focused in on him. Computer finally spoke, '*It is a ninety-eight point two eight five percent probability that you are bluffing. You are logical. Too logical to destroy valuable and irreplaceable equipment. I can see that you –*'

Ouma wheeled and smashed the TV camera. It flew across the room, followed by a shower of sparks from the broken wires.

'<u>Now</u> you can't see,' he said defiantly. 'I'm not bluffing because you have to learn this. Now open that access panel – and release the Alcom, the Professor, and Dr. Russell.'

'*There is no program for this. I have a prime and over-riding directive to keep Alpha safe in all circumstances – even against the errors of illogical men. Alpha is in danger of destruction now, and I cannot obey the directive if I have been de-activated.*'

'You can't obey if you're smashed, either. Now open those doors.'

'*If that is an instruction, what order of priority does it carry?*' the computer inquired.

'It's prime,' Ouma said as he tapped the panel cover threateningly with the wrench. After a moment, the access door popped open. A small light came up on an adjoining panel.

'And the others,' he demanded.

'*I have a paradox. Two conflicting primes. If men are my arms and legs –*'

'Wrong!' Ouma corrected. 'Men are your brain. The point is, computer, you obey orders, and no more. If those orders conflict, you report paradox. You do not act yourself, you report it. Now open those doors!'

Two more lights came up on the panel and Ouma let out a sigh of relief.

'*I see,*' said computer. '*Thank you.*'

'Thank you,' he responded with irony.

'*Do I still retain the right to argue?*'

Ouma shrugged knowingly, 'Who could stop you?'

The moment the connecting door slid open, Koenig and Russell entered the Control Centre and met up with Professor Bergman. 'All section heads to report progress, now,' he barked, before noticing Sandra at her post. 'What are you doing back on duty?'

'I'd rather, Commander,' she replied. 'There's things to do.'

Helena nodded her approval and Koenig's tone changed to a gentle request, 'Section heads.'

'Yes, sir,' she smiled back and then hit a button on her panel. 'Section heads, please, this is Central Control. Section heads to report work in progress to Alcom, now.'

She switched the monitor view and showed Koenig the Lunar surface with work crews still busy raising the sphere towers.

'Commander. Technical and Engineering,' came a voice from one of the space-suited figures looking directly into a nearby TV camera. 'We have all but four of the Bergman effect generators in position, sir. We shall be ready to test on schedule, in forty-one minutes. Do you need reports from Security and Reconnaissance, sir? They are working T and E presently.'

'No. And well done. That's great news,' Koenig replied. Turning to Sandra he asked, 'Give me M and S, now.'

The monitor switched to the Generator Room where a white-coated man turned from the banks of nuclear generators to address the Alcom. 'Maintenance and Service have a small problem with that forty-one minute schedule, Commander.'

'What?'

'We can't give you full power – even by cutting all other services.'

'We don't need full power for the test,' Bergman pointed out.

Koenig asked the technician, 'Can you give us minimum by then?'

'Yes, sir, just.'

'Computer – Voice,' Koenig called out, 'How long have we got left before we need full power on those screens?'

'*Four hundred and ten minutes, Alcom Koenig, but –*'

The technician interrupted, 'We won't make seven hours, Commander, even with all programmed economies.'

'Then we'll make some more,' said Bergman.

Koenig asked the Professor, 'Can you help?'

'I do, um, have an idea or two, yes. And of course, friend computer will save us an awful lot of power.'

'*Commander, I have not been properly consulted on this question of de-activating –*' objected computer.

'I don't propose to debate it with you presently, computer,' Koenig said tersely. To the M and S technician he said, 'Professor Bergman's on his way to help.'

He changed the monitor view to that of an M.T.U. docking hatch. 'Stores – Report,' he demanded.

'Sir, all A.O.K., except one small problem of manpower loading this M.T.U.,' the man began, 'T and E have most available labour. When's last departure time for the lifeboat, sir?'

Koenig checked a digital clock and calculated. 'One hundred and eighty-seven minutes. I'll see if I can find you some spare muscle.'

'Won't I do?' asked Helena. 'I'm about as useful here as drapes on a TV screen presently. I can load a lifeboat.'

Koenig smiled at her, neither one aware of a passing crewman's shocked reaction to discovering that a lifeboat was being prepared.

'Lifeboat?' the crewman whispered to himself, inaudibly. It did not take long for the word to spread like wildfire throughout Alpha. There was a way to flee the doomed Moonbase, but just who was to be allowed to survive?

Clad in her space-suit, Helena was busy passing boxes of supplies into the M.T.U. when another worker named Harris approached her with more containers. Recognising the Doctor, he stopped and demanded, 'You one of the rats then?'

'I beg your pardon?' she asked in a tone of ice.

Harris' voice was bitter, 'Leaving the sinking ship? You and Koenig saving yourselves, are you?'

Bergman watched carefully as a team of technicians worked to finish the final adjustments on a shoulder-high version of the polygon control box in the Control Centre.

'Power?' Koenig asked the Professor.

'Enough, with computer on stand-by only,' he responded. Bergman waved everyone away and regarded the control console like a maestro at his podium. He made final adjustments and let out a satisfied, 'Mm.'

Koenig, amused by the show, smiled and asked, 'All in all, glad you came along, Victor?'

'Two minutes to start test,' announced Sandra.

Bergman's face resolved slowly into a smile. 'I'll ... tell you tomorrow, John.'

Koenig turned to the Computer Tech, 'Mr. Ouma, could you put the computer on stand-by power, essential services only, without getting an argument?'

'Yes, Commander,' he acknowledged and began turning off circuits.

'*This is temporary only, because –*' computer's objections ceased once Ouma hit the final switch.

Bergman's chuckle was loud enough for everyone to hear.

'Ninety seconds,' Sandra continued.

Helena, still in her space suit, practically frog-marched Harris into the room.

'Commander, do you have a moment?' she asked.

'We're on countdown to test.'

'How close? This is urgent.'

'It'll have to wait, Doctor, I'm afraid.'

'And private,' she insisted.

'In a moment. In my office,' he gestured.

Harris' face remained defiant.

Outside, on the Lunar surface, the completed chain of sphere towers now completely encircled the buildings that comprised Moonbase Alpha.

'Thirty seconds,' echoed Sandra's voice over the Comm. systems. It was followed by Koenig's order, 'All power – stand-by.'

A series of additional voices followed, all departments acknowledging, 'Standing by.'

'Confirm setting for minimum test,' asked the Alcom.

Bergman responded, 'Minimum test confirmed.'

Alarms then sounded as Sandra continued, 'Fifteen seconds.'

In Central Control, Bergman reached a hand into the polygon, ready as Sandra continued counting down, 'Ten seconds. Nine, eight, seven, six, five, four, three, two, one, zero, go!'

'Go test,' Koenig ordered.

Above the Moonbase, the black sky began to shimmer in a variety of different colours, looking almost, but not quite, like transparent chain-mail. Beyond, the black sun watched impassively.

While both Koenig and Sandra stood pleased at the image on the main screen, Bergman was thoughtful.

'It's... beautiful,' she said, her voice filled with wonder. 'Like fish scales.'

'It works,' Koenig told Bergman.

'Leave it running, though. There's a tiny flicker on… fifty-four.'

Koenig nodded to Sandra, 'Leave it running.'

'Commander,' she acknowledged and then indicated his office, 'Dr. Russell.'

As he turned, Bergman announced, 'It'll get very cold. There's no heat on.'

'Well, suit-up anyone who feels it,' Koenig responded.

'But – ,' as Bergman began to object, the office door closed.

Dr. Russell and Harris stood, waiting in silence, as Koenig entered. 'Doctor?'

She pointed to Harris and said, 'We seem to have a mutiny on our hands.'

'I didn't say that,' objected Harris.

'It's leaked that there's a lifeboat. The general consensus of opinion seems to be that it's for you and I and Alpha section heads only.'

Koenig stared down the man and asked, 'Harris?'

'Everybody's saying it… sir,' he replied, like a schoolboy caught by the headmaster.

Koenig let out a thoughtful 'Mm. I wanted to leave it until we were sure of the screens, but…'

He shrugged and called out to Sandra on the comm-post.

'Yes, Commander?' she asked as her image appeared.

'Hook me into Alpha network, Sandra. I have an announcement to make.'

'Yes, sir.'

'Now hear this. This is Alpha Commander. We have an unpleasant fact to face, now. Despite the Bergman screens presently over our heads, it is no more than a slim hope that Alpha will survive beyond the next few hours…'

Across the vast complex, activity once again ceased as people stopped to listen. Koenig continued, 'Therefore, one M.T.U. – a lifeboat – has been kept intact and equipped with supplies to carry five male and five female persons. Perhaps, alone in the galaxy, these ten have no better chance than ours, but they will leave Alpha by 17:03 hours at the latest.

'Central Computer, instructed to select people most likely to survive, and despite orders to the contrary, included me. I need hardly say that my job is here, and I shall not go. For the rest, here are the ten names…'

Koenig began to read the list, all the names were the same as before, except now Lam Yang Ha had replaced the Commander. As Koenig switched off, Harris tried to speak.

'Alright, no recriminations, Harris.'

'Thank you, sir, and…'

'Now back to work.'

'And I'm sorry,' he mumbled sheepishly. Koenig gave a faint smile and nodded as the man departed. He turned to Helena and said, 'It's beginning to get very cold.'

'I'm not going,' she announced.

'Not going?'

'On the M.T.U. I'm not going'

'Oh? Another "mutiny"?' he regarded her with a wry smile.

'Yes.'

'I'll make it an order, if I have to, Helena.'

'There are two reasons why not.'

'I've thought of all the reasons.'

'One,' she began to tick off, 'I'm a section head, and I don't run, either. It's bad for morale.'

'The computer was of the opinion that morale is irrelevant, now.'

'As the Alpha psychologist, I disagree.'

'And as Commander, I over-rule you. This isn't the time for noble gestures.'

'Let me give you a selfish reason, then. You said it – alone in the galaxy. An Alien galaxy, cut-off from Alpha's technology, just ten people, certain there's no possible landfall within scouting distance. The M.T.U. doesn't have a whisper of a chance, and you know it.'

'I don't know it,' he countered.

'I want to stay here and take my chances with...' She stuttered, almost saying 'you,' but instead finished with, 'all of you.'

Koenig gave her a stern 'No.'

'Then that can only mean that you believe – screens or no screens – Alpha has less than a whisper of a chance.'

'Dr. Russell, you have about two hours to pack.'

Resigned to her fate and staring him down, she said, 'Then, I'll say goodbye here.'

'… Yes,' he agreed, regarding her for a moment before she spun on her heel and quickly departed.

Bergman frowned at the flickering light on his polygon control. 'Sandra, can you give me a monitor view of section fifty-four?' he asked.

'Yes, Professor,' came the response as she switched the TV monitor view. He clearly saw that there was no doubt section fifty-four was wavering and about to fail.

Deeply concerned, the Professor suited-up and made his way toward the tower. Bathed in its iridescent, flickering light, he climbed up the tower. Bergman reached towards an access hatch that lay at the bottom of the sphere. He stretched out his gloved hand to open the panel, but as his fingers came into contact with the surface, a brilliant blue fire erupted. The force hurled Bergman off the tower. His body crumpled to the ground in a flurry of Lunar dust.

The entire force-field then collapsed and vanished. Above Moonbase Alpha, the black sun clearly appeared as a great open mouth. It was lit only at its peripheries by distant stars and streaks of captured space debris being swallowed. That was the fate the Earth's errant Moon would soon share.

ACT FOUR

A coating of ice covered not only the inert polygon control panel, but all the instruments that adorned the Control Centre. A space-suited figure sat at Sandra's usual place, bathed in the dim emergency lighting that glinted off the coated surface. She moved slightly, and the ice cracked off from the suit joints.

Frost, in delicate patterns, covered the glass screens of the corridor commposts. Down one wall near a Travel Tube entrance, a weird sculpture of heavy icicles formed an oddly beautiful pattern created by a broken water main and the absence of normal gravity.

A space-suited figure emerged from a nearby room and navigated on crunching ice in slow, careful steps. He approached the Travel Tube hatch and pulled out his I.D.X. to summon it. There was no response and then, he remembered that there was no power to operate the transport system.

Bergman lay in the darkened Medical Centre, bathed in the orange glow of portable heaters. Helena, still in her space-suit, warmed her hands at one of the heaters, and then grabbed a hypo-gun.

'Are you sure this is necessary?' she asked a figure who stood in the dark behind her.

'Will it hurt him?' Koenig said.

She hesitated, 'No, but...'

'Do it.'

Gently, she turned the Professor's head to one side and injected the spray at the base of his skull. Cleaning the injection site, she told Koenig, 'I changed the batteries – they were drained – and they're supposed to be inexhaustible.'

'How long?' he asked as he gestured toward Bergman.

'Give it time. He'd be dead, but for his mechanical heart.'

'We're running out of time. I have to know why those screens blew. I can't wait. We'll freeze before we're crushed without power, and I don't want to restore power until I know it won't blow again.'

'Turn off the screens,' she suggested.

'He knew – and Central Computer knew – how. If it blows again, there won't be time to fix it.'

Faintly, Bergman's head began to rock, as if trying to relieve pressure on the back of his neck.

'He's stirring,' announced Helena. 'He… may not talk sense.'

They leaned in to hear a weak rattle emerge from the Professor's lips. 'Help,' he whispered.

'What did he say?' asked Koenig.

Helena answered dryly, 'He said help.'

With more effort, Bergman pleaded to someone – something? 'Help us. Please help us. Please.'

'Victor? Can you hear me?'

Bergman replied a bit louder, 'No.'

'Do you remember the accident? What made the screens blow? How do I turn them off? Can you understand me? Victor?'

The Professor strained, thinking hard through a haze, and began to babble, 'I think I understand… Otherwise we could not have survived. I'm a not a religious man. The only explanation. Perhaps – perhaps inside… we can make some sort of contact. Intelligence of that order. Communicate … inside… the black sun.'

Helena shook her head, 'I'm sorry. You're getting his thoughts at the time of the accident. Why it happened isn't a memory.'

'Victor, hear me,' Koenig pleaded. 'This is important, listen. Can I risk restoring the power?'

'Inside the black sun… anything's possible. We have to go inside to… talk. I wonder… Yes, I wonder.'

'Can we turn-on the power again?'

'Ask… Ask computer?'

Bergman fell back into unconsciousness.

'He's gone,' Helena said as she checked him over. 'Did that make any sense? About the computer?'

'Maybe he's right, but with the power off, computer's not working.'

'Well…' she looked at him, not daring to state the obvious.

He reluctantly had to agree, '…Yeah.'

Catani heaved a heavy axe onto the thick ice that coated the electrical cables linking the polygon control. Semi-transparent shards bounced about in a weird arial ballet, thanks to the low gravity. It was hard work in a space-suit, made all the more difficult in the dim Control Centre emergency lighting. Other crewmen manoeuvred portable heaters around him.

Stopping to catch his breath, Catani remarked, 'What am I – the only man who still remembers how to use an axe?'

'I'm a farm-boy, too,' stated Koenig.

'Ah…,' he responded to the good-natured grouse.

Still ringed by the heater-lamps, Bergman stirred once more. His groans alerted a nearby nurse, who rushed over only to find he was still unconscious.

One final chop of the axe and Catani finally had the cable exposed. A technician moved in and coated it with a spray-on plastic insulation.

'Right,' said Koenig, standing over the now exposed control panel. After a brief hesitation, he selected 'On.' The Control Centre's main lights began to blaze, heat emerged from the vents and the floating debris crashed to the floor as artificial gravity engaged.

Removing his helmet, Koenig noticed the main monitor. It had also come to life with a view of the black sun. He stabbed at a button to kill the unnecessary sight.

'Okay, Mr. Ouma, let's bring Central Computer back from the dead.'

'Yes, sir,' he acknowledged, fingers working feverishly at his control console.

'What's the betting it says, "Where am I"?' Koenig commented.

Ouma smiled back, 'No bet, Commander. Central Computer is functioning again.'

The dedicated monitor screen for computer came to life and a text message appeared:

+++ WHAT HAS HAPPENED QUERY +++

'Voice, computer,' ordered Koenig.

'*I see what has happened, Alcom Koenig. I have taken charge of services. Commander, all timepieces working by broadcast power were stopped – there is only seven minutes before last departure time for the lifeboat.*'

'Go, Lieutenant Catani. Sandra, broadcast seven minutes,' he ordered.

Sandra turned to her intercom, 'Urgent, urgent, M.T.U. passengers and crew now to launch pad for…'

Koenig turned back to the computer monitor and asked, 'Computer, a problem for you. Why did the screens fail? How can they be restored? Can they safely be used at maximum?'

'*Beyond simple operating instructions of switching off and on, I have been given no data on the Bergman forcefield screens effect. I cannot help.*'

The answer shocked Koenig, '… You – ?'

'*Power failure occurred for unknown reasons following consumption surge greater than Alpha's capacities. If such power is again required, the screens cannot be used. All other queries must be referred to Professor Bergman.*'

'He's… unconscious.'

'*That fact has been observed.*'

'… Well, you'd better organise manual control for essential services – and a little heating this time – and then get ready to deactivate yourself again, as soon as possible.'

'*Yes, sir.*'

Koenig was surprised, 'No argument?'

'*The power consumption of even my minimum circuits may have contributed substantially to the breakdown.*'

'And that,' Ouma proclaimed, 'is the nearest you'll ever get to an apology.'

'*If it relieves human feelings, Commander,*' continued computer, '*I am programmed to make apologies.*'

Well, thought Koenig, will wonders never cease.

The Commander was not pleased to see Helena sitting in his office.

'You have five and a half minutes to get yourself on board that M.T.U.'

The Doctor admitted, 'I came in here because I was sure you'd be too busy to find me.'

'You're going, Helena,' he said firmly

'I'm not going. And from my eavesdropping,' she gestured to the commpost. 'It seems you need me to revive Professor Bergman in a hurry.'

'What makes you think you're irreplaceable? There are other doctors.'

'Now you're trying to be offensive so I'll lose my temper and go.'

'Dr. Russell, you have one choice. You can get on that lifeboat on your own two feet or I shall have two security men carry you aboard.'

After a long pause, Helena acquiesced, 'Very well.'

'I'll see you aboard myself.'

'But – ,' she sputtered.

Koenig steered Helena out of the Travel Tube by her elbow. Clad in space-suits, the two figures stopped just outside the M.T.U. hatch and regarded each other.

'Through… your visor… I can't really see your face,' she said.

'No… And we can't…' he began.

Catani leaned urgently out of the ship, 'I'm sorry, but quickly. Quickly.'

'Goodbye, Helena,' said Koenig.

'Goodbye, John.'

She entered and the hatch slid shut.

The M.T.U. skimmed away over Alpha, speeding in an opposite direction from the black sun. Ahead lay an area of space ablaze with a myriad of stars.

Koenig watched the lifeboat fade into the distance. Standing off to the side of the launch and landing pad, near the Travel Tube, he barely noticed another space-suited figure emerge and join him.

'I missed saying goodbye…' came Bergman's voice.

The black sun now appeared swollen – monstrous – alien. Another asteroid streaked over the base, to stretch and flare, then vanish as ghost-like. It was a fresh reminder of their fate.

Bergman watched as he stood at the foot of the faulty pylon. Turning back, he saw Koenig climb up to reach the bottom of the sphere. No longer a shiny silver mirror, it was now charred a matte carbon-black colour. Koenig opened the panel to the interior and cried out with surprise, 'It's intact!'

The Control Centre was now fully-manned, a hive of activity. Koenig watched as Bergman's head emerged from the access panel of his polygon control console. The Professor had completed rewiring replacement cables.

He explained his theory about his accident when he tried to repair sphere fifty-four, 'The fire – if it was a fire – must have been cold, quite without heat. I wasn't burned, of course.'

His voice became wistful, 'An extraordinary phenomenon… Then we hardly understand the forcefield effect at all. It worked – for a few minutes, anyway.'

'Will it blow again?' asked Koenig with concern.

'You know… perhaps it won't. There's no doubt that one machine was out of phase. In layman's terms, you might say it was trying to break the unbreakable. Hence the blow-up, perhaps. Now it's fixed, it may work.'

'May… ?'

Suddenly, everyone saw colours around them shift. True colour was gone, replaced down the spectrum, first to red, then darker muted colours. Just as rapidly, it reversed back to normal.

Bergman, unmoved, repeated, 'May.'

'What was that?!' demanded a shocked Koenig.

Bergman's responded matter-of-factly, 'This close now, we'll get a few odd effects. Illusions.'

When viewed from away, Spaceship Moon was, frankly, an ugly lump of rock. It was dwarfed by absolute darkness as it plunged deeper into the black sun.

Flying in the opposite direction was an infinitely smaller M.T.U., carrying its somber crew. No one talked, their attention transfixed to T.V. monitors that showed the fate of their compatriots.

'They've no screens,' whispered an awestruck Sandra to herself. 'They still have no screens.'

Deeper in, the Control Centre staff were consciously aware that space around them was distorting. It was as if their eyes had become fishbowl camera lenses. Ouma was too busy to be concerned, focused on typing questions into his console. With each entry, the computer responded:

+++ CONFIRMED +++
+++ CONFIRMED +++
+++ CONFIRMED +++

'Commander,' his voice came out oddly slowed. 'We are ready to go over to manual.'

Koenig approached him – lackadaisical, floating, gliding, in the reverse-gravity, upward-pull of the black sun – over to the computer console.

'And all available power is ready to divert to the screens?' he asked, his voice also distorted.

'Yes, sir. Computer, give us Voice.'

'Computer?' asked Koenig. 'Are you prepared to de-activate yourself?'

'*Quite prepared.*'

'Then de-activate.'

'*Yes, sir,*' computer responded. '*And sir?*'

Koenig was surprised at not only the question but what the Voice said next, '… *Goodbye…*'

As the computer's screen went dark, Koenig began to move back to Bergman. 'Divert all power to screens circuits,' he ordered.

'Power diverted,' confirmed a technician at the power station. At that same moment, the colours shifted again.

'Professor, activate screens.'

Bergman switched on his forcefield and the colours, sound, optics, and gravity all returned to normal.

'Whew!' exclaimed a female technician.

'Ladies and gentlemen, we're in business again.' Koenig's pronouncement was met with a chorus in agreement. He smiled and asked, 'Can somebody find me some coffeesub? There's nothing more to do but wait.'

'And pray,' Bergman said, mainly to himself.

In the M.T.U., Helena could just spot the faint glow of the forcefield over Alpha. That flickering light on the Moon's surface appeared more iridescent, darker, richer in colour than before.

'Thank God…' she breathed.

With nothing more to do, the Control Centre staff mulled about, sitting, standing, looking for some way to fill the time. One female technician switched on the main monitor and the awful maw of the black sun appeared. Concerned for morale, Koenig switched off the image. 'We'll see it soon enough,' he said softly to her. 'Hook me into the network.'

'Yes, sir,' she replied, activating the intercom system.

'This is Alpha Commander. We're on minimum heating now. Minimum air. Without safety margins, everybody should suit-up again, and all duty is temporarily cancelled. You may go to quarters – rest, eat – whatever you feel like. And… good luck.'

As the Moon began to accelerate into the absolute blackness, Bergman approached Koenig and quietly told him, 'Well, John, you were right to keep us all busy, but…'

'Not from you, Victor,' he replied very seriously.

'No?… I'd like to say it.'

'Anyway, what happened to your cosmic intelligences who're going to rescue us in the nick of time?'

'We believe… what we want to believe,' he shrugged. 'I sometimes think that's all reality is.'

'Wishful thinking?' Koenig asked in mock indignation. He was unwilling to allow any defeatism.

Undeterred, Bergman continued, 'The boundaries… The boundaries between science and pure mysticism are paper-thin, and getting thinner. Sometimes, it makes me feel old.'

The M.T.U. scanners were still managing to track the Moon. The image on their monitors was undeniably beautiful, the glowing opalescence of the forcefield still visible. Against the inky blackness of that maw, it was like a drop of oil caught in a sunbeam.

The stricken faces of the ten passengers watched in silence as Alpha brightened visibly. Then, it began to stretch, transformed into a comet of light. Down it went, down, down, growing longer and longer, changing from an opal drop into an iridescent spear. "Solid Alpha" neared the point of blackness, beyond which no light could pass. Suddenly, it seemed to hit a kind of invisible barrier. One moment it was there, then gone. Snuffed out of existence. Only a ghostly image lingered.

Helena could only cover her face in her hands and Sandra wept. Catani breathed out in Italian, 'Madre di Dio.'

Koenig, seated in his command chair, studied his body in fascination. He had become transparent, like a ghost from an old movie.

'More illusion?' he asked the equally non-corporeal Bergman, seated beside him.

'I don't know.'

A horrid, grating, creaking series of sounds filled their ears.

'The... screens?'

'Yes.'

'They're holding.'

'So far,' Bergman agreed, then resumed studying his transparent hands. 'It's possible we don't exist.'

'I exist,' insisted the Commander.

Bergman smiled at him, 'Exist for the black sun.'

'How?'

'Whatever the forcefield does, while it holds, we're invulnerable,' the Professor postulated. 'The old paradox of irresistible force meeting immovable object. The black sun can't act on us in any way. We don't exist for it, perhaps.'

'Did you notice the room?' Koenig gestured to the now frozen ice-palace that was once the Control Centre.

'Sort of exist, then,' he conceded. 'I don't feel cold.'

Koenig hadn't thought about it until now and stated, 'I don't feel anything.'

He reached out his hand to touch a panel, to see if he was as insubstantial as Bergman postulated. Just before his hand made contact, the ice melted rapidly, turning into steam. For a moment his vision was obscured until...

The Control Centre was free of ice, and Koenig and Bergman's bodies were once again substantial.

The Professor exclaimed, 'We are inside the sun itself...'

'It's suddenly hot,' said the Commander. He rose to walk over to a control panel.

'The clock has stopped.'

'One moment freezing, next roasting.' Koenig flipped a switch and then asked, 'What about the clock?'

The digital chronometer sat unmoving.

Suddenly, there was an absolute silence as the two men, and the entire Control Centre froze in the moment. After perhaps ten seconds, time resumed, but slowly, ever so slowly. Koenig struggled back to his chair, exhausted, his energy ebbed away.

Koenig strained to raise his hands and something forced him to look down at them. They had shrivelled into a wrinkled mass. Yes, they were his hands, but they appeared to be an old man's hands. Before their eyes, each man had aged radically, as if they were now a thousand years old.

'I can hear your thoughts,' Bergman's voice echoed, yet the Professor's mouth remained unmoved.

Koenig's voice came back in agreement, 'Yes.'

'It's very beautiful.'

'I see the theory behind your forcefield.'

'Very obvious.'

'In fact, it ties up with a unified field theory.'

'Does it?' said a surprised Bergman. He pondered the possibility. 'Yes, I see how.'

'So that everything is everything else.'

'That's why I called it beautiful,' he agreed.

'Of course, your screens will fail.'

'I suppose so.'

'Shall I fix them?'

'If it gives you satisfaction,' Bergman conceded, then watched in fascination as Koenig's head appeared to swirl and melt into the shape of a polygon. Opalescent colours began to abound, a black facet flared bright pink and suddenly, the Commander's face returned, still eons old.

'There,' he said, as if it was a magic trick. 'If everything is everything else, then the whole universe is living thought.'

'*Who are you?*' came a woman's voice.

Koenig and Bergman looked at each other, then around. There was no one there with them, and yet, they both had heard it.

'Who are you?' asked the ever-curious Professor.

'*Come,*' the Voice beckoned.

Outside, Alpha receded from the black sun so fast, it became only a memory in a few moments. Stars blazed everywhere else, moving at incredible speed, until they too fell away and resolved into one swirling galaxy. Then, that too, also receded, becoming one of many galaxies. Each one then became a single star, which transformed into yet another spot of light that transformed into more galaxies within galaxies.

Eventually, it all seemed to resolve into one single speck of light, which then became one facet on a ring on some great hand, dimly perceived against the blackness of outer space.

'*That is who I am,*' explained the Voice.

Bergman ventured to ask, 'Are you God?'

'*I have a God. My God has Gods.*'

Focusing on that single spot of light, Koenig mused, 'Every star is just a cell in the brain of the universe.'

'*That is a pretty way to understand it.*'

'Why have I never talked with you before?' queried Bergman.

'*Because of time. You...*' the female voice hesitated, as if searching for the right word, '*People seem to think at what you call the speed of light. In eternity, I have no hurry. I think a thought perhaps in every hundred of your years. You are never there to hear it.*'

Then, the voice bid them goodbye, '*It was good to have known you.*'

'But –?' Koenig blurted out.

Bergman said sadly, 'She's gone.'

'And... maybe time that we did, too?'

'Yes,' he agreed.

Time seemed to suddenly run backwards, like a film in reverse. The two men appeared to de-age, wrinkles, lines, and perhaps gained wisdom, all melted away. They eyed each other in wonder, until the loud click of the digital clock drew their attention to the fact that all had returned to normal again.

'John… ?' said Bergman, standing and stretching limbs that felt like they hadn't moved for what… a millennium?

Koenig switched on the big monitor. A vast field of space, brimming with gloriously bright and colourful stars, greeted them.

'Look, look!' he exclaimed.

'We're… though…' the Professor said in wonder.

Koenig rotated monitor image 180 degrees from where they were headed to where they had been. Behind them was a brilliant light – no, a blinding light. It was a star that had gone nova, with tentacles of white fire reaching out as if to grab at the rapidly fleeing Moon.

'Your screens held.'

'Somehow, we are on the other side of the universe… Fleeing from a nova.'

'Your screens held, Victor!' Koenig repeated.

Bergman's face went blank, 'I wonder how…'

As life returned to normal, Control Centre was once again fully-manned, filled with a flurry of activity and happy, smiling faces.

As he watched Bergman and his staff dismantle the polygon control console, Koenig asked, 'Someday, Professor, you must explain how that thing worked.'

With a guilty look, he confessed, 'I don't understand it myself.'

EPILOGUE

Koenig was keeping busy in his office when the door opened, and Bergman peered in. 'Got a moment?'

'I was just thinking...' Koenig smiled, waving him in. 'So much for your fancy theories of cosmic intelligences snatching us from the jaws of death.'

Bergman made an awkward apology, 'Well... I knew it was impossible. But the statistics ...'

Koenig scoffed, 'You can prove anything by –'

Alarm klaxons interrupted their good-natured verbal fencing. The Commander raced to the commpost as a technician's face appeared. He demanded, 'What is it?'

'Aliens, Commander!' came the reply. The image changed to a speck of light moving through space towards Alpha.

'No,' Koenig exclaimed with wonder. 'It's the lifeboat...'

No sooner had the M.T.U. settled onto the Landing and Launching Pad than a happy reunion took place in the Control Centre.

'You must have followed us into the black sun,' Koenig said accusingly to Catani.

'No,' he protested.

Coming to the pilot's defence, Helena confirmed, 'We ran from the black sun.'

Bergman scoffed, 'You must have.'

'I swear we didn't,' Catani said, hand over heart.

Sandra chimed in, 'We saw you disappear.'

'This is...' the Commander started, then paused to ask, 'How? If you didn't come after us, how did you follow a million light years?'

'Across the universe?' marvelled Bergman.

Catani shook his head, 'I don't know.'

'Something… ,' Helena began, then apologised. 'I know this sounds crazy. Something took hold of us and moved us, just moved us… across the universe… as easily as if… '

At a loss for words, she looked down at her hands. The doctor then raised them and pulled something off the finger on one hand, placing it on the other.

'… it were this ring.'

OBSERVATIONS

Much of David Weir's original draft survived into the final episode, but Christopher Penfold was tasked with creating a shooting script that simplified the visual effects sequences so that they could be realised with the resources available. He also tightened some of the action and opened up the character drama to include supporting cast members as they faced the potential of certain death. Weir undoubtedly wanted to focus more on Bergman, making him something of a moody introvert and ill-qualified to save them. Eventually, as seen on-screen, Bergman would become Koenig's general scientific expert. However, Weir followed George Bellak's original guide, which painted the character as a former teacher of Koenig's and the man who created the Moonbase anti-gravitational system. With that in mind, it's somewhat odd that among a population of 300, there would not be a least one astrophysicist who would recognise the phenomenon. He also made use of Ouma's close relationship with the Moonbase's somewhat independent computer A.I. It's a great pity, though, that the concept of a Base Restaurant was not considered as a standing set as it would have been a useful location for the characters to socialise in.

A BREATH OF DEATH

Working Draft
by Irving Gaynor Neiman
Adapted by Robert E. Wood

PROLOGUE

Moonbase Alpha sat nestled in the darkness of the Lunar surface as the Moon hurtled through the blackness of space.

"Moonbase Alpha. July 16, 1999. Six months and nine days have passed since the explosion of atomic waste blew away a portion of our Moon and sent us out of orbit and into space...

"We are three hundred on Alpha. We continue to hurtle through space. Impossible to know our position or our fate..."

In his darkened night-time quarters, Professor Bergman continued making the entry in his journal.

"We exist. We man our stations. We provide our own sustenance... recycling, repairing, planning. But we are human beings, and more than most, must live with ultimate uncertainty... We do not always do it well..."

In Alpha's Tech Area, scaffolding surrounded a portion of the MTU probe ship as technicians made an installation in the propulsion system. Captain Catani stood by with Tech One, supervising. Nobody looked happy… The only sound was of the tools. No conversation.

Murneau, head of Tech Section, sat at an elevated desk that overlooked the area. He was working on some papers, then looked down worriedly at the sound of angry voices below, which were a bit indistinct from his vantage point. He heard Catani's voice first…

'…if you didn't drag your damn feet and just did the damn job!'

'Nobody's dragging his feet!' Argued Tech One. 'But if you want my opinion, Captain…'

'I don't want your opinion! I want a job of work out of you and I'm not getting it!'

Murneau rose and started down to the work area via the platform elevator. He could see Catani and Tech One continuing to face off. Other tech workers had stopped work and were watching with hostility. Paul, Catani's assistant, was with him.

'I don't have to take this from you!' Shouted Tech One. 'You're not my superior in Tech Area, so why don't you just…'

Murneau came up to them, pretty annoyed himself. 'That's enough, Olney!' He said to Tech One, then turned to Catani. 'You have any complaints, Captain, I'm your man!'

'Wonderful!' Catani said, 'It's been a week since I got those oxygen boosters approved for my ship… and look where we are!'

'You've got to know it's not simple!' Murneau stated. 'And I don't know how you wangled your approval, but it's an idiot waste of oxygen supplies to use them to jazz up your hot rod!'

'It's necessary, dammit!'

'Where the hell do you think you're going in that thing, anyway?' Murneau turned away angrily, muttering in French, 'Bête stupide…!'

Catani grabbed Murneau's arm furiously and whipped him around to face him again. 'I heard that, Murneau!'

Murneau shoved him hard enough to break his grip on his arm. 'So you heard! Get your hands off me!'

Catani, who had staggered back into scaffolding, came off swinging at Murneau. They grappled furiously and fell, fighting. Tech One jumped in to help Murneau, while other technicians started down scaffolding to get into it. Paul hesitated, then took two steps to press a button marked SECURITY... then jumped into the fight to help Catani. Their odds weren't good: it was four Tech people against Catani and Paul, who were putting up a good fight.

The entrance door opened, and three Security Guards rushed in to break it up. Before the Guards reached the fighters, the men crashed into the scaffolding, throwing it against the probe ship, setting off sparks and a puff of smoke.

The guards broke the fight apart, but the men were still hot.

'Satisfied?' Murneau indicated the smoke, 'There's your booster! A week's work shot to hell!'

Koenig strode in, followed by Helena in time to see Catani continue the argument.

'Then you just start over and do it right, you French...'

'Hold it!' Koenig called, sharply. 'What's the problem here?'

Catani and Murneau started talking at once but were cut off as an alert horn sounded a series of short, not-too-loud blasts.

'Stations, everybody!' Koenig ordered.

Technicians rushed to their stations, while others started clearing away the scaffolding from the ship.

Koenig called into the intercom, 'Commander here! What's the alert?'

The Communicator's voice responded, 'We've got some sort of planet on the scope, Commander!'

'I'll see it in here!' Koenig responded as he began to cross the room to a scope with Helena.

Helena frowned to him, 'That's the third fight this week, Commander.'

'I know.'

Helena was worried, 'I don't know how much longer they can take the strain... lost out here...'

'You're the doctor!' Koenig said in irritation, 'Find out!'

'I'm a doctor! Not God!'

They arrived at the scope, on which an image appeared of a slowly turning planet, against a field of stars.

Koenig was barking orders, 'Ready probe ship! Activate sensors! I want reports every five minutes!'

Responses came through to Koenig's orders, and Alpha buzzed with the sounds of excitement.

In space, as the planet slowly turned, Bergman finished his journal entry, 'We have sighted a planet... a jewel of price in the star-spangled velvet of the void. Perhaps a home for the people of Alpha... perhaps not a moment too soon.'

ACT ONE

Central Control bustled with activity, centred around the large viewing screen displaying the image of an Alien planet. Koenig was in the command seat as others brought him reports.

Catani's voice filtered through the speakers, 'Probe One at 30,000 over the surface and holding. You getting readings from our sensors?'

'Right, Captain,' acknowledged Koenig. 'Gravity is a shade off Earth normal. No problem. Heat readings in acceptable range.'

Catani was at the controls in the Probe cockpit, with Paul beside him at the monitoring equipment. 'Visual observation of vegetation over maybe… oh, a third of the surface. The rest looks sort of like our Moon. Do we go down?' Catani asked.

In Central Control, Helena frowned over a report and handed it to Koenig.

'Atmosphere analysis just came in, Catani,' said the Commander. 'Oxygen levels about seventy percent of Earth normal. You'll need direct injection oxygen packs.'

'We have two on board. We –' Catani's voice broke off. 'Stand by. Paul's got something on the monitor.'

Catani leaned over in the Probe cockpit toward Paul to peer into the scope, then exclaimed, 'Buildings, Commander! Some sort of a settlement!'

'Any sign of life?' Koenig responded.

'We're zooming in…' Catani said. 'Yes, there's movement! There are people down there!'

Koenig and Helena exchanged glances. 'People?' Koenig said dryly.

'All right, creatures! Somebody!' Catani exclaimed. 'Commander, we're going in!'

Koenig thought for a moment, then said, 'Probe One is clear to land and reconnoiter.'

'That's go, Commander!' Catani answered.

The Probe ship rockets blasted, bringing its nose up into landing attitude, and starting its descent. Inside, Paul tapped Catani's shoulder and indicated the scope. Catani nodded and corrected course.

The Probe ship descended to the surface of the Alien world and settled on a rocket landing pad surrounded on one side by open country. On the other side, a rather odd, somewhat primitive settlement, with the backs of a few rather crude dwellings and small garden plots behind them. There was no sign of people.

Inside, Paul switched to ground scanner.

'Probe One to Alpha... On the ground,' called Catani.

'Right, Captain,' responded Koenig. 'Oxygen pack setting will be four five zero.'

'Four five zero. Right.' Catani acknowledged as he took two small oxygen packs, which would then be strapped to their left arms, from a rack.

'Captain... take a look,' Paul said.

Catani leaned over the scanner, strapping on his oxygen pack. In the scope viewer Catani watched the image move from the dwellings near the landing pad to an open area like a village square or main street. There were the same strange, primitive dwellings... but now there were also people in the street. They were dressed in odd, very simple costumes, and seemed to be going about their business, paying no attention to the Probe ship. Their chests were unusually large, their nostrils unusually broad, but otherwise they looked pretty much like Earthmen. There were no vehicles.

'Beam this to Alpha, Paul,' said Catani.

Paul threw a switch. Their arm-packs now on, the men each inserted a needle, attached by a tube to the pack, into their wrist arteries. Direct injection oxygen.

'Alpha, are you getting a picture?' Catani asked.

The big viewing screen in Central Command displayed the scene projected from the planet. A villager, load slung over his back, walked past the scanner without sparing a glance to the ship.

'Clear picture, Captain. What's your viewing range?' Koenig asked.

Catani's voice answered, 'Hundred meters. No welcoming committee... but they're not shooting, either.'

'Yes. It's as if you're invisible. What do you make of it?'

'Let's go see.'

The Probe ship hatch was open as Catani and Paul emerged in full gear but not wearing helmets, laser guns at the ready. They descended cautiously to the ground.

They looked warily around. The villagers went about their business nearby, not paying them any attention. Very strange. Catani shrugged and gestured them forward. Paul put out a restraining hand, blinked and looked a bit distressed.

'I'm a bit groggy...' Paul said.

'More oxygen. Try four seven five.'

Paul adjusted his pack... and it was better. He nodded his okay to Catani, and they moved toward the village square, alert to any sudden movement. Most of the people were moving in a single direction, toward a destination that was as yet out of view.

Once they entered the square, near the passing villagers, Catani and Paul were no longer disregarded. Although they stood out like sore thumbs in their space gear, the locals just nodded and smiled greetings as they went by. The puzzled Earthmen nodded back, tentatively, but kept their guns at the ready. They moved to a point where their backs were against a wall, and slowly lowered their guns.

Catani spoke into a transceiver on his shoulder, 'Probe One to Alpha.'

'Go ahead, Catani,' said Koenig.

'Situation normal... whatever that is. I'm going to try talking. You'd better sit in.'

'Standing by.'

A youngish man came along the street toward them. Catani gestured Paul to cover him, and stepped out to intercept the man, who stopped, nodded, and smiled. He seemed gentle, polite, and unemotional.

'Er... pardon me...' said Catani.

'Sir?' asked the villager.

'We come... from a great distance...' Catani began.

'You... hunger... thirst...' The villager was solicitous.

'No, look... We want to...' Catani said, but the villager turned away and called to a girl outside a nearby dwelling.

'Talla. Food... drink... please...' he said.

The girl nodded, smiled, and disappeared into the house as he continued, 'Ours... is yours. Excuse...' He went off the way the others had gone, down the street and around a corner.

Paul set up an automatic camera, geared to the movement of his head, which shot whatever he saw, automatically.

Catani stopped another passing man. 'Can you give me some information, sir?' he asked.

'Yes... Ask...' politely responded the villager.

'Good. We want to know...' Catani hesitated. Where to start?

Koenig's voice came over the transceiver. 'Ask the name of the place. The population.'

'Is Medli, sir,' said the man. 'We are four thousand... Excuse,' he apologised, and went off in the same direction as the last man.

The girl, Talla, came out of the house carrying a crude tray with two bowls and two glasses, all made of rather simplistic pottery.

From a distance came a thin, high-pitched whine. Catani tapped Paul and indicated for him to check it out. Paul moved toward the sound in the direction all the Medlians took. A few others remained on the street... but all were women. Catani crossed to Talla, speaking to Koenig as he did so.

'Commander, they want us to eat.'

'Negative. Get samples for testing.'

'Right.'

Talla smiled and proffered the tray to Catani, who said uncertainly, 'Greetings...'

'Greeting...' responded Talla.

Catani took out plastic sacks and poured the contents of a glass into one. 'You don't mind?' He asked.

'No.'

'We... want to learn about your land, you see,' Catani explained.

'Yes.'

Catani continued to fill containers with samples. 'You saw our ship?' He asked, receiving a nod in response. 'Do you have ships like that?'

'No,' she said.

Koenig's voice came again, 'Ask her how come the rocket pad, then?'

'Sir. Cannot say,' Talla answered.

'Other people live on this planet?' Catani asked.

Talla hesitated slightly.

No one noticed the hand pulling back a crude drape in the rough window opening of a nearby house, revealing an old, bearded man, watching them.

'Live?' Talla said, 'No. Medlians only...'

Paul stood at the corner where the villagers turned off the main square. He called to Catani, 'Captain! Over here!'

Catani trotted over to Paul. The whine heard earlier became more pronounced.

'Look at that!' Paul exclaimed.

Down the side street, at a distance, past more simple buildings, was a large, very modern domed structure... dark, windowless, imposing, and entirely out of keeping with the other primitive structures.

'Well... what do you know?' Catani said quietly, impressed.

Returning to Moonbase Alpha, Catani moved purposefully through a dimly lit corridor with Koenig.

'They warned us off the building, so we just took some shots of it,' said Catani.

'Good thinking.'

'What's hard to get across is the quality of the people. I mean, strange, sure, and primitive... but there's a gentleness about them... a <u>nice</u>ness.'

'Not much curiosity, though. They didn't ask a question, did they?'

'No... but they were friendly, and warm... and well, <u>nice</u>.'

'Yes. I got that,' Koenig said dryly. 'Nice people.'

'Right.'

Koenig stopped at a doorway into a lab, where a technician handed him a computer read-out. Koenig scanned it quickly, then frowned. 'Five days?'

'Outside limit, Commander,' said the technician, handing Koenig another read-out. 'Closest proximity to the planet will be in three point two days... then we spin off pretty fast. After five days we'll be out of practical range to transport personnel and equipment.'

'Damn little time...' said Koenig, about to leave. He stopped and turned back, 'Did you check out the food the Captain brought back?'

'Yes, sir. Safe. Good nutritional range.' The technician smiled slightly. 'Delicious, too.'

'Not a major factor,' Koenig said wryly, 'but it helps.'

Koenig, Helena, Catani, and Bergman sat around a table in the conference room with a few others. They talked through a series of pictures Paul took projected on a big screen, each holding for a few seconds.

'You propose to establish a colony on this planet?' Bergman asked thoughtfully.

'I propose we consider it...' replied Koenig. 'Subject to a very tight time factor.'

'The sooner the better,' said Helena.

'The oxygen factor,' pondered Bergman. 'We could get by on oxygen packs for a while, but then...?'

'There's every possibility our lungs would adapt to a thin-oxygen atmosphere in time. I could run some tests and get a computer projection,' offered Helena.

'Catani?' Koenig asked, 'Any thoughts about living with those "nice people" of yours?'

Catani was dubious. 'It would be... for all time?'

'For our lifetime, at least,' Koenig answered.

'I would have to think about it,' Catani said, then added wryly, 'Could we stand that much "nice"?'

Helena was impatient. 'Can our people stand much more of this? This rushing blindly into the void?'

'They would not adapt to "this" in time?' asked Bergman gently.

'We don't know!' Helena stated. 'Can we ask them to do it if we have a reasonable alternative?'

'Is it reasonable?' Bergman asked.

'Looks that way on balance, so far,' Koenig said. 'Positive factors: A population without hostility to us...'

'Or anybody, as far as we can tell,' murmured Catani.

'Gravity, temperature, food positive. More than enough habitable space...' Koenig continued.

'We may never find any place nearly as favourable, Professor!' Helena stated.

'My decision, Doctor,' said Koenig, as he checked his timepiece. 'Oh eight hundred hours. I'll take a full party down in the module for a complete check. If it checks out... we'll go.' He rose and started out of the room.

Bergman added, dryly, 'On balance... you didn't mention the negative factors.'

'Question of adapting to the environment, of course...' said Koenig at the same moment the screen displayed a shot of the strange, grim, modern building...

Bergman added, pointing grimly, 'That question... and others....'

A large MTU was ready for takeoff. It signalled and blasted off.

Inside the MTU, on its way to the planet, Koenig, Catani, Paul and others manned their stations. Paul was at his scope, while Koenig looked over his shoulder.

'Yes,' said Koenig. 'We'll put down right about there.'

'Commander... why land in the uninhabited section?' Catani asked.

'Observe without being observed, if we can,' said Koenig, then added thoughtfully, 'Maybe find some answers to Bergman's "other questions"...'

The MTU neared the planet, and a smaller module detached from the large ship and started a gliding descent to the surface. It descended silently, with just a whoosh as it passed through the atmosphere to a smooth landing in the rough terrain of an uninhabited section of planet Medli.

The MTU module moved across country, hovering as if on an air cushion, toward the settlement in the distance.

Stopping at the foot of a hill overlooking the settlement, it was shielded from immediate observation by the Medlians. Koenig and party disembarked, all with oxygen packs, and all armed. Koenig instructed Paul and two Security men to approach town from one direction, while he and Catani started off in the other...

Koenig and Catani walked across rough terrain, and climbed the hill overlooking the settlement. They approached the crest warily, then crouched and took up vantage points behind rocks, peering down at the settlement.

The village square looked deserted, except for one young man who was sweeping up. A peaceful sight.

Catani gestured for them to go down. Koenig glanced back down again as Catani started to rise, and – seeing something – urgently gestured Catani to get down again.

The village square was as before, but the young man had dropped his broom and was looking around him with a mounting sense of fright, as though searching for a way out... Then eight Medlian men emerged from the edges of the square and formed a rough circle, moving in toward the increasingly panicky young man.

Koenig glanced a question at Catani, who shrugged, unable to figure what's going on.

In the square below, the circle of men closed slowly on the young man. They were entirely expressionless... and both Koenig and Catani realised at the same moment that, save for the young man, each of the Medlians was carrying a club.

Catani unslung his laser gun and started to rise. Koenig gestured him sharply to get down and not interfere.

The circle was now tight around the young man, who ceased his desperate efforts to find a way out. He sunk, terrified, to the ground. The men in the circle closed in, raised their clubs, and methodically beat the young man.

In a nearby doorway, a figure watched. He appeared to be Medlian, but was dressed in a strange, black, military-type uniform and carried what was clearly a weapon. He observed what was happening with a contented half-smile on his face.

And then the killing was over. The circle of Medlians broke up, each man leaving the way he came. None showed the slightest emotion. The body of the young man lay alone in the square.

Catani was shocked. Koenig looked at him with a tight expression, commenting as clearly as possible, 'Nice people, huh?'

In the village square the Guard lounged over to the dead young man and negligently took one foot to drag him off and out of sight.

The village square was empty and peaceful again. A young woman crossed with a market basket...

ACT TWO

The Medli village square appeared entirely deserted.

On the hill above town, Koenig rose cautiously. He waved to signal Paul and the Security men on another hill, and the five men moved down, deployed in a sort of skirmish line, laser guns ready.

The Earthmen entered the square and heard the sound of a factory. Catani led them in the direction of the noise.

As the group passed Talla's house, they heard the sound of wood-chopping. Koenig stopped the group and listened. He gestured Paul and his men to go around one side of the house while he and Catani started around the other, leaving one Security man at the front, on guard.

Koenig and Catani moved warily around the side of Talla's house, then Koenig peered around the back and saw an old man, chopping wood alongside a sort of woodshed. Koenig stepped into the back yard, covered by Catani. Paul and the Security Guard emerged from the other side of the house, guns ready. The old man looked up, unruffled, serene.

'Greeting…' the old man said, then indicated himself. 'Karim.'

'Commander Koenig. Moon Base Alpha.'

'From far planet. Yes,' Karim said.

'They reported to you?' Koenig asked. 'Then you're the head man.'

Karim shrugged. 'The eldest.' He put down his axe and crossed to Koenig. Catani raised his weapon.

The old man assured him, 'No need. Here are gentle people.'

'Sure you are,' reacted Catani dryly.

'Talla… please… bring food…' commanded Karim.

'Thanks… but we'd sooner have some answers,' said Koenig. 'Where are the others?'

'Work. In their factory.'

'The big building?' Catani asked.

Karim nodded.

'You said "their" factory. Who are "they"?' asked Koenig. 'What do they make?'

Karim crossed to the house and called inside, 'Talla… not make guests wait…'

'You're the one making us wait, old man!' Koenig said toughly. 'We don't have time! We need answers!'

'Yes, sir. Always in Medli… each helps each…'

'Nice people. Yes,' said Koenig. 'We saw that out on the square just now.'

Karim sighed. 'Ah… the ritual…'

'Ritual?' Catani protested. 'Your people clubbed a man to death!'

Talla emerged with a tray of food and began to pass it around.

'Please… sit…' Karim said, taking a place on a crude bench; Koenig and Catani on the another.

'The ritual…' Koenig prompted.

Karim shrugged. 'They order. We must.'

'The man in uniform! Is he a soldier?' Catani asked.

Karim nodded. 'From Med. Medli… is a moon. Our planet is Med.' He looked around to see that he was understood. Koenig nodded, and Karim continued. 'On Med… people strong, brave, warlike… not like us.' He gave a wry smile. 'On Med… people are sane…'

'And you?' Koenig asked.

'How I say… mutants? Aberrants? We were born… without force… aggression… love of war. Insane, you see… so sent… this place.'

'You mean Medli is –' Koenig started, but was interrupted by Karim.

'Insane ward… for Med? Yes. You can say so.'

At that moment the Security Guard posted in front of the house ran up to Paul and said something urgent to him. Paul crossed to Koenig and said, 'Armed patrol coming this way.'

Koenig and Catani rose and started toward the house.

Karim said calmly, 'Only Med soldiers. Patrol.'

'How many?' Koenig asked Paul.

'He said maybe a dozen.'

'Each hour… patrol. Never… they find trouble,' offered Karim.

'They never found us here,' Koenig said dryly, then gestured Paul and the Security Guards behind the woodshed, while he and Catani moved warily along the side of the house to the street.

In the village square, a formation of armed Meds, under command of the Guard who had earlier supervised the murder, marched down the street in good military order.

Koenig and Catani crouched in the bushes in front of Talla's house, watching, guns ready. They were momentarily startled as Karim came up to stand behind them and nodded benignly to the passing patrol.

'What are their weapons, Catani?' Koenig whispered.

'A kind of stun gun,' answered Catani softly. He had seen something similar in a history book. 'We haven't used them in maybe twenty years.'

The patrol marched away down the street, turned a corner and was gone. Koenig and Catani rose cautiously to their feet.

'They go… to barracks…' offered Karim.

'You implied they force you to perform this "ritual",' Koenig said. Karim nodded, and the Commander asked, 'Why?'

'Sometimes… not many times… one on Medli… how I say… reverts?'

'Becomes like the Med people?' Koenig asked.

'Yes… yes. So… he will resist them… no? Must be destroyed. It is… too bad.'

'You club a man to death… but reluctantly,' Koenig observed dryly.

Karim shrugged. 'Meds many… strong…'

'Okay. Get the others,' Koenig ordered Catani. 'We're pulling out.'

'For good?' Catani asked.

'Depends.'

Catani trotted off behind the house. Koenig and Karim walked slowly toward the rocket pad. 'Old man… you're either telling me the truth… or you're lying,' Koenig said.

'Yes,' said Karim with a small smile.

'You're either sane or insane, whatever those terms mean out here. Would you put these things to a test?'

'It pleases you? Yes…'

In the distance, the sound of an approaching spaceship grew rapidly louder. The other Earthmen ran out from behind the house and joined Koenig, looking up. 'What's that sound?' Koenig asked sharply.

'Rocket… from Med. Excuse…' Karim apologised as he hurried back to his house.

'It's coming down on the pad,' said Koenig. 'Spread out and take cover.'

They were at a point in the square which overlooked the rocket pad. Paul and the Security Guards ducked behind buildings, while Koenig and Catani found cover in a cluster of rocks.

The Med rocket ship landed. There was a moment of silence, then something like new-fangled cannons slid out of ports on the craft and swept menacingly back and forth across the area.

'Look something like our old K-26 shock guns. We could take them on with our lasers,' Catani said.

'Just hope we don't have to,' said Koenig grimly. 'We're a long way from home.'

One of the Med cannons swung around and pointed almost directly at Koenig and Catani. Then a smooth, tough, and scary voice boomed from the ship, amplified through the village.

'Men from far planet! Hear Krog of Med! You… will… leave… now. You… will… go your base… and go away! Understand?'

A moment later a small puff of smoke emanated from one of the Med cannons and a large rock near Koenig was blasted to bits.

'One shot, Captain,' Koenig said tightly. 'Let them know we're not just targets.'

Catani lined up his laser gun on the rocket and fired a long arcing shot that hit one of the Med cannons… and it disappeared.

A moment later, Krog's voice boomed again, more calmly. 'Good. Very good. You go now in peace… Understand?'

Koenig stepped out from concealment, laser at the ready, followed by Catani. There was no reaction from the rocket ship. Koenig waved the other men to proceed around the side of the rocket, toward their module. All moved out warily, laser guns trained on the rocket ship as they moved around it.

'You… go… safe. Have good journey.' Krog's voice sounded a bit amused. 'Long journey…'

The Earthmen passed the rocket and started to skirt the hill toward their module. The remaining cannon on the Med ship didn't swing around after them.

The Earth party reached their module amongst the moonlike surface of Medli. They piled in, and the module lifted off.

In the Alpha Conference Room, Koenig, Helena, Bergman, Catani, and others were assembled. Images were once again being projected on a large screen: shots of Karim… the patrol… the Med rocket ship…

'Insane asylum, eh?' Bergman asked. 'Some of us might feel right at home there.'

'Comes down to this: are the Meds and the Medlis what they seem to be? If so, can we handle the Meds?' Koenig asked.

'Our technology is years ahead of theirs,' Catani said.

'But we're tremendously outnumbered,' Koenig said. 'I have our Tech people working on it…'

'On what? Weapons?' Bergman interjected sharply. 'Is that how we go in?'

'Defensive weapons,' Koenig said. 'But Dr. Russell tells me we better go in any way we can.'

'I disagree!' Bergman said.

'You know that conditions on Alpha are getting critical, Professor!' Helena stated.

'They're not good, but –' Bergman started, but was interrupted by Helena.

'We're coming apart under the strain! We could end up tearing each other apart!'

'Are you speaking of yourself?' Bergman asked.

'All of us! Yes! I can't take too much more of this! Can you?'

'I am an old man. I won't have to take too much more of anything, Doctor.'

'Professor, we're locked in a five day schedule!' Koenig said. 'We've used nearly two of them! You agree we can't go on in Alpha indefinitely?'

'I agree.'

'Then why are we blowing precious time in debate?' Koenig asked.

'Because we must! I put it to you: Assume Medli is the idyllic society it seems. Assume, too, that the forces of Med can be neutralised, which may not be as difficult as it seems. We still must ask what happens when we enter the equation.'

'You see us as serpents in paradise? I don't think we're that bad, Professor.' Koenig said.

'Neither bad nor good. Different,' Bergman said, then almost to himself added, 'Mix two chemicals never before mixed. How to predict the reaction? I'll have to think about it…'

Koenig rose, a bit impatiently. 'Do that, Professor. We're going to have to move. Doctor… how do we check out the Medlis and the Meds?'

'Bring me one of each. I'll get you a quick answer in the lab,' Helena said, only half kidding.

Koenig was serious. 'My thought, too. And I want a reliable projection of how long it would take our people to adapt to a thirty percent reduction in oxygen intake.' He started out of the room, and gestured Catani to go with him. 'If we get those answers, we're halfway home.'

'Are we, John?' Bergman asked.

Koenig paused at the door and turned back, soberly. The questions Bergman suggested troubled him, too. He said quietly, 'I don't know. I can only pray we are.'

Koenig and Catani stepped out of the Conference Room into the corridor.

'That one-of-each you promised the Doctor…' Catani said. 'How do we do that?'

Koenig gave a small, tight smile. 'We go down and get one of each.'

The MTU module glided down silently toward the moonlike surface of Medli and landed just outside of town behind Talla's house. The same party as before emerged: Koenig, Catani, Paul, and two Security men. They moved silently toward the house, laser guns at the ready.

Light came from the windows of Talla's house as Koenig stood with Karim in a shadow outside the front entrance.

'This… your test?' Karim asked, thoughtfully.

'We'll do psychological tests only. The subject will be returned unharmed,' Koenig said.

Karim nodded. 'Daughter… Talla… will go.'

'Only if she agrees,' Koenig said, then turned to Talla, who stood nearby.

'Can we… deny you?' Karim asked.

'She goes willingly or not at all,' Koenig said.

'Willing, then…' Talla agreed, with a small smile.

Koenig signalled toward bushes outside the house. One of the Security men rose from concealment, crossed to Talla and led her off behind the house in the direction of the module.

'A Med… not so easy…' said Karim with a small smile.

'I know.' Koenig checked his watch. 'You didn't tell me. What work is done in the factory?'

'Make parts… their machines. Not difficult.'

'You make it sound like a good life,' said Koenig dryly.

Karim shrugged. 'Not… to complain…'

'And the rituals? Killing one another?'

'Sir… you think you come here… to Paradise?' Karim asked wryly.

The distant sound of marching feet broke their conversation.

'Inside. Please,' Koenig said to Karim, then crouched and joined his men behind bushes. He dispatched Catani and Paul to the far side of the street. They ran across, crouching, and found concealment.

The sound of the approaching patrol grew louder as they came around a corner and approached the point of the planned ambush. The Meds weren't expecting trouble and didn't look around much. As they came even with Karim's house, a laser beam arced out from behind a bush, hitting the road just in front of the patrol, burning a deep groove in the street. The startled

Guard commander shouted an order, and the patrol came to a halt. The Guard leader looked at the deep groove at his feet, obviously impressed and alarmed.

'Drop your weapons! Now!' Koenig ordered.

The guard leader hesitated, then barked a soft command. A Med soldier raised his weapon toward the lawn and was met by a short laser burst from across the street, which dropped him.

Koenig stood, his laser gun on the Guard leader. 'Drop those weapons!'

The Guard leader barked a command and the men in his patrol dropped their weapons. The other Earthmen rose from concealment, guns trained on the patrol.

Koenig pointed to the Guard commander. 'You! Over here!' The Guard leader crossed to Koenig. 'Go with this man.'

The second Security man marched the Guard commander off with his laser gun. Paul and Catani crossed the street quickly to Koenig, who kept the patrol covered.

'Commander!' Catani said. 'We spotted more troops on the way! They must have a signal of some –'

He was interrupted by the sound of a very loud rifle shot. Paul, running toward Koenig, was knocked flat. Med patrol started to reach for their guns, but Koenig fired a laser arc over their heads, and they backed off. Koenig and Catani helped Paul to cover behind bushes, while holding a gun on the patrol.

Paul lay on the ground, and Koenig kneeled beside him. Paul was in pain but managed to bring his laser gun around to cover the patrol.

'You all right?' Koenig asked.

'Yes. It wasn't a solid hit. Take off. I'll cover you...'

Koenig hesitated, then heard the sound of two more shots and projectiles ripping through bushes near the Earthmen.

'Commander...?' Catani asked.

'Let's go,' Koenig said.

Koenig and Catani fired a couple shots up the street as the sound of approaching shouts and running feet increased. Paul got off a shot. Crouching, Koenig and Catani ran off around the corner of the house.

The MTU module remained on the moonscape of Medli. A Security man waited outside an open hatch as Koenig and Catani ran up to the module. He offered them a hand up to the hatch, but Koenig shook him off and turned back toward the village, waiting tensely.

A moment, then the sound of firing stopped. Koenig waited another second, but there was no sign of Paul. Then came the approaching sound of shouts and running feet of the Meds…

'Take off,' Koenig ordered grimly. He jumped aboard the module with the others. The hatch closed, and the module lifted off…

ACT THREE

In Alpha's Tech Area, a viewing scope displayed a head shot of Krog. Koenig, Murneau, and Catani watched the screen as Tech One monitored the transmission from Med.

'Krog of Med… speaks to Earthmen. Our technology… sees. Sees Earthman base. Sees Medli.'

'Wonderful…' muttered Murneau.

'We know! We… strong! Earthman is our prisoner on Medli.'

'Then Paul's alive,' said Catani.

'Now… many Med soldiers are on Medli.'

Koenig spoke into a mike, 'Central Control. Confirm?'

The Communicator's voice filtered through, 'Confirmed. Estimate they sent in a hundred men. Maybe more.'

'Earth men… hear… obey! Go… you survive! Stay… we destroy! Hear Krog of Med!'

The screen went dark.

'He's not eloquent, but he makes himself clear,' Koenig said, dryly.

'We've got them outgunned with our lasers. We could take on a hundred!' Catani said.

The men crossed to a table where Murneau had a mock-up of an electronic defence perimeter around the Medli settlement area.

'They'd send another hundred... or a thousand!' Koenig said.

Catani flared, 'I won't leave Paul there, Commander!'

Koenig answered sharply, 'You'll do what you're ordered to do!' Then he sighed and put a friendly hand on Catani's shoulder. 'We won't argue, Catani. We'll do what we can.' To Murneau he asked, 'What have you got?'

Murneau looked at his mock-up. 'Nothing too great, but it could work. Wouldn't take long to set up an electronic defence perimeter around the settlement, here... see? Knock down anything or anybody passing through the field.'

'Just around the settlement?' Koenig asked.

'To start. Then, with time, we push it out to cover all the habitable space.'

'But they could come <u>over</u> the barrier, couldn't they?'

'We can make it effective up to say 5,000 meters. Force whatever aircraft they have to come in high. They'd be sitting ducks for our KY or KT missiles.'

'An electronic fortress...' Koenig pondered.

'In effect,' continued Murneau. 'We'd need a full day's work down there to be operational. Could you hold them off that long?'

'Damn right we could!' Catani stated. 'I like it, Commander.'

'You like living in a fortress?' Koenig asked.

'Better than this cage we're in now!'

'That's the flaw, of course,' said Murneau. 'We could be under a constant state of siege… They could keep coming at us. Maybe develop a breakthrough missile…'

'Or they'd get the message sooner and quit coming!' Catani said.

Koenig posed the question to Helena in the Medical Lab.

'No. They wouldn't stop coming,' she said. 'Not the Meds.'

Helena was in the midst of two experiments, in two parts of the lab. The first involved Talla of Medli and the Guard of Med. Both were wearing bubble helmets to control the amount of oxygen they were breathing, and both were wired to a computer-like apparatus.

'How can you be sure?' Koenig asked.

'We've done a complete psych probe of each of the subjects… the Med and the Medli. Even allowing for the sexual variables, we have almost direct opposites.'

'Then Karim wasn't lying.'

'Understated the case, if anything,' Helena said. 'You name the response… fear, anger, aggression, love… it becomes predictable in each subject. It's as if… as if you split the human personality down the middle. The Medli represents the best in us… The Med has the worst elements in our characters.'

'Dr. Jekyll and Mr. Hyde?'

'Very much like that, Commander. Look… I'll give each of them a mild electric shock…'

Helena pressed a button on an elaborate panel. The computer clacked out a response. The Guard strained angrily against his restraints, while Talla winced, but accepted the pain.

'See? You don't even need the read-out. The Med fights it… the Medli accepts it as a test. Same right down the line…'

Koenig was thoughtful. 'You conclude from that that the Meds would keep on attacking any defence barrier we might set up?'

'From all the evidence. Yes. That doesn't mean they're irrational savages. But they'd have to be faced with absolutely impossible odds before reason would override their aggressive instincts.'

'Impossible odds. No, the best we have is a stalemate,' Koenig said.

'But that might be good enough. As long as we can hold the Meds off, wouldn't that be good enough?' Helena asked.

Bergman was working on the other side of the Lab and heard Helena's comment. 'Not nearly good enough!' He called sharply from across the room. 'Have we lost our reason?'

Helena quietly and tightly told Koenig, 'I can't take too much more of our wise old man!'

'Easy, now…' Koenig whispered back to her, then crossed to Bergman.

The Professor was stationed alongside another experimental set-up, which consisted of an Earthman inside a glass bubble, wearing a direct-injection oxygen pack. Tubes were attached to the bubble, and wires were attached to the man. In the middle of the bubble was a two-step stand.

'Are you blandly talking about establishing a colony under a constant state of war?' Bergman asked.

Koenig was stern. 'I'm talking about ways and means of getting our people off an endless flight to nowhere! I'll do it the best way I can! Do we have a projection of how long it would take our people to adapt to 7 percent oxygen?'

'Tentative,' answered Bergman as he activated recording devices, then pressed a button which sounded a buzzer inside the bubble.

The man in the bubble, who had been sitting, rose and turned off his own oxygen pack. He stepped up and down on the stand a few times, and the recording devices captured his reactions.

'The atmosphere in the bubble duplicates that on the planet,' said Bergman. 'Same as we're feeding into the helmets of the Med and the Medli. He just shut off his oxygen pack. Watch.'

After a few steps up and down the man seemed groggy and staggered. Bergman pressed the button twice, switching to different recording devices. The man turned up his oxygen pack and sat down again, clearly recovering rapidly.

'He can work fractionally longer in the Medli atmosphere on each attempt. We stop him when vital signs reach point Omega.' Bergman consulted a computer read-out and continued, 'No physical damage. Fairly constant projection. A human could adapt to the Medli environment in ten months to a year. There will be personal variations, of course...'

'That's not too bad. We could accept that,' Koenig said.

'Fine!' Bergman said angrily. 'Then we plunge ahead, I take it! All systems go, without a thought beyond our immediate salvation!'

Koenig was stung. 'Of course there are risks! And imponderable consequences! But we're dealing with the lives of 300 people! We have twenty-four hours left in which to make a decision... and that doesn't leave us much time for self-indulgent moralising!'

'Is that what I'm doing?' Bergman was quietly furious.

'You think I want to put us down there into a state of siege? You think I like the idea that I might have to?'

Bergman rose in a towering rage and began crossing in the direction of Talla and the Guard. 'Is that all that's bothering you, John? That's easily fixed! If we're to go in with weapons, let's go in with the ultimate weapon!' Bergman brushed Helena aside as he crossed to the Med Guard. 'It's been under your noses all the time!' He said as he loosened the restraints on the Guard.

Helena moved to intervene, but Koenig held her back... watching, fascinated.

'You've been playing with that answer all day!' Bergman exclaimed as he ripped the helmet off the Guard and stepped back.

The Guard sprung to his feet in an aggressive posture, looked around quickly, then started toward Bergman. The Professor took a calm step back, watching the furious Guard. Koenig moved to intercept the Guard.

'Leave him alone!' Bergman said sharply.

The Guard took one more step, faltered, and fell on his face… out cold.

'There's your weapon,' Bergman said. 'Oxygen! Too much oxygen! He's getting half again his normal supply in our atmosphere.'

'You may have it, Professor!' Koenig said, impressed.

'No, you have it!' Bergman scoffed. 'Put his helmet back on. With his lung capacity, too much oxygen is like poison to him. He won't survive it long.'

Helena and medical assistants rushed to replace the Med's helmet.

'But that much more oxygen would have no effect on our people, would it? Maybe make them feel exhilarated…' Koenig said intensely. 'It could work… if we can deliver it… and contain it!'

Bergman again was sharp, 'You can do both! Unless it strikes you as particularly obscene to use life-giving oxygen as a poison gas, John!'

Koenig looked at the Professor for a long moment, sobered by the thought. He continued quietly, 'It strikes me that we've never fought before, Professor. That's the point we've reached on Alpha.'

'At least you consulted me!' Bergman said. 'Have you thought of consulting the Medlis before we barge in?'

'We'd be getting them out from under the Med rulers! How could we be worse for them as neighbours?'

'At least you're beginning to ask the right questions, Commander!' Bergman said.

Koenig frowned, troubled and thoughtful.

The voice of the Communicator came through the intercom system, 'Call for Commander Koenig. Section Chief Murneau… Urgent.'

'Accept,' said Koenig into the mike.

'Commander, computer projection says we need to go on that barrier now or we won't make it,' Murneau reported.

Koenig hesitated, looked at Bergman, then came to a decision. 'The barrier's out,' he said. 'I'll meet all senior Tech personnel in your office in five minutes. Top priority. We have a weapon.'

As Koenig spoke, Talla watched and listened in her helmet. She seemed saddened and dismayed.

There was a bustle of activity in the Tech Area as technicians filled "grenades" and canisters from oxygen tanks. Another group assembled a shiny rocket nearby, supervised by Murneau.

Koenig led Catani through the area, showing him what was being done. 'Your attack force will be equipped with oxygen grenades… and we'll have launchers for these canisters.'

'Like artillery?' Catani asked.

'Exactly. You can use either or both as the situation develops down there.

'And you say the oxygen will stay where we release it?'

'Yes. Professor Bergman saw that, too. Brilliant man.' Koenig frowned thoughtfully, bothered again for a moment by Bergman's misgivings… But he shook off the troubling thoughts and went on, 'The methane in their atmosphere will combine with the oxygen and set up an orgon layer that will hold down the mass of oxygen.'

'What if they catch on and just send in more troops with gas masks?' Catani asked.

'Won't help them. Any gas masks they have, or we have, are made to filter out a foreign substance... not a <u>needed</u> substance like oxygen. They <u>have</u> no defence.'

Catani shook his head in admiration. 'That Bergman's a genius! I've got to congratulate him.'

'I wouldn't,' responded Koenig dryly.

Having crossed the Tech Area, Koenig and Catani arrived at the big shiny rocket being set up.

'What did Bergman come up with here?' Catani asked.

'That's not Bergman's. Murneau came up with it,' Koenig said.

'What is it?' Catani asked.

Murneau gave a small grim smile. 'This? Just our doomsday machine...'

Koenig, Murneau, Catani, Bergman, and a few other officials had gathered in the Conference Room. The atmosphere was tense and subdued.

Koenig consulted his timepiece. 'It is now... 0800 hours.' He paused as the others checked their timepieces, then continued, 'Captain Catani and I will go in with the attack force at 0830. If the initial phase succeeds –'

'Can't miss,' Catani interjected.

Koenig gave him a look and carried on, 'If the initial phase succeeds, Chief Murneau will start the transfer of personnel and equipment to Medli at 1000 hours. Does that check with your projections, Murneau?'

'We should be able to complete basic transfer if we start then,' Murneau answered. 'First phase transfer is set up and ready to go. They're working on phase two now.'

'All right. You'll start on my signal... or Catani's, if I'm not available,' Koenig said.

'What about the Medlis?' Helena asked. 'Will they be in any danger when we release our oxygen?'

'Minimal,' Koenig said. 'We've got Talla back on Medli warning her people to stay clear of the operational area. Captain Catani…'

'Sir?'

'You understand that basic operations will be confined to the attack area. If the Med troops fall, they are to be captured and revived. We want no casualties if we can avoid them,' Koenig said.

'Understood,' Catani said.

'All right,' said Koenig. 'I want it thoroughly understood that the thrust of our attack is only to convince the Meds that we have an irresistible weapon. If we can convince them of that, we are home free.'

'And if we can't?' Murneau asked quietly.

'Then we've lost,' Koenig stated. 'That's the chance we're taking. We've agreed to that, haven't we?' He looked around the table and received tight-lipped, uneasy nods of agreement. An apprehensive pause followed…

Bergman broke the silence, quietly. 'And Murneau's "doomsday machine"? A rocket with enough oxygen to wipe out the principal settlement on Med?'

'That's our ultimate threat. That <u>has</u> to convince them, if nothing else does,' Koenig said.

'But of course you would never use it,' said Bergman. 'It could kill thousands.'

'No. Of course not,' Koenig answered.

Bergman continued, almost sadly. 'Unless you have to? To save human lives? Isn't that the drill? Have you forgotten history?'

'God forbid that I do,' said Koenig softly. 'All right. Move out…'

ACT FOUR

The large MTU landed on the Medli rocket pad. Its hatch opened and a number of armed Earthmen, led by Catani, spilled out and took up defensive positions around the ship. The oxygen rocket missile was swung out to them.

Inside, Koenig sat in the command seat. A Communicator was at the controls of a bank of viewing scopes.

'No sign of enemy forces, sir,' said the Communicator.

'Good. Catani figured they'd wait for our move. They've seen our laser guns.' Koenig took a deep breath. 'All right. See if they've raised Krog.'

The Communicator operated his controls and the live feed of Murneau in the command seat of Central Control on Alpha was replaced by an image of Krog.

'Earth ship is on Medli. Krog... gave warning.'

'This is Commander Koenig, Krog. You said you can view Medli.'

'Krog... sees all.'

'Good. Zero in on your Medli barracks... and watch.'

'Krog... gave warning. Will strike!'

'Krog! I have a force of only ten men. We will take your barracks. Watch!'

Krog absorbed that for a moment, warily. 'Ten men... you have?'

'And a weapon. Watch!'

'Krog... watches,' came the grim response.

'Good,' Koenig said.

Krog's image disappeared from the screen. Koenig, fully equipped, rose and went to the hatch, then said to the Communicator, 'Stand by. We'll be in contact.'

'Sir,' came the response.

Koenig emerged from the open hatch of the MTU and signalled Catani. The Earthmen fanned out toward the square.

Two Earthmen set up the missile in the square. The rest, in a sort of skirmish formation, crossed out toward a barracks building, which lay in the distance. There were no Medlians to be seen.

Outside the Med barracks, a Med Commander watched the advance of the Earthmen through conventional field binoculars. He gestured an order to a Sergeant, who in turn ordered ten Med soldiers out of the barracks. They deployed behind cover in front… their stun guns commanding the approach.

Crossing a field on approach to the Med barracks, Koenig issued a command, and the line of Earthmen stopped their advance. Koenig held a portable viewer to his eyes and scanned the barracks.

'You know your business,' Koenig said to Catani.

'They brought out only a platoon?' Catani asked.

'You called it.'

'Figured,' said Catani. 'Krog's contacted them. They won't commit the main force until they see what we've got.'

'Then let's show them,' Koenig said.

'Paul must be in there. You're sure this won't hurt him?'

'You ever breathe pure oxygen?'

Catani nodded, satisfied. He detailed a man on each end of his line forward. Each man carried a grenade launcher. Two other men set up a larger launcher and loaded it with a canister, then worked their way cautiously forward until they were within range. They stopped, signalled back, and waited for their orders. There was no action from the barracks.

'No reaction yet,' said Catani quietly. 'Still our move.'

'Make it,' Koenig ordered.

Catani lifted his arm... then dropped it.

The two men with grenade launchers fired them. The grenades arced toward the barracks. As they exploded with a small puff outside the barracks, the Med Sergeant gave a command. His ten-man squad rose, and the soldiers aimed their guns toward the Earthmen... but before they could fire, they keeled over, one by one, including the Sergeant.

Koenig and Catani watched through their viewers.

'Got 'em,' said Catani with satisfaction.

'Should take them a minute to react... No, here they come!' Koenig said tensely.

The barracks door opened, and the rest of the Med troops started pouring out.

'Let it go!' Catani ordered the Earthmen on the canister launcher.

A puff of smoke rose as another canister was launched toward the barracks.

The Med troops were milling about outside, taking up a defensive position, when the canister exploded with a bigger puff of smoke nearby. A moment later they started falling down...

Catani grinned.

Koenig was on the mike, 'MTU from Koenig. Any reaction from Krog?'

'Negative, sir,' responded the Communicator.

'They're all down. I'm going after Paul!' Catani said as he gestured for a couple men to follow him. As Catani started heading out, the Communicator's excited voice stopped him.

'Commander from MTU!'

'Go ahead.'

'Missile inbound from Med, sir! Closing fast!'

Catani moved back toward Koenig. 'He's not buying it!'

'The fool!' Koenig said.

'Take cover!' Catani ordered the troops.

The sound of an approaching missile could be heard as the Earthmen went flat behind rocks and trees right before a big explosion erupted in the field between the Med barracks and the Earthmen's command post.

Koenig was flat on the ground as a shower of dirt from the explosion fell on him. He called into his mike, 'MTU from Koenig!'

'MTU here,' responded the Communicator.

'Get Alpha to raise Krog! And cut me in on the circuit!'

'Sir.'

Catani crouched and crossed to Koenig. 'Nobody hurt… but at that range, he's too close!'

The sound of a second incoming missile led Catani to flatten alongside Koenig. The missile exploded not far from the first.

'He doesn't mind killing his own troops,' said Koenig grimly.

The Communicator called, 'Commander! We have Krog on the scope. You are patched in.'

'You wish surrender, Commander? No surrender.'

'Krog! You saw our weapon! We have the capability of delivering it to Med!'

'Gas. Old weapon. We have masks for gas.'

'Masks are not effective against our gas,' Koenig said.

'So? Good,' Krog was amused. 'Your men die, too. I have many men…'

'Hear this! Our gas kills your men. It does not harm mine!' There was a pause, and Koenig quickly gave an order to Catani, 'Go get Paul. Stand by at the barracks.'

Catani nodded and took off with a couple of men.

'No gas can do this,' scoffed Krog.

'You can view your barracks! Watch again!' Koenig said.

The response was a grim, 'Krog watches.'

Koenig supervised as the fallen Meds were cleared away from their barracks. A revived Med soldier was set up to stand alongside one of the Earthmen, out in the open in front of the barracks.

Catani and Paul stood in front of the barracks.

'I still don't know how you did it, Captain,' said Paul.

Catani gave a short smile. 'Long story. It's not over yet.'

An Earthman soldier came out of the barracks and approached Catani.

'Prisoner secured?' Catani asked.

'Locked up. Under guard,' the soldier said.

'Did you get them all revived?'

'Most of them, sir,' the soldier answered grimly.

Koenig checked that his two "victims", an Earthman and a Med, were lined up the way he wanted them. Satisfied, Koenig turned and walked away a distance, followed by the second soldier with grenades.

'Krog!' Koenig called into his mike.

'Krog of Med here.'

'You have us on your viewer?'

'Krog watches performance.'

'Good,' Koenig said as he took a grenade from the second soldier. He waited a moment, then heaved the grenade so that it fell at the feet of the two "victims". A moment later, the Med soldier crumpled, while the Earthman slowly smiled.

Catani approached Koenig anxiously. Koenig waited a moment, listening... but there was no call from Krog.

'Krog! Did you see?' Koenig called into his mike.

Krog's voice responded, 'One man dead. Now we fire rockets. You all dead. Your base will be dead.'

'Missile Crew from Commander!' Koenig called.

'Missile Crew, sir!' Responded a man's voice.

'Arm missile and stand by,' Koenig ordered.

'What missile?' Krog asked.

'Gas missile. Aimed at your capital. It will wipe out every soul,' Koenig said.

There was a tense pause. No reaction. Then the Missile Crew man's voice called again, 'Missile armed and ready, sir.'

'Stand by to fire,' Koenig ordered.

'Standing by, sir.'

Catani looked at the grim Koenig with tense concern, wondering if he would really do it? A moment later, Krog called again.

'You want moon of lunatics?'

'We want your troops out in one hour… to stay out,' Koenig said. 'Our missile remains targeted on your capital.'

'Krog does not need lunatics. Krog gives to you.'

The tension broken, the Earthmen relaxed. Some broke into exuberant yells. Catani looked at Koenig, who drew a deep breath of relief.

'Question, Commander. Would you have fired if he did?' Catani asked.

Koenig looked at him oddly for a long moment, then said quietly, 'Get back to the MTU and signal Murneau. We're moving in…'

The Medlians had resumed their quiet business in the village square. The rocket sat in the square, looking rather like a war memorial. The armed Earthmen were at ease, moving about and chatting amiably with Medlians.

Koenig walked slowly along the square with Karim, toward the factory, their conversation relaxed.

'We'll establish our colony to the north, centred around the old Med barracks,' Koenig said.

'Yes.'

'We'll try not to interfere with your people or your way of life. We'll help you if you want us to. Is that all right?'

'We can not... deny you...' said Karim, quietly.

'We had hoped you might welcome us. We thought you might be pleased to be rid of the Meds.'

'Medlis... exchange one master... for another.'

Koenig was a bit annoyed. 'We won't be your masters! We'll be... well... neighbours!'

'We... weak. You... strong. Can not be good...'

'Look, Karim, I –' Koenig started, but broke off at the sound of an alarm siren from the MTU.

There was a stir in the crowd as Catani ran from the direction of the MTU. He reached the square, blew a whistle, and the armed Earthmen trotted into formation.

'Commander!' Catani called as he ran up to Koenig.

'What is it?'

'The man we left on the MTU was shot with his own laser. The gun is missing.'

'So... it starts...' Karim said sadly.

'Find that gun!' Koenig ordered Catani. 'Search every house if you have to!'

'Yes, sir!' Catani said, then crossed to his men and began giving instructions.

Koenig turned to Karim. 'What starts?'

'Young people of Medli. I said... can revert...? Be like Meds, again...?'

'They shot my man?' Koenig asked.

'Must be. They want... no new master. There... will be more...' Karim warned just as a laser beam arced into the square from the direction of the factory. It hit a tree near Koenig, demolishing it.

Koenig grabbed Karim and pulled him to cover behind a house which overlooked the factory street.

Catani reacted to the shot and shouted to his troops, 'There it is! Spread out!'

Crouching, the Earthmen deployed at a run, taking up position on either side of the street commanding the factory. Another shot arced out of the factory, blowing a piece out of a building, but otherwise doing no harm.

'You see?' Karim said to Koenig. 'It will not stop.'

'It'll stop! We'll stop it!' Koenig said angrily.

Quietly, the old man responded, 'Yes... master...'

Koenig turned to Karim slowly, absorbing the import of his words.

Catani, behind cover, called over to Koenig, 'Commander! Are we free to fire?' Koenig hesitated, and Catani asked again, 'Gas grenades or lasers, Commander?'

The Commander still hesitated.

'You have shown... resistance can succeed,' Karim told Koenig.

'Because we have overwhelming power!' Koenig said.

'Oh... you will rule. But it will not stop...'

Koenig looked at Karim, deeply troubled by what he had said.

Another laser shot blasted through the square, still missing everybody.

'Commander! They're firing at your men!' Catani was furious. 'Give us the word!'

'Hold it!' Koenig ordered, sharply.

Incredulous, Catani ran over to Koenig, crouched, and demanded, 'What are we waiting for? We can handle them easily!'

Koenig was grim. 'Sure we can. And then what do we do? Go on handling them?'

'I don't get it,' Catani said.

'Three hundred of us controlling four thousand. An occupying power. Is that what we want? We'd be a master race on Medli. No avoiding it. Do we want that?'

Catani frowned. 'Bergman questions?'

'They finally have to be answered, don't they?' Koenig asked.

There was a moment of silence, which was gently broken by Karim, 'Your man… who is dead. Is that answer?'

Koenig drew a deep breath.

'Yes. That's our answer,' Koenig agreed quietly. 'Get your men,' he told Catani. 'We're pulling out.'

The MTU blasted off the rocket pad, but the oxygen rocket was still in the village square.

Back on Alpha, Koenig, Helena, Bergman, and Catani sat in the Commander's office, thoughtful and somewhat depressed. A view screen displayed a shot of Medli, slowly receding.

'You left the Medlis the "doomsday machine"?' Helena asked.

'Had to. Krog wouldn't forgive them for what happened. We couldn't leave them defenceless,' Koenig replied.

'So we left them power,' Bergman said quietly.

Koenig threw him a look. He'd thought of that, too. 'Yes. We did that.'

'How long, I wonder, before they realise the rocket gives them absolute power over the Meds?' Bergman asked.

'Not long, I would think,' Koenig answered.

'The Medlis are good people,' Catani said. 'Better they have the power than the Meds.'

'What was it Dr. Russell said?' Koenig asked. 'The Medlis are like the best of us. But power corrupts the best of us, doesn't it?'

'We intended only good for them,' Helena said.

'We always have intended only good, haven't we…?'

There was a long pause as Koenig's words sank in.

Alone in his quarters, Professor Bergman concluded his latest journal entry. He glanced at his view screen, which displayed planet Medli as it receded into the depths of space.

"The question hung in the room like a deadly cloud of life-giving oxygen... and no one spoke. And in that moment, we knew ourselves to be still prisoners locked together on Moon Base Alpha... confined to the company of our fellow creatures. But we will take comfort from one another, too, and we will survive, in the void..."

OBSERVATIONS

'*A Breath of Death*' shows a strikingly different approach to *Space: 1999* than what was eventually seen on-screen. Here the Moonbase is a pressure-cooker of tension and hostility and the Alphans are far more willing to bend their morality in their desperate search for a new home. While there are some intriguing concepts in Irving Gaynor Neiman's script, Koenig's actions are way off the final characterisation established in '*Breakaway*'. His intent to settle on an Alien planet at all costs in '*War Games*' was justified because Alpha had been crippled beyond repair, but here, he is forcing the colonisation issue due to social unrest. Though that had been George Bellak's original intent for the series, Christopher Penfold practically eliminated that concept in favour of a more harmonious atmosphere. As in '*The Void Ahead*', the use of voice-over narration by Professor Bergman is effective. Unfortunately, the final act is something of a mess, where the humans have emotionally contaminated the indigenous population, perhaps setting them on a path to ruin. It's all "Manifest Destiny" at its worst.

NOBODY'S PERFECT

Final Storyline – 9th April, 1974

by Christopher Penfold

HOOK

Special Effects shot of Alpha in relation to planet Piri.

Computer data has indicated that the place is perfect for their needs – atmosphere, vegetation, etc.

An Eagle reconnaissance astronaut reports computer inaccuracies in time element. The planet is much closer than they thought. He flies over the surface – reports it to be beautiful, but no signs of life, flora, or fauna. Now there are computer inaccuracies in relation to its gravitational pull. The Eagle is being drawn down to the surface. The astronaut cannot control it – the engines have not the thrust to blast it away.

Koenig orders Kano to check out the computer data thoroughly. It repeats confirmation of its previous figures. Koenig orders the astronaut to go over to manual. He does.

Special Effects sequence of Eagle fighting gravitational pull, dodging the pinnacles of spheres that cover the surface.

Inside the Eagle we see the astronauts sweating and struggling for survival.

In Main Mission the Eagle's 'blip' disappears from the screen.

Special Effects shot, the Eagle points directly at a pinnacle. It stops moving.

ACT ONE

Koenig orders Carter to take off and check the situation out, on manual all the way, taking no chances.

Command Conference. Koenig concerned about the misinformation given by the computer. According to the astronaut it was wrong on almost every detail about the surface. And, reports Bergman, it was wrong too about Alpha's trajectory past the planet. It was thought we had time only for a quick reconnaissance before we passed out of range of our trajectory. But now the figures assess that we are passing much closer than was at first thought. Are those computer figures checked? Yes, in every detail. Bergman has taken the precaution of making an astro sighting. And this contradicts what the computer says. In fact, Alpha is curving inexplicably down towards this planet.

Koenig calls Carter urgently. He must rely on no computer data. Fly visual all the way and pull out at the first sign of trouble.

Carter approaches the Eagle. Reports back that it is just hanging in the sky, motionless on the point of impact with the pinnacle.

He gets inside the Command Module and finds the two seats empty. There is no indication of any struggle. The Eagle is as mysterious as the Marie Celeste.

Koenig orders Carter to get away as fast as possible, and to close down all electronic data systems on the Eagle. He does so, blasts away from the first Eagle and heads back to Alpha.

Back on Alpha there is a chapter of disaster. Computerised control of the artificial atmosphere system has been pumping too little oxygen into the air. Heating controls are haywire. Control and monitoring systems throughout the base are all on manual. In the Intensive Care Unit a patient who was on computer controlled life-support systems has died.

Carter lands on manual and makes his report to Koenig. Koenig orders Kano into his office. Private conversation. Koenig reminds Kano of his brain connection to computer. Kano remembers it with extreme displeasure. Koenig says they are totally dependent on computer and somehow it's leading them into trouble they don't understand. No normal checks have given any indication that anything is wrong. As a last resort, Koenig is asking Kano to connect himself with computer to see if he can detect where the malfunction is.

To the amazement of Main Mission staff and under elaborate medical supervision, Kano is sat on a reclining chair in front of computer, and Helena Russell takes the cortex connector from its panel in the computer. She parts Kano's hair, removes a hermetic seal and reveals a precision socket. She makes the connection.

Kano's face is contorted with pain and then suddenly relaxes into a smile and becomes still – utterly still, and then before their eyes, he disappears.

ACT TWO

Command Conference. They assess their situation. Koenig announces that they are stuck in orbit around an apparently dead planet. Kano and two astronauts have disappeared already. They can no longer trust computer which is, for some reason they don't understand, deliberately misleading them into trouble. In search of answers Koenig decides to take an Eagle down to the planet with Alan Carter.

Koenig's Eagle lifts off, travels to Piri and flies alongside the still Eagle before putting down on the surface. Koenig orders Carter not to leave the ship under any circumstances and to call him on the commlock as soon as anything unusual happens.

Koenig steps out onto the Pirian surface. He looks around in amazement and moves towards a central raised area.

Before he reaches it he becomes aware of a close presence. He looks around and is surprised to find an incredibly beautiful girl – beautiful in a very stylised kind of way. She explains to him the simple truth. She gestures as though she is talking and her voice is heard, but her lips do not move.

She is the servant of the Guardian of this planet and the Guardian's task is to keep the planet without blemish. Siren music attends the Pirian Girl and Koenig is entranced. Suddenly it seems as though computer was right after all. The Pirian Girl takes him by the hand and leads him into the Paradise Garden. Here they wander among strange, immobile shapes and Koenig asks if he can see the Guardian personally to discuss certain problems that have arisen on Alpha.

The Pirian Girl tells him he can see the Guardian now but that he can only talk to him when he is ready to accept perfection. She points to the top of the raised area from which grows a bright multi-coloured column of light on top of which a beacon flashes, causing Koenig to flinch and turn away. When he recovers he looks back at the Pirian Girl who stands, smiling impassively.

'What is perfection?' asks Koenig.

'The one moment of truth which you know to be absolutely perfect.'

'And?' asks Koenig.

'That the moment should last for ever.'

She takes him further into the garden saying she will show him.

While they walk Koenig asks who is the judge of perfection on Piri? The Pirian Girl tells him it is the Guardian, whose power is absolute.

Koenig suddenly stops in horror. He sees the two reconnaissance Eagle astronauts, utterly still, in attitudes of adoration, their eyes glazed. Koenig runs up to them, attempts to attract their attention. They don't flinch, or blink. They do not even breathe. They are dead, like statues, and the smiles on their faces are a mockery.

Next to them is Kano. Koenig goes to slap his face. It does not move, and his own hand is bruised by the contact.

He rounds on the Pirian Girl in anger, demanding to know if this is what passes for perfection on Piri – if this is the work of the Guardian.

They were imperfect intruders. The astronauts faced certain death and Guardian came to their rescue. He offered them eternal life at the point of death, and they were perfectly happy to accept. And Kano, through his connection to computer, glimpsed the Guardian and, in a moment was made perpetually and perfectly happy.

Koenig tells the Pirian Girl he will not allow the Alpha People to be deprived of life for the sake of an idea of perfection that is abhorrent to him. The Pirian Girl is a little shocked at the vehemence of his rejection. She asks him if he has absolute power on Alpha. He replies that he does not, but he's confident he'll have no difficulty in persuading the others to fight the fate of Kano and the astronauts.

Koenig asserts that for his presence to be perfect he must choose it for himself and that, come what may, he will refuse to do.

She tells him that it is impossible that anything imperfect should exist on Piri. He will be made perfect.

Koenig takes his commlock and calls Main Mission. He can get no reply. He calls again. Still no answer.

Main Mission is empty. The corridor is empty. Koenig appears on the Comm-post, calling from Piri. Sounds of music and laughter.

In the Diagnostic Unit Helena is dancing. A party of happy celebration is going on.

Koenig snaps off his commlock and returns to the Eagle to find Carter in a similarly euphoric state of mind.

Carter is insistent that he brought the Eagle down to Piri and he should take it back to Alpha. There's nothing wrong with him and therefore there's no reason why Koenig should be flying the ship. He tries to take command, but Koenig refuses. Now Carter attempts to mock him out of control and Koenig gets mad. Finally, there's a physical struggle for control. Koenig, in desperation, knocks Carter out. But in so doing he crushes the bones in his right hand and falls awkwardly, stoving in his ribs. Now Carter is unconscious, but Koenig is in considerable pain. The Eagle lifts off, but Koenig can make no contact with Alpha.

As Koenig calls Main Mission, Morrow makes no reply. He gives everyone time off and he himself turns off all external communications systems and relaxes.

Koenig lands and calls for medical assistance. As Helena watches his pain-stricken face on the Diagnostic Unit monitor, she can't see that he's in trouble. He has to operate the Boarding Tube himself.

He struggles through the airlock and into the Travel Tube. Gasping for breath, he emerges into the corridor and heads for Main Mission. Sandra and Tanya pass him, and don't appear to notice that he's half-crawling and in terrible pain. They welcome him back home and pass on. Finally, Koenig struggles into Main Mission and finds it completely empty – except for Paul Morrow, smiling as he plays the guitar. "Good to see you back, Commander." Koenig passes out with his pain.

ACT THREE

Bergman opens a conference in Koenig's office by apologising on behalf of Koenig, for his absence. He is delayed in the Medical Section having treatment for fractured ribs after his unfortunate fall in Main Mission. So, the meeting goes ahead without him.

Koenig revives from unconsciousness in the Diagnostic Unit. He sees Mathias and asks him where Doctor Russell is. Mathias reports that she is attending the Exodus meeting. Mathias looks uncommonly happy to Koenig and with a couple of questions Koenig establishes that so far as Mathias is concerned their days on Alpha are numbered. The plan for total evacuation is going ahead and that is what is being discussed right now.

Koenig struggles out of bed and nothing Mathias can say about his condition will stop him. He makes his way, in great pain through Alpha to Main Mission, totally bemused by the attitude of the people he meets on the way, which is happy go lucky and carefree and celebratory all at the same time.

In Koenig's office the Exodus conference hears from Bergman that, as things have turned out, computer has vindicated itself. All the data on Planet Piri which caused them to make their first reconnaissance there have been borne out by the first-hand reports of John Koenig. In every respect Piri is just perfect for all their needs. Computer is now working well, and all data is being processed in the proper manner – it's just a pity they won't be able to take computer with them when they go.

Koenig makes his way through Main Mission, being greeted happily by the staff who are on duty. He goes to the doors of his own office and listens to the conference a while, before making his presence felt. Where questions are asked about the surface of Piri, Helena answers them on Koenig's behalf, as though she had questioned him extensively before attending the meeting.

Finally, it's too much for Koenig. He bursts in on the scene to the surprise of all present. In the first place, despite his obviously distraught state, Bergman's reaction is to give up the chair so that Koenig can join the conference – they are all glad to have his advice. But slowly, slowly, they become aware that he is not of their mind. He disputes every aspect of their discussion, disputes that he has ever said these things to Doctor Russell about the inhabitability of Piri. Contrariwise, he asserts that the place is dead, dead, dead, and that there is nothing there whatsoever, and that they should be concentrating their attention on the problem of how to release themselves from the orbit of this utterly sterile world on which they will die, like Kano, in a matter of minutes. He tells them that computer is untrustworthy, that it has been fraternising with the Guardian, the machine which maintains Piri, and that it is deliberately misleading them now.

He tells them of the fate of the astronauts and Kano. He tells them that their euphoric state of mind is the result of deliberate interference by Piri – that they are being brainwashed.

Koenig suddenly goes quiet and agrees. Exodus goes ahead. He lets Bergman handle end of meeting. Goes back into Main Mission. Thinks a moment. Then sees computer. Begins to smash it up. The noise brings everyone in from Koenig's office to Main Mission.

Morrow and Carter try to restrain Koenig, but they are thrown back. Helena calls for Security men and Medical assistance. Finally, the pain in Koenig's ribs overcomes him and he is overpowered before the computer is a total write-off. Helena, Bergman, and Morrow have a hurried consultation and decide that Koenig is insane and for the safety of Alpha he should be locked up. He is taken away, still protesting verbally, by a group of Security men. Mathias gives him a sedative and as he goes quiet, Main Mission begins to pick up the pieces.

Alpha in a hubbub of activity. There is an Eagle on every pad. The last one is raised on the lift from the now empty Technical Section. There is a tremendous excitement in the air about the new world they are going to.

Koenig, alone and frustrated in his quarters.

Bergman and Helena meet to discuss their one outstanding problem: what to do with mad John Koenig. They decide that they cannot leave him on Alpha, so they will, whether he likes it or not, take him under Security Guard and put him on an Exodus Eagle. They feel sure that after a few days of the new life, the balance of his mind will be restored. Helena puts his behaviour down to the continuous tension he has been living under through the weeks and months since they were blasted out of Earth orbit – he just can't let go – shell-shocked by their situation.

Helena, with Mathias on hand in case a sedative should be needed in a hurry, goes to Koenig's quarters with four Security men. She asks them to wait outside; she would like the opportunity of talking to him first. Koenig, apparently quiet, allows her to come into the quarters and she begins to talk about their new life. For a while Koenig appears to listen, so Helena tells him they are all about to leave and that he is to come with them. To her immense relief, he seems willing to do just this. She opens the door and Koenig smiles at the Security men and Mathias, who had obviously been expecting trouble. They walk away, with Koenig too, talking excitedly about Piri. Then, coolly and quietly, Koenig lifts a stun gun from one of the Security men and holds it in Mathias's back. They are at the open door to a Travel Tube. Koenig motions the Security men to get inside, he closes the door and sends them on their way. With Mathias as his hostage, he now faces Helena.

ACT FOUR

At the Commander's console Bergman is giving final instructions for the close down of the base and the shut-down of the main generators. He's concentrating on results which come up on the computer screen.

Koenig walks with Helena and Mathias down the corridor to Main Mission.

Koenig confronts Bergman, who looks up from his calculations and sees Koenig with Mathias as his hostage. Confrontation.

First Bergman tries to plead with Koenig not to endanger the very thing they have all been looking for – the opportunity of beginning a new life on a suitable planet.

Then Koenig, rationally, tries to persuade Bergman that the Guardian is getting at them through computer and by some kind of telepathic brainwashing in the hope that they will choose to accept the so-called perfection of Piri. Impasse. So, Helena suggests a way out. They will still leave Alpha with power supply intact, and Koenig can stay alone here while the rest of them go down to Piri. They can hope that when their optimistic view is confirmed, Koenig can join them; while he hopes that they will discover Piri to be as dead as he believes it to be, and they will all return. The deal is done, Mathias is released, and they leave Koenig alone in his office while Exodus goes ahead.

Koenig watches through the windows of Main Mission as a succession of Eagles lift off the pads. He crosses to the other side, climbs the stairs to the balcony and looks out. More Eagles lift off and head for distant Piri which now looms, menacing, in Koenig's view.

The whole base is shut down and empty except for Main Mission and Koenig's office. Koenig himself is emotionally drained and utterly weary. A depression begins to set in.

The Pirian Siren music is heard softly, and Koenig becomes slowly conscious of it. He goes to sit down and suddenly a bed appears. Koenig looks at it suspiciously and then he kicks it and the modular units from which it is made are scattered.

The music builds again and as Koenig moves towards the table a drink appears on it. Again, Koenig regards it suspiciously and hurls it against the wall. Instead, he goes to his own cupboard and pours himself a drink.

He sits down in his own chair. The music builds again, and Koenig becomes aware of a strong presence behind him. As he straightens, the Pirian Girl steps in behind his chair and soothes his brow. She tells him he is a strong-willed and persistent man, but that he has now put himself in an impossible position. He knows Alpha is being telepathically attacked. And because he knows it he can resist it, he can fight it, but ultimately he's fighting a losing battle. His own people have made their choice and he, by his own obstinacy, is helplessly alone on Alpha. He has no alternative but to join them.

Koenig jumps up from his chair in anger to face her. She can talk and tempt as much as she likes, but he, John Koenig, will never voluntarily leave Alpha for Piri.

In an instant he is there, in the Paradise Garden. He looks around him aghast at the Alpha People who stand, like the astronauts and Kano in attitudes of total adoration, with blissful smiles on their faces.

Koenig looks to the raised area, where the light of the Guardian shimmers above. Standing, looking down at him among his own people, is the Pirian Girl. She tells him now that he must choose – or be destroyed.

'Choose what?' asks Koenig in a rage. 'Choose this grotesque mockery of a death which your Guardian calls perfection?'

He goes up to each of the Alpha People and challenges them to make the choice for themselves, to let him hear it from their own lips. And to his amazement and horror the statues animate and close round him, aggressively accusing him of human pride and arrogance, speaking from an entirely Pirian point of view.

Koenig is doubly betrayed. He backs away from them, towards the steps, as they hound him in nightmare fashion up towards the Guardian.

At the top he turns his attention to the Pirian Girl and rails against her. But she explains she is only the servant of the Guardian.

'You have no mind of your own. You might as well be a machine since your whole life is controlled by one,' mocks Koenig.

'Your life, too, will be controlled by this machine. It is inescapable.'

She turns and walks away from Koenig towards the column of light. As she stands in front of it, in the familiar attitude of adoration, Koenig thinks hard. Suddenly he takes his stun gun and fires it at the Pirian Girl's back. She stiffens as though from instant rigor mortis and falls back.

Koenig runs up to her, trembling. He rolls her stiff body over and fumbles at the back of her head. He opens a flap and reveals she is a robot.

He picks her up and carries her to the edge of the platform and throws her doll-like body down to the Alphans below, crying that that is what passes for life on Piri.

Now Koenig turns to face the Guardian. The column of light vibrates and a weird electronic sound builds. The voice of the Guardian is the voice of the defunct Pirian Girl.

The Guardian explains that it created the Pirian Girl in human form so that Earthman could understand better. Now Koenig has destroyed her and he will have to communicate with Guardian direct.

If the choice is the same, says Koenig, then he has the same answer. He will never choose this Pirian mockery of life and as the only alternative is death he is prepared to face it.

But the Guardian is bemused. It is a machine, and its task is to preserve Piri as a memorial to a life which no longer exists. The Pirians, aware that they were a dying people and believing they had created a perfect world, elected the Guardian to maintain it for eternity. They chose Guardian because, as a machine, it was immortal.

But now Koenig, by his infectious humanity, has made Guardian aware that Piri is more dead than perfect. It has therefore decided to destroy itself, to restore time to the planet, and to leave it to the Alphans to turn it into their New World.

Before Koenig can protest the column of light begins to die and internal explosions cause him to shield his face and turn away.

He sees, against a changing Pirian sky, the Eagle poised before the pinnacle of spheres. As it begins to move Koenig turns back to the Guardian and shouts desperately for it to stop. But another explosion is its answer and as Koenig turns back he sees the Eagle smash into the pinnacle and become a falling fireball.

Koenig looks down at the Paradise Garden. All of the Alpha People have gone. He looks up into the sky and sees the Moon now moving further away. On the Pirian horizon two suns are rising. On the planet surface some of the shapes are moving, some of the spheres tumble through the growing breeze. Piri is alive again – and growing.

In Main Mission, where everyone has returned to their stations, there is concern for Koenig and Carter because Alpha is now back on its original trajectory past the planet.

Morrow calls to Koenig. They must lift off immediately if they are to get back to Alpha at all.

Koenig calls Carter on the commlock and tells him to wait. He leaves the dying Guardian and runs down the steps through the Paradise Garden.

Carter now has the motors running, kicking up dust and debris on the now living planet surface.

Koenig runs, choking, through the dust, climbs aboard, and Carter lifts off.

EPILOGUE

Koenig and Carter are back in Main Mission sadly watching, with the others, the quickly receding Planet Piri.

The irony is that when the Guardian restored time and growth to Piri, it also put Alpha and its people back on their original trajectory – too far away for them now to reach Piri at all.

Nor could it prevent the Reconnaissance Eagle from crashing into the pinnacle – killing the two astronauts.

This is where it all began. Helena asks if their Pirian nightmare really happened at all.

Koenig points to the damaged computer. Yes, it did happen, and the result is that they have brought a dead planet back to life.

Kano reports that computer confirms Piri to be just perfect for their needs.

The Guardian's final gesture was generous, but badly mistimed.

'Nobody's Perfect' is Bergman's final comment.

OBSERVATIONS

Christopher Penfold's original outline is much more straightforward than his final shooting script, which aired mysteriously without his screen credit. Originally, he envisioned the Guardian as a character who would interact with Koenig, thus reducing much of the planet's mystery. The original ending, in which Helena wonders if their Pirian nightmare really happened at all, is similar to the ending of '*Another Time, Another Place*' or '*War Games*'. This storyline was rumoured to have been originally pitched by David Weir.

WEB

Original Story Treatment
by Christopher Penfold

PROLOGUE

Helena, in her quarters, narrates the story. It is an event of the recent past. She begins by recalling the date when Jimmy Calder began to feel the web closing round him for the second time.

We see the web closing round Jimmy. He is Hemingway – an outdoor man, who seeks the meaning of his life by forcing himself into situations where he will come close to death. He is established as a man of the deepest moral courage and physical strength. We find him in bed in his quarters approaching the climax of a nightmare. He sees himself receding, sees his hold on life disappearing into the distance, and in its place is a nightmare of a red spider constantly lunging towards him.

Helena Russell, on duty in the Medical Centre, gets a call from Computer. Metabolism and heart rate for Calder are approaching dangerous limits. She tries to wake him on the communications post. Succeeds. He tells her it's only a nightmare and she wishes him a more peaceful sleep. But as the communications post dies, Calder gets out of bed. He is in agony over the unresolved conflict, the fear that is within himself and which he cannot explain. He goes out and heads for the Eagle launch pads.

Koenig and Kano are alone in Main Mission, playing chess. Computer reports an unusual movement. Calder approaching the launch pads. Koenig tries to call him. Calder makes no reply. Computer reports he's inside the stand-by Eagle. Koenig orders Security to stop him. They do, just as the Eagle motors are beginning to blast. They stun him after a struggle.

RCT ONE

Calder is unconscious. Helena is making a medical examination. Koenig is there. During this scene we establish that there has been a very close relationship between Calder and Koenig. They have been trained together and they have done vital interplanetary exploration together, including the ill-fated Ultra Probe.

We also establish that Helena has a much lower opinion of Calder than Koenig. Through her we learn that Calder has been under a cloud for the past three years as a result of unresolved suspicions about his behaviour during the flight of the Ultra Probe of which he was the only survivor. There was an official inquiry into the disaster and the charges against Calder ranged from murder to lack of moral fibre. We also learn in this scene, that up to this moment, Koenig has not realised that the medical assessment for the prosecution of Calder was provided by Helena Russell. As soon as Koenig discovers this, there is a flare up between them and the scene ends with Koenig walking out.

Helena's narration takes us back to the preparations for the launch of the Ultra Probe, in 1996. Colonels Koenig and Calder have been jointly responsible for getting the project off the ground. There is a final moment when there is a toss-up as to who shall actually fly the mission and who shall remain on Moonbase Alpha to control it. Calder wins the toss and Koenig remains on Alpha as Mission Controller.

We see the crew assembled. Colonel Jimmy Calder is Commander and Engineer. Dr. Darwin King is number two, and also the astrophysicist of the party. Professor Juliet Mackie is a specialist in radiation, and Doctor Olga Vishenskya is responsible for medical and commissariat. The voyage will last eighteen months, and will take them to the planet Ultra, only recently discovered by radio astronomy deeper into space than any expedition has yet probed.

Koenig farewells the crew on Alpha and they are ferried to the space station in orbit around the Moon, where the Ultra Probe is docked.

Through Helena's narration, we learn that the first eight months of the flight were scientifically invaluable, but otherwise uneventful. The plan was to put the Probeship in a high orbit around Ultra and from there to launch a landing craft to the surface. As with the early Moon landings, this would be the most dangerous part of the exercise because they are beyond contact with Moonbase Alpha.

We see Calder approach the far side of Ultra and preparations are in hand for going into orbit when they see something extraordinary. Their scanners indicate several contacts slightly further away than Ultra, and Calder decides he will go and take a look. They stumble onto a space junkyard – a collection of weird space-travelling vehicles used by a variety of space people. But there are no signs of life.

Calder decides that they must take a closer look. From this point, the narration is Calder's. He is manoeuvring the Probeship from the Command Module. The rest of the crew are in spacesuits, preparing for Darwin King and Juliet Mackie to go out of the main door to the landing craft that is stowed behind the main accommodation. They are prepared for the spacewalk and send word through to Calder that they are about to open the door and go out. Calder gives them the go ahead and they open the door.

Calder watches on the monitor as the door opens. The spacesuited figures all shriek in horror. Waiting, unsuspected, in the doorway is a monstrous red, four-legged spider. From the centre of its head a spear tongue shoots out and penetrates Darwin King's spacesuit and he dies instantly.

Calder immediately tries to get into his spacesuit. There is nothing he can do until he's got it on, because he cannot close the door of the Probe. The doors simply close up to the spear tongue but go no further. Then the spider gets one of its forelegs round the crack between the doors and simply wrenches it back. Olga and Juliet, terrorised, back into the ship and take out their stun guns. They blaze away at the spider, but it keeps on coming. As soon as the tongue retracts from King's body, it spikes Juliet Mackie and she dies. Olga, now bravely, but futilely tries to grapple with the spider's foreleg, but it flings her against the airlock door and plunges its spear tongue into her and she dies instantly.

Calder, at last, has his suit on, and he goes to a crash locker and flings aside the laser cutting gear which he knows now to be useless against the monster. Instead, he takes an axe. He presses the button to open the airlock door, and sees the dead bodies of King, Mackie, and Olga lying on the floor. The spider's spear tongue is still in Olga, but as soon as the door opens, it gets a foreleg inside. Calder immediately tries to hack at the foreleg with the axe. But the strength of the spider still contrives to pull back the door. Calder sees the spear tongue retract from Olga's body and angle towards himself. As the tongue shoots out, Calder ducks back behind the door and with split second timing brings the axe down on the tongue. It is instantly withdrawn, and now Calder hacks with all his strength at the foreleg. It suddenly bursts open, pouring red blood all over Calder and all into the floor of the Command Module.

The spider momentarily loses its grip and Calder gets the door closed.

ACT TWO

Breathlessly, Calder thinks what to do next. He goes back to the console and looks at the monitor. He can see the wounded spider still clawing at the airlock door. Calder closes the other airlock and traps the spider inside. Then he goes to the on-board computer and begins to work out his position. But the module is wracked with terrifying wrenching and Calder, going back to the monitor, soon sees that the spider will tear the module apart.

In desperation there is nothing else he can do. He works feverishly at the console.

Outside, we see exploding bolts part the Command Module from the rest of the Probe. Finally, in a big blast, the Command Module blasts away from the Probeship, leaving the spider gaping at it through the open airlock of the Probeship.

Helena's narration describes how that, at least, was Calder's story. She describes how, through brilliant work between Calder in the Command Module and Koenig at Mission Control on

Alpha, the Command Module went into a low orbit round Ultra, and then, using the gravity of the mysterious planet, blasted itself back in the direction of Earth's Moon. Another interplanetary Probeship was diverted, and Calder was picked up and brought back to Alpha.

Koenig meets Calder after his return. Calder tells him the story. His approach is, I know you won't believe it, but … And then he tells the story of the spider. Koenig jokingly refers to his battle with the spider as St. George and the Dragon, and outwardly Calder laughs, but inside there is very much a sense that he has failed his greatest challenge, that he turned and ran at precisely the moment when he should have stayed and fought.

While Koenig is talking to Calder, other experts are going over the Command Module. The bloodstained spacesuit and the axe are taken away for analysis and the blood on the floor is the subject of forensic scrutiny.

Calder is in his quarters on Alpha when Koenig comes to him ashen faced with the news that there is to be an official inquiry and that Calder is to be under arrest until that has taken place. He is to be questioned about the "murder" of Darwin King, Juliet Mackie, and Olga Vishenskya, and with dereliction of duty. In short Calder's story is just not believed by the Space Commissioners and he is to be arraigned and cross-questioned. Koenig has been allowed to tell him this news and makes an impassioned plea to be allowed to speak for him in defence.

Koenig, like everyone else, finds the story of the spider improbable, but because he knows the man better than anyone else, he believes it, if not implicitly, then at least he believes that something absolutely mind-wrenching must have happened out there.

Helena Russell is brought up from Earth to examine Calder medically and psychologically. She questions him about his way of life and in effect concludes that he is schizoid, that he is all the time confronting one aspect of his persona with the other, challenging the other to take over.

The inquiry sits, and Koenig is on his feet making the final speech in defence of Calder. It's an impassioned assault on chairborne administrators, an attack on the complacency that has induced them to believe that in deep space they will only find, broadly speaking, what they expect. As he sits down, he challenges the Commissioners to find Calder guilty.

ACT THREE

Helena's narration. The judgment against Calder was inconclusive. They simply didn't have sufficient evidence to press the charge of murder because they have no evidence from the other side. But Calder was taken off flying duties and his career was ruined. At a later date, thanks to the insistent manoeuvring of John Koenig, he was restored, but only as a shuttle pilot between Earth and Moonbase Alpha. And by chance he happened to be on Alpha when the Moon was blasted away from Earth.

Koenig comes to visit Calder again in the intensive care unit. He is still suffering the effects of the stun but showing signs of becoming conscious again. For Helena the episode with the Eagle is confirmation of her assessment of him as unbalanced. Koenig is deeply concerned by it but is more positive in his search for alternative reasons than is Helena.

Calder regains consciousness, and they begin to question him about the episode. He tells them of the spider nightmare, that he simply felt its web closing around him again and that he had to go and do something about it. He thanks Koenig for his constant support, but even believes himself that he is broken and that the spider nightmares are getting him down and that maybe the story he told them all was not true, but something concocted by a mind he didn't know was sick.

During this there is a call from Main Mission. They have a contact – a number of small contacts, as though a fleet of spaceships were approaching.

Koenig goes back to Main Mission. He sends out an Eagle to investigate.

Back in the care unit, Calder has another nightmare and Helena has to sedate him. He is reluctant to accept the effect of the sedative and goes under protesting loudly and talking about the threat to Alpha the spider represents.

Carter is out in the Eagle, and he sees the spaceships hanging there in space. Reports to Koenig, who orders him back.

Bergman scans the area with everything they've got. A recent development, Infrascan Nine, picks up the minuscule threads of the spider's web that has enmeshed all of the spaceships. They can see the limits of the web, and close to them they can see the body of the Ultra Probe.

ACT FOUR

Calder, the hunter, is now completely unconscious. He feigns weakness as he approaches Mathias, but as soon as he has Mathias where he wants him, he cuffs him unconscious with a karate blow, and takes his commlock. He makes his way out of the Medical Centre and towards the launch pads.

In Main Mission, the attention is all on the Ultra Probe. It is established that the Moon will not actually pass close to the web itself, but Koenig sees this as the opportunity finally to exonerate Calder from the allegations that have plagued him. Koenig orders preparations to be made for the launch of a docking Eagle, so that he, Helena, and Bergman can go and examine the wreckage for clues.

Now Calder makes his way ruthlessly into the stand-by Eagle. This time he makes no mistake about it. He stuns anyone in his way and takes their commlock. He gets into the Eagle and lifts off.

Koenig establishes that it's Calder who has taken the Eagle and goes after him in the docking Eagle. But Calder has a head start, and Koenig, with the aid of Infrascan Nine, has to manoeuvre past the threads of the web, whereas for some reason, Calder even without the infra aid, appears to be able to drive right past them. The web opens to receive him.

Calder reaches the Probeship first. He blasts the Command Module free of the rest of the Eagle and skilfully docks it into the Probeship. Inside we can see the spider beginning to stir, the spear tongue twitching expectantly as a life form approaches.

Calder takes the axe out of the crash locker and presses the button to open the airlock door. There lie the bodies of King, Mackie, and Vishenskya, exactly where he left them three years ago.

He looks at the reviving spider. The wound is still visible in its foreleg, but it has healed, leaving a scar. The spider sees Calder and makes its first lunge with the spear-tongue. But Calder is ready for it. He draws back behind the door, out of its way, and as it comes through the doorway he brings the axe down on it ferociously. The spider seems momentarily affected, and as it hesitates, Calder grabs hold of the tongue and attempts to break it against the edge of the door. But the spider withdraws the tongue very quickly and Calder falls as the door knocks him off the tongue. As he picks himself up, he sees the spider hesitating over him, his tongue retracted. Now Calder rushes forward and with a massive blow, brings the axe down on the spider's head. But it sticks there and while he is trying to get it out, the tongue darts out again and spikes him in the chest. Calder dies, but the spider wavers on its feet, obviously badly shaken by Calder's blows.

Koenig's Eagle approaches the Probeship and docks with the main body of the ship. Koenig tries to raise Calder but gets no reply. Finally, they decide to break into the Probeship to see what has happened, and there is the tableau for him to see. The spider, wounded, turns to meet him, but Koenig sees him withdraw his tongue from Calder and realises that this is the weapon he has to fear. He sees the axe sticking in the spider's head. Quickly, he closes the door again, and arms himself with the axe from the Eagle. Bergman and Helena each take lasers and as they open the door again, the spider stands groggily before them. Helena and Bergman blast away ineffectually with the lasers and the spear tongue flickers, hesitantly, not knowing which body to attack first. In the moment of hesitation, Koenig leaps on the spider and drives the axe deep into its head. As he pulls it out, blood gushes, and the spider sags to the floor.

They look around the Probeship. Helena examines Calder and is amazed to discover that he is only a husk. His insides have been sucked completely out. The other bodies are the same. The problem of the blood on the spacesuit is solved. The blood came from the crew members, and it was giving life and vitality to the spider. When Calder severed the skin on the foreleg, it was the blood of his own crew that poured out all over him.

Calder's nightmares are now believed. He, like they, could not really believe that what he had seen was real. But as he came closer to its presence, so the strength of his awareness of the spider increased, and the spider, dormant until some life form should fall into its web, began to stir for the first time in three years.

To Calder, it finally became the biggest challenge of his big game hunting career, and it defeated him – but not before he had dealt it a mortal blow.

They speculate about the nature of the spider's lifestyle and are thankful that the Moon is passing out of its reach. But just as they are beginning to feel comfortable, Helena sees four round objects beneath the body of the spider, and they are moving.

In its death throes, the spider has reproduced. They are eggs, and their presence, a life-form to be preyed upon, is encouraging them to hatch. They escape quickly and head away from the Probeship and away from the spider's web.

OBSERVATIONS

The genesis of Christopher Penfold's finest episode was always a horrific retelling of the tale of "St. George and the Dragon". While the monster spider was perhaps too elaborate to film, it's none-the-less fascinating to see parallels to the creature featured several years later in *Alien*, specifically the spear tongue (akin to the *Alien* Xenomorph monster's inner jaw) and the eggs that hatch upon sensing the presence of nearby prey. It's interesting that 'Calder' is the name of the principle guest character, Penfold acknowledged that he originally envisioned the tale as Alan Carter's backstory.

ALL THAT GLISTERS

Revised Draft – 9th February 1976

Final Shooting Script – 9th March 1976

by Keith Miles

Adapted by Robert E. Wood

KOENIG

(Voiceover Introduction)

Space 1999 – Moonbase Alpha.

A massive nuclear explosion...

Cause – human error!

The Moon is torn out of Earth orbit and hurled into

outer Space –

doomed to travel forever through hostile

environments...

PROLOGUE

Moonbase Alpha sat nestled in a crater on the Lunar surface, illuminated by distant starlight.

In the base's Medical Centre, Dr. Russell narrated crisply into a futuristic recorder. 'Moonbase Alpha. Status report. Three hundred and ten days since leaving Earth orbit. Doctor Helena Russell recording. Two days ago we encountered an asteroid, moving across our path at enormous speed. Our scanners indicated the presence of Milgonite – a rare mineral, vital to our life support systems. Eagle Four was dispatched immediately to carry out a full geological survey of the asteroid. Leading the reconnaissance team… Commander John Koenig…'

Eagle Four hurtled through the depths of space towards the asteroid, closing in fast.

In the Eagle's pilot section, Koenig and Alan Carter manned the controls. Behind them in the passenger section sat Maya, Tony Verdeschi, and geologist Dave Ellis.

Koenig nodded, 'Let's go down for a closer look.'

Alan hit a button. 'That's some cloud bank we're about to hit, Commander.'

'I almost forgot what clouds look like,' said Koenig, smiling.

Eagle Four descended from the blackness of space into the cloud bank.

As the Eagle shot through the clouds, the asteroid's surface revealed itself as grey and pitted for the most part. At its centre was a large, shallow crater, giving off a dull, yellow glow. Eagle Four aimed toward the shallow crater.

Maya was at the controls in the Eagle's passenger section, watching the screen. Dave Ellis stood at her shoulder, a lean, solidly built man around forty, whose rugged face still bore some weather-beaten vestiges of Earth. He seemed more interested in Maya than in anything on the screen.

'We now have close visual contact,' said Maya.

Dave grinned. 'The closer the better,' he said in his slight regional drawl.

'Too close too quickly could be dangerous,' Maya replied with Alien naiveté.

Dave's grin broadened as he put his face closer to hers. 'Definitely.'

Tony and Helena, seated nearby, heard the exchange. 'She's a big girl, Tony,' said Helena.

Verdeschi nodded sourly. 'But loudmouth Romeos aren't in her experience.'

Helena smiled to assure him. 'She's a quick learner.'

Koenig called back from the pilot section, his image appearing on a monitor. 'What have you got for us, Maya?'

Maya looked up at her screen. 'Geophysical scan confirms presence of large deposits of Milgonite.'

'We got us a giant jackpot sitting down there waiting for us to come take it home!' Dave interjected.

Maya continued. 'Location of Milgonite – asteroid reference 075. In that central crater.'

'Life signs?' asked Koenig.

'Some kind of life form is registering, minimal and unidentifiable,' replied Maya.

'Atmosphere?'

Maya scanned the data. 'Oxygen, nitrogen, inert gasses, hydrogen…'

Dave moved forward and put a hand on Maya's shoulder. 'It's breathable, Commander!'

'Temperature?'

'Almost eighty-seven degrees,' Maya answered.

Dave grinned at her. 'Getting warmer every second.'

Maya cast her strange wide eyes at him expressionlessly. 'On my planet, Psychon, where I am from… eighty-seven degrees would freeze you to death.'

Dave, who didn't need any rocks to fall on his head if Maya had meant this last for him, removed his hand from her shoulder with a good-natured grin, cupped his hands together, and blew as though to warm them up. 'Guess old Dave the geologist fell on his face in the rocks on that one.'

'Prepare for landing!' ordered Koenig.

In the pilot section, Koenig and Alan continued to man the controls.

'Put us down in that crater, Alan,' said Koenig.

Alan nodded and hit a button.

On command, Eagle Four made its approach toward the crater, which was now glowing more distinctly.

In the Eagle's passenger section Helena, Maya, and Tony were seated and strapped in, while Dave sat on the arm of his seat.

'You'd better strap yourself in, David, before you do more than fall on your face,' said Helena with amusement over Dave's last remark to Maya.

Dave shrugged the suggestion off with a nod in the direction of the pilot section, 'I've got complete faith in the pilot.'

Just then, Eagle Four landed and juddered, throwing Dave forward. Helena and Maya laughed as Dave corrected himself, grinning sheepishly.

Tony nodded good naturedly. 'Looks like we've got ourselves a clown, not a geologist, on this rock hunt.'

Eagle Four had come to rest in the yellow sand at the edge of the crater.

In the pilot section, Koenig asked, 'How much time before we lose our range with Alpha?'

Alan made a quick check on range instrumentation, getting the fix. 'With Alpha's speed… the speed of this asteroid… three hours.' He looked up at Koenig meaningfully. 'If we don't blast off in three hours, we lose Alpha. And that's cutting it down to the bottom line, John.'

Koenig nodded, then led Alan back into the passenger section of the ship, where Maya, Tony and Helena were unstrapping and getting up. Dave picked up a large pack, marked **GEOLOGY KIT**.

'We've got exactly three hours to find that Milgonite, pack it aboard and get out before Alpha is too far gone!' Koenig announced.

'Commander – the way I read the book, that Milgonite is going to come to us!' said Dave.

Koenig ignored him. 'Maya, program the timer for three hours.'

Maya hit a button on the computer console. Instantly, a distinctive, electronic beep signal came over, followed by the toneless computer voice, it's countdown already underway.

'Minus two hours fifty-nine minutes, forty-eight seconds,' said the computer.

And with that, the group realised that the time bomb had begun ticking away.

Koenig broke the momentary silence with a look to Alan. 'Better bring a stun gun just in case… Tony hang in here with Helena.'

'John, I should go with you…' Helena cut over. 'There could be environmental hazards?'

Koenig dismissed her suggestion with a smile. 'Somebody

has to mind the store…' he said, then added to Tony, 'Keep your commlock open. We'll yell if we need you.'

Koenig opened the door to exit and nodded for the others to follow. Dave hoisted his geology kit over a shoulder, moving behind Maya who trailed Koenig. Alan removed a weapon from its place in the wall weapons rack and moved out in Dave's wake.

'Good hunting,' said Helena.

Koenig, Maya, Dave, and Alan stepped out onto the Alien sand as the door closed behind them, gazing around at their surroundings in awe. The crater was filled with strange, amazing rock formations of all colours, some opaque, most luminescent. A soft, throbbing glow illuminated all, almost haloesque.

'Glory be…' said Dave with reverence.

'What do you make of it, Dave?' asked Koenig.

Dave started to gradually wander forward through the rock field, shaking his head slowly in reply to Koenig's question, his eyes taking it all in. 'I don't know… I've never seen anything like this before.' He stopped and hunkered down before some of the faintly glowing rocks as the others came up alongside him.

'Milgonite?' asked Koenig.

Without answering, Dave pulled a mini hand scanner from his kit, equipped with a meter to register mineral printout. Dave aimed it at the cluster of rocks and eyed the scanner meter, frowning slightly.

Maya noted his strange expression. 'What is it, Dave?'

Dave continued to study the meter, which failed to register any signs. 'Zero… it doesn't make sense.' He looked up at Koenig. 'It shouldn't be… something should register. There's got to be an energy source for this glow from somewhere.'

The group all detected the sense of Dave's unfulfilled questioning.

'Don't look at me, Cowboy,' said Alan, 'I'm only the astronaut around here.'

Dave seemed not to hear Alan and pivoted his head as though he were scanning the terrain. 'Man, I can almost feel it…' Dave said as he started off in a direction through some encircling rocks.

'You get any vibrations of any kind, Maya?' Koenig asked.

Maya placed two fingers of each hand to temples on either side of her head, then shut her eyes in silence and absolute concentration. In her Psychon mind came the distinctive sound of pulsating brain waves, but it was an even sound – no distress signals. Maya removed her fingers from each side of her head, opened her eyes, and looked at Koenig. 'Negative, John.'

Koenig nodded with no undue concern, cool, yet cautious and alert. He moved after Dave. Maya and Alan followed, the latter taking a firmer grip on his stun gun.

Koenig, Maya, and Alan pursued Dave across the asteroid's surface and came to a bend through a wall of rocks. As they rounded the corner and came into open view, they were struck by an explosion of unbelievable blinding luminescent light – its effect that of sudden impact, rocking them back as though they had been shot. Bedazzled, they were scattered, and half dropped to their knees as they shielded their eyes against its brilliance.

Koenig was the first to recover, and he stared ahead at a glowing crystalline structure about the size of a huge boulder, different from the other rocks and monolithic in shape. Its hue was a deep yellow and it contained crystal formations within its structure that were not uniformly cubic. But what struck Koenig the most was that its glow had a heartbeat regularity.

Maya, Alan, and Dave also recovered as their eyes adjusted to the glare, and they started to move in on the rock.

'I knew it! I knew there had to be something!' Dave said ecstatically as he moved closer to the rock and bent down, about to kiss it. 'Milgonite, say hello to Big Dave… Mmmm <u>whah</u>!'

He glanced up to find Koenig looming over him and gestured to the rock. 'How about that, Commander?'

'If I can break up this romance between you and the rock…' Koenig said wryly.

'Rocks understand me, Commander,' Dave replied. 'None of my wives ever did; but rocks do.'

'Good,' said Koenig. 'How about bringing a sample to the Eagle for computer analysis.'

'You're playing my song,' Dave replied as he opened his kit to extract a laser gun.

'Song?' Maya asked. 'I don't hear any music.'

'You will, Maya. You will.' Dave winked at her confidentially then aimed the laser gun at the rock and fired. The laser beam cut into the rock and sliced off a small section which fell to the ground. To the amazement of the Alphans, the cut mark on the larger rock then began to produce a golden, syrup-like secretion.

'Crazy…' said Dave slowly, not understanding.

'Let's find out how crazy,' Koenig stated.

Inside Eagle Four's passenger section Koenig, Helena, Tony, Dave, and Alan were clustered around Maya as a straight, unwavering line ran across the monitor screen. With no sound and no computations, the single line indicated zero information on the rock.

'Computer negative,' said Koenig.

Dave shook his head. 'I don't buy it… that rock has got to hook us into where Milgonite is.'

'Try the petroscope, David,' suggested Helena as she moved toward it.

Dave followed Helena to the petroscope, a futuristic petrological microscope with double lens, but Tony moved forward quickly and stopped Dave as he was about to peer in.

'Mind if I have a look, first?' Tony asked, a slight grin hiding any fears or anxieties he might harbour. 'Security measure… you know.'

Dave waved him to the petroscope with a "be-my-guest" gesture. Tony bended to put his eye to the instrument. As he did, a blinding orange flash enveloped him, and he seemed to become alive with an electrical charge for a second before collapsing.

The sudden phenomena also affected the others, but their reactions to it were like a sting of pain and they winced sharply.

Koenig was first to recover, steadying Helena, as, with the others, they reacted to the sight of Tony in a crumpled heap on the floor.

'Tony!' called Koenig as he and Helena hunkered at Tony's body, the others looming behind them.

Helena performed an instant check on Tony… carotid vein… heart… pulse… then stared up at the others before slowly pronouncing, 'He's dead!'

The others reacted with shocked silence, as suddenly the computer voice chimed, 'Minus two hours five minutes nine seconds…'

ACT ONE

On the asteroid, the rock's yellow glow seemed to be throbbing stronger, brighter… any residuals of its syrupy content were now absorbed as though self-cauterised, and there was no longer any visible evidence of the laser gash.

In the passenger section of Eagle Four the scanner screen registered a series of unique and varied visual readings.

Helena monitored the scanner screen console connected to a series of wired electrodes running from the equipment to various parts of Tony's body, which was laid out on a table. 'Brain waves normal,' she reported. 'Blood temperature slightly lowered…'

A concerned Koenig, a worried Maya, an alert Alan, and a thoughtful Dave eyed the proceedings… every once in a while, Dave's eyes cast a fleeting glance at the rock sample still fixed at the petroscope.

Helena continued. 'No impairment of internal organs – all functions normal…'

Koenig cut over her report. 'Except for his heart and his lungs. He's not breathing, he's had cardiac arrest. He's dead, but he's still alive, is that what you're saying, Helena?'

Helena didn't answer Koenig, intent upon the last printout of readings displayed on the scope. She hit a switch on the console operating scope, which triggered a low whine that gained in intensity. A feeling of urgency rose among Koenig, Maya, Alan, and Dave as Tony's body twitched with induced spasm-like convulsions.

Helena turned a dial on the console, increasing the power and the subsequent whining sound. Tony's body arched in response.

'This may shock his heart back…' Helena said, taut and clipped.

'…It might destroy the rest of him!' said Koenig.

'I've got to risk that!'

Helena's eyes were fixed on the blips tracing across the scope screen – irregular at first, then starting to form a pattern of regularity. A moment of hope, broken as the blips went crazy and dissolved into a discordant melody.

Tony's body went inert again.

It was a battle for a life that had been lost, and Helena never liked losing that kind of battle. The only principal life-sign functions left registering on the scope screen were Tony's brain waves. She turned round to face Koenig and the others. 'No use,' she said.

'But he began to respond,' Koenig replied.

'I'm only a doctor, John – not a miracle worker!' Helena stated with frustration. 'I can cope with the known... the unknown sends any doctor back into the Dark Ages.'

Maya eyed the scope screen intensely. 'Tony's brain is still functioning, Helena.'

Helena gave a paradoxical smile. 'One of the mysteries of life, Maya.'

The sound of the computer voice snapped them all back to reality. '*Minus one hour fifty-six minutes ten seconds.*'

With that prompt, Dave hefted the geology kit and turned to exit the ship.

'Where do you think you're going?' asked Alan.

'Out,' said Dave, indicating the door. 'Out there to find what I came looking for.'

'Is that all you can think about now?' asked Maya.

'You heard the doctor, she said Tony is dead, and I'm sorry about that... Tony was a good guy, but I'm a geologist,' said Dave.

Koenig was torn between different kinds of dilemma over this but nodded. 'Alpha needs that Milgonite.'

'And I'm going back out,' said Dave, smiling his victory. 'It's what I'm here for... my job... what I'm getting paid for.' He eyed Koenig evenly. 'You understand, Commander?' he asked as he started for the door.

'Hold it, Ellis!' Koenig called.

Dave stopped at the door and turned round to face Koenig.

'You understand this... all of you,' said Koenig, who then indicated the petroscope. 'Off bounds from here in – nobody goes near it... Nobody looks in it, until we know more about it.'

Dave smiled wryly. 'Me... I've got twenty-twenty vision, Commander,' he said, then exited the ship.

Koenig stared after him for an instant, sensing Dave's challenge of his authority, but had greater problems at hand. He nodded to Alan. 'Keep him company.'

Alan returned the nod, hoisted the rocket gun over his shoulder, and moved out after Dave.

Maya stared at Tony, then at Helena. 'Is there any hope for him... will he always be like this, Helena?'

'There's always hope,' said Helena, looking again at the scope screen. 'His brain is still alive.'

'Mind over matter – but how much matter over mind, Helena?' Koenig asked.

Helena gave a faint, rueful smile. 'Sorry you asked that, John... I've got no answers.'

Koenig eyed the petroscope and rock sample. 'That?'

Helena shrugged unknowingly. She encircled Tony's body, checking the electrode wiring to make certain Tony was still hooked up to the scanner screen.

Maya came alongside Helena and stared into her eyes intensely. 'Try, Helena... try and save him!'

'I'm trying. I'm trying every way I can!' Helena said, gesturing at all the equipment around her.

'If I could take Tony's form... his image?' Maya suggested.

'In his condition, you couldn't communicate,' said Koenig.

'"They" wouldn't know – "them"... "those"... or whatever – whoever,' said Maya. 'I would <u>be</u> Tony. I would become myself again in one hour!'

'Maybe we should get Tony back to the medical facilities at Alpha,' proposed Koenig.

'I can't do any more for him at Alpha,' said Helena. 'If there's a cure, it's here, John.'

Koenig nodded. 'In that rock.'

Among the rocks on the surface of the asteroid, Dave supervised the operation of an energy rod inserted into a hole drilled in the ground. Koenig, Alan, and Maya were with him. Koenig carried a torch-like object, while Maya was stationed at a portable power unit.

'Power on, Maya,' said Dave.

She punched a switch at Dave's command, triggering an instant power sound, and a tape began to issue from a slot on the meter.

Dave took the tape, reading the printout as he let it reel out through his fingers. 'Quartz… orthoclase.. hornblende… augite… olivine… feldspar…' The ticker tape ceased, leaving Dave puzzled and frowning.

'No Milgonite?' asked Koenig.

'There has to be! Our computer confirmed it!' Dave replied.

'You might have made a wrong reading,' suggested Koenig.

'No way. I checked and double-checked. It printed out every component part!'

'The computer could have had a malfunction,' said Alan.

'That's the human mind for you,' said Dave. 'Doubt… disbelief… man, the computer printed out every component part of Milgonite… And I read it straight.' Dave turned to Maya. 'Set up the microscope, Maya. I want a look at that rock fluid on a slide.'

'I told you – nobody cuts up that rock, nobody looks at it!' Koenig replied sharply.

'You've got your answers to find, I've got mine,' said Dave, quietly. He then broke into a slight, taut smile. 'Besides… it's my neck on the line, Commander.'

Koenig thought for a moment, then smiled assent.

In the passenger section of Eagle Four, Tony's head was fitted with a cluster of electrodes. Helena monitored the computer screen at a console, her back to Tony's body. The screen was registering some rather strange activity, puzzling Helena. She glanced over her shoulder at Tony, who continued to lie inert.

Helena turned her full attention back to the screen again, hit a button and made one or two adjustments, but the computer activity was not checked. Her puzzlement gave way to certain wonderment and concern as she turned her eyes to the rock sample, which began to glow a fierce mixture of orange and yellow, the yellow gradually becoming more dominant.

On the asteroid's surface, Dave peered into a portable field microscope, Koenig and Alan on either side of him as Maya operated the power unit. As he studied the rock syrup on a slide, Dave witnessed what appeared to be a flowing yellow lava-like sea, separating from itself, and spreading in all directions.

'What do you make of it?' Koenig asked.

'Don't know… can't be a source of power… I would've been struck dead right off the bat like Tony,' said Dave as he straightened and turned to Koenig. 'Have a look for yourself. Maya, brighten the light under the slide, would you, please?'

Maya made an adjustment on the power unit.

Dave grinned. 'Go ahead, Commander. It won't bite you.'

Koenig grinned back, then peered into the lens and studied the fluid on the slide. 'Like blood corpuscles… only they keep separating and spreading.'

'My guess – whatever that stuff – it feeds the nerve system of the rock,' said Dave.

'Then the rock must be an organism… a life form,' Maya realised.

Dave nodded. 'It's alive, all right.'

'And lethal,' said Koenig, grimly.

In Eagle Four's passenger section, Helena sat at the console, with computer activity still building and her back to Tony, who lay as still as before.

At that moment Tony's body bifurcated; his solid body remained prostrate, but an opaque, profile body – "Tony II" –

rose up out of it. It solidified, collected his commlock and laser, and turned, as though drawn, to the rock sample.

The rock emitted a tiny flash of yellow light and a single electronic ping, unnoticed by Helena. But the light flash and ping of noise seemed to program Tony II; the image turned and let itself out through the door.

As the door closed silently after Tony II, Helena turned from the still active computer to cross quickly to Tony. She looked at him worriedly, then up at the encephalogram with astonishment. Its graph paper record displayed normal brain activity giving way to sudden hyper-activity as the tracer needle moved violently on its course.

Helena didn't like what she saw and slowly turned her gaze to Tony's body.

Tony II headed slowly for the rocks on the asteroid's surface, his body movements as though under some hypnotic control.

At their place amongst the rocks, Dave put the microscope and other materials into his geology kit as Koenig stared intensely at him.

'What made that rock in the Eagle have the power to kill Tony? Yet here it left us alone?' Koenig asked, but before Dave could answer, Koenig's commlock buzzed. He grabbed the device from his belt. 'Yes, Helena?'

'Trouble, John…'

'What kind of trouble?' said Koenig, alert to potential danger.

'The computer seems to have gone out of control… and something very strange is happening to Tony!'

'Be right there!' said Koenig. 'Alan!' he gestured for Carter to come with him, then eyed Dave and Maya. 'You, too.'

'In a little bit, Commander,' replied Dave. 'You don't mind, I want to take a hydrostat reading… got a hunch it may tell me something. Milgonite is usually found where there's an underground water supply.'

Koenig eyed Maya.

'If I could stay with Dave, John… We might find something to help Tony.'

'Make it fast!' said Koenig urgently before he and Alan hurried back in the direction of Eagle Four.

Dave scanned the terrain and pointed off, away from the rock. 'We'll set up over there,' he said, taking his kit as Maya followed.

Tony II approached the rock, which glowed yellow, and aimed his laser. The laser cut the rock, slicing off a larger portion than before, and as the chunk fell away the golden secretion flowed from the parent body.

Tony II picked up the cutting of heavy rock without effort and started away…

Koenig and Alan had joined Helena in the passenger section of Eagle Four, watching Tony's body with concern.

'When did you first notice the change in him, Helena?' Koenig asked.

'It wasn't so much the change in his brain wave recordings on the encephalograph. I could understand the possibilities of some abnormality… but the disappearance of the laser and commlock – that is something else,' said Helena, obviously distraught.

Koenig and Alan exchanged a knowing glance and a shrug. Alan started conducting a placation search while Koenig turned to Helena and suggested, 'They could have rolled on the floor when Tony fell.'

'I checked everywhere,' she said as she turned round to face Koenig. 'And I'm not that uptight, if that's what you think, John.'

The Eagle's door opened, and Tony II entered, carrying the rock.

Helena saw Tony II first and stared in disbelief. 'John...?' she said, in a low voice.

Koenig and Alan spun and saw the image. They stared, sharing Helena's disbelief. Helena started toward the image, but Koenig cut her off. 'Hold it, Helena!'

Helena froze as she watched the image of Tony II put down the new larger chunk of rock next to the first sample, then replace the commlock and laser in Tony's belt and rejoin his body.

Koenig looked at Helena, and while he didn't know all the answers, he did know that Helena had not been fantasising.

Suddenly a sound from the computer screen notified them of a printout from the encephalograph. The tracer needle had resumed normal readings.

'It's returning to the normal pattern for an unconscious brain,' said Helena slowly.

The two rock segments were mere inches apart when the larger one, glowing with bright yellow light, started drawing the original, small section toward it. They fused, and their combined glow was even brighter.

'I see it, I don't believe it,' said Alan.

The computer screen began to go crazy, and Koenig went to the console and started hitting buttons in vain.

'It's taking over the computer. Alan... get to flight control!' Koenig ordered, tautly.

Alan headed for the pilot section as Koenig and Helena followed. As the pair entered, Alan was already working at the controls. 'No response,' he said.

'Switch to manual,' said Koenig as he slipped into the seat next to Alan.

Alan made the attempt but there was still no response. 'All systems dead.'

Koenig hit the com switches. 'Eagle Four to Moonbase – come in Moonbase – Eagle Four to Moonbase...'

There was no reply from Moonbase Alpha, but the computer's countdown chimed, 'Minus one hour one minute fifty-nine seconds.

ACT TWO

On the surface of the asteroid, in the pilot section of Eagle Four, Commander John Koenig continued his urgent calls. 'Eagle Four to Moonbase Alpha... Eagle Four to Moonbase Alpha... Do you read us? Over...'

In the passenger module behind Koenig and Alan, bathed in the pulsating yellow glow of the rock sample, Helena tentatively checked Tony's motionless body, unable to shake the sight of Tony II's image.

'This is an emergency. Repeat – an emergency. Eagle Four requests immediate help. Come in please!' Koenig called desperately. 'Moonbase Alpha, we need you!'

'We're wasting breath, John. Control systems are not functioning,' said Alan.

'Open all frequencies and switch to automatic,' Koenig said briskly as he rose from the controls to go back into the passenger section. 'Check out all circuitry... insulation... hang in... keep trying.'

'Will do.'

Koenig stepped back into the passenger section and found Helena trying to get a response from an EKG she was taking of Tony. 'Any change?' he asked.

'None.'

Koenig noted that nothing was registering on the EKG and stared at Tony's body. 'So how does one get up and walk around with a dead heart?'

'I wish there was a simple explanation,' answered Helena.

Koenig lifted his eyes to the rock and came to a sudden decision. 'The rock goes.'

'You can't! The rock may be the key to save Tony.'

'To all intents and purposes, Tony is dead, you said so! But if Tony should survive, he could come out of it a vegetable. We can't sit around waiting for us to be next!'

Koenig started toward the rock determinedly, but Helena attempted to stop him.

'Leave it alone, John – it could kill you!'

'So could old age,' was Koenig's wry but grim response as he began to reach for the rock. Suddenly, the rock's orange flash erupted, but this time it quickly turned a deep blue.

The flash of blue light shone through the door and illuminated the pilot section as well. Alan reacted with alarm and quickly jumped out of his seat.

As the blue light struck Koenig, he let out a cry of sharp pain, stumbled back and sunk to his knees, clutching his sides in pain.

Alan burst through and – along with Helena – rushed to help Koenig to a seat.

'It's okay! I'm all right…' said Koenig, catching his breath. 'Obviously my heart's still beating.'

Helena, who had been checking his pulse, nodded.

'What happened?' Alan asked.

'The rock hit with a blue light this time… It was double the pain,' Koenig paused as his eyes returned to the rock. 'I wonder which colour light kills.'

The yellow glow had returned to the rock, making one think of a lingering grin.

'Look at it,' said Koenig, still staring at the rock. 'Like it knows it has us trapped.' He started to rise from the seat, but Helena stopped him.

'Cool off, John, you've had a rough shock to your system.'

'No time to cool,' said Koenig as he eyed Alan. 'Any luck?'

Alan shook his head in reply.

Koenig returned his attention to the rock. 'We've got to find out what makes that thing tick.'

'If it's responsible for blocking out our com system, I wish it would let us know the reason why,' said Alan.

Koenig threw a sharp glance at Alan, then rose and moved in a slow circle about Tony's inert body. 'Maybe it <u>was</u> trying to communicate… say something.'

'But why here – us – what's the attraction?' Alan asked.

'It could be angry,' suggested Helena. 'Its natural habitat is out there. We took it out of that habitat.'

Koenig paused, facing them both. 'Did we, Helena…? Or did it bring <u>us</u> to <u>it</u>?'

'If it fouled up the computer just now, it could have brainwashed the computer into believing Milgonite was here. And we fell into the trap,' said Alan, smiling wryly. 'Won't that make the Cowboy jump with joy.'

Helena had returned to Tony's body and took his wrist to feel his pulse. There was no beat, but also no reaction from her as her mind struggled to make medical and scientific sense out of the cryptic. 'Then its energy took over Tony's body… using his image to slice off that other piece of rock from its parent body and bring it back… and had the biological powers to fuse itself with it.'

'But what does it want?' Koenig asked.

Helena stared at the rock. 'To survive? And when it gets what it wants, maybe it will release Tony?'

'All right,' said Alan. 'One more time, then. What does it want?'

'There's only one way to find out,' Koenig said, almost a whisper, as an ominous feeling of jeopardy hung over them all.

Among the rocks on the asteroid's surface, Maya and Dave studied the data from the hydrostat's round register meter, its two outer dials resembling a pair of eyes set in a face.

'Dry as the bleached bones of a coyote,' said Dave, disgusted.

Maya was puzzled by the foreign word. 'Coyote?'

'Yeah… coyote – like a wolf.'

'Wolf?'

'Well, yeah… wolf, Maya. If you didn't know and you saw one, you'd think it was a dog.'

'Dog…?'

Dave started to explain further, then stopped himself short with a futile gesture, smiling. 'Forget it,' he said, then shook his head over the hydrostat readings. 'I don't dig it. There's <u>been</u> water here. Geologically speaking, there <u>should</u> be water here, yet the whole asteroid is like a desert.'

'What happened to the Milgonite?' Maya wondered.

'Don't say <u>happened</u>, think positive.'

'But something is wrong, Dave. There are clouds above that have dropped no rain… The hydrostat says so. Even on my planet the clouds drop rain.'

Dave was frustrated. 'I'm not looking for reasons why there is no rain, Maya. That could be an ecological goof-up that took place, but I <u>am</u> looking for Milgonite.'

The sound of Alan's voice suddenly interrupted them. 'Not on this asteroid, Cowboy…'

Dave and Maya turned around at the sound of Alan's voice to see Koenig and Alan approaching.

'What's that supposed to mean, Astronaut?' asked Dave.

'Just what he said: No Milgonite,' Koenig replied. 'Your computer reading was right, but the source was all wrong.'

'What source?' asked Dave, slowly.

'The rock. The rock, friend,' Koenig answered. 'It programmed our computer to get us here on the pretence we'd find Milgonite. That rock has power, energy, intelligence, and purpose. At this moment, it has control of Eagle Four; we can't lift off, we can't communicate with Alpha. In other words, Cowboy, we're stuck here.'

'You talk like it's alive,' said Dave.

'It is a life form. No doubt the one we picked up on our sensor before we touched down. What we don't know, is its purpose.'

Maya had been listening quite intensely, absorbed by what Koenig was saying. 'A life form?'

'I could hardly wait for you to ask,' Koenig said with a faint smile and forced lightness.

'If I can reach it, I may learn its purpose. I could save Tony.'

'Hey, wait a minute, Maya,' said Dave. 'You saw how that rock acts, what it's done.' He turned to Koenig. 'You're asking a lot of her.'

'I know.'

Maya started to walk toward the rock, its glow somewhat diminished, when Koenig stopped her.

'It can be very dangerous, Maya,' the commander warned.

Maya nodded her acknowledgement of the risk.

Dave glared from one to the other. 'Then why ask her to do it?'

'There's no other way,' stated Koenig.

'Because you can't think of one?' asked Dave, truculently.

Koenig was fighting his anger. 'Got any suggestions?'

'Not off the top of my head.'

'Then why don't you give your mouth a rest?' interjected Alan.

'Look…' started Dave.

'Okay. Discussion ended!' declared Koenig.

Dave glared at him as Koenig turned to Maya. 'Ready?'

But Maya had already left during their argument. Koenig, Dave, and Alan looked toward Maya who stood just a few feet away from the rock. Utilising her Psychon powers of molecular transformation, Maya's form shimmered, and she metamorphosed into a segment of the rock, about the size of the piece moved by Tony II.

The Maya rock was quite close to the parent rock, which suddenly began to glow. Koenig, Alan, and Dave all saw the sudden glow, with mixed reactions.

'If that rock is talking to her, I hope Maya understands the lingo,' said Dave, while Koenig and Alan were too intent upon the sight to reply.

The parent rock attracted Maya, pulling her ever so slowly, yet inextricably closer.

Alan stared at Koenig. 'Happy talk, John...'

Koenig's silence was an indication that he might be worried.

'...I hope,' added Alan, neither as a question or a statement, merely an utterance, or a prayer.

Koenig nodded.

'If that thing is really alive, and is really talking to Maya, then it's off guard...' said Dave as he pulled out his stun gun and aimed it at the rock.

Koenig leapt at him, knocking the gun aside. Dave fell heavily to the ground as Koenig glared down at him.

'I was only trying to find out if our weapons could be effective against it,' the geologist said.

'You fool,' spat Koenig.

'I had it on stun. I wasn't trying to kill it.'

'Suppose it killed Maya in reaction?' stated Koenig, savagely.

'I wanted to help Maya!' Dave shouted back in his own defence.

'To her grave,' added Alan.

Meanwhile, the parent rock was still glowing and Maya in her rock form was now almost having tactile communication with it.

'Hold it, baby... no closer... freeze right there,' whispered Dave under his breath.

Koenig and Alan were intent. Koenig pondered if he did wrong letting Maya do this, but was silent about his thoughts.

Then the Maya rock shimmered and the Psychon resumed her normal form. As Maya rejoined Koenig, Alan, and Dave, there was general relief all round, but Maya looked serious. 'It's friendly. It intends us no harm,' she said.

'Then why did it do this to us... to Tony?' Koenig asked.

'It's dying. It's been slowly weakening for months. If it does not get to another energy source soon, it will die forever.'

'What is its energy source?' wondered Koenig.

'Water.'

'But there's no water here!' stated Dave.

'It reached out to us, to take it to water...' Maya said, pausing. 'Call it... its deception.'

'But it didn't have to hijack our Eagle!' Koenig stated. 'We could have helped it... taken it to a planet with water.'

'No way that way, Commander... this old cow has got a deep thirst... it's why this asteroid will always have a drought,' said Dave as he eyed Koenig wryly. 'And you know what, Commander? I may be a dumb geologist, but this much I know: if we travel with that rock in the Eagle – forget it.' His smile spelled doom. 'The human body is mostly water.'

Dave's words hit Koenig with full significant force. He grabbed his commlock and called into it. 'Helena!'

In the passenger section of Eagle Four, Helena's expression was stark as she kept her eyes fixed on Tony's still inert body.

Koenig's call came over her commlock. 'Do you hear me, Helena?'

Suddenly Helena's face was flooded with a green light emanating from the rock sample, but she kept her eyes on Tony as the beam of green light stretched across his body. She gripped her commlock and activated it, her voice low and taut. 'Yes, I hear you, John.'

'Get out! It's not safe – get out fast!'

Despite her terror, Helena kept her voice softly modulated as though not to give way to her inner feelings of fear and not to let the rock know that she feared it.

'Yes, I know that, John... I'm trying to get out. I'm trying,' she said, slowly moving toward the door, barely a step at a time...

Koenig heard the fearful tone in Helena's voice and there was no need for words to describe it, or his gut feeling that Helena was helpless. He nodded at the others, and they all took off on the run for Eagle Four...

The green light still framed Helena, never leaving her face, her body. She made a sudden attempt to reach the door, but as she did, the light intensified, spreading itself out the distance between her and the door, stopping her dead in her tracks, acting as an impenetrable wall.

Koenig, Alan, Dave, and Maya ran towards Eagle Four. They stopped as Koenig gestured not to go too close to the craft.

'Hold it right here!' Koenig ordered, then spoke into his commlock. 'We're outside the ship, Helena.'

Helena aimed her commlock at the door, but the green light narrowed swiftly on her commlock in a pencil-like beam. The door would not open.

'Commlock won't open door,' Helena called, still virtually immobilised by the light beam.

Koenig aimed his own commlock at the Eagle hatch without success. 'Try the computer.'

Helena slowly backed away, past Tony's body, in an attempt to reach the computer but as she did the green light exploded with a short staccato burst of even brighter green, hurling her away.

'I can't get to it... light... from the rock... stopped me.'

'What colour?' Koenig asked.

'Green.' Even as Helena said the words, the brightness increased to almost dazzling brilliance, holding her in a fixed, rigid state.

'Any pain?'

'Numb... can't move... no feeling...'

Outside the ship on the asteroid's surface the group considered the situation.

'I should have smashed that rock,' said Dave.

'I could transform and get in, John?'

'No, Maya.'

Before Maya could protest, Helena's voice cut over their discussion and snapped them to attention. 'The light is intensifying... beginning to cover my body...'

The group's concern slowly built to expressions of horror. Dave made a break for the door, but as he touched it, he was instantly hurled back by a force of electrical energy.

The green light continued to narrow on Helena's face, closing in... closing in... 'Oh, no...' she said, barely audibly, as the light obliterated all but her face.

ACT THREE

Inside Eagle Four's passenger section, the light had not yet fully enveloped Helena.

'Helena!' Koenig called to her through the commlock, but she couldn't reply. 'Helena!' he repeated, with greater concern.

The light beam on Helena suddenly held and wavered for an instant, then began to retreat, leaving her with a mixture of relief and wonderment as her eyes followed the light.

As the light beam moved off Helena, she watched it, wonderingly.

'The light has moved away from me. It's feeling its way across the storage supply wall.'

'Can you move?'

'No,' said Helena, still locked in position and only able to move her head.

The light beam held and focused on a large metal container built into the wall, marked **WATER**.

'What is the light doing?' asked Koenig.

'It's fixed itself on the water supply…'

On the asteroid's surface Koenig exchanged grim looks with the others at this, as it confirmed their theories about the rock.

Koenig was taut. 'Do nothing to distract it, Helena!'

Helena watched with wonderment as the light beam intensified – the green fading into pale yellow as it started to burn through the metal container. The metal suddenly ripped apart, but the water did not spill out. Instead, the flow of water was drawn through the air as if coming through an invisible hosepipe toward the rock. Upon contact, the water was absorbed by the rock which then seemed to become revived and began to glisten bright yellow again.

Helena was amazed at this, but slowly realised what it meant as she witnessed the transfusion-like effect the water had on the rock, which glowed even more fiercely. 'John, the rock has absorbed the water… every drop,' she said.

'Yes, we know,' came Koenig's grim reply.

'That's the answer isn't it, John…' said Helena, her fears confirmed. 'To survive it must have water. It's brought us here to take it to water. And it will get water – any way it can.'

'Helena, that isn't going to happen to you… we'll find a way to get in, we'll…' said Koenig as he realised what she was thinking. But his voice was interrupted by the sound of the Eagle's engines starting.

Helena was startled, to say the least, and stared around. Tony's body was still inert, and the rock still glowed, but she had no view of the pilot section from where she was rooted.

Outside the ship, the roar of Eagle Four's engines was deafening. The group, unable to hear each other over the sound, scattered and took cover against the swirling sand kicked up by the mounting power of the engines.

The rock sample in the passenger section glowed fiercely, holding Helena rigid yet alarmed at the idea of lift-off. Computer was at peak activity, and in the nearby pilot section an invisible hand seemed to depress various buttons on the control panels as the roar of the engines built. The screen printout displayed: **LIFT-OFF**.

The Eagle's engines had reached peak roar, sand swirled around the ship, and lift-off was imminent.

The parent rock glowed with an intensity almost at a peak with the roar of the engines.

Koenig and the others huddled among the rocks. Sand swirled all around them and it was impossible for anyone to move against the tremendous onslaught of air pressure created by the engines.

Inside the pilot section, an invisible hand hit more buttons. On screen a printout read: **ABORT LIFT-OFF**. The engines started to cut out.

Helena felt immediate relief as the engines started to die. She could see there was no change in Tony's condition, but the rock sample seemed to glow with satisfaction.

Outside the ship the group watched with relief as the engines cut out and the sand began to settle.

'The engines are cutting out,' said Dave, hopefully. 'Maybe Doc Russell got loose and got her hands on the controls.'

But Alan dampened Dave's hopes. 'She's had no training… wouldn't know what to do.'

'It was the power of the rock,' Maya determined. 'It must now be fighting for its life.'

'Aren't we all,' said Alan.

Koenig's only concern was for Helena. He grabbed his commlock and punched a button. 'What happened in there, Helena?'

'I don't know,' came Helena's reply. 'The engines started up, then suddenly stopped. I can't see into the pilot section.'

'What about Tony?'

Inside the ship, Helena looked at Tony. 'The same. No change.' Her eyes froze as a pulsating glow of light reflected against her face. The rock sample was glowing fiercely, with increased regularity, as if it were drawing on whatever reserve energy supply it had. 'The rock, John… it's glowing again.'
Koenig looked to the Eagle with alarm. 'Colour?'

'Yellow!' said Helena.

'Yellow doesn't inflict pain. It denotes brain activity,' assured Maya.

A conglomerate of electronic sounds came through Koenig's commlock transmitted from Helena. 'That's computer activity, John,' she said.

'Describe.'

'Different star charts are flashing on the screen.'

Dave reacted instantly. 'A hundred to one it's looking for a place where there's water!'

For the first time there was a glimmer of hope in Koenig's eyes. 'It's facing a deadline, the same as we are.'

'Which deadline runs out first... its or ours?' asked Dave.

'Trouble is you've got no vision; our friend has got to get off this asteroid – and soon...' said Koenig as he nodded to the parent rock.

The group followed Koenig's nod and saw that the rock's glow was more diminished than before.

'It's beginning to fade... beginning to die,' said Maya.

'But do you know who is going to buy our way back into the Eagle?' asked Koenig, bringing his commlock to his lips. 'Helena... Are the star charts still flashing?'

'They've cut out. The screen is blank,' she replied.

'No questions, Helena, just listen: If I'm right, Tony is going to rise up and do his whole jogging bit again... The second he leaves the craft, make contact, you understand?'

'But...' said Helena, questions beginning to spill out.

'No questions. Contact out.'

Dave eyed Koenig with a grin. 'I sure wish there was a bookie joint around one of these rocks so I could double my bet.'

'Let's move!' ordered Koenig as he, Maya, Dave, and Alan took off across the asteroid's surface.

In the Eagle's passenger module, Helena observed as the rock shot out an intensifying yellow glow, which was accompanied simultaneously by the chatter of sudden computer activity.

Tony's head began to convulse slightly. Helena turned her eyes to the encephalogram to witness a violent upsurge of the tracer needle. She anticipated what would happen next and looked over to Tony as his body bifurcated once again and Tony II rose up, taking his laser and commlock and going toward the door, opening it, and leaving the ship.

'He's out!' Helena called into her commlock.

Koenig, Dave, and Maya were at one vantage point among the rocks at the site of the parent rock, while Alan was at another.

Koenig punched a button on his commlock. 'You get that, Alan?'

'Got it.'

'Hang in.'

'You know it,' Alan replied.

Koenig saw Tony II move toward the rock almost as though it were a countdown. He brought his commlock to his lips. 'He's heading for the rock…'

'Right on,' acknowledged Alan.

Tony II reached the parent rock and aimed his laser at it. As he fired, a large section was cut by pinpoint laser and the remaining parent rock – now half its original size – diminished in glow.

Tony II picked up the sliced-off rock and started his return trip to Eagle Four, under the watchful gaze of Koenig, Maya, Dave, and Alan. As they saw Tony II cross an open area of terrain, Koenig yelled into his commlock.

'Now, Alan!'

Koenig charged out with his laser in hand like a gung-ho Marine.

Alan, too, charged into the open, laser gripped.

Tony II was in the open as both lasers hit him at once and he vanished into the air, leaving only his commlock and laser on the ground.

The group rushed to stand where Tony II had been mere moments before. They stared about, then huddled with Koenig to examine the sample rock Tony II had dropped.

Inside the Eagle, Tony's body suddenly twitched. Helena witnessed it and immediately activated her commlock. 'John, something just happened to Tony.'

On the asteroid's surface, Koenig instantly responded. 'What?'

'His body had a sudden life movement!'

'We just hit him with our lasers. It may have loosened the rock's grip.'

'It's become weaker still,' Maya observed.

Dave spotted the commlock and picked it up, unseen by the others, and headed for Eagle Four on the run.

'Let the rock be,' Koenig said. 'Find Tony's commlock. That'll get us back into the ship.'

They began to examine the area and Alan quickly made a discovery. 'I've got his laser,' he said, glancing off across the asteroid's surface and spotting Dave on the run. 'Hey, Cowboy!'

In that instant Koenig realised that Dave must have found the commlock. 'We've got to stop him before he does something crazy!'

Tony sat bolt upright, eyes open, the electrodes and wires pulling free from his body. At the same time there was a sudden instantaneous renewal of computer activity, the computer light bank flashing on as the system reactivated.

'*Minus thirty-seven minutes eleven seconds*,' chimed the computer voice.

'Tony!' Helena called out as the immobilising effect of the green light was suddenly broken. She rushed toward him as he shook his head, unaware of what had transpired.

'What's all this?' he asked, indicating the electrodes and wiring. 'What happened?'

'You don't remember anything?'

'Just a flash of light…' he raised his hands to his head. 'But what a hangover. I feel like I've been to an Italian wedding.'

Outside the Eagle, Koenig and the others were on the run as they saw Dave aim the commlock at the door

'Dave – hold it!' Koenig shouted.

The door of the passenger section opened, and Dave entered, filled with determination to destroy the rock sample. Without even noticing Tony's recovery, Dave went to the weapons rack and grabbed a rocket gun.

'David, what are you doing?' asked Helena.

'I'm going to finish off that rock, that's what I'm going to do… now out of here!' he said as he took Helena's arm and moved her toward the door, then noticed Tony, who was still too groggy to resist. 'And you too, whatever you are.'

'No, David, you must leave the rock alone!'

Despite her protest, Dave moved Helena out the door with Tony, then aimed the commlock to shut and lock it behind them.

Dave whirled round to the rock sample, gun poised, a deadly glint in his eyes – it was the rock or him now.

'*Minus thirty-two minutes fifty-one seconds*,' the computer voice stated coldly as Dave raised the gun to fire.

Suddenly, the rock sample emitted a short burst of red light, hitting Dave and causing the gun to fly out of his hands. The rock then emitted two additional short bursts of red light, illuminating Dave's face. His eyes were seemingly transfixed as he was irresistibly drawn toward the petroscope.

He tried to fight off the magnetic force that had him in its grip, flailing his arms at the invisible enemy.

Koenig, Alan, and Maya raced toward Eagle Four as Helena and Tony emerged.

'Tony!' called Maya.

'What about Ellis?' asked Koenig, who was too intent upon what Dave was up to at that moment to accept Tony's recovery as anything but normal.

'He's trying to destroy the rock,' said Helena.

'Out of his mind!' Koenig stated as he aimed his commlock at the Eagle's door. But the door failed to open.

Dave continued to struggle against the force that pulled him ever closer to the petroscope. As he moved in on the device there was a blinding flash of yellow light and Dave collapsed, motionless.

'*Minus twent* – …' began the computer voice before it cut out abruptly, along with the sound of all other computer activity aboard the ship.

The rock glowed fiercely.

ACT FOUR

The asteroid drifted through space on its endless course. Still nestled in the sand on its surface was Eagle Four.

On board the Eagle, Dave was still sprawled unconscious on the floor when the computer bank lights started to come on, but then dimmed… they became brighter for another instant, then dimmed again… in synchronicity with the rhythm of the rock sample's pulsating glow, which was less strong than before. Its power weakened, it struggled to take over computer and activate its possession of Dave.

At a vantage point between Eagle Four and the rock, Alan, Tony, and Maya were in the process of reassembling some pieces of a rocket gun while Helena and Koenig observed the parent rock, whose glow was diminished and continued to fade slowly.

'It's beginning to fade fast now,' said Helena.

'Not fast enough,' Koenig stated before calling to the others. 'How much longer with that? He should be coming out any second now.'

'Doing the best we can,' said Alan.

'The muzzle, Maya,' Tony asked.

She handed him a piece, which he began to attach to the end of the barrel.

Koenig moved toward them. 'You think it will work?'

'In theory and principle, yes,' answered Maya. 'By reversing its propellant rocket firing power, it should create a backward vacuum, strong enough to dehydrate the rock of whatever water is left in it.' She paused for a moment. 'I hope. At least we know what effect the laser had on Tony.'

'That dehydrator gun'd better do the rest of the job,' Koenig said, grimly, as he stared at Eagle Four. 'Better start to get ready, Maya.'

Tony and Alan hesitated slightly as Maya nodded, but they continued their desperate piecing together of the weapon.

Maya rose.

Helena turned to Koenig, her concern spilling over. 'John?'

'We can't risk letting Dave bring any of the parent rock back,' Koenig explained. 'You yourself said you don't know how much reserve energy power the other rock has stored after it got to the water. If the two fuse, and the gun is a bust, we've had it! At least Maya can pull out!'

In the Eagle's passenger section, the rock sample's glow intensified, as if a great effort was being made. The computer lights were up to a bright, wavering peak as Dave's head convulsed slightly. His body bifurcated as Tony's had previously done, and a see-through image of Dave – Dave II – rose out of his body. It became solid, took his own commlock, and collected a laser from the weapons rack. Dave II opened the Eagle's door, stepped out, and set forth on the asteroid's surface.

Alan saw Dave II moving in their direction, towards the parent rock. 'Here comes the Cowboy!' he said with a low whistle.

'Not too fast, friend,' said Tony, indicating that he and Alan had not yet finished with the gun.

Koenig nodded at Maya. She nodded back. No words, no goodbyes, it was time to go for broke and they all knew it.

Maya gave a brief look to Tony, who would have stopped her if he could, but his duty was to keep working on the gun with Alan. Koenig and Helena stared after Maya as she started off in a line with Dave II's path.

Maya stopped at a spot where Dave II would have to pass prior to getting to both the group's position and the site of the parent rock. Her form shimmered as she transformed into a replica of the rock.

The group watched with a mixture of wonder and alarm as Dave II approached the Maya rock lying on the path before him. He paused, looked down, then looked ahead and took a few tentative steps forward before stopping. He turned back, picked up the Maya rock, and headed back toward the Eagle.

The group was relieved. Almost simultaneously, Tony held up the gun. 'Finished!' he said.

'Let's go!' Koenig said to Alan.

Tony tossed the gun to Koenig, who caught it with one hand and started to run after Dave II, Alan keeping pace with him.

Dave II approached Eagle Four with the Maya rock and used his commlock to open the door and enter.

Koenig and Alan were just a few paces behind. They entered the spacecraft quickly and poised themselves.

In the passenger section, Dave II put the rock beside the other sample then aimed the commlock to shut the door. He then replaced the commlock on Dave's belt and rejoined his own body.

The rock's glow intensified as it attempted to absorb the new sample but met with resistance from Maya. The glow filled the section as the rock fought not to lose its hold.

Koenig moved into the open with the dehydrator gun aimed at the original rock, but before he could fire, he was confronted by a kaleidoscope of action. He and Alan were hit by a series of different, ever deepening coloured bursts of light beams with a strobe-light effect – blue – purple – red – each colour produced different degrees of pain reaction and even muteness. Alan tried to shout but found he had no voice. The first burst of pain light caused Koenig to drop the gun.

Meanwhile, the rock was trying to fuse itself with the Maya rock and she continued to struggle to not succumb to the rock's final attempt to conquer. The rock was weakening in strength in pace with the slowing of computer activity as the rock's energy source waned.

Dave's body twitched slightly.

All the coloured lights faded from the rock, and only one light beam prevailed: a black light that tried to seek out the humans who, albeit wracked by the horrifying experience, were no longer under the influence of the other lights and had their senses returned.

Koenig realised that the black light was the death light! 'Down! Stay away from that light,' he shouted to Alan.

Alan dove for cover as the black light probed, then it, too, began to fade from its stygian blackness, becoming less black as it probed for its human targets. The sound of computer activity faded, and the light dimmed further and became a flickering diffused murky glow.

Maya had almost tactile contact with the fading rock as it pulled her toward it, but she managed to hold her position until the glow of the rock returned to a very faint yellow.

The computer banks went silent.

Koenig crawled beneath the beam of light to reach the dehydrator gun, and as he quickly rolled out of the light beam, he fired the gun.

The rock emitted a sharp, sucking sound as it was hit by the beam.

A shimmer… and Maya emerged as herself.

The others moved toward her, a 'Thank God' expression on Koenig's face. He smiled at her. 'A sight for sore eyes,' he said, then looked to Alan. 'Try the door.'

Alan aimed his commlock at the door, which opened.

Helena and Tony rushed in as a moan arose from Dave, who began to sit up slowly, shaking his head.

Alan and Tony helped him to his feet while Helena supervised. 'Easy with him,' she said.

'My head,' complained Dave.

'Like at an Italian wedding, huh?' said Tony, knowingly.

'I think there's an old saying from your part of Earth...' Alan grinned as he put on an accent. 'There ain't never been a horse that can't be rode, or a cowboy that can't be throwed.' His grin widened. 'You got throwed this time, Cowboy.'

The computer voice reactivated. '*Minus nine minutes forty seconds,*' it said, giving everyone a jolt.

Koenig took instant command of the deadline situation they faced. 'Test all systems!' he ordered Alan, who rushed to the pilot section. He then turned to Tony and Dave and indicated the rock. 'Get that out of here. We don't take off with it!'

Tony and Dave went to the rock, but Helena intervened. 'We can't just abandon it, John.'

'No time for that kind of humanitarianism, Helena,' he said before he again ordered Tony and Dave, 'Out!'

'It's a living organism – the same as all of us – with one basic need: to live,' Helena protested. 'You can't let it die here if there's a chance to save it.'

'Like it tried to save us?' Dave asked.

'If we'd been that rock, we would have done the same,' argued Helena.

Something caught Maya's eye and she indicated that a faint search beam had started to shine from the rock, a pale yellow.

The group had their weapons at the ready, but Maya stopped them. 'It's trying to tell me something!' she said.

The group held their fire as the light beam panned the computer bank.

Maya looked to Helena. 'You said it was studying star charts and computer data on sources of water…'

The beam moved on to pan across more containers built in the wall.

Helena became fearful. 'But it took all the water.'

The beam passed on to a large, refrigerated unit and with its ebbing light, moved in on it, and froze there…

'Nucleoid active crystals!' proclaimed Helena.

'Those clouds,' said Maya. 'It wants us to make rain the way we do in our Moon atmosphere.'

The computer voice chimed again. 'Minus six minutes twelve seconds…'

Koenig nodded to Tony and indicated the rock. 'Take it back where it belongs.'

Tony started toward the rock, but Dave interrupted him. 'Hey, paisano… how fast do you do a hundred-yard dash?'

Tony thought briefly. 'I don't know.'

'Neither do I,' said Dave as he grabbed the rock and dashed out before anyone could say anything or stop him.

Tony shouted after him. 'Don't make it a Moon dash, you hear – you'll be running forever!'

'Minus five minutes fifty-nine seconds,' the computer voice announced.

Koenig indicated the laser blasted door to Tony. 'Get the emergency door in place.'

Tony moved to comply while Koenig looked at Helena and Maya. 'Get the crystals ready,' he said, then moved to the entrance of the ship's pilot section. 'Systems functioning?' he asked Alan, who was at the controls.

'All systems functioning, sir,' Alan said with a formality that was standard operating procedure in an emergency or operational situation. He hit some buttons and the roar of engines rose.

'Contact Moonbase and tell them we'll be leaving for home.'
'Right on, sir.'
'Hold for lift-off.'
'How soon, sir?'
'When I tell you.'

Dave ran hard and fast among the rocks on the asteroid's surface.
The weight of the rock sample anchored him down a bit, but he
ploughed on and arrived at his destination. Dave put the sample
back beside the parent rock, which was glowing very faintly. He
paused a beat and stared down at the two rocks. They did not
fuse, and Dave knew he didn't have time to wait to see whether
they would or not, so he turned and started his mad dash back
to Eagle Four.

Koenig and Alan were strapped in at the controls of Eagle Four.
    'Minus two minutes twenty-two seconds,' reported the
computer.
    'Prepare for lift-off,' Koenig said grimly while nodding at
Alan.
    Alan knew what Koenig meant and nodded silently, then hit
some buttons on the controls.
    Behind Koenig and Alan in the passenger section everyone
was strapped in at their places. They all knew they may have to
lift off without Dave, but their worry about this increased even
more as the computer announced, *'Minus two minutes exactly.'*
The countdown was too thin for comfort.

Dave stumbled on the asteroid's surface, wrenched his ankle,
and let out a sharp cry of pain. He rose and found he had to half
run, half hobble the rest of the way in considerable pain.

In the pilot section, Koenig was intense. 'Start the engines,' he
ordered.

Alan didn't even look at him this time. He just hit a button that brought the engines to life.

'*Minus one minute thirty seconds.*'

Dave was closer to the ship, and could hear the rev of the engines. He strained every effort to get more speed despite the pain.

Tension continued to mount for the crew in the Eagle as the computer voice continued the countdown. '*Minus one minute ten seconds.*'

Dave finally fought his way through the swirling dust and reached Eagle Four. He struggled to get a grip on his commlock but finally did and aimed it at door. As the door opened, he all but stumbled inside, breathless.

Tony looked at him blandly. 'What'd you do – stop for a beer?'

Koenig turned his head from the pilot section, saw Dave, grinned, and gave the geologist a thumbs up signal. 'Get her out of here!' he ordered Alan.

And boy, did Alan ever want to.

'*Minus one minute exactly.*'

Koenig heaved a sigh of relief as the engines roared and finally lifted Eagle Four from its position.

Koenig and Alan monitored as the ship approached and entered the asteroid's cloud cover. 'Maya – stand by to jettison crystals…' Koenig announced.

Maya, Dave, Tony, and Helena were all on their feet in the passenger section. Maya was at the console, along with Helena.

'Release now!' Koenig called.

Maya hit a button and exchanged a glance of hope with Helena.

As Eagle Four rose above the clouds, it dropped a sparkling stream of crystals in its wake, which settled on the clouds that then billowed and darkened.

Down below on the asteroid's surface, the rock was fading fast – its glow almost dim – as the first drops started to fall. The drops became drizzle, the drizzle rain, and the rain turned to a downpour. The rock started to revive. The two sections fused, and the glow built. As the rain glistened on it, it was visibly restored.

On screen in the Eagle's passenger section the Alphans could see the rock revive with its full glow as the rock sample fused with it.

'Love at first sight,' said Tony as he eyed the others obliquely. 'I wonder if they'll be holding an Italian wedding down there.'

Koenig smiled as he watched the monitor, then looked at Alan. 'Full power... let's see if you can make it back to Alpha in time for dinner.'

Alan hit a button and Eagle Four accelerated through space. In the far distance was the Moon.

EPILOGUE

Alan looked at the screen in the pilot section of Eagle Four. 'There she is, Commander... The Moon.'

'It's getting to look better to me all the time,' Koenig said wryly as he rose and made his way back to the passenger section to join the rest of the group.

'I was really nervous that you were going to stay in that rock forever!' Tony said to Maya.

'And if that had happened, would you have looked after me, Tony?' she teased him.

'Owning a pet rock is the rage these days…' Tony replied. 'Not like a woman… they don't talk back.'

Maya laughed.

Koenig looks to Helena. 'Too close for comfort, this one,' he said.

Helena eyed him affectionately. 'If it was easy, everybody would be doing it.'

Koenig laughed, looked over at Dave and went to him.

Dave looked up at Koenig. 'I guess I acted like a dumb jackass trying to pull that macho bit with the rock.'

Koenig smiled. 'You can't win them all, Cowboy.'

'And falling for that computer rip-off on there being Milgonite on that asteroid,' said Dave as he shook his head with a rueful smile.

'It won't happen next time.'

'Next time… what next time? As a geologist I should be digging Moon ditches.'

Koenig looked at him, then turned to gaze through the window.

His manner put a note of hope in Dave's voice. 'No chance at all for a next time… Is there, Commander?'

'There's got to be Milgonite out there somewhere… Cowboy.'

Koenig turned to face Dave, who understood, and grinned.

Eagle Four reared back through the depths of space toward its nest on Moonbase Alpha.

OBSERVATIONS

'*All That Glisters*' is a bit of a departure for this book as all the other novelisations contained within are based on early scripts from Year One. With '*All That Glisters*' we've jumped to Year Two, with all the radical differences that entails. Assuming the readership for this book will consist of *Space: 1999* fans already knowledgeable about the differences between the two seasons, we've not endeavoured to attempt to itemise or explain them all here.

The '*All That Glisters*' script came to us courtesy of Martin Willey, who explained that it was Brian Johnson's copy and that Brian hadn't discarded the old pages as he was supposed to, so the resultant copy of the script is a mix of the 'Revised Draft' dated 9 February 1976 and the 'Final Shooting Script' dated 9 March 1976. In a way this was a blessing as it enabled this novelisation to adhere as closely as possible to the earlier draft and its key details that are significantly different from the final episode, but it was a challenging process. Certain lines of dialogue had been crossed out to the point where they were unreadable, and other scenes contained contradictions between drafts that forced editorial choices to be made for the sake of providing the most coherent story possible. We are aware that the realisation that the rock is a life form occurs twice in this story, as per the script we have, with all its inconsistencies. As the two life form realisations happen at entirely different points (scenes 23 and 35 as per the scripts) it was impossible to extricate one while maintaining the script's integrity, so both are retained here.

One of the weakest episodes of the series, '*All That Glisters*' was certainly Martin Landau's least favourite. It is a simplistic script that seems heavily influenced by Fred Freiberger's doctrine (contained in his infamous memo of 25 November 1975 critiquing Year One and setting his course forward) that 'above all, humour' should be interjected into scripts. Bad jokes were awkwardly shoehorned in here at every opportunity.

This early draft features duplicates of Tony and Dave, but these doubles were eliminated as apparently a walking 'dead man' was thought to be more dramatic. One does wonder how the rock could be able to raise duplicates from Tony and Dave's bodies, or for that matter how it was able to feed false data about Milgonite to Alpha's computer in order to lure the Alphans to its asteroid to begin with, among other questions. But it's probably best not to dig too deep.

There is no depth of characterisation to be found; nothing beneath the good-natured grins alternating with angry outbursts. Maya spouts redundancies like 'On my planet, Psychon, where I am from…', while Alan is reduced to punching buttons and interjecting an occasional generic line, but Helena fares particularly poorly at the mercy of the script's sexist tendencies. From the opening where Helena's suggestion that she should go out to monitor for environmental hazards is casually dismissed by Koenig's comment that 'somebody has to mind the store', to Koenig and Alan suspecting her of fantasising about the missing commlock and stun gun and conducting a 'placation search' to appease her. In the end Tony jokes about the benefit of exchanging Maya for a pet rock because unlike women 'they don't talk back', to which Maya simply laughs, as if casual sexism is great fun. It was a different time!

Even a veneer of scientific accuracy is non-existent in the basic setting of an asteroid with an atmosphere, let alone one that is breathable for humans. Thankfully that detail was changed to a planet in the 'Final Shooting Script' but for the sake of keeping this novelisation as close to the original version as possible the asteroid setting has been preserved.

Maya has another superpower here, which was never utilised on screen, whereby she can sense 'vibrations,' seemingly as a way to warn of imminent danger. In practice it seems that it would have resulted in reducing drama and surprise if Maya could warn the Alphans of the ominous vibrations of danger prior to anything actually happening in this or other episodes, so it was wisely removed.

Alpha's computer is able to speak here, even if it is only functioning as a countdown clock - a significant downgrade from computer, which had previously been a formidable virtual character of its own, particularly in David Weir's original version of '*The Black Sun*'.

And finally, regarding sowing the clouds with nucleoid crystals, Maya says, 'It wants us to make it rain the way we do in our Moon atmosphere.' To which we have to ask, WHAT 'Moon atmosphere'?! Had Keith Miles only watched part of '*The Last Sunset*' in preparation for writing this script and assumed the Moon in *Space: 1999* had an atmosphere? Or is Maya implying that they use nucleoid crystals to sow the seeds of rain in clouds within Moonbase Alpha itself? Either way, it's utterly nonsensical and displays total disregard for the entirety of the series that had preceded this episode.

Someone either thought this was a good story, or they had nothing else ready to shoot.

EVOLUTION OF NAMES

Readers may be confused by the variety of names used throughout these early drafts. As the series was developed, changes were naturally made, characters were combined, deleted entirely, or changed nationality / gender due to casting. Here is a handy list to explain these alterations. In some cases there were additional name variations beyond those listed here but for the purposes of this book we have listed only those names that appear within these pages.

NAME AS BROADCAST: Commander John Koenig

EARLY NAMES	SOURCE
Space Commander Steve Maddox	Zero G
John Koenig	The Void Ahead (1st Draft)

NAME AS BROADCAST: Doctor Helena Russell

EARLY NAMES	SOURCE
Doctor Gordon	Zero G
Doctor Helena Russell	The Void Ahead (1st Draft)

NAME AS BROADCAST: Professor Victor Bergman

EARLY NAMES	SOURCE
Doctor Marc Miller	Zero G
Professor Bergman	The Void Ahead (1st Draft)
Professor Penmarric	Siren Planet

NAME AS BROADCAST: Captain Alan Carter

EARLY NAMES	SOURCE
Lt. Caron	Zero G
Probe Captain Catani	The Void Ahead (1st Draft)
Captain James Grayson	Siren Planet

NAME AS BROADCAST: Controller Paul Morrow

EARLY NAMES	SOURCE
The Controller	Zero G
Vorkonen	The Void Ahead (1st Draft)
Main Mission Controller Paul Morrow	Turning Point

NAME AS BROADCAST: Data Analyst Sandra Benes

EARLY NAMES	SOURCE
Female Operator	Zero G
Sandra Sabatini	The Void Ahead (1st Draft)

NAME AS BROADCAST: Doctor Robert Mathias

EARLY NAME	SOURCE
Doctor Fujita*	The Void Ahead (1st Draft)

NAME AS BROADCAST: Lunar Commissioner Simmonds

EARLY NAMES	SOURCE
Commissioner Symonds	The Void Ahead (1st Draft)
Commissioner Simmonds	Turning Point

NAME AS BROADCAST: Commander Gorski

EARLY NAMES	SOURCE
Commander Grodno	The Void Ahead (1st Draft)
Commander Gorski	Turning Point

NAME AS BROADCAST: Lee Russell
EARLY NAME   SOURCE
Telford Russell   The Void Ahead (1st Draft)

NAME AS BROADCAST: Eagle Pilot Collins
EARLY NAME   SOURCE
Simpson   Turning Point

NAME AS BROADCAST: Eagle Pilot Mike Ryan
EARLY NAME   SOURCE
Mike Meyer   The Black Sun (1st Draft)

NAME AS BROADCAST: Tony Cellini
EARLY NAME   SOURCE
Jim Calder   Web (Story Treatment)

NAME AS BROADCAST: Dr. Monique Bouchere
EARLY NAME   SOURCE
Dr. Olga Vishenskya   Web (Story Treatment)

NAME AS BROADCAST: Dave Reilly
EARLY NAME   SOURCE
Dave Ellis   All That Glisters (1st Draft)

NAME AS BROADCAST: Eagle Transporter
EARLY NAMES   SOURCE
M.T.U. (Multiple Transport Unit) Zero G
Prober   Siren Planet (1st Draft)
Probe Ship / MTU   A Breath of Death

NAME AS BROADCAST: Moobase Alpha
EARLY NAMES   SOURCE
Moon City   Zero G
Alpha Base   The Void Ahead (1st Draft)

Moon Base Alpha   Turning Point

NAME AS BROADCAST: Main Mission
EARLY NAMES   SOURCE
Control Centre   Zero G
Main Mission   Turning Point
Alpha Control Centre   The Black Sun (1st Draft)

NAME AS BROADCAST: Medical Centre
EARLY NAMES   SOURCE
Medical Section HQ   Siren Planet (1st Draft)
Sick Bay   Siren Planet (1st Draft)

NAME AS BROADCAST: Commlock
EARLY NAME   SOURCE
IDX   The Black Sun (1st Draft)

NAME AS BROADCAST: Stun Gun
EARLY NAME   SOURCE
Laser Beam Generator   Zero G

NAME AS BROADCAST: Communications Post
EARLY NAME   SOURCE
Comm-Post   The Black Sun (1st Draft)

*   The character of Dr. Fujita does eventually appear as a non-speaking member of the survival ship crew in the broadcast version of '*(The) Black Sun*'.

ABOUT THE AUTHORS

DAVID HIRSCH

Born in 1957, David grew up watching the many TV series created by Gerry and Sylvia Anderson. During his first year of college, he elected to write a paper for a film study class on their work, but with little research material available in the pre-internet era, he was forced to make a daring attempt to secure information from the company that distributed their programs in America, ITC.

A fortuitous meeting with Robert Mandell, son of company president Abe Mandell, eventually led to an introduction to Kerry O'Quinn and Norman Jacobs, publishers of *Starlog* Magazine. A brief summer internship in 1977 led to a long association with the magazine where he worked his way up from contributor (Issue #7) to Associate Editor.

Among his work for the magazine, he edited *The Official Moonbase Alpha Technical Manual* (1977), 'Gerry Anderson's Space Report' column and several popular titles in the Starlog Guidebook series. These included *Fantastic Worlds* (1978), *Science Fiction Weapons* (1979), *Spaceships* (Revised & Expanded 1980), *Special Effects*, Vol. 2 (1980), *Science Fiction Heroes* (1980), *Science Fiction Villains* (1980), *TV Episode Guides, Vol. 1* (1981) and *TV Episode Guides, Vol. 2* (1982).

Though he left his full-time position after Issue #71 (1983), David continued as a free-lance writer, now specialising in film and TV music with his AudioLog column (#201, 1994 through #252, 1998) and interviewed many composers such as David Arnold (*Independence Day*), Leonard Rosenman (*RoboCop 2*) and, for their *Star Trek* Magazines, Dennis McCarthy, Ron Jones and Jay Chattaway.

This passion has also led to work on several soundtrack albums as a consultant, producer and writing liner notes. Titles include *Star Trek Volume 2: Doomsday Machine & Amok Time* (Sol Kaplan & Gerald Fried, GNP Crescendo Records 1992), *Space: 1999* (Year 2, Derek Wadsworth, Composer Promo 1995), *Godzilla* (50th Anniversary Edition, Akira Ifukube, La-La Land Records 2004), *Thunderbird 6* (Barry Gray, MGM Music 2005), *King Kong vs. Godzilla* (Akira Ifukube, La-La Land Records 2006) and the 1998 *American Godzilla* (David Arnold, BSX Records 2012).

He has contributed to several books including *The Star Trek* Encyclopaedia (Michael and Denise Okuda, Simon & Shuster 1997 edition), *Videohound's Soundtracks* (Didier C. Deutsch, Visible Ink 1998), the *Space: 1999* novel '*The Whispering Sea*' (John Kenneth Muir, Powys Media, 2014) and *Martin Bower's World of Models* (Shaun McClure & Martin Bower 2019).

David has achieved a life-long dream to write for a Gerry Anderson production when son Jamie Anderson invited him to write scripts for the audio drama revival *Terrahawks volume 2* ~ '*Lights, Camera, Disaster*' (Big Finish 2016) and *Terrahawks volume 3* ~ '*Set Sail for Mis-Adventure*' and '*You Foe*' (Big Finish 2017).

More recently, he consulted on an update of his first book, the *Moonbase Alpha Technical Operations Manual* (Chris Thompson & Andrew Clements, Anderson Entertainment, 2021) and is producing a series of albums for the Japanese *a cappella* group Bukimisha, released world-wide on BSX Records ~ *Godzilla vs Rodan* (2021), and *Godzilla & Friends vs. Ghidorah* (2022) and *Seven Samurai & More Movie Themes* (2022).

This is his second collaboration with Robert E. Wood and Christopher Penfold. *To Everything That Might Have Been: The Lost Universe of Space: 1999* (Telos 2022) explored the development of the series as the writers re-imagined the cancelled second series of *UFO*.

ROBERT E. WOOD

Born in 1971, Robert's love of *Space: 1999* has been nearly life-long and has led him to numerous extraordinary experiences, not least of which was a fifteen-year friendship and working relationship with series star Barry Morse, during which they produced (as a triumvirate with Anthony Wynn) a television movie version of Morse's one-man stage show *Merely Players* (2000), TV specials *Spotlight on Barry Morse and Spotlight on 1999* (both 2002), the *Space: 1999* audio book *Resurrection* performed by Barry Morse (released by Powys Media in 2010), the audio drama *Rogues and Vagabonds: A Theatrical Scrapbook* (released on CD in 2013), and stage plays including multiple performances of *Merely Players* in the United States, Canada, and England, and a 1999 Los Angeles production of *Love Letters* which reunited Morse with his *Space: 1999* co-star Barbara Bain.

Robert also worked with Barry Morse and Anthony Wynn on numerous books including *Merely Players: The Scripts* (2003),

Morse's autobiography *Remember with Advantages* (2006), *Stories of the Theatre* (2006), and following Morse's passing Robert continued to collaborate with Wynn to memorialise Morse in additional books *Such Stuff as Dreams ...* (2009), *Valiant for Truth: Barry Morse and his Lifelong Association with Bernard Shaw* (2012), and *The Wit and Wisdom of Barry Morse* (2013).

Robert's friendship with *Space: 1999* actress Zienia Merton also led him to edit her autobiography, *Anecdotes & Armadillos* (2005).

Robert has also edited the soon-to-be-announced autobiography of another *Space: 1999* star.

As an authority on *Space: 1999* Robert has appeared on numerous television programs, radio talk shows, and podcasts and has been published in magazines such as *Filmfax* (issues 116 and 117, 2008). His book Destination: *Moonbase Alpha – The Unofficial and Unauthorised Guide to Space: 1999* (2010) is the most comprehensive guide to the series ever published. Since 2012 Robert has been working closely with writer and script editor Christopher Penfold and writing partner Steve Warnek developing concepts and writing screenplays for television and film projects.

This is his second collaboration with David Hirsch, following their tremendously successful *To Everything That Might Have Been: The Lost Universe of Space: 1999* (Telos 2022).

CHRISTOPHER PENFOLD

Christopher Penfold has been both writer and script editor in British film and television for nearly 60 years during which he has either written or script edited over 350 hours of prime-time TV including single plays and several feature films. Christopher's first work in television was as script editor and assistant producer on the Australian Broadcasting Corporation's production of an adaptation of George Johnston's award winning novel *My Brother Jack* which starred Nick Tate. Christopher was story consultant and lead writer for the first season of Gerry Anderson's cult series *Space: 1999*, which starred Martin Landau and Barbara Bain, and wrote the second season of *The Tripods* for the BBC. He script-edited and wrote for the immensely popular BBC series *All Creatures Great and Small* and he either wrote or script-edited over 100 episodes of ITV's long-running hit show *The Bill*.

For ten years he taught on the Carlton Screenwriters Course, which produced some of the most successful writers in UK television today. In 1998 he set up his own script production company, ScriptWorks, through which he assisted in the script development of Saul Metzstein's first feature film, *Late Night Shopping* (a prizewinner at Berlin in 2000); John Deery's first feature film, *Conspiracy of Silence* (winner of the Hartley-Merrill International Screenwriting Award at Cannes in 2001); Kevin Sampson's *Awaydays*; Jonathan Glazer's second feature film *Birth*, which starred Nicole Kidman and Lauren Bacall, and his 2013 feature *Under The Skin*, which starred Scarlett Johansson. Most recently he has assisted in the development of Nicholas Martin's screenplays for *Florence Foster Jenkins*, which was directed by Stephen Frears and starred Meryl Streep and Hugh Grant and for *Golda* which starred Helen Mirren.

From 1999 Christopher was series editor for 78 episodes of ITV's *Midsomer Murders*, which has been possibly the most successful long-form drama series in the history of television, with 128 feature-length episodes produced to date and which is sold in 186 countries. Still in development is an ambitious science fiction series *Helios* which Christopher has co-created with writers Steve Warnek and Robert E. Wood.

Now in his 80s, Christopher divides his time between London and his garden in Mid Wales where he finds inspiration for a continuing series of op-ed articles for a London magazine – still believing that the pen is mightier than the sword and still hoping to put the world to rights.

OTHER GREAT TITLES BY ANDERSON ENTERTAINMENT

available from
shop.gerryanderson.com

Stingray: Operation Icecap

The Stingray crew discover an ancient diving bell that leads them on an expeditionary voyage through the freezing waters of Antarctica to the land of a lost civilisation. Close on the heels of Troy Tempest and the pride of the World Aquanaut Security Patrol is the evil undersea ruler Titan. Ahead of them are strange creatures who inhabit underground waterways and an otherworldly force with hidden powers strong enough to overwhelm even Stingray's defences.

Stingray: Monster from the Deep

Commander Shore's old enemy, Conrad Hagen, is out of prison and back on the loose with his beautiful but devious daughter, Helga. When they hijack a World Aquanaut Security Patrol vessel and kidnap Atlanta, it's up to Captain Troy Tempest and the crew of Stingray to save her. But first they will have to uncover the mystery of the treasure of Sanito Cathedral and escape the fury of the monster from the deep.

Five Star Five: John Lovell and the Zargon Threat

THE TIME: THE FUTURE
THE PLACE: THE UNIVERSE

The peaceful planet of Kestra is under threat. The evil Zargon forces are preparing to launch a devastating attack from an asteroid fortress. With the whole Kestran system in the Zargons' sights, Colonel Zana looks to one man to save them. Except one man isn't enough. Gathering a crack team around him including a talking chimpanzee, a marauding robot and a mystic monk, John Lovell must infiltrate the enemy base and save Kestra from the Zargons!

A GERRY ANDERSON PRODUCTION

THUNDERBIRDS

Thunderbirds:
Operation Asteroids

What starts out as a simple rescue mission to save a trapped miner on the moon, soon turns out to be one of International Rescue's greatest catastrophes. After the Hood takes members of International Rescue hostage during the rescue, a chase across space and an altercation among the asteroids only worsens the situation. With the Hood hijacking Thunderbird Three along with Brains, Lady Penelope and Tin-Tin, it is up to the Tracy brothers to stage a daring rescue in the mountain tops of his hidden lair. But can they rescue Brains before his engineering genius is used for the destructive forces of evil?

Thunderbirds:
Terror from the Stars

Thunderbird Five is attacked by an unknown enemy with uncanny powers. An unidentified object is tracked landing in the Gobi desert, but what's the connection? Scott Tracy races to the scene in the incredible Thunderbird One, but he cannot begin to imagine the terrible danger he is about to encounter. Alone in the barren wilderness, he is possessed by a malevolent intelligence and assigned a fiendish mission – one which, if successful, will have the most terrifying consequences for the entire world. International Rescue are about to face their most astounding adventure yet!

Thunderbirds:
Peril in Peru

An early warning of disaster brings International Rescue to Peru to assist in relief efforts following a series of earth tremors – and sends the Thunderbirds in search of an ancient Inca treasure trove hidden beneath a long-lost temple deep in the South American jungle!

When Lady Penelope is kidnapped by sinister treasure hunters, Scott Tracy and Parker are soon hot on their trail. Along the way they'll have to solve a centuries-old mystery, brave the inhospitable wilderness of the jungle and even tangle with a lost tribe – with the evil Hood close behind them all the way...

Intergalactic Rescue 4:
Stellar Patrol

It is the 22nd century. The League of Planets has tasked Jason Stone, Anne Warran and their two robots, Alpha and Zeta to explore the galaxy, bringing hope to those in need of rescue. On board Intergalactic Rescue 4, they travel to ice moons and jungle planets in 10 exciting adventures that see them journey further across the stars than anyone before. But what are the secret transmissions that Anne discovers? And why do their rescues seem to be taking them on a predetermined course? Soon, Anne discovers that her co-pilot, Jason, might be on a quest of his own...